Would I LIE to You?

Aliya Ali-Afzal

HEAD
of ZEUS

First published in the UK in 2021 by Head of Zeus Ltd

9 7 5 3 1 2 4 6 8

A catalogue record for this book is available from the British Library.

ISBN (HB): 9781800245662
ISBN (XTPB): 9781800245679
ISBN (E): 9781800245693

Typeset by Divaddict Publishing Solutions Ltd

Printed and bound in Great Britain by
CPI Group (UK) Ltd, Croydon CRO 4YY

Head of Zeus Ltd
First Floor East
5–8 Hardwick Street
London EC1R 4RG

WWW.HEADOFZEUS.COM

Would I LIE to You?

ALIYA ALI-AFZAL has a degree in Russian and German from UCL and worked as an Executive MBA Career Coach in London. While helping her clients to pursue their dream lives and careers, she decided to take her own advice and become a writer. She is studying for an MA in Creative Writing at Royal Holloway, is an alum of Curtis Brown Creative, and has had her writing longlisted for the Bath Novel Award, the Mslexia Novel Competition, the Mo Siewcharran Prize and the Primadonna Prize. Aliya has lived in London all her life, since moving there from Pakistan as a young child.

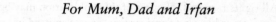

For Mum, Dad and Irfan

Prologue

September

Her face flashes in his mind.

He walks to the end of the rooftop terrace and looks at the view, squinting in the sun. City icons stand like sentries along the skyline: the Shard, the Gherkin, St Paul's. His eyes are drawn, as always, to the different office blocks he's worked in over the years. Toy trains slither in well-worn grooves, converging at stations to catch their breath and people rush along pavements, going nowhere.

He grips the Perspex railings and looks straight down. It would only take a second...

One

The last thing you need to hear when you're waiting to get Botox at a Harley Street clinic, is that your husband may be about to lose his job.

I was at my first Botox party, although it felt more like a field trip for the Year 12 mothers. I'd started questioning the wisdom in coming as soon as I'd stepped into the clinic, but then Lizzie's excitement began to rub off on me. I noticed that I was the only brown face there but I was used to that, especially with this group. I tried to get into the spirit of things. I reminded myself that this wasn't just about the Botox, but also hanging out with my friends. I didn't want to be the odd one out. We flicked through the menu of face 'enhancements', laughing at options such as 'Temptress', 'Diva' and 'Supermodel'. I was joking that there should be one called 'Normal', when Tom called my mobile.

'We just got an email from the CEO. "Due to the current economic climate, the Bank is restructuring with immediate effect". They're laying off half the London team. Bob's

3

calling us into his office one by one. The HR director's in there too.'

Shit.

I got up to walk to the far end of the waiting room. Lizzie stood in my way. She was smiling.

'Welcome to the club, Faiza! Here's to your first time!'

She raised a glass of cold-pressed kale juice towards me, as did Anna, Cora and Bella, who all stood behind her. I smiled automatically and gave them a thumbs up. On the phone, Tom was still talking. He said three people from Syndications had just been escorted away by security to clear their desks. I mouthed a silent 'Sorry' to Lizzie, pointing to the phone, and hurried to the window, away from the others.

'How can they do this? Are you all right, darling?' I said.

'I'm fine, don't worry.' He spoke in his office voice. 'I'm sure I'll be OK. I've met all my targets this year and I'm about to close that deal in Sao Paulo.' He paused. 'I won't let them fire any of my team. They're all good kids. They've worked hard.'

He kept on talking, upbeat, faster, listing the reasons why he would keep his job: he said more in those few minutes than he normally would in a week. I hated to think of him all alone in his office, high above The Royal Exchange, and wanted to rush to him. They should allow family members to be present if they're about to make you redundant, like they do for other bad news, like telling you that you might have some terrible disease.

Goosebumps flared a path down my arms. I knew I shouldn't have come. We were supposed to be on a budget. I'd tried to stay away, I really had. I'd made some excuse the last time Lizzie had asked me along. But I couldn't stand my crumpled forehead any more, when I compared it to the smooth ones topping my friends' faces. It seemed almost rude to cart that forehead into people's houses. Like turning up without brushing your teeth. Still, now I felt like a criminal.

'Sweetheart, I'm sure you'll be—' I said.

'They're calling me. I have to go.'

The line went dead.

As I walked back into the party, Anna held out a tray of miniature brownies.

'Have one of these, Faiza. Do you fancy a make-up lesson? There's a make-up artist doing demos.'

I shook my head.

'I'm sorry, but I need to go home.'

'Why? Is everything OK? It's not one of your parents, is it?'

'No, no, they're fine, thank you. It's just a plumbing emergency, but I need to go.' The words tripped easily from my lips.

I scooped up my bag. My phone clattered to the floor. Before I left, I needed to get my money back. I hurried to the 'treatment concierge' desk in the corner.

'I'm so sorry but I can't have the treatments today. My builders have hit a pipe and my kitchen's flooded. They've had to call the Fire Brigade.'

This had, in fact, happened last year. I could have said one of the children or Baba was ill, but that would have been tempting fate.

'Of course!' said the receptionist. 'I'll cross you off the list. Good luck!'

She looked back down at the papers on her desk. I stood, not sure what to do. I held out my debit card to the top of her blonde bob.

'Excuse me... for the refund?'

She looked up and frown-smiled at me.

'I'm so sorry but we charge a 100 per cent cancellation fee for less than twenty-four hours' notice. It's clinic policy.'

I opened my mouth to argue, but nothing came out. The packed waiting room was silent behind me. I looked down. My face felt hot.

'Why don't you just have the treatment?' I didn't want the kindness in her voice. 'We can have you out of here in twenty minutes.'

'You can go first, Faiza, before the rest of us,' said Lizzie.

The nurse was standing in the doorway. She checked her clipboard.

'We can take you in now, Faiza. Follow me.'

I hovered between the desk and the door. Nothing had happened yet, had it? There was no need to assume the worst. I refused to think like Ami. By now, she'd have fast-forwarded the scenario to a sorry end: Tom getting sacked, then having a heart attack, the house being repossessed and all of us moving to a concrete estate at the tattered edges of London, the children becoming knife-wielding gang members! She'd be on her prayer mat, begging God to have mercy on her daughter and grandchildren, and to save her son-in-law's life.

I followed the nurse down a corridor, hugging my coat to my chest. I heard myself replying to her comments about the tube strike and the weather. I checked my mobile to make sure the ringer was still turned on. They wouldn't sack Tom. He'd been nervous when he'd first joined the bank, but as the months passed, I'd heard snippets about 'million-dollar wind farms' and 'solar projects in Brazil', and he began to sleep properly again as the deals started to come in.

I lay down in the treatment chair. My foot started to shake.

'Nervous?' said the nurse. 'Let me put some numbing cream on for you.'

She smoothed icy gel onto my forehead. I shivered, wishing that it would seep into my mind as well. I imagined Tom walking into the room to hear his fate, his mid-life heart hammering, trying to appear composed in the open-plan fish bowl that magnified every emotion for those watching the show.

'This should start working soon.'

The nurse smiled and took off her gloves. I dabbed the tears in the inner corners of my eyes with my index finger, pretending to dislodge a speck of dirt or an eyelash. I wasn't there just to indulge myself. The Botox injection was supposed to vaccinate my relationship against a marital superbug: the usual viruses that weaken long marriages – time, money, juggling three children, four parents, two cultures. I didn't want to add another item to the list by 'letting myself go' and have him go off with someone else. It had happened to our friends Amanda and Johnathan. As Lizzie said, 'Men become silver foxes, women just become silver.'

The highest divorce rates were for people in their forties. I hadn't dared to google the stats for a mixed-race couple. I'd always had to work hard at looking good and the older

I got, the harder I had to work at it. Not having the Botox would have been a false economy in the long run.

Dr Curtis entered, his age-neutral face and uniform tan highlighting his transatlantic credentials. My phone rang.

'I'm so sorry, Doctor, I have to take this.'

I escaped into the corridor.

'I've been let go. They've had to restructure due to losses across EMEA. They can only keep one Team Head. They're keeping Matt.'

He repeated the HR spiel they must have rolled out for him.

'Darling, I'm so sorry.'

I wanted to wrap my arms around him. They had no right to do this to Tom. He hadn't done anything wrong. I began to pace the corridor, pressing the phone hard into my ear.

'Look, it's going to be OK,' I said.

But thoughts exploded like grenades in my head, despite my verbal bravado. How would Tom cope with losing his job? How long would it take until he found a new one? Sofia was in the middle of her A levels. We couldn't pull her out of Brookwood High. Ahmed had finally settled down at the new school. I couldn't move him again. Not after last year.

'You'll find something else,' I said.

'I'm not so sure. The market is dead.'

'What kind of package are they giving you?'

It was important to know what kind of cushion we had.

'Nothing, just one month's salary.'

'But that's impossible! Don't they have to give you at least three months' pay? What about your bonus? What about BUPA?'

Ahmed's treatment was being paid for by the insurance. I sank down on a stool in the corridor and leaned back against the wall.

'One month is all that I get. That's the contract I signed, remember. No bonus either. They say the bank hasn't made enough profit.'

'But we have some savings, right? We should be OK?'

He looked after all of that.

'I've been using the savings to pay the school fees. That account's almost empty. I was going to put my bonus in there next month.'

We'd been planning how to use this suddenly non-existent bonus for months.

'Don't worry, Faiza,' he said, listening to my silence. 'We still have the emergency fund. That should keep us going until I find something else.'

The emergency fund.

The room spun. I clutched the side of the stool, afraid I was going to fall. I leaned forwards and rested my elbows on my knees, gripping the phone tighter. I focused my eyes on the blue and yellow diamond pattern on the carpet and counted the tiny blue squares between my cream suede ankle boots.

'Yes, of course,' I managed to say.

I wasn't sure about the balance in that account. I'd been dipping into it for months, maybe more. Money for birthday parties, school trips, Ubers, Deliveroo, presents, furniture, dinner parties, concert tickets, clothes, spending money, Ami and Baba's cleaner, Lingo Bear, the Botox party… The statements were lying unopened in my 'documents folder' – an old LK Bennett shoe bag – at the back of my cupboard.

It was easier not to see what I'd spent. I'd planned to put the money back by getting a job one day, when Alex was older. I never imagined we'd need that money so soon, if at all. I couldn't have spent that much, though. I was probably worrying unnecessarily.

'Are *you* OK?' I asked.

That was what really mattered. He didn't deserve getting fired in a five-minute conversation, by a boss ten years younger than him. He should have been safe by now. That was the plan he'd slogged and sacrificed towards for twenty-five years.

'They're taking away my phone so I won't be able to call you till I get home. Where are you?'

'Peter Jones.' It popped out easily. I couldn't tell him where I really was. 'I'll head home too.'

The nurse waved at me, to hurry me along.

'I love you,' I said, but Tom had gone.

The nurse ushered me back to the doctor. As the needle sank into my forehead, I wondered what Tom would think, if he saw me. A tear slipped out from the corner of my eye. The doctor apologised for the pain.

I ran out of the clinic and zigzagged my way through the snail-slow crowds on Oxford Street. A cyclist just missed me as I darted across the road, his 'Stupid bitch!' still ringing in my ears as I ran down the escalators and jumped through the tube doors just as they were beeping shut.

At Waterloo, I caught the train to Wimbledon. I leaned my head against the window. Everything looked the same as it had that morning: the London Eye peeking out above the station wall against a matt grey sky, the usual people sitting around me, reading the *Metro* as if nothing was wrong. I wanted to text Tom to check if he was all right, but there was no way to contact him. I'd been trying to do a mental tally of how much I might have spent, but I had no idea. After avoiding the statements for months, I couldn't wait a second more to check them. I had to get home before Tom.

Two

He'd beaten me to it.

I found him at the dining table under the Murano chandelier. He was hunched over the laptop with his back to me, scrolling through the 'E-Financial Careers' website. His blue suit jacket lay discarded on a dining chair, the sleeves slumped on the floor like a dead body, his yellow silk tie scrunched up into a ball. He didn't stand up or turn when he heard me come in. I put my arms around him from behind and leaned forwards, pressing my cheek into his from the side, skin to skin, rubbing against a hint of stubble. I slid my hands down his forearms, until they came to rest over his.

'This looks promising,' I said.

There was a long list of jobs on the screen.

'I've applied for a couple already. I'm going to call up John and Tig and the old gang. I got David his role at Nomura, I'm sure he'll help.'

I bent down and kissed the sliver of neck between his collar and hair, forgetting that I was supposed to keep my head upright after the Botox. His shoulders slumped. He turned around to face me and pulled me on to his lap. There were blue shadows under his eyes.

'Stefano doesn't know how to tell his wife what's happened. She's just had a baby and they bought a new house a few months ago.'

'Poor guy,' I sighed, and kissed his forehead.

He stood up and stretched his arms above his head, flexing his shoulders. He tipped my chin up, then moved his hand to cup my cheek. I leaned into it. I could always tell how he was feeling from the temperature of his skin, or the colour of his eyes. I was relieved to see that his eyes were a calm light blue. He looked at me and smiled.

'I don't want you to go into one of your worrying overdrives, OK? We're going to be fine.'

'What was all that "dead market" doom and gloom?'

'That was just the shock talking. I'll look after you. I always have, haven't I? I've already fixed a meeting with a headhunter for tomorrow.'

He put his arms around me and I let myself slump against him. The beat of his heart seemed to confirm his optimism. My breaths started to come more easily again and in time with his. Even though he was so much taller than my five-foot three frame, and his body was still hard with muscle memory while mine was slim but soft, we slotted together perfectly. Whenever I imagined worst-case scenarios, like tsunamis, or nuclear war, or if I was dying of cancer or even old age, I knew that so long as Tom was holding me, it wouldn't be as bad. His arms tightened.

'It might take a while to get another job, that's all. But we have enough for next month's bills, and then we can use the emergency fund.'

I froze. I struggled to keep my muscles limp and my breathing steady. I counted to a hundred and waited until I could extricate myself without arousing his suspicion. As soon as he was back at the computer, I went to our bedroom.

I shut the door and tapped the front of my ceiling-high wardrobe. It sprang open and I knelt down, removed several cardboard shoeboxes from the bottom section, then thrust my hand to the back of the cupboard. I had to lie almost flat on my stomach, on the cool parquet, to reach in. My fingers had just found the edge of the cotton shoe bag with the statements, when I heard Tom calling me.

'It's your mother on the phone.'

I'd forgotten about Ami and Baba.

'Just a sec!' I shouted.

I pushed everything back, stood up and ran downstairs. I was supposed to take Ami and Baba to Tooting to buy a freezer-full of halal meat and a cash-and-carry-sized bag of rice. We could have bought it all at the local supermarket in half the time, but for twice the price. That was both illogical and unacceptable to them.

'I have a bit of a cold coming on, Ami, so I came home early,' said Tom.

So that was how he wanted to play it. I nodded to show him that I understood, as he handed me the phone.

'Salaam alaikum, Beti. I've been so worried. I thought you'd had an accident. I didn't want to call your mobile in case you were driving,' said Ami.

'Wa-Alaikum salaam, Ami, I'm so sorry, I should have called. Tom came home and I completely forgot.'

I thought about my parents waiting for me on the TV room sofa, their matching navy raincoats on in advance and

Baba's walking stick standing to attention in his hand. I didn't know how long they must have stayed like that.

'I needed to collect my warfarin as well. You know I can get a blood clot if I miss a dose. But I don't want you to leave Tom if he's sick. Does he have a temperature? Make him honey and lemon with black peppercorns. Take some chicken wings and make some soup as well. Put lots of ginger and garlic in it. Do you want me to make it?'

'Thanks, Ami, but Tom's fine. It's just a cold. I'll swing by the chemist on my way to get the boys. I'll drop off the warfarin before your nine o'clock dose.'

I could shoehorn in the chemist if I left straight away, but then I wouldn't have time to check the papers. I had no choice; the statements would have to wait.

After dinner I made blueberry pancakes for dessert, a Saunders' family tradition for birthday breakfasts and Sunday brunch. We ate in front of the TV, watching an episode of *Friends*. Tom and I sat on the sofa, our hips and knees stuck together. Ahmed, who at twelve was still amenable to physical contact, sat near me, his football-scabbed knee poking out of his rugby shorts and thrown across my leg. Alex, six, with his baby blond head bent in concentration, transported small pieces of pancake on wooden Thomas trains on the dark oak floor, changing his voice for each different engine. Sofia, excited about her school trip to Barcelona, had been persuaded to leave her room. She sat curled up in a cavernous, sky-blue armchair, at enough of a distance to disassociate herself from us, her open laptop a further shield.

The pancake stuck in my throat. I struggled to swallow each mouthful. I waited for a chance to get away to check the statements.

'Mum!' Sofia was waving her phone at me. 'Why are we having pancakes today?'

I felt Tom's body tense.

'Are you getting divorced? Is this to help us feel good before you tell us?'

'Have we won the lottery?' asked Ahmed, jumping up to sit on his knees on the sofa.

Sofia's brown eyes, with expertly flicked wings of black eyeliner, narrowed at me as she waited for an answer. She was biting the tip of her thumb, which was half in her mouth. Her dark brown hair, an exact colour mix of Tom's light brown, and my black, fell in waves to her waist. She'd recently started wearing red lipstick, which made her look like a young Sophia Loren, but reminded me of a day when she was three; she had sneaked into my room to decorate her face, the walls, the windows, and even my computer, with one of my lipsticks. Ahmed leaned forwards, caught up in the moment and nothing else. His blue eyes shone, amused at his own joke. He looked just like Tom, only with darker skin and hair. I'd waited so long to see him like this again, laughing and carefree. I hoped that this was here to stay.

'Goodness, what imaginations! Nope. Happily, we are not getting divorced and, sadly, we have not won the lottery! We're celebrating because Dad's got a new project. He'll be working from home for a few weeks so we get to see more of him. Isn't that great?'

Sofia and Ahmed looked suitably disgusted as I laid my

head on Tom's shoulder. I laced my fingers through his and he held my hand back tight. It anchored me. It always had, since that first time we'd held hands, on a platform at Piccadilly Circus tube station, twenty-one years ago. He'd held it through every illness, every worry, every stressful day. He'd never let me down.

'Emergency! Emergency!' Alex frowned at an overturned train and slapped his forehead with a small hand.

Tom went down to the floor, folding his six-foot two frame inside the train track. He fixed a piece that had come undone. Alex gave his father a high five, then pushed some pancake from the floor into Tom's mouth as a reward. Tom ate it with a grin, shaking his head as he caught my eye.

I grabbed my car keys, yawning.

'I'd better drop off the medicines.'

'I'll drive you,' said Tom.

In the car, he was silent. I turned towards him.

'You OK?'

No reply. His eyebrows frowned, the way they did when he was worried. I longed to smooth them back, and kiss his jaw until it relaxed.

'Look at the bright side – at least now you know I'm not with you for your money.'

I squeezed his thigh and grinned, but his expression didn't change.

'There's no doubt about that. I haven't exactly brought in the millions, have I? You married the wrong sort of banker,' he said.

His mood had slumped as we'd driven away from the house.

'Well, A, I didn't marry you because you're a banker, and B, you've brought in plenty, thank you.'

I took his hand.

'You've just had some bad luck, that's all. Lots of people are in the same boat. The "poor me" act isn't going to work. You're not after some redundancy sympathy sex, are you, Sir?'

'Worth a try.' A half-smile on his face.

I let myself relax against the headrest.

'We need to cut right back now, Faiza. I never thought you'd stick to our budget, but you've been great. We need to see where else we can economise.'

The credit card usage showed exemplary restraint on my part because I'd been paying for the extras from the other account. He was right, though. This was a crisis. I would stop.

'Yes, darling, absolutely.'

'Can you please give me the emergency account statements when we get home? I want to transfer that money to the current account so all the direct debits are covered. We should have enough savings for six months, maybe even eight.'

Did we? I had no idea.

'OK.'

'I made a spreadsheet for that account a while back. It will have the exact balance. I'll check it when I get home. Then I'll draw up a monthly budget to see how far we can stretch it.'

The emergency fund was the only account that I 'looked after'. A couple of years earlier, Tom had moved the money to a new account with a better interest rate. He was in South Africa when the paperwork came and he asked me to file it away. After that he got busy at Apex and, as we weren't using that account, he never needed to see the statements. It had fallen off his radar and into my lap.

I turned on the radio so that U2 filled up the space left by my silence. I knew that the balance would not be what he had on his spreadsheet. I also knew that I could never let him see the statements and find out that I'd been using our savings.

Once we got home, I locked the bedroom door and retrieved the LK Bennett shoe bag from the back of my cupboard. I undid the knots on the nylon drawstring, my nail snagging as I struggled. Most of the money was still there, I was sure it was. I peeked inside the bag, full of statements, unopened and unread. I pulled out an envelope at random, ripping it open. Too scared to look at the statement directly, I squinted at it through screwed-up eyes, holding it away from me at arm's length. I opened my eyes slowly. I needn't have worried: the balance from March, around two years earlier, was quite healthy.

Relieved, I tipped a flurry of white envelopes on to the floor and started to open them one by one, looking for the latest statement to see how much we had in the account now. After a few attempts, I found it. My eyes darted to the balance, locking on to the figure. I kept staring at it, until the numbers swam and became jumbled up. I held my breath. At first, I thought it must be a mistake, that I was reading the statements incorrectly. I ran my nail across the line, following the string of numbers with my fingertip. However many times I checked it though, the figure remained the same. There was nothing left. I had spent almost seventy-five thousand pounds.

I stuffed the ripped envelopes and the roughly folded statements back into the bag. My arms felt like lead. I was breathing too fast, but I couldn't stop. I grabbed some Sellotape and wrapped it around the bag several times over, so the fabric was almost completely covered with tape and it was impossible for anyone to look inside. I hid it back in the cupboard then stayed on the floor, hugging my knees to my chest and rocking myself. My mind was a blank. I wanted to run – and keep on running. I pulled myself up, holding on to the bed. I went downstairs slowly, leaning on the banister.

I watched Tom from the living-room door as he sat on the sofa, watching *Columbo* in a pool of lamplight. He looked up and patted the seat next to him.

'We haven't seen this one for ages. Come.'

He shifted and put his arm around me, making space on the footstool so that I could put my feet up next to his. I put my arm across his stomach and pressed myself into his side. I stared at the colours and shapes on the screen, not hearing anything.

We checked in on the children before we went to bed, for a change, together. The boys were asleep and Sofia was finishing off an essay in bed. I put away phones and books and hung-up sweatshirts and school ties, dropping a kiss on Sofia's head, despite her 'Go away, Mum!' All the time, my mind was screaming, 'What have I done?' I watched the boys as they snuggled in soft, heavy duvets, sleeping towards the future we had promised them. The future I had taken away.

As I brushed my teeth, Tom came up behind me. He grinned and put his arms around me. I covered his hands with mine. They had not changed at all over the years and I stroked the golden hairs on the back.

'Screw the job, at least we still have each other,' he said.

I looked at us in the mirror and smiled.

'That's all we need.'

I glanced down, hiding behind my individually attached lash extensions, so he couldn't see the look in my eyes.

Tom fell asleep almost immediately. I tried to calm myself. He was confident, even though his default setting was caution, that he would find something soon. After all, he'd managed to get an interview within twenty-four hours of leaving Apex. With the redundancy money, and some holiday pay, we had enough in the current account to last us six weeks. I curled my hands into fists and squeezed my eyes shut. Tom would have a job before we needed the emergency fund money. I was sure he would.

Three

Tom left early the next morning, before the children were awake. Richard, the headhunter, was squeezing him in for a pre-breakfast coffee at Waterloo. He wore his 'interview outfit', a navy suit, a starched white shirt, silver cufflinks and a blue and pink Hermes tie, which I'd bought him for his fortieth. His hair was slicked back, still damp from the shower.

'Good luck!'

I pinched his bottom. I stood on tiptoe in my bare feet and pressed my lips lightly on to his. His hands went around my waist.

'It sounds like he's got something. That's why he wanted to meet me as soon as possible.'

I held up both hands, fingers crossed, and smiled. He'd woken up with his usual energy restored. His mood was a constant that I could rely on and looked forward to when he came home: a calm, reassuring positivity. It wasn't that he expected things to always be OK. It was that when things went wrong, he was still OK.

His hands moved lower and pulled my hips close. We had made love earlier.

'Sorry to be so quick this morning.'

He grinned and a lock of damp hair fell across his forehead. I pushed it back.

'I'm a very busy woman. That's all the time I had anyway!'

While he was at his meeting, I was driving the boys to school.

'Mum, tell him to turn the music off!'

Alex had woken up cranky. He hadn't finished his cereal and had left his reading book at home.

'Ahmed, darling, just turn it down a bit, will you?'

Some band I didn't know was blaring a song I didn't recognise from his phone. Ahmed had entered that pre-teen zone, where I no longer knew the music he listened to or the meaning of the words he used.

'He's just being a brat, Mum.'

Ahmed turned back to stare down Alex, before complying, or pretending to comply, with my request. I wondered if they had picked up on my tension. Moods were as infectious as norovirus or flu in families. Once one person had it, it was bound to spread. I tried to inject some therapeutic cheer.

'Listen, if you both behave, I'll take you and one friend each for bowling or pizza this weekend. Deal?'

I kept glancing at the numbers on the dashboard clock. Within the hour everything could be back to normal for us.

After the school run, I ignored the unmade beds and the post-breakfast tsunami in the kitchen. I needed to call the surgery about Ami's physiotherapy referral, order a textbook for Sofia, cook something for lunch as Tom would be home, and call Tom's Mum, Victoria, to arrange a time to take her to John Lewis to buy a new microwave. I also wanted to pick up some groceries for Ami and Baba, as they'd missed their shopping trip with me. Instead, I sat down with a cup of coffee and opened up a pack of Jaffa cakes.

Two hours had passed since Tom's meeting. I wanted to text him and ask what had happened, but decided to wait. I didn't want to pressure him. I drained my cup and propped the mobile up in my eyeline against the tall steel pepper mill. I traced the light grey veins on the marble kitchen table as I waited. Finally, it rang. I jumped up. The phone wriggled out of my hands and fell to the floor. It wasn't Tom anyway, but Ami, reminding me about Baba's cardiology appointment the following day, which I was driving them to.

I went into the living room. I checked Tom's WhatsApp and saw he hadn't been online since 7.30 a.m. He might have been sent to an interview straight away. I stood in the middle of the room, not sure what to do. I looked around. The emergency fund was everywhere. Above the sofa hung an enormous seascape oil painting which I'd bought from one of the art galleries in the Village. I'd told Tom that it was from a graduate art show and had cost next to nothing. A large Pakistani rug, the traditional tree of life, its navy and pale green silk woven into intricate birds of paradise, deer and lions, dominated the floor. A friend's husband had a carpet shop in Knightsbridge and he'd given me a hefty discount. The rug would be a family heirloom one day. It had seemed like an investment, not just an indulgence, and always drew gasps of appreciation when we had people over. The pale grey sofa from John Lewis, which I told Tom had been 75 per cent off in the sale, and the Murano glass lights, which I'd said were from Homebase, but had been bought on the New King's Road – all these things taunted me. My house was a crime scene. There was enough evidence there to sink me.

To distract myself and get the house into a decent state, I started the well-choreographed routine of picking up shoes, straightening duvets and plumping cushions with the imprints of the children still in them from the night before. I gathered up the daily mounds of clothes that seemed to appear on their bedroom floors overnight. But I kept walking into the bathroom when I had meant to go to my bedroom, or picking up a jumper or a towel, with no idea about where I was supposed to put them. I couldn't bear it any longer. I texted: *Hi, when will you be home?* The message was delivered but not read.

Tom came home an hour later. I ran to meet him, but stopped when I saw his face. He tossed a tightly rolled up edition of Thursday's *FT* onto the console table and loosened the Hermes noose.

'No luck, I'm afraid. He said there are things in the pipeline but nothing concrete at the moment.'

I took his hand and we walked into the living room together.

'He's not the only headhunter in the City, is he?' I said. 'Why don't you sign up with a few more?'

I bit the inside of my cheek, keeping my face in neutral.

'I met David for a coffee afterwards. He said the same thing. It's all about headcounts and hiring freezes at the moment. Everyone says the market should pick up in the next quarter, though. That's not too bad.'

The next quarter meant three more months of mortgage payments, a new term's school fees for Sofia and Ahmed, and three months of bills.

Tom went to change and I started to pace the room. I wiped my hands on the front of my jeans. My chest was tight and I rubbed it, trying to ease the burning. We didn't have enough money for three months.

'I have to tell him. I have to tell him!'

The words ricocheted inside my skull. I had to do it. The sooner the better. Once he knew, we could take steps to manage the situation. We could borrow money from the bank, maybe, and use credit cards if we didn't have cash. We could prepare ourselves. I had to do it.

I gave him some tea when he came down. He sat down on the sofa and I stood by the window, looking out at the garden, watching the birds at the far end, sitting on the garden chairs that were still wet from the rain. I couldn't face him when I told him. I waited a few minutes, getting myself ready. I scrolled through my phone, pretending to read an email. My lips were dry. I opened my mouth but I couldn't string the words together. I didn't even know which words to use. I knew that once I started speaking, my marriage would be over.

I couldn't stop thinking about the last time. Six years ago, just after Alex was born, I'd got into some trouble with money. In a way, it had also been Tom's fault – to start with, anyway. He had a habit of checking every item on our monthly credit card bill before he paid it off. He'd go down the list, reading every single payment out loud, whether it was a TFL charge for the tube, or a particularly large grocery bill if we were entertaining. When he came across something he didn't recognise, he'd ask me about it. I knew that he was just 'being a banker', and looking out for fraudulent transactions, but I hated it. It triggered memories of the endless arguments Ami and Baba had about money when I was growing up. The soundtrack to my childhood.

Ami grew up on a ten-bedroom, five-acre estate in Lahore, and her wealthy parents, who owned several factories, had objected to her marrying Baba, who was still a graduate student, from a modest background. After their wedding they had moved to London as Baba had a scholarship to study at UCL. Ami's past had not prepared her for the tiny flat in South London, which was all Baba could afford when Farrah and I were young, or life on the salary of a junior, and then middle manager in an engineering firm. Ami's 'essentials' were Baba's 'frivolities' and this argument swirled, circular and never-ending in our house.

Despite vowing never to be like my parents, somehow, I'd ended up in the same place. For Tom, money was utility and security. For me, it was a solution to all sorts of problems. We had never found a middle ground.

When Tom used to ask me about the credit card bill it felt as if he was asking me to justify every purchase. He said he was only keeping track of our spending, as I couldn't be bothered. I started to call him controlling. He called me irresponsible. It had felt like déjà vu. It was my childhood nightmare all over again. We never fought about anything else.

One day, when I was offered a store card in my name only, I signed on the dotted line. I'd needed to buy a new dress for Tom's work summer party. I was still overweight after Alex and these parties always made me nervous. It felt wonderful to spend the money without having to give an explanation, the way it used to feel when I had my own salary going into my account. It wasn't that Tom would have stopped me buying the dress, but he would have passed comment or judgement. For me, that was almost worse.

I used the card again a few times: clothes for Sofia, toys for Ahmed and Alex, some make-up, a couple of lamps and some bed linen. I spent a few hundred pounds. Then I stopped and cut the card up so I was not tempted further.

When the bills came, I tore them up and threw them away. I knew I'd need to pay them eventually, but I thought that it could wait a few months, even a couple of years. There was an initial interest-free period, though I didn't check exactly how long that was for. I didn't want to know. I pushed it all to the back of my mind, and then got so caught up in the daily whirl of the children and Ami being ill, that I lost track of time. I didn't know when the invoices turned into final demands, or legal notices, because I never opened the letters. Tom found out when he answered the phone to a debt recovery agency one evening, who told him they'd be sending their 'colleagues' to collect property unless the debt was repaid within twenty-four hours. With interest, the bill had spiralled into thousands. He'd paid them off, but he had been livid. Seeing how mortified I was, and that I was still suffering from that sleep-deprived exhaustion of having a new baby, while also looking after Ami, who was recovering from gall bladder surgery, he'd forgiven me. I'd blurted out how much I hated the way he questioned me and explained why. He had agreed to stop and I had agreed not to overspend. I had sworn it would never happen again.

But it had. This time, he was in no position to bail me out. Nor would he forgive me, I knew that.

I decided not to say anything. We still had money for a few weeks; he'd only just started his job search – something was bound to turn up.

Over the next few days, he heard the same message repeated, over and over again: no one was hiring at the moment, not at his level. Contacts that he'd emailed and friends who'd snatched a few minutes to meet him for a drink, all told him it could take weeks, if not months, before the market picked up.

He came home after yet another networking meeting in the City.

'No luck, I'm afraid. Back to square one.'

He walked past me without saying anything more. He took his laptop and sat down on the sofa, not loosening his tie, or taking off his jacket. He fixed his eyes on the screen, and remained at the same spot until the children came home. At one point, I wedged myself between him and the laptop, pushing it aside. I put my hands on either side of his face. His eyes looked trapped and helpless in an intricate cobweb of lines. The flecks of grey in his temples, which I loved to stroke when we lay in bed, suddenly made him seem older. I bent down to kiss him. His lips didn't move. He glanced up at me once, with a flicker of a smile, then put his hands around my waist and moved me aside. His eyes went straight back to the screen.

I went to the kitchen. I grasped the edge of the butler sink and took a deep breath. The blossom tree outside the window had exploded into bubble-gum pink. There was nothing I could do to make Tom feel better.

Tom had asked me to transfer the money for next month's mortgage and bills from the emergency fund into the current account. He wanted to see the bank statements too, so he could manage that account himself going forwards. I told him I couldn't remember where I'd kept the papers, but promised to look for them. In the meantime, I'd make the transfer myself, since I had a card for that account, but Tom's had been kept safely with the statements.

'Make sure you transfer the money before May 30th, OK? The redundancy money will be finished by then and all the bills will be due.'

Something fluttered in my throat. I checked the calendar on my phone.

We had six weeks till May 30th. That was when all our money would be gone. We'd miss the mortgage payments. We would be bankrupt. We would lose everything.

My breathing was fast and shallow. I tried to take a proper gulp of air into my lungs, but it got stuck in my throat.

I put the phone face down on the counter, and threw a dish towel over it. I started preparing after-school snacks for the children on auto pilot. I washed grapes – green for Sofia and Ahmed, black for Alex – and took out bananas and satsumas. Ami had given me a box of fresh jalebis for the children when I'd popped in to see her yesterday. I placed the sticky sweets on a plate, then tore off three pieces of kitchen towel and folded them into triangles. I arranged everything on the table. When there was nothing else left to do, I sat down and let my head sink into my hands. I closed my eyes.

A time bomb started to tick in my head.

Four

Six weeks to May 30th

Tom was meeting another headhunter the next day. Six weeks was plenty of time for first and second interviews. He could have a new job within a month. It was possible. But what if it didn't happen before our deadline?

Dead. Line.

The words thumped along with my heartbeat as I lay in bed, until my mind grew numb and darkness swallowed me up into a restless oblivion. My eyes snapped open at six, an hour before the alarm. Purple crescents dented my palms and I rubbed them gently with my thumb. I sat up, suddenly alert. An idea had slipped into my mind while I was half asleep.

There was a way to fix this. I didn't need to find seventy-five thousand pounds. I just needed to find a job. If there was enough money coming in each month to cover our bills until Tom was working again, he need never find out what I'd done. I'd tell him we should use my salary and leave our savings intact. I knew he'd agree. 'Never touch savings if you can help it.' It was Tom's mantra.

The only problem was that I hadn't had a job for fifteen years. I didn't even have a CV.

I was meeting Sam and Naila for coffee that morning. Sam had gone back to work recently after ten years at home with her kids – she'd know what to do.

I waited in the warm cocoon of a Wimbledon Village coffee shop, watching a constant stream of women enter the café with their regulation size-six bottoms, carrying enormous designer bags in butter-soft leather with discreet logos. These women in their thirties and forties had better skin than the twenty-something baristas serving them coffee.

I looked at the mound of shredded tissues lying in front of me and pushed it aside. I'd decided not to tell my friends about the emergency fund. What would they think of me if they knew what I had done?

My story was that I was ready to go back to work; the children were older and I was bored.

I spotted Sam rushing into the café. She always looked as if she was late for an appointment, although she was usually early. Even her clothes looked thrown on. She alternated between identikit shift dresses in navy or black, worn with ballet pumps for the office, or skinny jeans and trainers with jumpers she had owned for years.

She started talking before she sat down, unrolling the long red scarf from around her neck and waving to the waitress at the same time.

'I just came from Mum's so I haven't had any coffee yet!'

'Did you manage to find a carer?'

Her mother had just been diagnosed with Alzheimer's.

'Yes, but it's not really a long-term solution. I want to

make a little granny annexe, but James is working all hours on some mega case, so I haven't talked to him yet.'

Naila arrived and we all hugged.

'I love your outfit, Naila,' said Sam.

Naila was wearing a white cotton salwar kameez with pink embroidery and a matching pink dupatta.

'Thanks,' said Naila. 'I'm going for lunch at a Pakistani friend's house later. She has a lot of older "aunties" coming too, so I thought I'd go trad.'

As soon as our coffees came, I plunged in.

'Guess what? I've decided to go back to work,' I said.

I smiled as if I was talking about a weekend away with Tom.

'How come?' they said together.

'I think it's time I expanded my horizons beyond the school's charity ball circuit,' I laughed.

'Good! I don't know how you put up with all that rubbish anyways,' Naila said. 'I can't believe you had a class Botox party!'

Naila was always shocked by the extravagant extra-curricular activities of the mothers at my children's schools.

'I was at work, so I got out of it. It's not really my thing, as you can see,' said Sam.

She frowned, then smiled, pointing to various parts of her face, to demonstrate her lack of cosmetic paralysis. Sam's daughter was at the same school as Sofia, Brookwood High.

I smiled.

'Sam, can you please help me write a CV? Actually, could we please do it now? I want to start applying today.'

'What's the hurry?' said Sam.

She took a hairband from her wrist and tied her blonde curls into a messy ponytail.

I looked at the tables on either side, to make sure there was no one I knew, then leaned forwards to whisper.

'Tom's lost his job.'

Sam's hand went up to her mouth.

'That's terrible! When did this happen?'

'Just last week. Please, please don't tell anyone, not even your husbands. Tom wants to get used to the idea himself first.'

'Of course; it's no one's business anyway,' said Sam.

'I don't think you should tell anyone at all, not even when Tom gets used to it,' said Naila. 'Do you remember when Rani's husband lost his job? People just stopped inviting them over for dinner. Everyone still talks about it even though he's been back at work for ages.'

I didn't want to tell anyone either. I didn't need to be gossip fodder for some people, or the object of pity for others.

'Is Tom all right? Are you?' said Naila.

I dug my nails into my hands to stop the sudden tears gathering in my eyes.

'He's OK, a little shocked of course. I'm just so angry. He hasn't done anything wrong. It's so unfair.'

'Try not to worry, Faiza. I'm sure he'll find something else soon,' said Sam. She paused a second, looking down and brushing away a non-existent crumb from the table. When she spoke again, it was more slowly, as if weighing each word.

'At least banks give good packages,' she said.

Sam and I could talk about anything, but there was one

34

topic that we never discussed: money. I knew Sam had sex with James for the first time, in his office, that her father had cheated on her mother with her mother's younger sister, and that one of her twelve-year-old twins was in therapy for still wetting his bed. I was the first person she called when she found a lump in her breast. She knew about Ahmed's anxiety, the hiccups in my marriage I would never tell anyone else about, my frustration at my sister not helping to look after our parents, and the racism I came across on the tube or, more subtly, at dinner parties.

But we never discussed how much our husbands earned, what our houses were worth, how much we had in savings or what we paid the cleaner or the taxman.

I cleared my throat.

'Actually, the packages aren't that great these days.'

Sam knew Tom didn't earn the sort of bonuses that her husband James accumulated year on year. James was a partner at a Magic Circle law firm, something he told you when he introduced himself for the first time, as if it were an extension of his name.

'They're still better than for most people, Faiza. I don't know what we'd do if Tariq lost his job. IT doesn't pay like banking,' said Naila, not suffering any such qualms as Sam.

I wanted to tell them we were broke, but then I'd have to tell them why. The words vibrated on my lips, like an itch I needed to scratch. What if I just vomited out the truth, so that it lay exposed on the table in front of us? These were my closest friends.

Naila and I had met as teenagers, forced to attend Urdu lessons every Saturday in Worcester Park. We'd sit at the back, reading *Cosmo*s hidden inside our text books, bonding over the strange, uncharted dual-culture life we were creating for ourselves. I met Sam when our boys were at nursery nine years ago. She was kind, calm and a free spirit who didn't care what people thought about her. We'd met for coffee and power walks on the Common almost every week since. Now Sofia and Sam's daughter Sienna were in the same class too.

The fact that I loved these two so dearly, though, was also what stopped me from telling them. What I'd done was so selfish and reckless that it was bound to change the way they looked at me. The easiest thing would be to just say nothing. I wouldn't have to feel ashamed and they wouldn't have to worry about how to react.

I nodded.

'Yes, nothing to worry about on the money front, thankfully. Not for now, anyway. I just think it will be so much easier to get used to working again while Tom is still home with the kids. That's why I'm in such a hurry.'

'What do you want to do?' said Sam.

'I worked in the City before I had Sofia, at UBS.'

Sam shook her head.

'That won't be easy. Not after such a long break.'

I chewed my lip.

'Let's do your CV first, then you can look at your options,' she said.

She went into action mode, jotting down points in her red notebook, which she'd pulled out of her enormous blue tote. We all chipped in with suggestions.

Naila's neat, dark bob leaned across the table, her gold hoop earrings shaking. She always frowned a little when she listened, as if she wanted to catch each word. I loved that about her. Sam was brisk and business-like, which always made me feel calmer.

'I remember Lingo Bear!' said Naila.

The largest section on my CV was 'CEO Lingo Bear UK'. In reality, all I had to show for being the CEO was a teddy bear graveyard: twenty cardboard boxes crammed into the garden shed.

The bears recited pre-recorded phrases in Mandarin and Russian when their paws were pressed. I knew parents who took their bumps to French films and spoke to their uterine-darlings in a second language to give them a head start. The idea of teddy bears propped up in cots and high chairs, reciting formative phrases in Mandarin, was bound to be a hit. I planned to get bears that spoke Urdu too because Ami and her friends were always complaining that their grandchildren didn't speak Urdu. The possibilities were endless.

They sold well, but then I started to receive irate emails demanding refunds. After a few days of use, the only thing they recited was a high-pitched squeak. But at least it padded out my CV.

'Done!'

Sam tore out the pages and gave them to me.

'Thank you so much!'

'I hope you're coming to Julia's for the charity auction committee,' said Sam.

I groaned.

'Yep, the highlight of my week!'

'What's that? Another yummy mummy meet-up?' said Naila, her gold hoops shaking with disapproval. 'All these auctions and balls, dressing up for committees and lunches! It sounds exhausting.'

'It is a bit crazy,' I admitted.

'I don't understand why you bother paying for private schools at all. If a child is bright, they will do just as well at a state school.'

'That's true,' I said.

This was a discussion we'd had before. I'd never told her my reasons for choosing these schools, or what had happened to me.

She'd tell me I was wrong, that things had changed, times were different and I shouldn't let my one bad experience dictate my decision-making now. In my mind, I'd have to agree; but my heart still held that fear. I couldn't forget. Brookwood had been my safe place and so I had sent Sofia there. For Ahmed I had always chosen tiny prep schools.

I shrugged.

'I was at Brookwood and so was Farrah. It just didn't occur to me to send them anywhere else. My parents were so lucky though, because they didn't have to pay fees! We both had scholarships.'

It was what I always said when family or friends questioned our decision.

'Besides, this committee mafia isn't just a private school thing,' I said.

'That's true. My sister's always complaining about her sons' state school too. The cliques, the showing-off, all those dinner parties like *MasterChef*,' said Sam.

'My kids' schools aren't like that,' said Naila, unconvinced. 'Or the ones I teach at.'

Naila was a supply teacher for Wandsworth council.

All too soon we were checking watches and phones as the to-do lists of our lives called us back to reality. We got up reluctantly, but I was also eager to get home and type up my CV. I could already feel the knots in my neck dissolving. Spending time with my friends was like exhaling deeply. If I'd told them about the money, our conversation would have been very different. I was glad I'd kept it to myself.

As I drove away, a thought dropped like a rock into my chest. This was the first time Tom had been alone at home. He'd been talking about sorting through all the old mail and papers that I tended to stuff into drawers and forget. I sped up, trying to remember if I'd left a random bank statement tucked under some papers in a hurry, instead of hiding it away in the LK Bennett bag. I hoped he hadn't started looking through the drawers yet.

It wasn't safe having all the papers in the house.

Five

5½ weeks to May 30th

Sam and I were at Julia's house for the first committee meeting of the annual charity auction. I was grateful for the distraction. I hadn't received any replies to the dozens of job applications I'd sent off but Sam said that was normal and I had to keep applying. At least Tom had an interview coming up in two weeks. There was a job and he was on the shortlist.

I'd dressed carefully, choosing colours and styles that would make me look like any of the other women there. I wore a blush-pink silk dress and high wedge heels, both from Butterfly, the go-to boutique in the Village. I had straightened my hair, which fell past my shoulders and wore a sheer pink lipstick. My clothes were like an invisibility cloak that helped me fit in with this crowd.

When Sofia was younger, the mothers in the park, or at nursery, had often mistaken me for the nanny. The brown-skinned woman pushing around a fair-skinned, light-haired child. Since then, I had learnt to wear clothes and carry bags that would immediately make them see me as one of them.

While the others milled around in the hallway, their chatter swirling up into the high ceilings and hitting the sparkling chandeliers, Sam and I sat down in the vast, sun-filled living room, interior-designed to look like a stately home in the country, even though we were a twenty-minute Uber ride from Marble Arch.

Sam dumped her bag on the floor.

'Bloody in-laws! Or rather, bloody James! He's rented a crazy villa in Tuscany for our summer holiday and invited not just his parents, but Rupert and his family too. He's very pleased he found one with seven bathrooms, because the one Rupert rented in Nice last year only had five. Honestly, they're like two-year-olds!'

'I feel a bit sorry for poor James,' I said. 'Imagine your parents pitting you like that against your only brother.'

She looked at me, her face flushing. 'Sorry, that was so crass. Tom's not working and I'm...'

'Don't be silly. A problem is a problem. I won't judge your obscene holiday villas!'

I couldn't help thinking, though, that two weeks' rent for their villa would probably cover our mortgage for several months.

'How's Tom? Has he had any luck?'

'Not yet. He says there aren't many jobs around but he has one interview with a bank...'

A cloud of Chanel No 5 descended and Julia loomed over us. She bent down to kiss Sam. I waved. She wouldn't have stooped to kiss me anyway.

'Who has an interview?'

I froze. I didn't need Julia to know my business, especially as she liked to know everyone's business.

'Thanks for hosting us – again!' said Sam.

Julia smiled and shook her sleek blonde bob.

'Pleasure! You're right, this is no time for gossip.' She winked. 'Let's catch up later.'

Julia clapped her hands twice until all fifteen women on the committee were seated in a semi-circle. She stood like a conductor at the head of an orchestra, glistening with honey-blonde highlights and nude lip gloss. Her gesticulating hands were flashes of French manicure and diamond solitaires.

Julia was married to a multi-millionaire, something she saw as a personal achievement, like running a marathon or having a PhD. We had two things in common. Our daughters were in the same form and we were both friends with Sam. She and Sam had met at NCT and Sam said Julia 'wasn't that bad when you got to know her'. I thought that pregnancy must have dulled Sam's usual ability to spot arrogant, self-obsessed snobs.

Julia started to assign duties. I shrank into my seat, dreading what she would lumber me with.

'Sam, can you please ask to do something not too labour intensive? You have your hands full with your mum and I'm job hunting. Then say that I'll help you,' I whispered.

We were put in charge of ticket sales, which involved turning up for an hour at morning drop-off once a week till the end of term.

'Our target this year is to break all previous records and raise £20,000!'

Everyone clapped and Julia held up her hands, her eyes shut for a second, as a shaft of sunshine fell on her like a spotlight. She was wearing a white broderie anglaise sleeveless dress that showed off the tiniest waist I had ever seen on a grown woman, and her long, tanned legs looked like she had rubbed highlighter in a line down her shins.

'The tickets start at £200 for a regular, then £300 for silver and £400 for gold. This is per person, so just double it for couples. Harry will be at a conference in Bali, unfortunately, but we will still sponsor a golden table for eight. It's the least we can do.'

I had never seen Julia's husband, Harry, at any school events since they'd moved to the Village a few months ago, but we heard about Harry all the time. If Julia bought new shoes, she said how Harry loved it when she treated herself. When he missed netball matches, she told us how he took their daughters, Amber and Elle, riding on Wimbledon Common when he wasn't travelling, and always video called them from his office when he was working late. Once, during one of our periodic coffee morning discussions about cheating husbands, Julia had announced that the key to having a faithful husband was to keep your sex life so full that your husband had neither the inclination, nor the energy, to cheat.

'We have sex every day, even when he's travelling,' she had said.

The other women had listened, rapt, to details about sexting, FaceTime striptease and video-sex. Some seemed to be taking mental notes, while others looked worried, probably calculating the inclination and energy levels of their own spouses. I wondered how Julia's husband would feel if he knew she was spilling his bedroom beans? Tom would have hated it.

Lizzie sat down next to me, kissed me on both cheeks,

and started chatting. She was a little older than the rest of us, in her early fifties, but her yoga-toned body and clean-eating regime defied age. Her blonde hair shimmered in gentle waves past her collar bone, a testament to the bespoke herbal shampoo that her facial reflexologist prepared for her every month. She'd offered to get some for me too, but even with the emergency fund it had been too expensive. Lizzie was eco, but eco-luxe.

In the teal and copper kitchen, we were led to a marble-topped island. Amongst the pastel cupcakes, and small glasses with chopped-up fruit salad, there was an elegant chocolate cake, decorated with tiny fresh flowers in pinks and reds, and a silver candle.

'Happy birthday for next week, Sam! I baked it myself this morning,' said Julia, putting her arm around Sam.

Julia's smile seemed genuine and I wondered, as I sometimes did, whether I was simply being mean-spirited or over-sensitive about her. Everyone else seemed to love her and she was always at the centre of every group and the top of every guest list. People said how helpful she was, sending food if someone was unwell, and how thoughtful, giving lifts to other people's children. I'd never warmed to her, though, and the feeling seemed mutual. But if Sam liked Julia, there must be some good in her. I would look for it a little harder.

As we ate, the conversations revolved around university choices, but I stopped listening – I was thinking of an excuse to miss the auction. I couldn't afford the tickets now but the date was months away, in September, so I didn't know what I could say so far in advance and committee members were expected to set an example and buy the tickets first.

'Faiza?' Lizzie was touching my arm.

'Sorry?'

'Has Sofia decided what she wants to study?'

'She's not at all sure, but maybe Spanish? She likes languages.'

'Does Sofia speak your Pakistani language?' said Julia.

'Urdu,' Lizzie corrected and I smiled at her.

Lizzie always had my back.

'She understands Urdu, but she can't speak it that well,' I said.

'How does she communicate with her granny? I saw her with your mum in the Village. Your mother was wearing her gorgeous eastern dress. Such vibrant colours,' said Julia.

I frowned, unsure what Julia was asking.

'I mean, if Sofia doesn't speak...' Julia paused, as if the next word required oral gymnastics or painful regurgitation, '*Urdu*, can your mother speak English?'

I wasn't as shocked as I could have been at this question. I just sighed inwardly and smiled.

'I hope so, seeing as she has an MA in English Literature from King's.'

Julia beamed, as if genuinely thrilled about Ami's academic record. I was afraid she might clap.

'Well, isn't that just fantastic!'

I didn't know what to say and was grateful when Lizzie changed the subject. Despite their matching millions, Lizzie and Julia could not be more different. Lizzie wore her Botox and vintage designer clothes like a uniform, merely as something expected in her role as professional wife to a CEO. Julia, on the other hand, used her wardrobe to generate the sort of envy that she seemed to thrive on.

'Don't worry, Maddie still hasn't decided on her degree either,' said Lizzie.

'The problem with Amber is that she has too many choices,' said Julia.

'What do you mean?' said Sam, who had joined us.

'Well, she is a very talented artist, so art school is a possibility, but she also excels at sciences and my husband is keen for her to have a "proper" degree, ideally at Oxford, following in his footsteps. Then, last week, a modelling scout stopped us at Waterloo. I checked him out and it's all above board. He said she had exactly the sort of look the agency wanted. I just don't know what she should do. It's really stressful, to be honest.'

There were cries of excitement from the other committee members about the modelling scout, and commiserations about Amber's difficult life. A couple of women, eager to talk about their own daughters' similar struggles, compared notes with Julia.

Sam and I moved away to get some coffee.

'Poor Amber!' I laughed.

'Faiza!' said Sam, grinning back.

Some of the women asked us when we'd start selling tickets.

'In a couple of weeks,' said Sam.

James always bought a full 'golden table', inviting the most senior partners at his firm and their wives as his guests. He might miss parents' evenings and school plays, but he was always at the head of his table at the charity auction, trying to outbid the other alpha fathers. Charity wasn't the only aim of the charity auction, we all knew that, but at least most of the money would go to the children's hospital, as I always reminded myself.

I had to say something to everyone, so that later, when I didn't buy tickets, it wouldn't seem as if I was trying to hide something.

'I have a horrible feeling the auction is on the same night as a big party for my aunt's golden wedding anniversary. We have relatives flying in from Dubai, Pakistan and New York.'

I arranged my face in a suitable grimace.

'That's such a shame,' said Lizzie, who had joined the group, along with Julia. 'We'll miss you.'

Lizzie's baby-pink maxi dress was as soft and gentle as her. Her eyes would have crinkled when she smiled, if her laughter lines hadn't been zapped into oblivion at the Botox clinic. That was her one concession to unnatural practices on her body.

'Don't worry, Faiza,' said Julia, 'this year, the committee members will donate the price of the tickets even if they can't attend. That way you can still contribute.'

'That's a great idea. It is for charity after all, and we can all afford it,' said Lizzie.

I gripped my cup tight. If I didn't buy a ticket or make a donation, questions would be asked – and I would have no answers.

Six

'Can you please give me the statements for the emergency fund when you get back? I need the account details,' Tom called out, just as I was leaving to pick up Alex and Ahmed from school.

My heart started pounding.

'I'm sorry, darling, I still can't remember where I put them. You know what I'm like!'

'Yes, I do know.' His voice was terse, without a hint of indulgence.

Normally, he would have faux-frowned at my lack of organisation, before smiling and telling me I was lucky to have a husband who was so devoted to filing. I'd have teased him back, mocking his obsession with paperwork. This time, he just snapped, 'It's fine. The next statement should be coming soon. Or I'll just go to the bank myself.'

'No! Don't waste your time doing that. I know the papers are here somewhere. There's no urgency, is there? You have your interview coming up. Just focus on that.'

I left and drove to the Village, going too fast, hoping the

speed cameras had no film. I couldn't find parking so I left my car in a 'permit holders only' bay, and ran to the bank.

I smiled at the cashier; a friendly woman called Linda.

'I'm afraid we've had some problems with our post. Would you please hold on to my statements, so I can collect them from the branch myself? You hear such awful stories about identity theft these days.'

Usually, I was alone when the statements came, and hid them before Tom got home. Now, this would be impossible. She agreed to keep them for me and confirmed that none had been posted out yet for that month.

'Why don't you go online? I can set it up now?' said Linda. She tapped her keyboard and it was done.

Just as I was about to leave, I stopped. It was a joint account. Even if Tom didn't have the online passwords, he could still walk in and ask for a statement. I retraced my steps, as if walking a tightrope, and popped a smile on my face.

'I almost forgot! My husband wants to remove his name from this account so can you please change it to my name only, Linda?'

She frowned and looked at her colleague in the next window. I swallowed. Did she suspect something? They might call Tom and tell him that I was trying to take his name off the account. I twisted the leather strap on my bag around my palm.

'I'm sorry, I didn't catch that.'

She hadn't even heard me.

'My husband wants to take his name off this account. He doesn't really use it and keeps getting marketing emails.'

'Certainly. He just needs to come in and sign a form.'

I clutched my keys. The sharp edges bit into my palm.

'Right.' I frowned. 'The problem is, he's always at work and he can never get to the bank.'

I shook my head as if exasperated by his hours.

'We don't usually allow it, but as I know you, I'll just give you the form to take home. Please ask him to sign it, then you can drop it back,' said Linda.

I felt relieved, but also ashamed because of her trust in me. We always chatted when I came in to the bank. At least there were some advantages to being an identikit Wimbledon Village mother: women who occupied themselves with benign activities, like after-school ballet, cheering at rugby matches, Friday night dinner parties and mid-morning coffee dates, although of course, this was never the whole story. I knew people saw me like that too. That was my 'subcategory' anyway. The initial classification was, of course, always, brown, Muslim, and of Pakistani origin.

As I came out, I saw these women, like me, running errands in skinny jeans and blow-dried hair, making sure that family lives ticked along to the meticulous standards their spouses and offspring had become accustomed to. Harmless women, conducting harmless lives. No wonder the cashier had bent the rules for me.

I hurried to my car, wondering how I'd get Tom to sign the form. I'd have to pretend that it was something for school, maybe. It wouldn't be easy though. He never signed anything without reading it twice. I stumbled, tripping on the pavement. What if he didn't sign it? What if I signed it instead? The children always joked that his signature was so easy to copy. I shook my head, to expel that thought. No, that was forgery. It was betraying Tom.

I sped away, as if escaping a moment of madness. When I got home, I hid the form under a stack of papers in my bedside table drawer then went down to the kitchen.

Tom was standing inside the fridge door, shaking his head. 'There are so many things here that are about to expire tomorrow. Then you'll say they're not safe and throw them away. It has to stop.'

He was right, but I didn't like his tone.

He went on, 'I'm going to make a meal plan and a daily spending limit. I'll stick it up so everyone can see. And we'll all eat the *same* meal. The children are spoilt. I'm going to make the spreadsheet now.'

I tried not to get angry about the way he had spoken. I started washing the bunch of coriander that I'd bought from Tooting, rather than the supermarket, where it would have cost three times as much. He was wrong. I *was* trying to be careful. The shellac on my nails had started to peel and I had left it, instead of going to the nail bar. I'd cancelled my hairdresser appointment too.

I was putting away the coriander when Sofia came into the kitchen and started eating a satsuma.

'How was school? Are you hungry? I've made your favourite, lamb biryani.'

'Thanks, Mum, I'm starving. I came top in the Spanish test and Miss Haynes has a friend who's an artist so we're going to his studio in Barcelona.'

'Sounds amazing!'

'Oh, and she needs the money for Barcelona on Monday. Sorry, I forgot to give you this.'

She passed me a crumpled letter from her backpack.

'I thought it wasn't due till July?'

According to the letter, the final instalment of four hundred pounds was due in four days.

'No, Mum, I told you about this. You just didn't listen.'

I stared at the letter. I still owed Lizzie £100, for a spa day she had organised for Sam's birthday treat. I had to give her my share.

After dinner, Tom pinned his meal plan up in the kitchen then put his arms around me and sighed.

'I'm sorry about earlier.'

'I should hope so too!' I said. 'Not only does my husband lose his job, he seems to have lost his marbles too!'

I shook my head, but smiled to let him know that it was OK. I pulled away a little, to look at him.

'Tom? I've been thinking. Why don't we sell my car? We don't really need two cars. We shouldn't touch the emergency fund if we can help it. Once the cash is gone, that's it, isn't it?'

I tried to use his spirit of economising, to persuade him. I couldn't sell the car unless he agreed.

He laughed.

'Steady on darling. I was thinking more about switching supermarkets, not selling off cars!'

He pulled me close again. 'I have plenty put aside for us. Relax.'

He dropped a kiss on my head and when he let go, I wiped my eyes.

'Don't cry, darling. Everyone is healthy, the children are happy, I have you, we have money in the bank.'

Tom had started filing all our outstanding paperwork. It wouldn't be long before he wanted to do the same for the emergency fund. The next day, when he was at the budget supermarket, armed with his meal plan, I took out the bank form and sat down at the dining table. I practised his signature on a piece of paper. I did it again. It was identical to Tom's.

I signed the form and took it to the bank. Tom was immediately locked out of our account – and I had committed fraud.

Seven

5 weeks to May 30th

The school fees were due.

Tom had printed out the invoices and asked me to pay from the emergency fund. He had a meeting with the headhunter.

I parked by Wimbledon Common. I needed space to think. School fees had always been vaguely abstract concepts to me. I didn't even know exactly how much we paid. My role was to analyse school league tables, go to Open Days, Parents' Evenings and uniform fittings at Peter Jones. I was shocked when I saw the sum in black and white. It was an impossible amount.

I remembered a letter saying that if the fees weren't paid, students would have to stay at home until the accounts had been settled. I imagined Sofia or Ahmed being pulled out of class and sent home.

When Tom had lost his job, I had considered, fleetingly, moving Sofia and Ahmed to other schools. Alex was at the local state primary, so that wasn't an issue. It seemed a cruel and short-sighted option, though. Sofia was in the middle of her A levels; she worked late into the night on her essays and talked about her history coursework with the same enthusiasm she normally reserved for K-Pop bands. She was on track for Oxbridge. More than that, though, she was happy. She had been at the school since she was seven years old. It was her world.

Ahmed's recovery was still fragile. He was finally making friends at Clissington's. He no longer cried every morning, begging me to let him stay home, as he had at his old prep school. Most days back then I'd find him hiding in the loos at pickup time, pale and trembling, often in tears, crouching, feet up, on the lid of a toilet. On the way home, he was sick so often that I kept a kitchen roll and extra plastic bags in the car.

He started asking why he had an Arabic name, when Sofia and Alex didn't. I was surprised but told him I'd just always loved that name. What he didn't tell me at the time was that a group of white boys had been taunting him, saying that his surname could not be 'Saunders' if his first name was 'Ahmed'. They followed him around calling him 'Asshead Ahmed' and started to bully him.

'Don't pretend you're like us.'

At the same time, the two Asian boys in his class said he was 'weird' to be called Ahmed but have an English surname and blue eyes. They didn't bully him, but simply never accepted him into their group. For Ahmed, that was just as bad.

In the end, I decided to move him to Clissington's six months ago, a small prep school next door to Sofia's school. Now that my baby was happy and settled, I'd do anything to keep it that way.

I thought about the jewellery lying at the bank.

Unfortunately, most of my things had been stolen in a burglary a few years ago, including my traditional Pakistani wedding 'sets' and gold bangles. I still had a few pieces left, though, that Tom had bought me over the years. If I sold these, I'd have enough for the fees.

At the bank, I plunged my hand inside the metal safe deposit box, feeling the pouches nestling there, like tiny velvet creatures hibernating. I took everything out – earrings, pendants and rings – and put them into my handbag.

There were two other black velvet cases lying in the safe, each with curled up, acid-yellow Post-it notes. Sofia's name, scrawled by Diana, Tom's late grandmother, was on one, and Ahmed's on the other. These were family heirlooms that she herself had been presented with as a young bride by her husband in the 1940s. For Sofia, there was a gold brooch and for Ahmed, her diamond engagement ring, which she'd worn every day for sixty-two years.

I'd never had these pieces valued because I'd never measured their worth in terms of money. As things stood though, it might be good to know how much I could get for them. It would have to be the nuclear option and I realised that I might need one. I slipped them into my bag as well.

In the jewellery shop in the Village, the owner didn't hide his surprise when I said that I was selling, not buying, and asked if I could get cash for my items, that day.

'If the items are suitable for us. May I?' he said.

I sat down at a small, green, felt-covered table. He sat up a little taller. The power shifted in the room. The atmosphere became more business-like, for both of us.

I spread out my treasures across the table and he started examining them. The eye evaluating the stones had a contraption held up close, to help him look inside the stones. His other eye, free from examining the jewels, seemed just as adept at seeing right through me. I squirmed as his eye darted to my navy Prada handbag. I could almost hear his mind whirring as he tried to reconcile my long, highlighted hair and pale grey cashmere peacoat with my request for cash.

He put down the long diamond earrings that Tom had bought me, sat back and trained both eyes on me for the first time.

'I'll give you three thousand.'

'For the earrings?'

'For the lot.'

I started to scratch the eczema on my hand. The rasp of my nails on the skin was the only sound in the room. Despite his scrutiny I couldn't stop. A streak of blood broke through, making my skin burn.

I did a quick tally of what Tom had paid for these things: the earrings, an anniversary gift; the pearl pendant, which he'd slipped round my neck on my fortieth birthday four years ago, flying back overnight from Kazakhstan so he was with me when I woke up; the cocktail ring which he'd put into a Burger King bag along with a Whopper, which was all I had craved the week before Ahmed was born; aquamarine earrings that he'd put on my pillow when Alex had been a week old, as I rubbed cream into my cracked nipples, tears running down my face. Each piece was a nugget from our marriage, a memento of a happy milestone. There were several other pieces too. Tom must have spent over twelve thousand.

'But they're worth a lot more.'

'You must understand that you won't get what you paid

for them. If you had brought me gold, or antique pieces, perhaps I could have offered more.'

It was a sign.

I opened my bag, imagining Diana's reaction if she saw me flogging her beloved things. At the same time, I was relieved that I still had a way out. I handed over the pieces as if they were contraband.

'Now, this looks much more promising.'

He licked his lips, almost salivating. I was breaking my promise to Diana and losing the only link the children had to her. I silenced my doubts as I watched him finger the items. Sofia and Ahmed wouldn't miss these things, they'd never really had them. They needed the money more.

He picked up a larger eye piece set in brass and began examining the brooch, holding it right up to the lens and turning it over to see the back as well. There was a plaster on one of his fingers, with dirty edges peeling off. The room grew hot and I shrugged off my coat.

He took a sharp breath in. Maybe this would solve all our problems in one go.

'Fake!' He spat out the word and pushed the pieces back towards me as if he couldn't bear to touch them anymore.

'What?' I frowned. 'That's impossible. These belonged to my husband's grandmother.'

My voice was shrill. This man was a crook.

'I'm afraid it's true. You're welcome to take them to another jeweller but they'll tell you the same thing.'

His voice softened as he saw me slump. A stray tear slipped out and I swatted it away quickly before it could track down my face.

'They are beautiful pieces and I could give you a few

hundred for them, but I would advise you to keep them in the family, for sentimental value.'

Why had Diana lied to me? All pretence gone, I leaned forwards.

'Couldn't you give me a better price for the other things? Perhaps four thousand?' My throat was clogged. 'Please?'

Before he could reply, a woman around my age came in and sat down. She slanted tanned legs under the table. The silver bracelets on her wrist tinkled as she pushed her blonde hair back and smiled.

I pleaded with my eyes, but he shook his head.

I dropped the jewellery into my handbag. My coat got caught in the chair legs as I stood up and it tipped to the floor with a thud.

'Sorry!'

As I bent down to pick up my coat, my bag slipped out of my hands, scattering my keys, purse and the jewellery on the floor. A ten-pence coin rolled into the corner of the room and spun noisily on the floorboards on one spot. Tears sprang to my eyes. I straightened the chair, aware they were both watching. I bent my head low and scooped everything back into my handbag. Clutching my coat to my chest, I fled.

To anyone watching, I would seem like someone who had just treated herself to a purchase. If they looked closely, though, they would see that my shoulders were slumped and my head bent as I searched for answers in the dirty grey slabs of the pavement.

As I passed my bank, I happened to look up. A brightly coloured poster shouted at me in capital letters: 'PERSONAL LOANS'. It urged me to come in and 'see if we can help'. I followed its command.

Eight

The manager, Roberto, first name only, trendy glasses and a Scottish accent, led me to his office.

'I'd like to take out a small loan, please.'

'Certainly, Mrs Saunders,' he said, as if I was ordering a cappuccino.

'Please call me Faiza.'

He smiled.

'Let's start by looking at your transaction history,' he said, and started scrolling through his computer screen.

I fidgeted in my chair, unable to sit still, unable to do anything but watch on in horror. My transaction history was my walk of shame. My life was being strip-searched. Everything I'd hidden from Tom, my parents, even from my friends, was being examined in intimate detail by a stranger sitting right in front of me. I had never been able to look at these gory details. I always threw away receipts and never checked statements or downloaded banking apps.

He could see the freefall of our savings and how I had

haemorrhaged thousands of pounds, bleeding my family dry. It was all there, exposed to his scrutiny.

I had thought that using the emergency fund was the perfect solution. Tom didn't have to worry about money and I could make sure that the children didn't feel left out and different from their friends, the way I had growing up. It also meant Tom and I never fought about money, the way my parents had.

I had always planned to put the money back.

I waited for the manager's disgust at what he'd seen but when he spoke, it was only to murmur, 'Hmm. How much were you looking to borrow, Faiza?'

Relieved we were still on track, I smiled and sat back.

'We have a temporary cash-flow problem. My husband's between jobs and I'm interviewing as well. I need to borrow money for the school fees, please.'

His expression didn't change at the thousands of pounds that I was asking for. He tapped it into his computer.

'So, reason for loan, school fees for the year,' he said.

'No, that would just cover the fees for one term,' I said.

At this, his eyebrows shot up. I rubbed my neck, which was beginning to itch.

'I know, it's expensive, isn't it?'

It was a lot, but we weren't the only ones paying it. Besides, I had my own reasons to keep my children inside the hermetically sealed bubbles of Brookwood High and Clissington's. I had never forgotten what I had been through before my parents moved me to Brookwood. The boys at my old school spitting at me as I walked home, the whole class laughing that my mother wore pyjamas when she picked me up from school wearing her salwar kameez, and the girls who wouldn't sit next to me because I 'smelled like a dirty Paki'.

The minute I'd won a scholarship to Brookwood, everything had changed. I hadn't had a single racist comment thrown at me for the seven years I was there. So, when it was time to choose a school for Sofia, I made an emotional decision and decided on Brookwood. We'd been able to afford it back then.

'The problem is, Faiza, that one of you needs to be in employment for the loan to be sanctioned.'

I tried to slow my breathing, and not to sound as if I were explaining something to a three-year-old.

'That's a bit tricky, Roberto. You see, the reason we need a loan is because neither of us has a job.'

I smiled and shook my head as if amused at the trick life had played on us.

'I'm afraid, unless there's a mechanism for repayment, we can't proceed.'

Easy-going Roberto had somehow transformed into jobsworth Roberto, without me noticing.

I leaned forwards, and gripped the edge of his desk.

'Roberto, I've been a customer here for over twenty years. I opened this account when I was at university. Look at our spending – we earn a lot of money. Can't you help me out? Please?'

The last word shot out in a whisper.

'As a goodwill gesture for your long association with the bank, I can lend you five thousand pounds. It will be at a higher interest rate, though.'

All I heard was that he'd give me five thousand pounds. I

signed whatever he put in front of me and didn't probe him about the higher interest rate.

'Once you have your job, we can discuss other options like credit cards or further loans,' he said.

I felt as if Roberto had removed a knife from my chest. I could breathe again.

When I came out of the bank, it was pouring. I leaned forwards, fighting against the wind as it pushed me back. Icy spurts of water blinded me. With the three thousand I could get from the jeweller, I had eight thousand for the schools. I'd tell them I'd pay the rest in a month. Tom's job should have come through by then.

I didn't have an umbrella and started to run towards the jewellers. The owner opened the door for me.

'I'll take the money, please,' I said.

'Hey you! Wait your turn!'

A sing-song voice teased me. I spun around. Julia was smiling at me. She had scooped her blonde bob up in one hand, and was stroking a string of diamonds encircling her smooth neck. I swallowed, wondering if she'd heard what I'd said.

I caught sight of my face in a mirrored panel behind the counters and saw streaks of mascara on my cheeks. I tried to rub them away.

'I've known Ralph forever and he still won't give me a discount!' she pouted, smiling at the owner.

'You don't need a discount!'

They bickered like old friends.

'What are you buying, Faiza?' said Julia.

I wanted to say, 'I've seen some earrings that I like', but

as the jeweller was listening, I decided to go with a version of the truth.

'I'm recycling some old pieces I don't wear anymore.'

'Oh, *that's* why I heard you asking for money,' she said.

I turned to Ralph. 'You're busy. I'll come back later.'

My hand was already on the door knob when she added, 'How's Tom, by the way? I saw him dropping Sofia off. How come they let him out for the day?'

I pretended I hadn't heard and escaped. Water seeped in through the collar of my coat, cold rivulets trickling all the way down my back. I didn't care. I had the money for the fees. Well, most of it.

Bumping into Julia had been a close call. If she'd walked in earlier, she would have seen me begging Ralph for an extra couple of thousand, and being told that my family heirlooms were fake. I stopped walking for a second. She and Ralph were friends. As far as I was aware, jewellers took no oath of confidentiality. He could be telling her everything right now...

Nine

I had forged Tom's signature, taken out a bank loan, sold all my jewellery, as well as Diana's. My guilt felt heavy. It was a lump in my throat and a burning in my chest when Tom smiled at me, or hugged me as we lay in bed.

I had never expected us to end up like this, with a wall of lies between us. Pretending – in one way or another – had always been part of my life, but with Tom I could just be myself.

That was why I'd fallen in love with him. With Tom, I didn't have to be the peacemaker daughter, always thinking before I spoke. I didn't have to be more English or more Pakistani than I was, depending on my target audience, or, like at work, smooth away any quirky ethnic edges in my appearance or conversation so I could blend in. Tom just saw Faiza.

My first sight of Tom was of his six-pack stomach. I was smitten. I had walked into my friend Ella's flat for a dinner party and, in the middle of the living room, I saw a very tall man, reaching up to change a bulb in the ceiling light.

His T-shirt had ridden up and his stomach muscles, covered with coiled, light brown hairs, were visible. His arms looked strong... I couldn't tear my eyes away, even though I knew I should.

Ella worked with me, and Tom had been at university with her boyfriend. We all worked in the City and Tom was often at after-work drinks, weekend brunches and dinners with the same group that I was friends with. The more I saw him, the more I liked him. And this was a problem. Ever since I could remember, I'd been told I must only marry a Pakistani man, a suitable one at that, and one introduced via approved matchmaking channels. Dating was not an option. Having a crush on someone who didn't meet these criteria was most inconvenient. When my obsession with Tom did not lessen, as I had expected it to, I decided to try and neutralise it. Instead of admiring him from afar, I started talking to him more, hoping that, up close, I'd see all that was wrong with him. I'd used this tactic before, to quash past infatuations. Friend-zoning, as Sofia would call it now. She didn't know that I was an expert at it before they coined the phrase.

Instead of seeing flaws by spending more time with him though, I saw how funny he was and how kind. He was different to the other men in the group, with their loud laughter and banter. They seemed like boys, and Tom was a man. Tom didn't say much, but when he spoke, everyone listened. I saw humour under his serious expression and, when he did smile, his face lit up. I was fascinated by his eyes changing colour to different shades of blue, not just in the light, but depending on whether he was concentrating on watching a film, or laughing, or when he was tired. I loved his hands, his forehead, the way he never said anything bad about anyone.

Tom asked me questions about myself and what I wanted to do in life, and when I replied, he listened. When someone commented, as they inevitably did, that I was a boring teetotal, Tom didn't say, 'Oh go on, just have one!' as people usually did. He asked me if he could get me a coke or a juice instead.

Tom didn't seem to want anything more than the easy friendship we had struck up and I was relieved. My one-sided desire had nowhere to go and would have to die at some point. I wanted to get back to a life without the constant agony of wanting to touch him and longing for the moments I could see him again.

One day, we both left the pub together. The tube was packed but we found a pocket of space to stand in. My hand couldn't reach the rail at the top, which he had grabbed before the tube started to move. I swayed and he put his other hand on my arm to steady me.

'I've got you,' he said.

The tube jerked again, pushing me against him, and his arm went around my back, to steady me. I looked up and saw that his eyes were the deepest blue. My head tilted back as if by itself, his face moved closer. I looked down again and his arms tightened around me. I shut my eyes and leaned against him, my heart hammering.

As we got off the tube, he took my hand for the first time.

'I thought you weren't interested,' I said.

'Ella told me you're not allowed to date and all the stuff about your parents. I didn't want to scare you off.'

He invited me for a picnic the next day.

'Just to be clear, it's only the two of us – and it's a date.' Tom didn't play games and was straightforward in his invitation.

I didn't tell Ami and Baba about Tom. At first, I thought there was no point, as Tom would probably leave me after a few months. It was all too complicated. When he asked me to marry him, I decided to be completely honest with Ami and Baba. I couldn't hide behind a lie to smooth things over as I usually would, not if I wanted to be with Tom.

I was suddenly the cause of turmoil in our house and in their relationship. They blamed me and each other for ruining my life and theirs and for bringing shame on the family. The temptation was high to give in, to accept their decision and go back to my role in life – soothing, appeasing, calming things down.

But I couldn't give up Tom. For the first and only time, I risked everything by showing my parents who I really was and what I really wanted.

I sighed, looking at Tom as he slept next to me. I should have told him the truth when I found out the emergency money had gone. Now, there had been too many lies and it was too late. The sooner I got a job, the sooner I could replace the money and we could get back to being us again. But I still hadn't heard back from any of my applications.

One morning, while the children were at school, I was curled up on the sofa, hugging a cushion to my chest and refreshing my email. Tom stood in front of me. He was looking happier, after a successful first interview with an American bank a few days before.

'What's wrong?'

'Why doesn't anyone call me? I've applied for so many jobs!' I wailed.

'These things take time. To be honest, you've got such a long gap on your CV that they might not even look at your application. Let's ask my headhunter if he can help. Come here.'

He pulled me up and brought his lips down on mine. A comfort kiss. I kissed him back, putting my arms around his neck. He started grazing my lips gently with his teeth, then moved my hair back and kissed the side of my neck. I arched towards him and his hands moved down to my bottom. I closed my eyes and forgot everything. I wanted to forget.

'I'll email Richard now,' he mumbled against my skin. 'There's just something I need to do first...'

He took my hand and we ran upstairs. I closed the bedroom shutters, then we both took off our jeans. I felt his weight on top of me as soon as I lay down. We were quick, not bothering to take off the rest of our clothes. It would've felt strange to be naked in the middle of the day, and besides, I didn't want the glare of the sun on my skin. I was getting too old for that.

Afterwards, I snuggled my head into position on his shoulder. He pushed up my T-shirt and drew soft circles on my breast with his fingertips.

'I can't believe how you're getting a job to help me out. You're something else, kid!'

I flinched at the love in his voice. I forced myself to smile.

'I'm not helping you; I'm helping us. We're in this together – kid!'

He laughed.

'You're worried you haven't got any interviews, but at least you've been out of the market for years. Think how I feel. I've only had one so far.' He smiled. 'At this rate, I'd earn more if I dropped dead.'

'Hey!' I elbowed him gently in his side. 'You don't get out of this so easily. You'd better stick around to share all the fun with me!'

'Are you sure? My life insurance is £150k.'

I climbed on top of him.

'Chicken feed! I'm afraid you'll just have to get a job after all,' I said.

We laughed and he pulled me down so that I was lying on top of him, my face resting on his chest. He started to stroke my hair and I blinked back my tears.

'See, it's not all bad having an unemployed husband. When was the last time we did this in the middle of the day?' he said.

'Darling, I appreciate the post-coital romance, but can you email the headhunter now? I want to find a job.'

I smiled and handed him his iPad.

I had to fix things. Tom could never find out what I'd done. It would devastate him and destroy us.

Ten

4½ weeks to May 30th

Everyone came to my parents' annual Eid party: extended family, old friends who often brought along their own extended families, children and grandchildren. Naila, who Ami called her 'third daughter', her husband Tariq, who was a good friend of Tom's, and their two teenagers, would also be there.

I'd hung up our Eid clothes, new salwar kameez suits for us all, including Tom, and was going to help my parents set things up, before coming back to change.

Tom's final interview at the American bank was in ten days. We alternated between getting excited, then reminding ourselves that there were no guarantees. I'd allow myself a sliver of hope for a few seconds, as if taking a deep breath of clean, fresh air, imagining what life would be like if he got the job, before diving back underwater into the gloom that was our current reality.

When I got to my parents' flat, there was a whirlwind of activity.

Baba, immaculate in his ironed pale-blue shirt and a

tie I remembered from my childhood, was sitting at the dining table, making egg sandwiches, cutting them into delicate triangles, as per Ami's instructions. I laid the table with serving dishes for their usual Eid spread of seekh kebabs, parathas, dahi baray, chickpea chaat, haleem, naan, pakoras, samosas, fruit chaat and mithai, then took out crystal glasses to serve mango and orange juice. I took out the chocolate cake, which I'd baked and Sofia had decorated with 'Eid Mubarak' written in white icing. I cleaned the guest bathroom, put out fresh towels and loo paper, and vacuumed and dusted the living room, before arranging the dining chairs in semicircles so we had enough seating, and putting pink gladioli in a vase. I'd cooked some of the dishes at my house the night before, and now helped Ami finish off the others, that she didn't trust me to cook properly by myself.

She was chopping pistachio nuts into thin slivers and I watched the sharp knife, so perilously close to her fingers. She passed me a small bowl of the sayviyan, her Eid speciality. I breathed in the saffron and ate it up quickly, needing the sugar rush.

'I miss your sister so much, especially at Eid.'

'We'll FaceTime her later, OK?'

I put my arm around Ami.

Farrah blamed our parents for the breakup of both her engagements. She told me the reason she was too afraid to commit to marriage was because she'd witnessed the turmoil in our parents' relationship. I used to get annoyed that, as a grown woman of thirty-eight, she still used them as an excuse, but recently I'd been wondering if she had a point. Would I have dodged every awkward conversation about money with Tom, if I hadn't been so terrified of ending up like Ami and Baba?

Later, as Tom and I drove to the party with the children, the car was silent as I scolded Sofia.

'Why couldn't you just wear your Eid clothes? I bought them specially.'

'I didn't want to, OK? I don't even want to go to this stupid party but I'm coming. Isn't that enough?'

'There's no need to speak to Mum like that,' said Tom.

Tom turned on the radio and started to sing along to some Eighties pop and soon had the children joining in. I looked out of the window, wondering what would happen to our family if Tom didn't get this job.

I had to stop worrying. The bank had all but offered Tom the job. You didn't get to the final stage for such a senior role unless the decision had been made. Tom was smiling more these days, talking about the people he met at the last interview and how well they got on, and what a relief it would be to have a salary again, so we didn't have to use our savings.

The car turned and I almost dropped the plate of samosas that I was holding. I tried to shield my electric blue-silk salwar kameez from any oil. My matching chiffon dupatta, edged with tiny pearls, was folded up in my bag. I was wearing blue and silver glass bangles on each wrist and red lipstick.

I always had a stack of crisp £10 and £20 notes in my bag to give out as Eidi at the party to all the children there. This year I'd just have to pretend that I had forgotten to bring the money with me. I couldn't just not give it, and nor was I in any position to explain why.

Once we got there, I was enveloped in countless hugs as I went from person to person, wishing Eid Mubarak to all the friends squeezed into my parents' flat. I loved the way everyone came together at Eid. There was such a feeling of family, even if you weren't related by blood, and a warmth that extended across generations. The aunties and uncles who had asked me about my university choices, were now asking Sofia about hers. They gave advice, they told you off, they hugged and kissed you, they fed you.

When I was younger, I used to wish that my parents' friends, and the Pakistani side of my culture in general, had some boundaries or filter. My English friends never had to put up with such inquisition and interference. Over the years, though, I came to realise that if these elders felt the right to question and guide everyone, it was because they genuinely cared, and this capacity to care for so many people was something extraordinary. They had been there through every stage of our lives, good or bad.

Tom was shaking hands with two of the uncles.

'How's work, Tom?'

I froze. I'd forgotten to warn Tom not to say anything yet. My parents had no idea about Tom's job and this was not a bombshell to drop in the middle of the Eid party, where it would circulate with a velocity that would hit Ami and Baba within seconds. I shouted out to Tom before he could answer.

'Tom, I have a samosa emergency! Sorry, Uncle!'

I took Tom into the guest room.

'Darling, fifty people are going to ask you about work today, but please don't say anything.'

'I think it's OK to tell people now. It's been a while,' he said.

'No! I can't let my parents find out. Not like this. You know they'll freak out and it's dangerous for Baba to get stressed. Anyway, you'll have a new job soon. Why do we need to tell anyone at all?'

'What am I supposed to say if someone asks about work?'

'Just say, "Oh, you know…" and then start asking them about their work or their children. Please.'

I had to supply a template lie because I knew he wasn't very good at it himself.

He still looked unsure but when he saw my face he said, 'OK.'

After the feast had been devoured, all the children received their Eidi and sat counting their loot. Tariq and Naila helped us clear up, all of us squeezed into my parents' tiny kitchen.

Tom and Tariq went to fetch more plates.

'Why isn't Sofia wearing her Eid clothes?' asked Naila.

'Because she's a brat!'

'You shouldn't let her get away with it. It's disrespectful.'

Naila was always talking about the importance of traditions. Her children attended Urdu lessons and she chided me for not enrolling mine but letting them learn informally from Ami. Seema, her sixteen-year-old, had come dressed in salwar kameez. Naila's mini-me.

She was wrong about Sofia being disrespectful, though. Despite not wearing her Eid clothes, she served tea to all the guests, carrying a huge tray from person to person, the way Ami liked. She said 'Eid Mubarak' and chatted in broken Urdu to her grandparents' friends, not because they wouldn't have understood English, but because it made them happy.

Maybe I was being too harsh. Two of the aunties were also wearing trousers and neither Ami nor Baba had complained about Sofia's clothes. My parents and their friends had mellowed and adapted, with age and time. These days they were just as excited if a young person wanted to become a musician or a fashion designer, as when they followed the more traditional careers of medicine or law. Dating was now acceptable, and although they may have preferred it if their grandchildren married other Desis, it was now not unusual for them to dress up and dance at weddings where cultures and races combined.

It was Eid, and I didn't want to be fighting with Sofia.

I handed Naila the dishcloth.

'Actually, do you mind if I go and have a word with her?' I said.

'Good idea. Tell her how important it is to show respect on occasions like this,' said Naila.

Sofia was sitting on the living-room sofa, between Ami and Zeyna Khala, each of them holding one of Sofia's hands and talking across her. I waved to her and she escaped gratefully to the guest room with me.

'Maybe I overreacted about the Eid clothes,' I said.

'You always do, Mum.'

'I just wanted everything to be perfect, you know?'

'I can't be like you, Mum. I can't pretend to be different people all the time You have Eid clothes and you have Christmas and Easter dresses for Granny and Grandpa. You wear different clothes to your Pakistani friends' houses and then completely different ones for your English friends! I just want to be *me*.'

I put my arm around her.

'How did I produce such a wise soul as you?' I smiled. 'I love that you want to be yourself. That is exactly what I want for you, sweet Sofia. That's what I want for myself too.'

She looked at me as if she could see inside my head.

'Go on then, Mum, I dare you! At Christmas, wear your Pakistani clothes to Granny and Grandad's place with Uncle Peter and Aunt Lucy and all the English neighbours. And next Eid, wear one of your little flippy dresses and ankle boots from Butterfly!'

'OK, now I feel ill!'

I tried to imagine how it would feel to just 'be myself'. The idea made me anxious. I didn't know what 'myself' would look like. Or rather, it made me anxious to imagine how other people would react if I was simply 'myself'.

Sofia put shots of her henna-decorated hands on Instagram before getting up to leave. She stopped at the door and turned around.

'Look, promise you won't tell Naila Aunty, but I saw Seema on the bus with her friends, and she was off her head. She was so drunk she didn't even notice me.'

'Oh no! Are you sure it was her?'

Naila would be devastated.

'It was her. I know everyone thinks she's wonderful, and Naila Aunty was telling Nani how Seema listens to her Namaz app every night, but she obviously isn't that perfect. Anyway, I don't want to snitch on her but yeah, at least I don't do that, even if I didn't wear my Eid clothes!'

Poor Naila. I wondered if she knew? I wasn't sure what to do. If I told Naila that Sofia had told me this, she might not believe it. Sofia had also asked me not to say anything.

I went to find Naila.

'We've declared a ceasefire!' I smiled. 'It's so confusing, especially for our kids. All the culture mish-mash. And I don't want to be too strict. I want to make sure that Sofia can talk to me.'

'That's true.'

'Does Seema talk to you about parties and stuff? This is the age they start trying all kinds of things, right? Alcohol, boys. Terrifying!'

I laughed, watching Naila's face for clues.

'Seema knows what she's allowed and what's off bounds. I'm sorry you're having issues with Sofia, but you really need to define the boundaries more clearly. Luckily Seema's not the rebellious sort.'

I put my arm around Naila, pulling her close.

'Ah, it's hard being mums to teenagers, isn't it?'

I'd keep reminding Naila to check in with Seema. I was sure Sofia didn't tell me everything, either.

Eleven

4 weeks to May 30th

Tom dropped his iPad next to me on the bed. I scanned the email. The American bank had postponed the final interview due to a three-month hiring freeze.

I felt myself shaking and bit my lip, trying to control it. That meant no interview until August. Tom stood at the window with his back to me, his head bent.

I went up to him.

'I'm so sorry, darling. I'm sure they'll still call you for the interview in a few weeks.'

'You're sure, are you? What if they extend the hiring freeze? How do you know I'll get a job ever again?'

He was shouting but he stopped when he saw my expression.

'I shouldn't be taking it out on you.'

'You can take it out on me!' I said.

I smiled and took his hand, just wanting to take his pain away somehow. He put his arms around me and I held on to him, clutching his shirt. Our lives felt precarious, as if any sharp movement would make everything collapse.

I rubbed his back gently. 'Why don't you come to the hospital with us?' I said.

I was taking Baba to have an ECG at St George's and I felt uneasy leaving Tom alone. There was a new kind of panic in his voice, that I'd never heard before. It scared me.

'I'm fine, don't worry. I'm going over to Mum and Dad's. Their lawn mower is broken. I'll see if I can fix it.'

By the time he got back, I'd be home.

My chest felt tight. We'd been relying on this job. The headhunter had said the interview was just a formality, and that the American bank had already decided to hire him. We had twenty-eight days before all our money finished. In four weeks, we'd be penniless, homeless. The words expanded inside my head until I felt them pressing against my skull.

Everything was suddenly clear.

'Tom, I think we should sell the house.'

'That's not...'

'Just hear me out. We can move out of the Village, get something smaller. The job market is so uncertain and you don't need this kind of stress.'

What I could never have contemplated a month earlier seemed the obvious choice now. I loved this house, but I loved us more.

He took my hand and held it to his chest. I felt his heart beating.

'I've thought about that too, but the property market has crashed, Faiza. We'd lose money if we sold now. It would take months, anyway, and by then things will have stabilised in the City.'

'There's no harm checking. It would give us so many more options. Maybe you could start that solar power business you've always talked about? And we don't want to use up all our savings either, do we?' I said.

I felt his muscles relax a little. Perhaps I could persuade him.

'OK, but let's revisit this in three months?'

I didn't argue. I knew what had to be done. I'd get the house valued and get a quick offer. I was sure that he would feel relief, not anger, once it was a real possibility. He'd agree to sell it once I presented it to him as a ready solution to our problems.

As soon as he left, I called Naila. Her brother Shaan was an estate agent. When I told her that under the circumstances – the economic slump, the job market – I thought it would be wise to buy something smaller and free up some money, she didn't agree.

'I think it's a terrible idea. Once you move out of the Village, you can never afford to buy back. You live right next to Wimbledon Tennis. The value's just going to go up in future. Besides, you have three kids, so you can't get something that much smaller, can you? What about their schools and their friends? Who will drive out to see you in the middle of nowhere? What will everyone say? And what about your parents? They only bought their flat to be close to you.'

I had agonised over the same things, but none of those mattered any more. If we defaulted on the mortgage, we'd lose the house anyway.

Tom was still subdued when he got back. There had been a phone-in on the radio earlier, when I was driving Baba to the hospital. The discussion was about a recent spate of City suicides. Middle-aged men, with families but without jobs, jumping off buildings. It had broken my heart to hear about them, but it had also left me terrified when I thought about Tom. Stress was a killer, they'd said. I knew selling the house was the right decision.

Twelve

I lay in bed, listening to the sounds of our sleeping house; the mechanical hiccup of the digital clock, air bubbles gurgling through the pipes in the radiators. I forced myself to stay still, so that I wouldn't disturb Tom. My stillness intensified the thoughts churning in my head, the questions on a loop, without any answers. How would we pay the bills? How could I put things right? What would happen if he found out what I had done? It had been like this all week.

Images would flash into my mind unexpectedly, like vicious kicks catching me off guard; as I ate lunch with Tom, took a shower, watched Alex at football practice, or at school pickup as I chatted in a group. I imagined the fear on Tom's face, bleeding into disgust as he realised the money was gone; Tom not loving me anymore and leaving me; the looks on the children's faces when I told them they'd have to leave their friends, their schools, our home. My parents' eyes, full of worry and reproach. The shock might be too much for Baba.

A tear trickled down my cheek and pooled into my ear. As others followed, it became difficult to quell my snuffles. I slipped out of bed and went downstairs, huddling my feet up on the sofa and pressing my fingertips against my swollen eyelids.

Shaan, the estate agent, was coming over the next morning, but I still needed to find a job.

I turned on my laptop. Sam said I had to keep applying and that it was a numbers game. Tom's headhunter had not been optimistic for me, but said he would let us know if something came along. It would be easier to tell Tom the truth, once I had a job. I could offer him something besides my betrayal: a job, a plan, something to show that I was trying to put things right.

I trawled through the jobs website but I was getting nowhere. I texted Sam. It was late but she would see it when she woke up the next morning.

SOS. Any more ideas re job hunt?? xx

She replied instantly.

Let me think. Why are you up? xx

Why are YOU up?!! xx

Sam was always in bed by ten, whereas I loved to stay up once everyone was asleep, and have half an hour to myself, watching Netflix, scrolling through Instagram, or buying dresses online that I hid before Tom got home from work.

We decided to speak on the phone instead of texting.

'Do you remember my friend Daniella? She's a top headhunter in the City. She's away right now but I'll call her as soon as she's back and ask if she can help,' Sam offered.

I started to feel calmer.

'So, why are you up so late?' I said.

'Admin for the builder. Guess what else I'm doing at half-past midnight on a Wednesday?' said Sam.

'Eating chocolate, watching porn, buying boots on Net-a-Porter?' I laughed.

'I wish. So, Rupert was throwing a big do for the in-laws' fiftieth anniversary in October. It was all decided, but James says that, as the older brother, it's his place to host the party, not Rupert's. Rupert was getting a celebrity chef, *Tatler*, all his usual over-the-top-stuff.'

She paused to take an angry breath.

'OK...?' I said.

'James wants to make sure we outdo whatever Rupert was planning. His mother keeps texting me Rupert's plans, expecting us to match them. I just got a text saying, "Rupert was having Jamie Cullum". That was it. The whole text!'

'Oh no, that is a nightmare, although her text is funny in a grotesque way.'

'James really believes that if he doesn't do a good job, his parents won't love him. He might even be right.'

That was some high-level dysfunctional shit, I thought. To Sam, I said, 'Listen, you're juggling so many things. Get a party planner, you can afford it. In fact, ask your mum-in-law to text the party planner direct. Tell her it's your new number exclusively for the party. Actually, we should all have burner phones just for our mothers-in-law!'

Sam laughed, then sighed.

'This party means so much to James. I have to get it right.'

I decided to check my emails before I went to bed. The one from Ahmed's therapist jumped out first: Outstanding invoices.

Ahmed was still having fortnightly sessions for his

anxiety and we couldn't risk stopping them. I'd asked the GP to refer him to the NHS. The GP, a young woman wearing a designer shirt-dress and an Apple watch, had been understanding.

'Of course. There is a waiting list, as I'm sure you can imagine, of around sixteen weeks. In the meantime, if things deteriorate to the point where he ever mentions harming himself, or…' She paused, then continued, 'Or, if he mentions suicide, then we can get him seen urgently.'

I nodded mutely. The image of Ahmed harming himself made me feel sick. His therapist had never mentioned anything like that, nor had Ahmed. The thought lodged itself like a bullet in my brain. I couldn't let this notion exist anywhere, not even just in the GP's mind.

'I think you may have misunderstood. My son does need to continue the therapy because he was bullied and it's led to some anxiety issues – but there's never been any suggestion that he… I mean, his therapist has never mentioned…'

I couldn't bring myself to even say it. I felt the tears in my eyes and looked down, embarrassed.

'I'm so sorry. Of course, I don't know your son's case and I didn't mean to suggest he might harm himself. It's just something we need to tell everyone who is on the waiting list, in case their situation deteriorates. I should have made that clearer.'

The visit to the GP had not solved the immediate problem. I had to find the money for the private sessions until the NHS referral came through.

Even if Daniella could help me get a City job, it would take weeks. I decided to search for something that I could start straight away in the meantime. I froze when I saw, 'Butterfly,

Wimbledon Village. Sales Assistant Immediate Start'. Biffy, the owner, might overlook my lack of experience because my friends and I were great customers. I was an expert in her merchandise.

The job was perfect, except for one thing. When I imagined myself standing behind the counter, instead of at the other side, I knew it would spark off the gossip mill. It was too close to home. It would be better to be working away from the Village so I applied for three similar jobs in Covent Garden instead.

Not that the salaries any of them were paying would be enough to save our house.

Thirteen

26 days to May 30th

Shaan, the estate agent, was coming to do the evaluation. Tom had taken Sofia and her friends to their cross-country training in Guildford and I suggested he popped in to see his parents while he waited for Sofia to finish so he'd be out all morning.

When I called Shaan, initially he also advised me against selling in this market. However, if I was determined, he knew people, some overseas, who were looking to pick up bargains at the moment. He could probably find us a buyer within a few days, he said.

'Maybe we can get a famous tennis player to snap it up.'

I led Shaan from room to room and he took measurements with his laser tape. I kept thinking, irrationally, that Tom might come home and catch me in the act and, more rationally, that I was a terrible person to have someone sizing up our house, our home, behind Tom's back. This was no longer a little lie about how much a dress had cost, or paying an exorbitant amount for a birthday party that Ahmed had set his heart on. I had deliberately constructed

a scaffold of lies around myself to keep Tom out. I knew
it was wrong but I was only doing this to protect him, to
protect us. It didn't make me feel any better, though. My
stomach churned with shame and regret.

Shaan took photos on his phone, admiring the minimalist
marble of the white kitchen, the gleaming parquet, the walls
painted the sheerest dove-grey, the Murano chandelier and
the pitch-perfect shutters on the windows. As he shot each
room from various angles, I saw what he couldn't: the
different stages of each child in every room. The long-gone
highchairs in the kitchen, the skittles Ahmed set up in the
hallway to improvise a bowling alley, Sofia and me watching
In the Night Garden after nursery on the TV-room sofa.
The dining room with French windows looking onto the
garden, and the long table, where every family birthday had
taken place: Tom's, mine, the children's, Ami's and Baba's,
Farrah's, Tom's parents', and his brother Peter's. So many
cakes, so much happiness, over so many years. We'd moved
here when Sofia was just two.

'I'm going to put these photos in an e-brochure and send
them out to potential buyers this afternoon. It's a stunning
house,' said Shaan.

It all sounded positive. I didn't think about losing our
home or what I would tell people. I only focussed on saving
my family. Once Shaan had a buyer, I'd speak to Tom, and
persuade him that selling the house made sense. He might
secretly be relieved, under the circumstances.

In the utility room extension, Shaan paused to peer
behind the tumble dryer, using the torch on his phone. Then
he pushed the dryer aside to look more closely. He went out
to the garden, saying that he had to check something. I read

my texts to make sure Tom hadn't messaged that he was coming back early. I was eager for Shaan to leave as soon as he could.

When he came back in a few minutes later, Shaan was frowning. He had the same expression on his face as when he was eleven and Naila and I used to shout at him to get out of the room.

'What is it?' I asked.

'How long's this crack been in the wall?'

'I don't know. Why? We can get it fixed, don't worry.'

'I'm afraid it's not that simple,' he said.

I felt the nerves in my neck harden. I couldn't bring myself to ask him why.

'I'm so sorry, Faiza Baji, but this is subsidence. I don't know the extent of it without getting a survey. It may not be bad, but there's no way you can sell the house quickly in this state. This could take months to sort out.'

Shaan touched my arm. I tried to say something, but couldn't.

All our safety nets had disappeared.

Fourteen

25 days to May 30th

When I woke up my heart was racing, even though my head was still on the pillow and my only activity so far had been to open my eyes. It felt as if my insides were being trampled by a runaway horse.

I grabbed my phone and as I did every morning now, before anything else, opened up the calendar. Twenty-five days. Less than a month.

My breathing got faster, out of control. I went down to the living room, but there was no escape. I sat in my silent house, clenching my hands until they hurt. I looked around at the family photographs and Alex's drawings, which I had pinned up on the bookshelves. It felt as if I was taking inventory of a life that was about to disappear.

I'd been rejected for the sales assistant jobs in town. The house could not be sold, and there were no more interviews for Tom. The advert for Butterfly was still up.

I was driving to Lizzie's house for the second auction committee meeting when I took a sharp turn towards the

High Street. I had time to go to Butterfly first. The steering wheel was slippery. I gripped it tighter. I thought back to my absolute confidence that I would be able to replace the money 'one day', when I started using it. I had no plans back then, just vague hopes.

I realised that I was dressed head to toe in Butterfly. It was a sign. I was wearing skinny jeans, soft leather ankle boots with a block heel from a hip Italian brand, and a pale-blue off-the-shoulder cashmere jumper. I had completed the outfit with my Prada bag and a chunky silver bracelet. I knew exactly what the customers in Butterfly needed to wear to look the part for any event. I had studied that in great detail years ago.

I rubbed my chest. If I was working there, anyone could see me through the large glass window by the till: the children's friends, the mothers from school, our friends, people who knew Ami and Baba. A couple of Tom's ex-colleagues also lived in the Village. Ami's bottle of Gaviscon that I'd picked up for her from the chemist was lying on the seat next to me. I took a swig, grateful for the pink gunk trickling into me, soothing the fire in my chest.

I paused outside the glass door, decorated with bunches of white paper flowers. Inside, I could see the famous ceiling-high ferns and 180-degree mirrors, including the mirrored 'catwalk' in the centre of the shop. I went in.

My ears started to throb. When I told Biffy, the owner, that I wanted the job, she was sceptical. She was also desperate though, as she'd had no suitable applicants. I could see her wavering.

'Listen, I know your customers. I *am* one! I understand their needs. I want to start an online fashion business one day and if I work here, I can learn from the best. I'm serious about this.'

This would be my story for everyone, that working at Butterfly was a means to a suitably lofty end.

Biffy agreed to a week's trial. Alice was still working for a few more days so if I started straight away, she could do a handover.

As I drove towards Lizzie's house, it hit me. I shouted at the top of my voice, 'Yes! I have a job!'

Lizzie led me to her living room, which was a haven of eco-calm. One entire wall was studded, floor to ceiling, with lush, green plants. I sat down on a pale-blue sofa upholstered in organic fabrics, dyed using chemical-free colours, and ergonomically arranged for optimum energy flow. Clear crystals glistened as they hung from the ceiling like frozen dew drops and the soft scent of aromatherapy oils swirled in the air. I felt healthier just walking into her house.

Julia, Sam, Anna and the other members of the committee were already there. Once we'd all given our updates for the auction, we were allowed to eat lunch.

A table had been set up next to the natural swimming pool, where tall green plants edged the clear water. We sat under pale-grey awnings, at a long table covered with a white gauze tablecloth. An oversized vase, flowing with sweet peas like a floral fountain, was surrounded by large platters of salads, poached salmon and risotto, with tiny flags saying if the item was gluten-free or vegan. Lizzie, a flash of cobalt blue in her flowing maxi, invited us to help ourselves.

Sam sat next to me. She was the only one who hadn't succumbed to the yummy-mummy uniform. She wore jeans, ordinary gym trainers and no make-up.

'Sorry, ladies, but it's my day off so I need to slob!' she grinned.

She didn't seem the least bit embarrassed to stick out.

'I'm so jealous!' I said to Sam. 'I wish I could wear trainers.'

'You can! Why not?' said Sam.

'I'm not as cool as you?' I laughed.

I didn't say that she was white, rich, and one of them. She would always belong, whatever she did. I hated myself for feeling this way, but I knew I wasn't that far off the mark.

I decided to tell everyone about Butterfly myself. It was best if I gave them my version.

I waited until dessert. I'd wanted to tell Sam first but I'd taken too long trying to summon up my courage and think up my speech. I had to do it before people started to leave.

'I'm going to tell everyone some news. Sorry, I didn't get a chance to tell you before,' I whispered to Sam.

I waved at Lizzie.

'I'd like to tell everyone some news, Lizzie!'

Lizzie tapped her glass gently with a spoon. The conversations around us stopped.

'Faiza has an announcement,' said Lizzie.

'I'm going back to work, ladies! At Butterfly!'

'Fantastic! Are you going to be Biffy's new business partner? I know she's been looking for an investor for ages,' said Lizzie.

I swallowed, trying to keep a smile on my face.

'No, I'm going to be working there. Alice is leaving, so Biffy was in a bind.'

'You're going to be a sales assistant?' said Anna.

Her mouth twisted in distaste.

94

My whole body was burning. If they hadn't all been looking at me, I would have fanned my face and twisted my hair into a bun.

'Well, I want to start an online fashion business when Alex is older. So, I thought, why not get to know the industry by working at Butterfly? I'll be styling, too.'

'You'll be brilliant at that. I've always been so jealous of your clothes,' said Sam.

'It sounds like a great idea,' said Lizzie.

'Yes,' said Julia. I smiled, surprised at her support. 'Especially under the circumstances. I heard that Tom lost his job.'

The table fell silent. People stopped eating. I hadn't told anyone about Tom's job, except Sam, and Naila. Julia looked thrilled at dropping the bombshell. I felt everyone's eyes on me.

'Not quite, Julia. Tom didn't lose his job, he left Apex himself, to start his own thing with a couple of friends.'

The words were out before I realised that it would be easy enough for Julia to check this wasn't true.

'You didn't say!' exclaimed Lizzie.

'It just happened. I'm still getting used to having him home.'

'Still, at least one of you is earning now,' said Julia.

'I'm sure they don't need Alice's salary,' said Lizzie.

Sam and Lizzie laughed, along with some of the others. Julia frowned at their reaction.

'Actually, you're right, Julia. I *am* getting a job because Tom's home,' I said. 'I know he'll be there if the children need something.'

'Goodness! I could never turn Harry into a house

husband. There's something so emasculating about that, don't you think? Besides, I thought the women in your culture had more traditional roles?' said Julia.

I didn't know what to say for a second. What culture did she mean? Fourteen out of the fifteen women sitting around the table were in the 'traditional roles' of housewives or stay-at-home mothers, depending on how they wanted to identify themselves. Why was she bringing up 'my' culture?

I decided to ignore her and looked around the table.

'You must all come to Butterfly and see me.'

Lizzie raised a glass.

'Here's to Faiza's fashion empire! Biffy is lucky to have you. Cheers!'

The clink of cutlery on china resumed as people went back to eating dessert. I didn't look at Julia again.

'I don't know what's gotten into Julia. That was quite bitchy,' whispered Sam.

'Actually, that was quite "Julia". I've told you, she's not a nice person. What was all that culture shit?'

Sam shrugged and shook her head.

'How does she know about Tom?' I said.

'I don't know. Her husband works in the City. Maybe he heard about Apex?'

I didn't want to think about Julia any more.

'Talking of husbands, I saw yours at St George's on Wednesday. Please tell him I'm sorry I didn't say hello. I was helping my mum with her walker.'

Sam took a sip of her wine then frowned.

'On Wednesday? Impossible. He was in Paris for the day and didn't get back till very late. He must have a doppelganger!'

There was no doubt that it was James I'd seen. A doppelganger wouldn't be dressed like James and carrying the weathered tan briefcase that was his trademark. I'd tried to catch his eye at the hospital and had wondered if he'd seen me too, but he'd walked away, talking on his phone.

Wild possibilities ran through my head. Could James be terminally ill but didn't want Sam to know? Or had he fathered a love child and had been visiting the maternity ward? It was probably something much more prosaic, but I couldn't understand why he'd told Sam he was in Paris.

Maybe Sam was covering up for him. I stirred my coffee and took a bite of my cheesecake. I glanced at her. She was talking to Lizzie now, smiling as if everything was fine. No, Sam would have told me if James was ill. It was James who was lying to Sam. I gave her a tight hug as we said goodbye.

Just as I got home, I got a text from Sam: *You were right! James was at the hospital. He had some dental appointment before work, but he didn't tell me because we never see each other or even have time to talk! Paris was the day before. I lost track. I'm really going crazy with the annexe and the party! xx*

I texted Sam: *Good. At least this means I'm not going crazy! Xx*

I smiled. Perhaps I'd inherited more of Ami's Bollywoodesque, dramatic way of thinking than I liked to admit!

I found Tom in his study. I had to tell him about Julia's announcement. But first I wanted to tell him about my new job.

Fifteen

23 days before May 30th

Now that Julia had told everyone about Tom, we had to tell our families too.

I told my parents at our monthly lunch date, a treat that Baba ringed in red on their kitchen calendar.

Ami and Baba wanted to go to Cote in the Village, rather than their other favourite haunt, a Pakistani restaurant in Tooting. At least at Cote we were less likely to bump into their friends and I could speak Urdu when I told them the news, without worrying that the waiters or the people on the next table would hear me.

They were in a cheerful mood as we walked in the restaurant, my two tall parents and then my tiny figure in between. Ami was wearing a camel cashmere wrap over a bright blue salwar kameez, and her hair was coiled in a grey chignon, befitting her regal posture. Baba would have dressed more casually, but, for Ami, he had put on smart trousers. He was as tall as Tom and his lifelong love of playing tennis meant that he was still lean and trim.

I wanted everything to be as normal as possible when

I told them. I'd straightened my hair and worn make-up. They could spot a hairline chink in my armour. I knew this would be a blow to them. They'd worry non-stop until Tom got another job.

We ordered from the special lunch deal. The amount of money saved gave them as much pleasure as the food itself. These days they were both on the same 'bank statement' page when it came to money. A few years ago, the fights just stopped. I'd asked Ami why they decided to wait until I left home to live harmoniously. She said when her parents died, she realised that throughout her marriage she'd been trying to prove to them that she hadn't lost out by marrying Baba. She'd been spending for her parents and her sisters, who looked down at her lifestyle, rather than for herself. As well as that, once Farrah and I were grown up and Baba felt he had fulfilled his duty to look after us, he relaxed more about spending. They just stopped arguing about money.

Baba put his arm around me and I leaned into him. His blue and white checked shirt was as soft as a comfort blanket. He'd become thinner in the last few months.

In the roar of the lunchtime bustle, I had to repeat myself three times for Ami, who was a little hard of hearing. I slipped into Urdu.

'Tom's company have had a bad year, so they've had to let a few people go.'

Baba stopped chewing.

'Tom?' he said.

'Yes, but it's fine. He's already at the final interview stage for another job.'

This was true. It was just that the interview was on hold.

Ami took a sip of water. Her hand stayed on the glass after she had set it down, as if it was stuck.

I watched Baba carefully. I didn't want his blood pressure to shoot up. The cardiologist had said that could be 'catastrophic'. Perhaps I shouldn't have told them?

'Tom's very sensible. He must have put enough money aside for emergencies like this,' said Baba.

'Yes, absolutely. In fact, he set up a £250,000 emergency fund for us ages ago.'

I wanted a figure so big that it would buffer them from any possible worry.

'We don't have to worry about money at all,' I said.

I sometimes wondered when my lying had become so finessed. It was almost like a sixth sense. Sometimes it even felt like the truth. I was relieved to see the lie banished their worries, as they both exhaled.

Sam and Naila invited me to a celebratory coffee before I started at Butterfly. On the table there was a slice of lemon drizzle cake and a card saying 'Woohoo!'. They were both excited for me, but disappointed that I wasn't working in the sort of shop where they could use my employee discount.

I told the children that night after dinner. I'd been dreading it. Tom had to take a last-minute phone call. In an almost prophetic twist, after what I'd told Julia, he and two former colleagues had just started a consulting project for a client in Argentina. Although there was no salary, only a success fee when the project closed in three to six months, it was exactly what Tom needed. He jumped out of bed in the mornings and spent most of the day on the project, doing what he did best. It wasn't an immediate solution but I had Butterfly for that.

As it was getting late, I told the children by myself.

'We'll just have to be a bit more careful with money, like in *The Railway Children*,' I said.

Ahmed nodded.

Alex shook his head.

'Oh no! Are we poor?'

'Is that why Dad's been home? Why didn't you tell me?' Sofia fixed me with an accusatory gaze.

'We're not poor, we just need to be a little careful.'

'Can I still have my eighteenth, though?' said Sofia. She was looking at her phone, chewing her thumb. 'It's OK if I can't.'

A mini shrug of her shoulders.

Sofia and her friend Meg were having a joint party. I'd already paid a hefty advance and we wouldn't get a refund anyway. Besides, it was her eighteenth. I'd been thinking about using the money in a building society account that Ami had opened for her when she was born, and into which we had been adding a little every year on her birthday. It had around seven hundred pounds in it. I'd also paid the balance for the Barcelona trip from it.

'No, it'll be fine. We have money for your party. Maybe you should get a Saturday job, though, for clothes and spending money for the trip? I've got the job at Butterfly, remember? I know it's for my business, but it will also help with money. You know I worked at Fenwick's every Saturday when I was at sixth form.'

'You didn't have the academic pressures we have now, Mum. I can't get a job in the middle of my revision!'

She stormed out of the room.

I couldn't stop thinking about Sofia's reaction. I may have given my children a charmed life so they never felt left out, or were left wanting, but I wondered if I had gone too far? I'd worked every Saturday and throughout my summer holidays. I'd assumed that my children would do the same. It seemed not.

Ahmed hadn't said anything at all yet, and when Sofia and Alex left, I sat down next to him. He was biting his nails and watching the TV screen, even though the volume was off.

'Will I have to leave my school?'

His words, spoken quietly, without emotion, felt like a punch to my chest.

'No, of course not. You don't have to worry about that. Look at me, darling.'

I smiled, trying to reassure him that nothing would change, but I felt sick. Even with my job at Butterfly we couldn't pay the fees unless Tom got a job so I knew that my promises were empty. Perhaps he did too, because he went to his room without saying anything.

That evening I didn't hear him laughing as he usually did while playing PlayStation with his friends. When I went into his room he was lying on his bed, still in his uniform. I bent down to kiss him and told him to get changed, but he didn't reply. His eyes were fixed on the light on his ceiling and, despite my attempts to make him look at me, or make him laugh, they did not flicker or move.

I stood outside his room, unable to move. That haunted look in his eyes, which I thought we had chased away forever, was back.

Sixteen

21 days to May 30th

Sam and I were at Sofia's school, selling the charity auction tickets.

She had discovered the source of Julia's information about Tom. It was the Headmistress. The Head and Julia had become good friends. They played tennis at The Hurlingham and had even been on a girls' trip to Milan. When I'd asked the school for an extension to pay the balance of the fees, I told the Headmistress that Tom had lost his job. I was furious at the breach of confidentiality, but I knew all rules could be bent under the weight of Julia's hefty cash donations to the school.

I was surprised at the unexpected kindness of people when I told them Tom had lost his job. My hairdresser hugged me and told me to come on training Thursday and he would do my hair for free. Our babysitter said I could always call her and she would be happy to help me as a friend. At a rare trip to our local Chinese, the manager gave us a 50% discount on the bill.

The chatter in the corridors died down as the bell rang

and the first lesson of the day started. Sam and I sat at a small table outside the school office, as Julia handed us a stack of receipts, saying, 'We're going to ask for a deposit today, in cash, and the rest to be paid online. They're more likely to pay the rest if they've already paid half upfront.'

She reached into a spotless grey leather tote and took out a metal box, two keys, a receipt book, four pens and a calculator.

A queue of Year 12 and 13 mothers had already started to form, chatting as they waited to pay.

Sam handed over the black and glitter-pink receipts for the ball in return for wads of fifty- and twenty-pound notes, while I ticked off the names on our lists.

Julia sat with Anna in the corridor, looking at us periodically, as if checking that we were performing such a complex operation adequately.

When the last ticket had been sold, Sam started counting the money.

'We need to put it in the safe in Mrs West's office.'

I went to the loo, passing Julia and Anna, who smiled at me. When I was coming out, I heard Julia say my name and stopped just inside the door. I stayed absolutely still, straining to hear what she was saying.

'Faiza won't be able to pay the fees working at Butterfly. It was embarrassing the way she pretended it was for a business.'

I pinched my lips together, holding my breath.

'She's very nice, but let's face it, she's not really suitable, you know, for a CEO's wife. Her husband would never have been promoted to the top, not with her background,' said Anna.

I clenched my hands, trying to steady my breathing. I pushed the inner door of the bathroom so that it banged, to let them know that I was coming out. They smiled at me, the way they always did, and I walked away quickly to sit back down with Sam.

I pretended to check emails on my phone, as Julia and Anna walked past, calling out to say, 'Bye.'

I was so angry that for several minutes, I couldn't speak.

'What's the matter?' said Sam, looking at my face.

I wasn't sure I could bring myself to tell Sam what they'd said. Not yet. My mind was still reeling. Besides, I wanted to ask her advice about Ahmed.

'Ahmed's taken the news about Tom's job really badly. I can see all the same patterns starting up again.'

She put her arm around me.

'Listen, last time this happened, he wasn't having therapy, was he? You told me his doctor's very good. I'm sure she'll talk to him about it. Maybe he just needs time to get used to it.'

That made sense. Perhaps I was panicking.

'Thanks, Sam. When I saw him last night, everything came rushing back. I felt so helpless. It's such a strange illness.'

She sighed.

'I wish there was a pill, an antibiotic, or a steroid for the mind too,' said Sam.

'Exactly that.'

She shook her head.

'It must be so awful for you, too,' I said.

She nodded. I knew she was thinking about her Mum.

'Is James looking forward to the auction?' I asked.

'Not really. We're not getting a full table this year, either,' said Sam.

'Wow. James is OK with that?'

'It was his idea, actually. He may need to travel around those dates.'

'Is he still very busy at work?'

'It's awful. They've cut down his team, which means he's doing the work of three people now. He's too old for all this, Faiza. It's not good for his health.'

As she left, she hugged me. 'Ahmed's going to be fine, don't worry.'

In my car, I tried to stop myself from crying. It wasn't just Ahmed. I knew what Julia was like, but I'd thought Anna was my friend. The way she'd said 'background'. I knew what she meant.

Seventeen

20 days to May 30th

It was my first morning at Butterfly and I'd just received an email from Ahmed's therapist. Dr Keane had seen an escalation in his anxiety symptoms and advised more frequent sessions. I felt as if the world was suddenly spinning a little faster, as if any minute it might spin completely out of control. Ahmed *couldn't* fall sick again. I'd get him as many sessions as he needed.

Alice, Biffy's assistant, was watching me with proxy disapproval in Biffy's absence.

'Biffy doesn't like us using mobiles in the shop,' she said. I went to the bathroom to reply to Dr Keane. I had to control my anxiety around Ahmed. He was probably picking up on my stress.

'Welcome!' said Biffy, when she got back. 'Alice is going to explain the till, then I'll show you the stockroom.'

I spent the morning in the basement, opening stacks of cardboard boxes from Milan. Biffy had given me a little knife to open the tape, an inventory list to check each tag against, and a crash course in using the steam iron. There were sixty-five items to unpack and put out on the shop floor.

'We're just popping out to get coffees,' said Biffy, as she and Alice took their purses. 'Just stay by the till and we'll be back before you know it.'

I stood by the large display window, feeling like a mannequin. On my mobile, I calculated how much I'd earn in two weeks, factoring in a conservative estimate for any commission. It was more than I had expected. It wouldn't cover all our bills, but Tom's project client was going to give him three thousand pounds as a sign-on bonus. We would have enough for the direct debits due on the thirtieth and to pay for extra therapy sessions – but only if I made commission too.

I saw a movement outside and put away my mobile in case Biffy was back, but it was a group of women looking at the clothes in the window. I glimpsed long blonde hair and a red Burberry jacket that looked familiar, then saw the woman's face in profile just as she pushed open the door. It was Hannah, Augustus's mother from Ahmed's school. Hannah and I were school-gate friends. I only met her a few months ago when Ahmed started at Clissington's. She had immediately invited Ahmed to Augustus's sleepover when she heard that I'd been at Brookwood High – that gave me an 'access all areas' pass for Ahmed. The friendship with Augustus had also meant that Ahmed was suddenly invited to many more sleepovers and birthday parties by Augustus's group. I knew how Hannah would react to seeing me working in a shop.

I dropped to the floor, hiding behind the counter. I crouched, listening to Hannah and her friends chatting.

'Hi, anyone here?' called Hannah.

I didn't know what to do. Before I could make a decision, it was made for me. Biffy and Alice walked in and said hello to Hannah and the other mothers from Ahmed's class. I stood up before they discovered me and it became obvious that I was hiding.

'Hi! Sorry, I was just picking up my earring!'

Hannah smiled as I went around to double-kiss her. She seemed to think that I was on that side of the till simply to retrieve my earring. Then Biffy spoke.

'So, you know Faiza, my new sales assistant?'

Hannah's mouth dropped open and stayed that way. Biffy looked on uncomfortably as Hannah had processed the information.

'You're *working* here?'

'Yes! I'm thinking of starting an online fashion business and I thought this would be the best way to learn about the industry.'

Hannah smiled, visibly relieved, as if her world had corrected itself on its axis, and sat down to try some ankle boots.

'Do you mind being our guinea pig for the shoe sales protocol? I want to show Faiza,' said Biffy, coming up to us.

I stood with one of the shoes in my hand, trying to look as if Biffy was going to impart some vital insight.

'So, the focus is on the whole *experience*.' Biffy took the other boot out of the box. 'I love the rustle of the tissue, don't you?'

Hannah and I looked at each other and smiled.

'First, you offer the customer a sock, if they want one.' Biffy pointed to a stack to the side. 'Then kneel down and put the shoe on the customer yourself. We provide a luxury service.'

Neither Hannah nor I could look at each other. Biffy was waiting and I dropped inelegantly onto the floor and knelt down at Hannah's bare feet, with their French-manicured toenails.

'Oh, there's no need,' said Hannah, about to take the boot from my hand. Biffy stopped her.

'Do you mind if Faiza practises on you?'

I undid the zip on the boot and held the opening wide for Hannah as she slipped her foot in. I zipped it up and Biffy left.

I was biting the inside of my cheek, trying to hold myself together. Hannah's face was red. She hobbled over to the mirror in one boot, then took it off herself and walked back in bare feet. She pulled on her wedges.

'I didn't realise the time! I'll have to do this later. Bye, ladies!'

She left, almost running out of the shop.

I busied myself putting the boots back in the tissue. I imagined Julia coming in and waiting for me to put socks and shoes on her feet. It seemed like a bad dream.

I went to the bathroom and inside the cubicle I dabbed away my tears with some loo paper before they could ruin my make-up. I reminded myself that I was doing this for my family, for Ahmed, for Tom. I was doing this to save myself. I couldn't linger; Biffy had said a bathroom break should never be more than five minutes, max.

But the day got better: I helped two women to get outfits for a summer ball, along with matching shoes and bags, which meant two hundred pounds of commission.

Eighteen

18 days to May 30th

A couple of days after I started at Butterfly, I woke up to see Tom already sitting up in bed, staring at his phone. Someone had dug up an article about the Argentinean client being declared bankrupt. The consultancy project would have to be shelved.

He lay back down, facing away from me. He never usually let setbacks at work affect him. He always said, 'You win some, you lose some.'

'Are you feeling OK, baby?' I said and bent down to stroke his hair.

He pulled away. This was bound to be a blow. He'd worked hard on the project, and was relying on the fee to boost the emergency fund.

'Listen, you have a lie in. I'll drop the boys today. I have time before Butterfly.'

All day at work, I kept worrying about him. I took extra bathroom breaks so I could text him and see how he was. He just answered *Fine*.

That evening, when I got home, he was still wearing the

T-shirt he'd slept in and sweatpants, not jeans and a shirt as he normally did. He hadn't shaved or showered and his hair wasn't brushed. His eyes seemed to still be in a state of shock and he went up to bed as soon as we'd eaten. When I went upstairs, he was sitting up in bed, with all the lights off, his face glowing in the light from his iPad screen. He didn't look up. I heard a 'swishing' sound and then a 'tap, tap' again and again. When I looked at the screen, I saw he was playing Solitaire.

I lay down next to him but decided not to say anything. He needed some time to get over the disappointment of the lost project. He would be himself again soon.

But he was the same the next day and the day after. He stopped going for his morning run, and if he wasn't playing Solitaire in bed, he was shut away in the study while I ate with the children. No amount of cajoling or reassurance from me seemed to lift his mood. I kissed his forehead in bed and wrapped myself around him, wishing there was something I could do to make him feel better.

There was one thing guaranteed to make Tom happy: sex. I realised it had been weeks since any such interaction, so a couple of days later, I locked the door and put on some music so the children wouldn't hear us. He continued to swipe cards on his phone with his fingertip. I stripped down to my underwear and went to stand next to him by the bed. He protested as I took the phone away, but ignoring his outrage, I climbed on to the bed and straddled him. I bent down to hold him close. His body relaxed and his arms went around my bare back.

'Off with them, then.' I pointed to his PJs and began to

slide down the waistband. At the same time, I pushed up his T-shirt.

'Not now, OK?'

He shifted so suddenly that I lost my balance and tumbled onto the bed, as if I'd been thrown off a rodeo horse. He pulled his T-shirt back down over his stomach and picked up the phone to resume his game. I wasn't giving up that easily.

'Come on! It's like going to the gym. You just have to force yourself and then you feel so much better.'

I grinned and touched his leg. I reminded myself that he wasn't rejecting *me*, he was just going through a tough time.

'Not now, OK?'

'No probs. We can work out tomorrow.'

Tom carried on playing Solitaire for another hour.

In his face, I could see my fear reflected. Without the project, we wouldn't have enough to pay the bills. My salary wouldn't cover everything, unless I could make a lot of commission. I'd have to make sure I made as many sales as I could. I was grateful for the job at Butterfly. The humiliation was worth it for the peace of mind.

Nineteen

16 days to May 30th

Towards the end of the week, Lizzie and Julia came to the shop, along with Anna and some others. They all asked me to style their outfits, except for Julia, who said, 'Biffy knows what I like.' Julia and Biffy sat gossiping, rather than looking at clothes, and I saw them glance at me several times.

After what Anna had said about my 'background', I made sure that I showed her the most expensive pieces in the store. Lizzie bought three outfits and several bikinis for her holiday but they were all on a major shopping spree; by the end of the week my commission was double my pay.

'Do you have time for a drink?' said Biffy as we locked up the shop at the end of my first week.

The boys would be home in half an hour after their Friday playdates and I was planning to check in on Ami and Baba before going home. Baba hadn't been feeling well and I wanted to check his blood pressure. Sofia was having friends for a sleepover and I wanted to help her organise sleeping bags and dinner. However, Biffy was now my boss and I was about to get paid, so I said, 'Yes.' Besides, it was nice of her to take me out.

It was a warm summer evening and we sat outside the bar in the Village, at a round metal table on the pavement, sandwiched between after-work drinks and pre-date meet-ups. I sipped my Coke Zero slowly. We talked about my children and hers, who were both in their twenties and at university, and then we conducted forensic discussions about the best treatments for sagging jowls.

Biffy set her wine glass down and I checked my watch under the table. I could still squeeze in a quick hello with my parents if I left soon. She smiled and leaned closer.

'It's been so great having you in the shop, Faiza.'

'Thank you! I've loved it. I think we make a great team.'

She winced, as if in pain.

'The thing is, I don't think it's going to work out. I'm sorry.'

The chatter in the bar fell away. I gripped my glass, which was slippery with condensation.

'I thought I'd done very well. I've sold over five thousand pounds' worth of clothes, I've learnt the till, I did everything you asked me to. I even vacuumed the shop and cleaned the windows when the cleaner was ill. I-I don't understand.'

She looked at me with eyes that showed no emotion. The creases around her lips deepened as she started to speak.

'One of the customers, someone who knows you, actually, mentioned that the school mums are finding it awkward having you serving them. She says people have asked Alice when you'll be at lunch so they could pop in then. She's one of our biggest spenders. Times are tough at the moment. I can't afford to lose any sales.'

She shook her caramel highlights and shrugged.

'You don't need this job to learn the trade. When they see someone like you, one of them, working in the shop, it reminds them they're human too. It's bad for business.'

I rubbed the back of my neck. I'd pulled a muscle on my first day and had been living on paracetamol all week. I nodded. I remembered Hannah's face when she fled from the shop and the way Julia had kept looking at me during her tête-à-tête with Biffy. I knew instinctively that it was Julia, not Hannah, who had got me fired. Why did that woman hate me so much?

'Here's your pay for the week.'

She handed me a brown envelope.

'It's cash, £400.'

'What about my commission, another £800?'

'No, darling, there's no commission in a trial week.'

A minute later I was walking towards the Common. I started to cry, and afraid that someone would see, I rang Tom and asked him to pick me up.

He put his arm around me and led me to the car. Seeing me like that seemed to jolt Tom back into himself. He smiled his usual reassuring smile.

'At least you won't have to hide in the loos every time you need to send a text,' he said.

I snorted through my tears and laughed, before starting to cry again. His kindness made me feel worse. I shouldn't have lost that job.

He left me in the living room with a hot-water bottle for my back, a cup of tea and a lemon cupcake from Sofia's stash. None of it brought any comfort. Waves of fear washed over me. My worries worked their way up into my chest until it felt as if someone was clutching my throat. Biffy's job had been my last chance to fix things.

I heard Alex singing Thomas songs with Tom in the kitchen and could feel the music thumping from Sofia's room upstairs. The sound of Ahmed shouting with his friends, as they played some online game, was the best sound of all – but what would happen to our family now? Dr Keane was already concerned about Ahmed relapsing. What if all this made him spiral into a place from where I couldn't get him back?

Sofia came to get me for dinner. She shuffled from one foot to the other in her school socks.

'I've got a Saturday job at Zara.'

I jumped up and pulled her into a hug. She patted my back.

'OK, Mum, it's not such a big deal.'

'It is! I'm so proud of you.'

Later in bed, Tom and I lay facing each other. The moon seeped in through the shutters, falling on his face. The tree outside the window swayed in the wind, periodically blocking the moonlight and plunging us into darkness. Our arms reached out towards each other, and we held hands in the middle of the bed, our fingers intertwined.

'Tom?' I said, looking away. 'Would you ever stop loving me?'

'Only time will tell.'

I heard the smile in his voice.

'No, seriously. What if I did something bad? Would you love me whatever I did?'

'It's hard to say.'

Sometimes I hated his devotion to the truth.

'Why? What bad thing have you done? Murdered someone? Robbed a bank? Had an affair with a toy boy?'

My heart was pounding. His eyes travelled over my face, and then he smiled.

'If I've put up with you for twenty years, I suppose I could do twenty more. Is that OK?'

'I'm sorry I lost the stupid job.'

'It's not your fault. You haven't done anything wrong.'

His words were drowned out by the drumming in my ears. In fifteen days, we would be facing bankruptcy. I could feel the terror, tight and sharp, under my skin.

I had no choice but to tell him about the money now. But it was Sofia's birthday party that weekend. I'd tell him after that.

Twenty

15 days to May 30th

Sofia's and Meg's party was in full swing. Tom and I sat at a table in the corner, chatting with Meg's parents, shouting over the music. The girls were dancing in the middle of the dark club as the blue and pink lights throbbed, picking out the faces of their friends. Afterwards, we all gathered around as they cut their cakes in front of the bar, where I'd put giant pink metallic balloons with the number eighteen. The girls smiled shyly, their arms around each other, as their friends started to chant 'Speech, speech!'

Sofia was wearing my LK Bennett heels and a short black dress. Her face was dappled with excitement, as if she couldn't wait to start this new era of being 'an adult'. I was glad I'd raided her building society book and that we'd gone ahead with her party. This moment would not come again. Tom put his arm around me. I leaned into him.

'Our baby, Mashallah!' I said.

I knew that he perhaps didn't believe the way I did, in saying 'Mashallah', which was to thank God and ask for his protection for this beautiful person we had somehow produced, but he smiled and said, 'I know.'

Sofia came and gave me a hug and said that her friends thought I was 'very cool, and very pretty'. She seemed pleased and I was relieved, though surprised, that I'd passed the hardest of litmus tests, teenage girls. I was wearing a red 'flippy' dress and gold heels, with thin gold hoops and red lipstick, all approved by Sofia in advance.

I had danced with Sofia and Tom, eaten birthday cake, chatted to Meg's parents, clapped and cried at Sofia's speech. All the while, I'd been gripped by a feeling of dread that hadn't left me since the moment Biffy fired me. I felt it crawling under my skin, making me restless. It was a constant buzzing in my ears, and a punch in my guts. It felt like the sudden terror of coming across a stranger on a dark road, but having that moment of fear replayed over and over again. It would not let me go.

Twenty-One

14 days to May 30th

The next day was Ahmed's school fete. I went in early to help Hannah set up the lucky dip stall, before coming back to collect Ahmed. Although Ahmed's school, Clissington's, and Sofia's school, Brookwood, were next to each other, they held separate events. I was glad I wouldn't see Julia there as she didn't have a boy at Clissington's.

It was the first time I was seeing Hannah after the Butterfly incident. I didn't know her well enough to laugh it off, as I could have with Lizzie or Sam. She came forwards quickly to double-kiss me, as if we were meeting after a long time.

We chatted about the boys' homework. Neither of us mentioned Butterfly and soon we ran out of things to say. Silence seemed dangerous, suddenly, and I was grateful when she launched into details about the new students joining our class after the summer.

'There are a couple of Indian boys too. Won't that be nice for Ahmed?' she said, smiling. 'The Head is keen to have more diversity.'

I wasn't sure how to respond. Although I was very happy

that there would be more brown faces at school, I felt uncomfortable at the way she immediately classified Ahmed into a specific box. The funny thing was, that all my British-Pakistani friends considered my children 'white', and all my white British friends immediately put them in the 'brown' category. No, I was being too sensitive. She was right. It would be great for Ahmed to see someone from his Asian culture too. At the moment Clissington's was 95 per cent white.

'That will be nice,' I said.

In her own way, I knew Hannah was trying to make me feel more welcome.

By the time we waved goodbye, all awkwardness from the 'shoe incident' was gone. It was a relief.

When Ahmed and I got to the fair an hour later, it was already crowded.

I'd watched him carefully all morning, praying silently as he got dressed and had breakfast. I was afraid he might say that he didn't want to go, even though he'd been excited about it for weeks. But I was delighted to hear him grumbling in an everyday way, about too little jam on his toast and asking me if he could have extra one-pound coins for the stalls. I tried to keep my elation in check. I knew his mood could crash in an instant, but I allowed myself to be thankful that, for now, he was fine.

He ran off to find his friends. I saw clusters of women in skinny jeans and ballet pumps, wearing sunglasses and brightly coloured tops, or little sundresses, swaying like tulips as they chatted and laughed. I joined the parents from Ahmed's class but I only caught snatches of the conversation around me, about Common Entrance exams and holiday plans for Barbados or Cornwall. As the talk turned to which classroom our boys would be using next year, I couldn't help worrying what would happen if Ahmed had to leave...

Someone touched my arm and for a moment I lost my bearings. It was Naila.

'Hi!' I hugged her tight. 'This is a lovely surprise! What are you doing here?'

She smiled, nodding towards the playing fields, where her son, Adil, was bowling to Ahmed.

'Adil said Ahmed had told him anyone could come, so...'

'Of course! It's so good to see you,' I said.

Her eye darted around the stalls. Was she worried that Adil would get corrupted in the presence of such blatant capitalism? She was frowning at the designer T-shirts and truffle oil stalls.

'I know, it's very OTT. Some of the stalls are really good, though. You should check out the children's bookshop and the mini-donut machine.'

Adil came running up after a few minutes, his face red and his fringe sticking to his forehead. I gave him a hug.

'Sorry, Faiza,' Naila said quickly, 'we're late for a birthday party. We have to leave.'

As they rushed off, Hannah came up to me.

'I saw you talking to the new mum. I was going to introduce you but you found each other! Isn't she great?' she said.

She was so pleased I'd found another brown friend, that I almost didn't have the heart to correct her.

'No, actually that was an old friend of mine. I haven't met the new mum yet.'

Hannah frowned, looking embarrassed about her 'brown person' mix-up. But when she spoke again, I realised that she hadn't been embarrassed, only confused.

'Sorry, I didn't mean your friend. I meant that lady who just left, Naila. We thought it would be nice to invite all the new parents and pupils to the fete today...'

I heard Hannah's words but they didn't make sense.

'What's her full name? And her son's?'

Naila wasn't the only Naila in London.

Hannah handed me the paper she was holding.

'This is the list of new parents. They all signed up for a class tour.'

I scanned it quickly and saw Naila and Tariq's names, then Adil's, their address, Naila's email address and mobile. My hand tightened. I read it again, blinking my eyes, even though I knew it was true.

Adil must have sat the exam weeks ago.

As we drove home, I kept thinking about Naila. Why had she lied to me? She must have known I'd find out soon enough. I was furious as I thought about all the jibes she'd thrown my way about private schools, making me feel as if I was doing something morally wrong. Now she was sending Adil to a fee-paying school, the same school as my son, and she hadn't even had the decency to tell me. She suddenly felt like a completely different person, not my friend of almost thirty years.

I might have hidden my spending from Tom, but I'd only done that to protect our family. Naila had been a hypocrite. She'd spent years judging me for making a socially deviant choice and making me feeling guilty. Now this.

Twenty-Two

13 days to May 30th

On Monday, I didn't want to wake up. I wanted to keep my eyes closed and press 'pause' on our lives. If this day carried on, I'd have to tell Tom about the money. I'd promised him that I would have transferred the money by now. We were careering towards the thirtieth and nothing would change in the next thirteen days. Unlucky 13.

That morning, I had another stint selling tickets for the auction after drop-off, but I'd be back by ten. I would tell him then.

Tom was still asleep, and I was staring at a tiny spider on the ceiling when my mobile rang. It was 7 a.m. I shot up, worried it might be Ami. Tom also woke.

It was Dr Keane. My heart started to thud. She never called unless something was wrong.

'Is there a problem with Ahmed?' I said, not letting her speak.

Tom leaned towards me, hearing Ahmed's name.

'No, things are improving. Sometimes the anxiety does

spike like this so I'd still like to continue with extra sessions for now. I'm calling about something else.'

I puffed a huge sigh of relief, feeling suddenly drained. I gave a thumbs up to Tom, who started scrolling through his phone. I lay back against the headboard, waiting for her to continue.

'I'm sorry... This is a rather delicate matter,' said Dr Keane.

I frowned, confused.

'Your direct debit payments have been rejected.'

I jumped out of bed, afraid Tom had heard, but his eyes were on his phone screen. I went downstairs as Dr Keane continued.

'I know you've just paid the outstanding bill for last month but three invoices are still unpaid. As you know, we need to take advance payments from now on. I'm afraid the practice has an automatic policy to send unpaid invoices to a debt-collection agency. We also pause sessions. Since I know you, I wanted to tell you myself, rather than have the secretary call. Once it goes to a debt agency it can cause all sorts of ramifications on your credit score and...'

'I'm so sorry, Dr Keane. I can't think what's happened, but I'll sort it out.'

'I've asked the office to give you another ten days before takings things further. That's the most I could request.'

My forehead was tight as I drove to Sofia's school. For once, I was glad she was silent, absorbed in her headphones and Snapchat in the car.

Normally, I would have put on make-up and decent clothes to sell the tickets, but I had no energy for any of that. I just brushed my hair and pulled on one of Tom's sweatshirts over leggings.

As I handed over ticket after ticket, I couldn't help thinking that I'd only need a few of the crisp fifty-pound notes I was collecting, to pay Dr Keane's bill. I rubbed a note between my fingertips. The debt collectors would not be put off.

I sighed at the ridiculous thought. I may as well go and rob a bank.

I took the money to the office safe. I'd collected twelve hundred pounds, which I put in the safe.

As I was about to lock it, I glanced at Mrs West. She sat at her desk, with her back to me, glancing from the papers on her desk to a spreadsheet on the computer. If I took a little money, just a thousand, perhaps, no one would see me. I knew there were CCTV cameras out in the hallway, but I saw nothing in the office. I could say that I sold fewer tickets than I had. My heart was thumping and I stood still, not moving, not daring to breathe.

I couldn't do it. I slammed the safe door and locked it, dropping the key into my bag. I was frightened that the idea had even entered my head. This was charity money, for sick children in hospital.

I rushed to my car, my panic subsiding the further away I got from the school. It had been a moment of madness, I consoled myself. I wasn't a thief, even if I was a liar. I put on the radio, grateful for the pounding music. Everything would've changed if I'd taken that money.

My thoughts churned inside my head. They had nowhere else to go. If this had been any other problem, I could've told Tom. He'd have held me and said, 'Let's see how we can fix this.' I wanted to confide in Sam. She'd have listened and given me practical advice, then fed me cake and made me laugh somehow, despite everything. I longed to sit with my head in Ami's lap and tell her while she stroked my hair. I wished Baba could hug me into his tweed jacket, where it always felt safe.

I couldn't tell them about the emergency fund, though. My guilt had been festering inside me since the day Tom lost his job, growing more rancid, and now, seeping its poison straight into my mind. It was as if my whole being had malfunctioned. I had almost stolen money. Everything I had been all my life had mutated, even if only for a few seconds, into something so ugly that it had left me feeling afraid of what I might do next.

I drove around for ages, wracking my brains to see how else I could pay the doctor's bill. I thought about the seascape painting hanging behind the sofa. That was it! I'd ask the gallery to buy it back.

I bought the painting for five thousand pounds, using the emergency fund, just before it was my turn to host the end-of-term party for the first time at my house, when Sofia had been doing GCSEs. Twenty mothers were expected, some of whom I didn't know at all. When I saw how people reacted to the oversized painting with its muted blues and greens, I didn't feel guilty for spending so much, or for telling Tom that I'd bought it for a couple of hundred pounds from a graduate art show.

The painting, the colour of my walls, the type of flooring in our house, the wine I served, the clothes I wore – they were all a shorthand for anyone coming to my house, to reassure them that I was just like them.

People relaxed when they saw the seascape painting hanging in my minimalist décor. They didn't ask me where I was 'really from', nor did they question my right to exist in that particular gilded enclave they had constructed for themselves. Not as much as they had before, anyway.

Now, the painting, and everything else, felt like a mistake. Had it been worth risking everything, just so a particular group of people believed that I was just like them? I knew the answer to that. I just hoped I could put things right.

When I got to the gallery, the assistant told me the owner was away for two weeks. She said that even if he agreed, they'd only pay me once someone else had bought the painting from them, however long that took.

I walked out, feeling numb.

I was late to pick up Alex, but even though I wanted to rush, my feet dragged. I felt as if I was walking in the sea, heavy waves up to my face, pushing me back, as if the whole of the high street and all the shops, the cafés, the hairdressers, were submerged. Every step seemed to take all my energy and it felt as if, at any moment, I'd lose my grip and be swept away.

Twenty-Three

When I got to Clissington's with Alex, Ahmed wasn't at the gates. I waited as other parents and children drifted away. Alex was tugging my hand, saying he was hungry and wanted to go home.

Something started to twist inside me. Ahmed was never late.

I went inside the school, pulling Alex behind me, shushing his stream of complaints and questions as I tried to stop myself running through the corridors towards Ahmed's classroom.

It was empty, the chairs neatly pushed under the desks. I ran to the boys' toilets and then the playing fields at the back. Alex started crying.

'I want to go home!'

I went back out to the gate in case we'd crossed each other. The area was now deserted.

I was panting now, almost in tears. I kissed Alex, saying we had to find Ahmed and maybe he was sick.

I called Daniel's mother, then Hannah, then the parents of his other friends. Had I forgotten a playdate or an after-school match? I heard the women turn to their boys, asking quickly, urgently, if they'd seen Ahmed, but they couldn't remember seeing him after the last lesson. I heard my own panic in the women's voices too.

I called Tom as I walked back towards the school office. No reply. Then Sofia. Was Ahmed home? He wasn't.

The school secretary gave Alex some biscuits as he sat in my lap and I buried my face in his little back. Then she called the porter to check the grounds and the swimming pool area. An image of Ahmed, lying face down in the pool burst into my mind. I started to shiver and feel sick. I prayed to God to let Ahmed be safe. I didn't care what happened with the money, with the house, even with Tom. Please, just let my baby be OK.

They couldn't find him and he still wasn't home; the secretary called the police for me, giving them all the details when my sobs wouldn't let me speak.

As I drove home, Alex was silent, a look of fear I'd never seen before on his six-year-old face. Tom had called, saying he was going to drive around to search for Ahmed.

The look in Ahmed's eyes when he'd asked me if he would have to leave his school had frightened me. Clissington's was the first time he'd been happy and had close friends. What if he thought that he'd be taken away from it all? He hadn't been himself the night before. Why hadn't I stayed with him and tried to talk to him? My chest got tighter as I got closer to home, knowing that Ahmed wouldn't be there.

For the first time since he was born, I didn't know where he was or if he was OK.

I gripped the wheel tighter. I didn't want to think of the terrible possibilities barging into my mind. I ran through a red light without noticing until the car to my left almost hit me and beeped its horn violently.

Tom called on the speakerphone. I waited a second, dreading what he might say, then answered quickly.

'We found him! He's safe.'

I had to pull over because I was crying too much to see the road.

When I got home, the police were already in our living room. Two huge officers sat on either side of Ahmed, who was looking down, his face expressionless.

'Son, you mustn't do this again,' said one. 'Look how worried everyone is.'

Ahmed nodded, as if on auto pilot. I rushed over to him, squeezing in next to him. He shrugged off my arm as I tried to hug him.

Once the police left, Ahmed went straight to his room.

'I just want everyone to leave me alone,' he said.

Tom held me as I cried.

'I'm going to spend more time with him,' he said. 'We've forgotten him in the middle of everything.'

I called Dr Keane, then Tom and I sat with Sofia and Alex and tried our best to reassure them.

Ahmed didn't leave his room or eat dinner. I couldn't sleep until I'd spoken to him so, later, I took his favourite cherry jam crumpets and chocolate milk to his room. He sat up in bed and ate, while I perched at the edge of the bed, pretending to scroll through my phone. Once he'd eaten, I

edged towards him, and when I pulled him close, he let me.
I stayed with him stroking his hair.

'What happened, darling?' I said after a while.

'I don't know.'

Twenty-Four

It was almost midnight when Sofia came into our room. Tom and I were still awake. We wanted to make sure Ahmed was asleep before we talked, and when I popped my head into his room, I saw that he was sleeping peacefully.

Sofia sat down on our bed.

'I asked Ahmed why he ran away,' she said.

I sat up quickly. He had refused to answer any of my questions.

'Did he tell you?'

'He went to the Common and walked around.'

'But why would he disappear like that? Did something happen at school?'

'No. He says he just kept thinking about what would happen if his friends turned against him like they did at his old school. He didn't want to come home so he just ran to the Common before you got there.'

If I hadn't been late from going to the gallery, he wouldn't have had time to run away.

I stroked Sofia's hair. She was chewing her thumb and staring at the floor.

'I'm so glad you talked to him. We just need to let Ahmed know we're all here for him,' I said.

'Don't worry, Sofia, he's safe now and he didn't go far. Get some sleep now, darling,' said Tom.

I walked her back to her room with my arm around her and tucked her into bed. I could see she was still shaken.

So was I. Ahmed had always come to me when he was feeling upset or worried. Why did he feel that I couldn't help him? He must have felt so alone.

That night I couldn't stop thinking about the turmoil inside Ahmed, and the turmoil I was about to unleash into his life – into all our lives. I had to protect him, whatever it took.

I looked at Tom as he slept. My life had changed the moment I'd met him. I watched his eyes move under closed eyelids and reached out and stroked his hair carefully. I couldn't lose Tom. If I did, I'd lose everything.

My eyes snapped open.

I tried to guess what time it was. I woke up like clockwork two or three times a night: at 2 a.m., 4 a.m. and 5.50 a.m. The last slot was the worst as it didn't leave enough time to get back to sleep before the morning alarm went off at 6.45. I checked my phone. It was only midnight. I seemed to have added another insomniac pit stop to my routine.

I crept downstairs and paced the room, but my worries chased me wherever I went. It felt as if I was standing by the side-lines, waiting for my family to be destroyed. There was no one I could ask for so much money.

Ami and Baba had very little savings, less than ten thousand pounds. Their money was saturated with sacrifice and the stress of living as frugally as possible for their entire lives, so they could safeguard their future. Baba always said that they didn't want to be a burden on Farrah or me. If I asked for any of their meagre savings, I'd also have to tell them we were having money troubles and Baba's last check-up had been concerning; I couldn't risk his health.

Farrah had used up her savings to fund her stay in America. In fact, I helped her pay some of her rent from the emergency fund.

Theoretically, I could've asked Sam, but it wasn't an option. Years ago, she'd told me how her father and uncle had fallen out over money – they were still estranged twenty years later.

'I wouldn't even lend money to my children. It destroys relationships,' Sam had said.

I ran my hands through my hair as I stood at the French windows and looked straight into the eyes of a fox as it darted across the garden. It was just the two of us, alone in the dead of the night.

I looked at my phone. If I could find some sort of work that paid daily, I could settle Dr Keane's bill. I'd do anything. I googled and searched page after page, but there was nothing that started immediately or wasn't commission-based. I was about to log off when a banner started dancing cheerfully across the screen.

Want some money today? Payday loans £££. Apply now.

It had never occurred to me to get a loan from anywhere besides the bank. My hand shook as I opened up the tabs, rushing, tripping over the keys.

The process was user-friendly. There was an arrow on a sliding scale to choose the amount you wanted to borrow; I chose fifteen thousand and, for the repayment period, I chose a year.

I couldn't believe it. The solution had been here all along! It would solve everything, and could keep us going until Tom or I got a job. I whizzed through the form, filling in my bank details. The money would go straight into my account within twenty-four hours.

I watched the circle turning on the screen like a roulette wheel as the loan was processed. A message flashed up: *Application declined; unable to offer unsecured loans to those not in employment.*

I tried other loan sites, to borrow less and pay more interest, but I was rejected every time.

Twenty-Five

10 days to May 30th

In the middle of the project collapsing and Ahmed's disappearance, Tom hadn't asked me whether I had transferred the money from the emergency account. He would, though, and soon, because the direct debits were due to go out in ten days. It was just a matter of days, or even hours before he discovered the truth.

My heart raced continuously and nothing would slow it down. That was how hearts really broke, I thought, from fear and regret.

Tom had kept up a cheerful front around Ahmed and the other children, but when we were alone, he was back to either staring silently into space, or at his iPad. As I drove to school, I couldn't stop thinking about Tom's face. It was drained, defeated. I had tried to distract him, given him chores, held him and kissed him, but nothing worked.

Only one company had contacted me from all the ones I had applied to, a temping agency for office work on minimum wage, all over London. They emailed weeks ago but couldn't offer a date for interview until three weeks later. The time had passed and the appointment was today. I decided to go. I had nothing else and I could perhaps earn enough to cover Dr Keane's direct debits. We couldn't stop the sessions now.

As I left for the interview, I heard the now-familiar and maddening sound of Tom playing Solitaire on his phone. I told him I was going to meet a headhunter. He was slumped on the sofa, hair rumpled, still in his pyjamas, bare feet on the floor and eyes glued to the screen.

I sighed at my frustration. His only crime was playing Solitaire on a loop. Mine was to bankrupt us. I stood behind him and put my hands on his shoulders then kissed his head. He didn't wish me luck.

At the temping agency, the twenty-something executive told me that they couldn't help me as I didn't possess any of the skills on their checklist. I had wasted my time. I wanted to rush back to Tom and be there when Ahmed got back from school.

At Waterloo, all the trains were delayed. I paced the platform. I'd make some sweet-and-sour chicken for dinner, I thought. The children loved that. And Ahmed and Tom's favourite, prawn dumplings. I couldn't think about what would happen next. My mind had shut down.

I managed to squeeze onto the first train I could, but it moved much slower than usual. I didn't know what I'd do when I got home. Would I finally tell Tom that I had lied to him, or would I wait until the deadline got closer and he discovered the truth himself? Waiting seemed like the better option. I couldn't actively destroy everything.

When the train suddenly stopped on the tracks between stations, I looked at the sealed windows and doors, feeling as if I might suffocate. To calm myself I tapped my phone. The last search results for the loan site came up and I started to click link after link, still hoping to find one company that might give me a loan. As I was tapping, my screen was suddenly filled with pert nipples pointing straight at me, attached to naked women with long hair and pouting red lips. *Become an escort, start earning today.* My fingers moved as if of their own volition and clicked an icon saying fees and services. The figures for various 'services' flashed up. I closed the page, my face burning, too afraid to check if the man sitting next to me had seen my screen.

What was happening to me? I couldn't believe I had considered, however fleetingly, that the fees on that page might be an answer to my problem.

This had gone too far. I had to tell Tom about the money as soon as I got home. I tried to rehearse what I'd say. I kept stopping when I got to, 'Tom, I'm so sorry...'

Twenty-Six

The platform was packed as we pulled into Wimbledon station. Makeshift metal barriers had been set up and we were herded into single files as we got off the train. Station staff, some wearing high-vis jackets with the words 'British Transport Police', moved us along. I wondered if there had been a bomb scare?

A woman's voice floated over the heads of the crowd towards me. 'Someone jumped in front of a train at platform six.'

Another woman replied, 'No! Did they die?'

'I think so. It's not the first time, is it? I just wish they wouldn't do it at our station. Bloody selfish, if you ask me. I should have been home three hours ago.'

'Imagine being that desperate though. How awful...'

The voices moved away but the words kept ringing in my ears. I glanced back. It had happened just a few feet away. I shivered. Who knew what desperation could drive you to? If anyone had told me, a year ago, that I would be forging Tom's signature, selling family heirlooms and looking at dodgy loan sites or how much escorts made, I would not have believed it.

I thought about the person who had jumped. I'd seen the trains thunder past platform six. I couldn't imagine how anyone would step off the platform and let themselves fall onto the rails, knowing that they would be crushed, sliced, run over, between the tracks and the trains. It was guaranteed death.

I was doing the right thing, telling Tom. The man who jumped might not have had anyone to turn to. I still had Tom.

A woman was handing out leaflets from the Samaritans.

I took one. *Whatever you've done, we are here to listen.* I couldn't stop staring at the words.

An elderly woman standing near the exit spoke to me.

'Terrible, isn't it?' she said. 'I heard it was a banker who got fired today. He was sitting at the station for ages and then suddenly got up and jumped.'

I walked away quickly. I called Tom, needing to hear his voice.

'Hi, I'm waiting for the bus,' I said.

'All right.'

He sounded low.

'How are things?' I asked.

'How do you think things are?'

In the bus, I worried about how he'd react when he found out about the money and my lies, when he was already so down.

I was almost at my stop. I thought about the man who'd killed himself: someone's son, someone's husband and someone's father, maybe. Tom was not himself. It was as if he'd lost his balance, the way Alex did after he'd been spinning round and round in the garden. I'd never seen him like this.

If he found out about our financial situation on top of the hopeless job search and the cancelled project, it might be too much. I still had ten days before the thirtieth. I'd tell Tom that there was a slight delay in transferring the money from the Post Office, as I was waiting for a bond to mature, but that it would be in the account by the thirtieth for sure. I'd use this time to lift his mood and get close to him again, before the truth came out. I'd been so busy trying to get hold of the money that I hadn't been able to look after him at all. I'd remind him of what we had, not just what we had lost: that we loved each other, that we had three wonderful, healthy children.

It would give me time to help Ahmed too, time for him to feel stronger after what had happened yesterday.

My confession would have to wait.

Twenty-Seven

7 days to May 30th

The next few days were wonderful.

Once I'd stopped worrying about raising thousands of pounds, I could shift my attention back to Tom and the children. Like someone with a terminal diagnosis or on death row, I was aware that this might be the last time we were all together like this.

The change in my mood had a ripple effect. In the mornings I blasted music in the kitchen, flipping pancakes and cutting Alex's French toast into small squares, just the way Baba used to cut it for me when I was his age. I could sense an easing of the children's tension, even Ahmed's. We laughed at silly jokes in the car like we used to. I felt affection and amusement at their spats, rather than tearful frustration.

Tom had been more difficult to cajole out of his emotional coma. At night, I rolled towards him, pressing my body into his. He put his arms around me, but wouldn't let me take it further. Well, if sex wasn't going to work, then perhaps a different kind of fun would.

The next day the children were at school and we were having coffee.

'Do you realise we've hardly spent any time together since you left Apex?' I said. 'I know it's awful that you're not working, but let's take advantage of it. Let's be tourists in the city. Remember our walks along the South Bank? We used to love taking the river taxi from Putney pier. We could go to Richmond for a picnic or maybe see a film in the middle of the day?'

I saw something flicker in his eyes. I perched in his lap and his arms circled my hips.

'I can't remember the last time we did anything like that,' he said.

He went to get ready and I closed my eyes. I was getting him back.

We walked from the Royal Festival Hall along the Thames, right up to the Tate Modern. I pulled him inside, protesting, to look at some sculptures, and he stopped me, wanting to listen to a busker singing Beatles' songs.

Tom and I were opposites in everything. He was serious and I tried to joke about life. He loved sports, both playing and watching, and I had to force myself for a thirty-minute session in the gym. He spoke very little, and I talked non-stop, but he loved to listen. Between the two of us, though, we had found the perfect middle.

We walked across the wobbly bridge, our eyes swivelling from one side to the other, exhilarated by the view of skyscrapers gleaming in the sunshine. He put his arm around me and the wind blew my hair into his face as it fluttered happily in the air; he tucked a strand behind my ear, his fingertips warm on my skin.

We picked a different location every day. We ate churros and samosas from stalls in Borough Market, perching on walls or benches when the weather was good, and if it was raining, we sheltered under shop awnings, wolfing down shawarmas, sauce dripping on our chins. Instead of buying dessert, we had mini bites of the free samples, feeling like university students.

It was lovely to be us again. And I didn't have to lie all week.

In the evenings, Tom started sitting with me and the children on the sofa again instead of going up to bed early. He helped Ahmed with his homework and cuddled Alex. He got Sofia's favourite ice cream from the late-night supermarket when she was up till 1 a.m. doing an essay. He even started shaving.

One night, he stopped me as I was changing my clothes before bed and started to undress me himself, slowly taking off my jeans, my knickers, my T-shirt, and then my bra. He kissed me, then mumbled straight into my mouth, 'No PJs,' and led me to bed.

Despite the joy of our time together, I was always aware of the impending deadline. Most of the time I pushed the thought away, so that its presence was like a nightmare you remembered only vaguely, but at night I couldn't sleep.

Six days before the thirtieth, I was lying in bed staring at the dark, when my chest started to burn. I rubbed the spot, trying to ease the pain, but it became sharper until it hurt to breathe. I sat up, my face hot, my heart racing. I knew these symptoms from Baba's cardiology appointments. I tried to slow my breathing. Was I having a heart attack? A shot of fear ran through me.

Then, another unexpected thought burrowed into my head, overtaking fear. If I died, right at that moment, would it be such a terrible thing? The idea felt seductive. It felt like peace. No more explanations or worry. I rolled over to Tom, who had his back to me and wrapped myself around him. If I was going to die, I wanted to be close to him.

'I love you,' I whispered into his back.

He turned around and pulled me close to him, wrapping his legs around me. The pain was sharp again. I didn't want to die. I couldn't leave my children. I imagined them seeing my body in the bed.

'Tom, wake up!'

I pushed my hands against his chest.

'I'm feeling sick.'

He sat up, suddenly wide awake.

'What's wrong?'

'I have a pain in my chest.'

I was gasping and crying now. He felt my forehead with his palm and then put his hand on my breastbone. The room was starting to spin.

'Do you have pain anywhere else? In your left arm or in your jaw?' he asked.

I shook my head. As he spoke, I started to feel better.

He got me some Gaviscon and held me in his arms.

'Let's give it ten minutes and see how you feel,' he said.

He kept holding me and after a few minutes the pain went away.

'Maybe it was something you ate,' he said.

I googled my symptoms. It sounded as though I'd had a panic attack. I may have made Tom feel better, but my trick hadn't worked on me.

I was lying awake again, a couple of nights later, when my mobile flared just before midnight. It was Sam: *Daniella is back. She wants to meet you tomorrow. Send your CV xx*

Twenty-Eight

5 days to May 30th

I meandered along the sharp turns and winding streets near Bank station, out of step with the people rushing past like smudges of black and grey. They disappeared into neck-craning skyscrapers or ancient City fortresses guarded by spiked metal doors. The directions to Daniella's office had been familiar. There are some things you never forget: Threadneedle, Cornhill, Leadenhall; long lost friends of another me.

Daniella spread my CV out on the polished mahogany table.

'Sam told me you're looking for a PWM job after a long career break? I have to be honest; it's not going to be easy.'

As she talked, she glanced at her mobile. It was clear that although she was meeting me as a favour to Sam, that was the extent of her interest in me. I wasn't ready to dismiss my life as quickly as she was.

'I don't mind going to a junior role. I'll do a trial if they don't want to commit to a permanent contract, and take a lower base if they prefer a bonus or commission structure.'

I slipped back into banking-speak to impress her.

'Listen…'

She drew the word out too long, as if pulling back a deadly arrow before shooting it at me.

'I admire what you're trying to do but think about it from my clients' perspective. Why would they hire you? I'm sorry, but—'

'They'd hire me because I'm great at client relationships. I know the clients the bank is targeting. I have dinner with them at the weekends, I go skiing with them, their children go to school with mine. I speak their language – literally – some of them anyway. I have a degree in Russian.'

'You do? Russian?'

She looked at my CV as if she was reading it for the first time. She probably was.

'Are you fluent?'

'Yes.'

I could be fluent again.

'This might be a long shot, but I have a six-month contract. Someone on the team left suddenly so they're desperate. The key requirement is Russian. They're holding final interviews this afternoon. I know they don't have anyone who can start immediately.'

Another plastic visitor's badge and a lift to the twenty-fifth floor. The reception with views of St Paul's, white Barcelona chairs, art on the walls, the *FT* and *Economist* on coffee tables, and the scent of money coming in through the air conditioning. It all made you sit up straighter, be a little more on guard. I felt like an extra on a film set.

My worries about the unexpected interview were compounded by another terrifying thought. What if the interview was in Russian? It had been years since I'd spoken a single word. I couldn't remember a thing.

I was led into a boardroom with two men and two women sitting around an oval table. One wall was glass with vertiginous views of the City.

'Hello, Faiza. I'm Sergio Lucattini, the team head.'

Sergio wore a perfectly fitted charcoal suit and a lock of black hair fell over his smooth forehead. I couldn't remember bankers looking so glossy before.

He introduced me to the team, who all waved. Sergio offered me a seat at the head of the table and sat down to my right.

'Tell us a little bit about yourself,' he said.

My instinct was to look over everyone's heads but I knew that I had to make eye contact. One woman smiled encouragingly, while the other checked her phone under the table. One of the men started directly at my breasts. It felt as if I was on a roundabout. The faces around the table spun and Sergio's shiny black shoe started to move impatiently.

I cleared my throat and flicked my carefully blow-dried hair over my shoulder.

'Thank you. I'll start with the gory details then.'

Silence. This was a tough crowd to crack.

'I read Russian at Oxford and joined the graduate scheme at Citi. From there I was headhunted by UBS where I grew sales by 150 per cent over a ten-month period and was made VP Sales and Trading on the accelerated track.'

My face was burning so much that I wondered if Sergio, sitting just a couple of feet away, could feel the heat coming off me. He smiled. I didn't know if it meant anything, though.

He looked like the sort of person who smiled whatever he was feeling, a bit like me.

'I had a career break to raise my family. I was worried about the impact on my career, but in fact, it turned out to be an asset. I've been mixing with the sort of High-Net-Worth individuals we would target as clients – and, of course, I'm fluent in Russian.'

My heart was racing so fast, I thought it might trip and stop. Say something, please. When Sergio spoke though, it just made me more nervous. He fired a missile I could not dodge.

'Why should I hire you rather than the other two candidates who are currently working in banks in PWM?' said Sergio.

Clearly these people didn't mince their words.

Because I'm desperate, because I need this job for my children and to save my marriage, I thought. Sergio was beginning to finger his mobile on the table and I could feel it all slipping away from me. Tom had told me to be confident when I'd called to tell him about the interview. This job could change everything. I took a deep breath.

'I know ten people in my immediate network, at least, with over five million pounds to invest. People who know me socially, and in the City, who would take a meeting with me straight away,' I said.

It did the trick. He was really listening now. I probably only knew one person who fitted that description: Natalya, who'd been my partner for a cancer research fund-raising walk, and who I still had coffee with from time to time. I was sure I could tap into her network though, if I asked her.

I crossed my legs and my skirt rode up a fraction to mid-thigh. Sergio's eyes followed the movement.

'Yes, that network is a potential goldmine. You're older than the others in the team, but you don't look like a mother, which is great.'

He probably thought that was a compliment.

'And how would you feel about travelling, socialising? Would you be able to manage that? With your children?'

'Of course. I know what this work involves. Travel, love to. Socialising, yes please! I have a full-time housekeeper; the family runs itself really. I can focus on work 100 per cent.'

I'd heard enough horror stories from the few working mothers at school to know that you never admitted a chink on the family front. You might take the day off if your child had the vomiting bug, but you told the office that you had a gas leak. Property care was acceptable – childcare never was. If I'd mentioned elderly parents too, he would have thrown me straight out.

My teeth were clenched as I waited.

'We are getting a lot of requests from clients about investing for their children. You, being a mother, might be a selling point,' he said, as if thinking aloud. '*Allora*! I've never hired anyone over thirty-five before, and I rarely hire mothers, but I'm going to give you a shot!'

I couldn't stop smiling. The salary was higher than expected and would cover our basic monthly bills. If I met my targets, I'd get a bonus at the end of the six-month contract, with which I could replace the emergency fund. The only worry was the one-month probation period. I would have to prove myself quickly, but I'd do whatever it took.

I asked HR to print the contract out for me and rushed straight to the bank in the Village to show Roberto. As promised, now I had a job, he authorised another ten-thousand-pound loan.

I asked for it to go into the emergency fund first, and then I transferred it into the current account. That way, Tom would think that the money was from our savings, not a loan.

When I got home, Tom lifted me up and swung me around.

'Well done, my brilliant Faiza!'

He ordered takeaway pizza to celebrate. Before we ate, he raised a glass of water and told the children to do the same.

'We have very exciting news! Your clever Mum has got a fantastic job in the City. Here's to Mum! Cheers!'

Ahmed and Sofia asked what I would be doing, where my office was and how much I would get paid. Alex was quiet.

'What do you think, Alex?' I said.

'Who'll pick me up from school? Lucy's mum works and she never picks her up. She has to go home with Mrs Najeeb, her next-door neighbour. Mrs Najeeb never lets her have crisps.'

'I'll pick you up,' said Tom.

'But you don't know about my snacks.' Alex turned to me. 'Will your boss let you stay home for Sports Day?'

His eyes held mine, as if daring me to admit that his life would be adversely impacted by this thing we were so brazenly celebrating.

'I'm not sure...'

I didn't want to tell him no outright, but Tom interrupted me.

'No, darling, Mum can't take time off straight away.' Alex's face crumpled. Tom grinned. 'Tell you what, I'll get all the instructions from Mum.'

Ahmed and Sofia, happy that one of their parents was working so they didn't have to worry about their school fees, were full of laughter and jokes, so that by the end of dinner Alex had agreed to give Tom a chance to prove his skills as a replacement for me.

Tom turned and cupped my face in his hands.

'I'm so proud of you! This is phenomenal, to go back after all this time.'

We couldn't stop smiling and laughing. His face looked shiny, as if the layers of worry had been scrubbed away.

There was money in the bank and I had a job. Everything was going to be OK.

Twenty-Nine

2 days after May 30th

I asked Sam to meet me for a quick coffee on Sunday afternoon. I wanted to get some tips from her about how to behave at work. I needed to make the right impression from day one.

The sky was a perfect deep blue and the Common was teeming with children and dogs attached to adults in T-shirts and shorts. Sam and I got our coffees from the Windmill café and started to walk down a track with some shade.

She put her arm around me and gave a squeeze.

'This is so exciting!' she said. 'Hamilton Hughes are at the top of their game.'

'It's all because you sent me to Daniella. Thank you soooo much. I'm very nervous about tomorrow, though. I don't even know how to act or what to do after all this time. I need your advice.'

We sat down on a bench. In the distance, two swans glided on the lily-pad strewn pond. The air was still.

'OK. Right, first, look confident; second, get to know everyone in the team – especially the secretary! Then make absolutely sure you tell your boss everything that shows you in a good light – be your own PR machine. Plus, of course, the number one rule. *Never* talk about your children, your husband, or your parents. Faiza, you'll be fine, I promise.'

Sam was watching the swans. She had dark circles under her eyes and she looked tired, as she suppressed a yawn.

'How are things with you?' I asked.

She didn't reply straight away, then, watching a small puppy going past us, her lips lifted into a sad smile.

'Tired. Tired of everything. James, his parents, the party, the annexe, the children's endless pick and drops.'

She yawned again.

'And then I've dragged you out for career advice!'

'No, it's a tonic to see you.'

'At least you have your birthday trip coming up,' I said.

Sam and James went to Florence every year for her birthday weekend. It was the only thing he cleared his diary for.

She shook her head.

'James can't get away from work.'

I could see she was upset.

'Oh, that's such a shame! I hope you can go another time soon.'

She nodded, then sighed. I put my arm around her and laughed.

'Just think of all the millions he's making!'

She smiled, but only barely. I'd always been glad that Tom hadn't been the sort of millionaire husband I never saw. Despite it all, though, James was devoted to Sam, something you'd never guess when you met him and saw the slightly arrogant, City-lawyer vibe he gave off.

Sam took a sip of her coffee and said, 'What do you think Julia will say about your job?'

I frowned. 'Julia? I'm sure she'll find a way to bitch about me working. She's talented that way.'

'I mean, about you working for her husband,' she said.

'*What?*'

I swallowed my coffee too quickly and started to cough.

'You know Harry's a partner at HH, don't you?'

'Julia's husband is going to be my boss? Are you sure?'

'Yes. He was one of the founding partners. I thought you knew?'

All my excitement disappeared. I should have known it was too good to be true. A knot twisted in my stomach.

'I'm screwed, Sam! If Julia finds out I'm working there she's going to say something about me to her husband. He's probably as obnoxious as her. She got me fired from Butterfly, I'm sure she did. This is awful. What can we do? Please don't tell her.'

'Of course I won't,' said Sam. 'But Harry will recognise you and tell Julia, won't he?'

'I've never met him. He never comes to school stuff and I'm not invited to their parties.'

'So…?'

'So, how about I pretend that I don't know who he is? I don't tell him that Sofia's at Brookwood with his daughter, or that I know Julia. I'm sure he'd never expect a school mum from Wimbledon Village to be working in his company.'

Sam's lips twisted.

'I don't know. Your daughters are at the same school. You're bound to bump into him one day.'

'I have one month to prove myself and I don't want to

start off on the wrong foot. If you hadn't told me that Julia's husband worked at HH, I really wouldn't have known, would I? So, I'll just pretend I don't know the connection. Trust me, it'll be fine.'

I couldn't shake off my unease, though. According to Julia, she and Harry were soulmates. I wondered if they gossiped about their day, the way Tom and I did? If so, would Harry mention that someone called Faiza had started at his office? Would he say that it was someone coming back to work after a break? If she had even the slightest suspicion, she would start digging and it wouldn't take her long to uncover my secret.

'What if her husband tells her about me, though?' I said, suddenly unsure, as Sam hugged me goodbye.

'I wouldn't worry. I don't think you'll even see him, or speak to him. He's a founding partner, you're just a manager.'

'Why did this have to happen?'

'Relax. I'll tell Julia you're doing some admin role in Central London, to throw her off the scent.'

'OK,' I grinned.

In my car, I looked at Julia's husband's profile on the HH website. Harry Wentworth. His career was peppered with high-profile investment banks, he had a Harvard MBA – and had been at the same college at Oxford as me, although he'd graduated seven years before me. He looked like a million other bankers in the City, although slicker, like a Brooks Brothers advert. He wore tortoiseshell glasses and had thick salt-and-pepper hair. He fitted right into Julia's brand.

As I drove home, Naila called. I had to get this over with so I put her on speaker.

'Congratulations! I heard about your amazing job!' she said.

'Thanks.'

My voice was icy, despite my attempts to sound normal. There was silence for a few seconds. Naila cleared her throat.

'Actually, I have some good news too. Adil got into Clissington's! We just found out. I wanted you to be the first to know.'

She must have found out months ago. I wanted to call her out, tell her how hurt I was, but I couldn't. Now that Adil was going to be at Clissington's, I would have to deal with that awkwardness on a daily basis if we fell out.

'That's brilliant! Well done to Adil. Ahmed will be thrilled.' Then, when I couldn't carry on, 'Sorry, Naila, Ami's calling.'

I hung up. I felt stupid for having trusted her so completely.

I thought about us when we were fourteen, sitting cross-legged on my bed, giggling, feeling that we were soulmates, and then the conversation we'd just had.

I didn't know if I would ever feel the same way about her again.

I didn't tell Tom that Julia's husband worked at HH. I knew he'd tell me not to lie, but he didn't understand.

Tom tucked me into bed, pulling the duvet up to my chin. 'Get a good night's sleep. You have a busy day tomorrow.'

'Will the kids be OK?' I said.

'Yes.'

'Will you be OK with the kids?'

'Yes.'

'Will I be OK at work?'

'Yes.'

I grinned.

'OK, then.'

As I fell asleep, I decided to put Julia and her horrible husband out of my mind. I had happier things to think about. I smiled into my pillow. In a month's time a regular salary would start coming into our account and, with each deposit, I hoped that I could build up a little safety net around my family and feel a little less guilty about what I had done.

Thirty

Two months after Tom had lost his job at Apex and fifteen years after my last day at UBS, I was back in the City.

I exited 'the drain' – the Waterloo and City Line – at Bank station and was swept along in a wave of people. The crowd shuffled up the narrow stairs of the tube station and, once released, scattered in different directions. Dry-cleaned raincoats and suits in grey, blue and the occasional moss green, mingled with dresses in muted colours. I hurried along as fast as the people in front, behind and alongside would allow. The City swallowed me up.

Earlier that morning, as I blow-dried my hair, Tom insisted on feeding me a few mouthfuls of scrambled eggs, even though I felt as if I had lost the ability to swallow.

'Remember, you've done this before. These guys were in nappies when you were making mega sales. You'll be fine!'

He grabbed my bottom. 'I like this skirt.'

'I'm so nervous,' I said.

'It's only natural, but there's no need. I'm very proud of you.'

I'd been concentrating so hard on getting a job that I hadn't once thought about what I'd do once I had it. I was expected to deliver results and I only had one month. I'd done it before, but that felt like another lifetime.

When I called Daniella to thank her, she said, 'You need to get those sales in quickly. Remember, I won't get my commission either, unless you pass your probation!'

The weekend before I started, I spent hours reading articles on PWM and researching the latest deals and investment portfolios in the market. I'd also spent every spare moment brushing up on my Russian.

Just as important was what I would wear. The urge to go and buy clothes was like an unbearable itch. I needed the armour of new clothes for my new identity. The only saving grace was that the dress code in the City was more relaxed these days. I wouldn't look out of place wearing the dresses that I wore on more formal social occasions, in my role as 'corporate wife' and 'yummy mummy'.

I trawled through my wardrobe, looking for anything with a designer label and a hefty price tag. I knew how much the aura of money mattered in the business of making money. The solitaires, designer watches, handbags and coveted logos were all symbols of success that City slaves collected, to proclaim their dominance. That hadn't changed since my days in banking.

I chose a navy Hugo Boss dress, a Gucci belt and nude, high-heeled courts. I carried my Prada bag. For once, I was grateful for the money I'd splurged from the emergency fund.

The children were still asleep when I left. I left a note for Alex next to his cereal bowl: *Have a brilliant day. Good luck with your spelling test. Love, Mum.* I had a feeling he might scrunch it up or fling it to the floor. He wasn't happy that I was going to 'leave him' every day.

Sergio was in New York, so Sabine, who had dismissed my answers at the interview with a 'Pah!' and a shake of her glossy bob, took me up to the offices on the twenty-fifth floor. Despite a warm 'Bonjour!' she made no further attempt at conversation.

We stood at the edge of an open-plan office, with around ten desks, each with six or seven people, who were already talking into phones and looking at computer screens. I walked on the hard, dark-grey carpet, past walls that were unadorned except for whiteboards covered with black and red numbers, and punctuated by occasional steel filing cabinets. There were no windows, except at the far end of the long room. I could barely make out the other buildings outside and a tiny patch of dirty sky.

At my interview, I'd only seen the lobby, with designer furniture and floor-to-ceiling windows. The bathrooms had been luxurious, with green marble and wood-panelling. This was very different.

We stopped at a desk in the middle of the large room.

'This is your spot.'

The team, who I'd met at my interview, sat around the desk behind their computers and stood up to shake my hand.

'Hi, lovely to see you again,' I said to Teresa, who'd been the only friendly face at the interview. She was around my age and wore a wedding ring.

'Anything that you need, Faiza, let me know. Anything at all.'

'So, you managed to tear yourself away from your children, then?' said David, addressing my breasts, as he'd done the last time I met him.

Ivan stood up, even taller than I remembered.

'*Privet*!' He said hello in Russia.

'Sergio has his own office, like the directors, at that end.' Sabine pointed towards a partition at the far end of the room.

It was only when I sat down at my computer, next to Teresa, that I noticed a large whiteboard next to the desk, with the names of everyone in the team, including mine. It all came back to me: the sales board. Every team member's progress, or lack of it, was charted there for all to see. Next to my name someone had written 'monthly and quarterly targets' with numbers that looked frightening in their finality.

'You've got some catching up to do,' said David, when he saw me looking up at the board. 'Annie, the woman who you're replacing, was a bit of a rocket.'

'Why did she leave?' I asked.

No one replied for a minute, then Ivan said, 'Personal reasons.'

'I'm sure you'll do very well,' smiled Teresa.

'Here's a list of Annie's clients.' Sabine passed me a thick file. 'IT haven't set you up yet so just find their details in here. Sergio's afraid her clients may be starting to feel neglected. He wants you to start calling them this morning.'

'Sure,' I said. 'Where can I call them from? Is there an office I can use?'

Everyone laughed.

'This is our only office, I'm afraid. But use your

headphones and you won't even notice anyone else,' said Teresa.

Ivan brought me a steaming cup of coffee and put it down without a word before sitting back down.

I had no idea what I was going to say to the clients. I was aware of the others sitting just a couple of feet away and was anxious that they would hear my calls.

I decided to start with a woman, someone who was an existing client. I rehearsed my script in my head. I'd introduce myself as Annie's replacement, tell them how to contact me, ask them if they needed any help and make some small talk. I scanned the list and picked Melody Carruthers, CEO Nail Emporium. A woman, English, probably older as she was a CEO, maybe around my age, and in a business I felt comfortable in, beauty.

I bent my head as I dialled the number, trying to hide the terror rushing through me.

'Yes?'

A woman answered, sounding displeased, as if I was interrupting her in the middle of something.

'Good morning, may I speak to Melody Carruthers, please?'

The rest of the team seemed to stop what they were doing, to watch me. I looked down at the client sheet. I had to forget about the others and concentrate.

'Who is this?' The voice at the other end sounded impatient, angry even.

I smiled. I couldn't let the team see that my first call wasn't going well. Besides, I'd read somewhere that if you smiled while talking on the phone, your conversations were more productive.

'I'm calling from Hamilton Hughes and my name is Faiza Saunders. I've taken over from Annie Dill. It's a pleasure to speak to you Ms Carruthers—'

'What the hell?'

'I'm sorry, have I caught you at a bad time?'

By now I'd forgotten about the others watching me and became flustered as I tried to salvage this conversation. I didn't know what I'd done wrong. Opposite me, David snorted loudly.

'I can call you back later if—'

The phone slammed down at the other end. I tried to pretend that I was going to end the call myself, so though the line was dead, I carried on speaking into the phone.

'Of course, I understand if you're busy. It's no prob—'

'Which idiot is calling me on my extension and pretending to call a client? Do you really think I'd find this kind of thing funny?'

I looked up and saw a woman with East Asian features, a cropped dark pixie cut, and wearing a tight-fitting red dress, coming out from behind the partition. She was around my age. She may have been petite, but her voice filled the office and boomeranged back from the walls. Everyone sat up a little straighter as she approached.

'Well? Who decided to disturb me as I finished the Nordic tech projections? Hmm?'

My team all looked at me, waiting for me to confess. My face burned. The people on the other desks had paused what they were doing.

I put up my hand and said, 'Me. I'm so sorry. I must have misdialled by mistake.'

David's shoulders shook and his hand covered his mouth.

'Who are you? Stand up.'

I stood up slowly.

'I'm replacing Annie. My name is Faiza.'

'Ah, Sergio's "experiment". Welcome, welcome! Tilly Madison – I'm one of the directors.'

She came forward to shake my hand and said, 'Can someone please show her how to use the phone?'

Tilly smiled, as if she was sharing a joke with me, not making one at my expense. The whole office erupted in laughter and, as she walked away, I heard her say, 'Don't they have telephones in suburbia anymore?'

I dug my nails into my palms to stop myself bursting into tears and making my humiliation complete. Instead, I smiled as if amused at my mistake.

'OK, OK, at least I've provided everyone with some entertainment,' I said.

'Did you dial 900 first, for an outside line?' Teresa leaned across and whispered.

I shook my head. She showed me how to dial for an outside line and gave me the team's security code, which I also needed to enter. I wrote it on a piece of paper.

'You must have gone through to Tilly's internal extension. Anyone could have made the same mistake,' said Teresa.

'Absolutely,' said David.

He started laughing.

'Stop it,' said Ivan.

Later, when the others were away from the desk, I decided to call the clients again, but I couldn't find the paper with the security code. I was too embarrassed to ask Teresa again. Instead, I took the client list down to Starbucks and made the calls on my mobile.

As I was going back up to the office, the lift door was just about to shut when a large, trainer-clad foot inserted itself between the doors, so they jerked back open. A tall man, dressed in shorts and a T-shirt, muscled legs on show, stepped in. As I moved back to give him room, my client list fell to the ground.

'I'm sorry, my fault,' he said.

He sounded amused, rather than apologetic.

We bent down to get the papers at the same time and his hands touched mine. I stood up quickly as he handed me the papers. I felt self-conscious as he looked at my face, smiling as if he was admiring something he liked. I didn't know if he was being friendly or flirtatious.

'Thanks,' I said, wishing that my office was not on the twenty-fifth floor.

I wasn't used to handsome men looking at me like that. It wasn't the harmless flirtations that I usually came across, from waiters or shop assistants, and nor was it the unwelcome attention from men at parties who complimented me on my 'eastern beauty'. This man's eyes showed clear interest and attraction.

While the lift moved slowly, I stared at my papers as if I was trying to understand a complex problem and didn't look at him again. He also got out on my floor, letting me go ahead, and when I looked back, he'd disappeared.

For the rest of the day, my eyes kept darting to the partition where the directors' offices were. That's where Julia's husband was also sitting. He wasn't on another floor, in a penthouse, away from the lowly workers, but just a few feet away from me. Sam was wrong that I was unlikely to come across him. I'd already met Tilly within half an hour of being at work. She seemed to know about me as 'Sergio's experiment'. What if Julia's husband was also curious and came out to see me, then later told Julia about a woman called Faiza, who had just joined HH, and who, until recently, was a full-time mum?

My head started to hurt. This was too risky. I wouldn't be able to get away with it. I pretended to read through my notes, wondering what I should do.

'Si, can you pass me your stapler, mate?' said David to someone passing.

I had an idea. I had to hide anything that could give me away. I looked at the team and said, 'Oh, guys, I didn't say this at the interview, but everyone calls me Fi. It's my nickname, and clients also find it easier to pronounce.'

Later, Teresa asked me about my children.

'I have two boys,' I said, thinking it would be best if no one knew that I had a teenage daughter at Brookwood.

'And you live in Wimbledon, right?' said Sabine.

'I did for years, but we moved to East Sheen a couple of months ago. We needed somewhere bigger now the boys are older and everything in Wimbledon is so expensive.'

All the years of thinking up quick-fire, appropriate answers for each parent to keep the plates spinning when I was growing up, had paid off. If Ami told me to lie about her secret shopping to Baba, I would. If Baba bought me a treat when he got a bonus, he often asked me not to tell Ami about his windfall. If either of them probed my lies, I had to think up additional answers in a split second. It was no trouble at all to think up my alter ego. I had found a solution to the 'Julia angle'.

Now, I was Fi, who lived in East Sheen and had two boys.

Thirty-One

My first client was Thomas Seddon QC, a top divorce lawyer. I carried my brochures and navigated my heels along the cobbled square in the hidden legal enclave near Temple. I'd made a good start and was going through my proposal when Teresa walked into his office. I was surprised but relieved. I was feeling out of my depth. Instead of supporting me, though, she proceeded to demolish my proposal and suggested a different portfolio, winning the pitch from the client and leaving me looking like a fool.

The sales numbers went up against Teresa's name, not mine.

Sitting on a bench outside St Paul's, I called Tom, too upset to eat my sandwich.

'It was so humiliating.'

'You'll get better at it. At least now you know you can't trust Teresa.'

After dinner, Tom gave me an update on his job search. The headhunters all said he had a stellar profile and a great reputation, but that jobs at his level were few and far between. He had to be patient.

'I don't know what that means? Two months, six months?' He sighed. 'It's good that you're working, at least. Our savings wouldn't have lasted at this rate, not without your job.'

I wondered if that would be true in four weeks, if I kept having client visits like the one that morning. My euphoria at getting the job had turned almost instantly into nervous panic.

'I heard some news about Sam's husband too,' said Tom. 'One of the headhunters mentioned James's firm. They're cutting a thousand people globally. I hope James isn't one of them?'

'No, he's safe. Sam told me they've fired three people in his team so he's doing their work too and staying late every day. I don't think they can afford to fire him!'

I missed having my coffees with Sam and Lizzie. Naila had been texting me but I couldn't bring myself to reply to her. All I could focus on, for now, was passing my promotion.

That night, I sat cross-legged on the sofa, laptop perched on my knees, researching all the products and portfolios that we offered in as much detail as possible. I was not going to let myself look like a fool again. After the headhunter's prognosis, my job was our only lifeline.

Every night in bed, I asked Tom to test me on the latest products I'd been studying. Sometimes, as I stood at the foot of the bed in T-shirt and knickers, I pretended to do presentations and pitches, while Tom fired questions at me in a client's tone of voice. He told me I was 'killing it' and gave me tips when I stumbled on a question. It was like having my personal business coach in bed.

'You can do it, I know you can,' he said.

After a while, I started to believe it too. I no longer stayed silent in team meetings and I began to feel a little less like an imposter.

The loan from Roberto was getting used up, so I hadn't been able to send Farrah any money for ages. I told her that I would, once I got my salary. I'd been helping her out from the emergency fund, before Tom lost his job. I worried about how she'd manage.

'Don't worry, Baba sent me three thousand pounds,' she said.

I was furious.

'Farrah, how could you? That's half their life savings!'

'It's not "half their life savings" – Baba cashed in those shares he's had forever. He got ten thousand, plus they have ten thousand savings. He told me exactly how much they had when I was refusing to take any money from them.'

'You have to pay them back.'

'Of course I'll pay them back. I wouldn't be in this mess, though, if it wasn't for them, would I?'

I wondered if I would have taken the money for Dr Keane if I'd known about my parents' savings? No. It would have meant telling them why I needed five hundred pounds when Tom had a £250,000 safety net. I couldn't have put them through that kind of stress.

I was glad I hadn't known. This was my mess and it was only right that I sort it out myself.

Thirty-Two

The spa was the last place I wanted to be. The weekends were the only time I had now, with Tom, the kids and my parents. I knew Sam would be disappointed, though, if I missed her celebration and I hadn't seen her for ages. Besides, I'd paid my contribution – a hundred pounds, which had seemed nothing a few months ago – to Lizzie weeks ago, so I put on a suitable dress and a smile, and went.

Inside the spa, six of us stood in the dark, oak-panelled hall, looking through a menu of massages, manicures and facials. As well as Julia and Lizzie, there was Anna, and Sam's friend from work, Beth. Everyone was wearing pale pink, and even Sam had stuck to the theme Lizzie had planned, by wearing a pink T-shirt from a breast cancer charity. The rest of us were in cotton summer dresses, looking a bit like a hen party.

We each had to pay for our own treatments. I'd already thought of a way to get out of it. Every penny of my salary was accounted for to pay our bills and it still wasn't enough.

'I'm going to skip the treatments. My eczema has flared up,' I said.

I held up my scratched red hand as evidence.

'Have some hot stone therapy,' said Sam.

'Or a pedicure,' said Lizzie. 'You can't just sit here alone for hours while we bliss away!'

Julia was watching me. I felt my face flush, but at least no one could see it on my skin.

'Better not risk it. I'm going to zone out in the relaxation room. That's pretty blissful too!'

The rose-scented candles felt suffocating as I lay down on a chaise in the relaxation room. A therapist offered me a tall glass of water with ice and thin slivers of lime, and a tray with chilled face towels rolled up with symmetrical precision. Across the room I saw three women, in their fifties, maybe, all very tall, very thin and very blonde. Their fingers and toes were tipped with matching orange gel polish. I pulled the oversized white robe around me and closed my eyes.

I had to be careful not to slip up and mention HH in front of Julia. It made my heart race as I thought about the complex web of lies I was caught up in. I had to be on guard all the time. At work as Fi, at home with Tom, and even with my friends. I couldn't tell anyone at school about HH as it was bound to get back to Julia.

Later, we all sat in the conservatory restaurant, at a round table with a starched linen tablecloth and views of a mature, landscaped garden. Outside the French windows, rabbits and squirrels bounced around as if putting on a show just for us. It wouldn't have surprised me if that was true and the spa had trained the poor rabbits to prance around and add to the carefully curated ambience. I was desperate to leave.

As we ate the calorie-controlled meal that we'd paid so much for, with no comfort food in sight, the talk turned to the money-guzzling and time-consuming aspects of body maintenance.

'Well, I'm lucky, I have good genes, so I haven't really needed to do much since I first started dating Harry,' said Julia, pushing shredded carrots around her plate.

Julia was forty-eight and it was clear that there had been more than just divine intervention on her face. Despite their zealous pursuit of youth, the women were still coy about their cosmetic enhancements. Botox and fillers were acceptable, but boob jobs and liposuction were never owned up to. There was always gossip though, about tummy tucks and thread lifts, in the perennial school-gate game of 'spot the plastic surgery'.

All the women I knew were getting younger and looking better as the years passed. I wondered what it would be like for Tom to be the only man turning up with a wrinkled wife, when other women my age still looked as if they were in their mid-thirties. Sometimes it felt as if I was decomposing. Tom still told me I was beautiful, but I wondered if he was just being kind. He was like that.

I heard a groan from Sam.

'I'm glad I don't need to date any more,' she said.

'It was fun, though. The one-night stands, sex with different men, the excitement of what will happen next,' said Anna.

A collective sigh went around the table like a Mexican wave.

'The good old days,' said Sam's friend from work. 'I could tell some stories that would make you blush!'

'It *was* fun – but imagine having to do that now? No thanks!' said Lizzie, her eyes widened in horror. 'Can you imagine getting naked in front of a stranger and getting into funny positions?'

'Oh yes! I imagine it quite often,' said Anna, and the group exploded with laughter again.

I laughed too, grateful to forget my worries for a second.

'Never say never. I still get hit on. I was at a wedding in Ireland last week and this very sexy man flirted outrageously with me,' said Julia.

'Well, we still need to feel we could if we wanted to!' said Lizzie. 'Stewart still tells other women they look beautiful. I don't mind.'

My mind flipped to the man in the lift and the look of naked admiration in his eyes.

I had seen the playful flirtations at dinner parties, when usual marital constraints were loosened by good food and drink and an array of bare legs and décolleté. It was pretty innocent and never went further than sitting closer than normal or a slightly longer kiss or hug when saying goodnight.

My own experience of the attention from the other husbands at dinner parties was quite different. There were some who ignored me or kept a polite distance, as if wary of approaching me at all. Then there was the other group, who immediately picked me out. I didn't get the usual teasing, funny double entendres or playful compliments, though. With me, they went straight for the jugular. The comments were more sexual – and always focussed on my 'exotic' appearance.

'Your skin looks delicious. Like milk chocolate. De-lic-ious.'

'Your hair is so thick, so luscious. I bet it would be incredible to grab at the right moment, if you get my drift!'

'Your eyes are so beautiful. Very dusky. They're almost black, aren't they?'

'I love eastern women. So elegant and gentle. And experts in the Kama Sutra, right?'

They probably thought they were complimenting me, but it made my skin crawl. I never told them they were being racist or inappropriate. Instead, I'd learnt to move away quickly, the minute I saw where the conversation was headed. Although it didn't happen every time I was out, it was frequent enough that it would cause too many scenes if I called them out. These were the husbands of women who I'd see the next day at school pickup. I never told Tom either, not after the first few times. He was always furious when someone treated me like that and it would just have upset him.

Thankfully, there was also a third group, men who I knew well, such as my friends' husbands like James and Stewart, Tom's colleagues and our friends, and now Sergio and Ivan, who talked to me as if I was a person and not a walking, talking ethnicity.

'It wasn't all fun and games,' said Lizzie. 'I made some very questionable choices. I'm glad I'm an old married woman.'

She turned to me and asked, 'You and Tom are so loved up. Did you have to kiss a lot of frogs before you found him?'

I'd been avoiding eye contact, hoping they'd forget about

me. When the question came, I was unprepared. All my focus had been on avoiding any talk about work. I shook my head and tried to pitch my laugh at the appropriate level of amusement and horror.

'Thankfully, no! Tom was actually one of my first serious boyfriends. I got lucky.'

'So how many boyfriends did you have before Tom?' asked Julia.

She always knew when to keep prodding.

There was no way I'd ever have told them that Tom had been my first and only boyfriend. It wasn't just my embarrassment at this fact, I also knew that the shock of that confession would be something they'd discuss for months at dinner parties. Besides, my sex life was no one else's business.

'Just a couple at university.'

There was silence and all eyes were now fixed on me. I wished I'd been better prepared and invented a lengthier list of boyfriends. My face was hot and I just wanted someone to change the subject.

'*What?*' exclaimed Julia.

Her eyes widened.

'You *did* get lucky,' said Lizzie, cutting in.

I smiled.

'Ugh, I had forgotten about all the creeps I had to go through. You and Tom are perfect together,' said Sam. 'Now, where's my birthday cake?'

'But how does she know that Tom's perfect if she hasn't got much to compare him with?' said Julia.

I glared at her now, unable to hide my anger. On rare occasions in the past, when I'd mentioned my lack of romances pre-Tom, people had been surprised, but thought it was quaint and romantic in an old-fashioned way. No one had reacted like Julia.

'No offence, Faiza, I'm just curious. I knew Harry was the best sex I'd ever had because I'd tried out plenty of others. I'm going to tell my girls to make sure they play the field before settling down!'

She winked at the others and laughed, as if she wasn't taking a dig at me, but just an innocent trip down memory lane. Perhaps this wasn't directed at me? But then she said, 'To be honest, Faiza, it seems positively barbaric to marry your first serious boyfriend. It's a little backwards, don't you think, in this day and age?'

Julia and Anna exchanged horrified glances.

'Well, clearly it's worked out for me,' I said.

Julia ignored me and started talking about how she had been right about Harry. She cited her evidence with a look of bashfulness mixed with pride.

'He still,' she began, and leaned forwards to whisper the rest of the gory details to everyone around the table. If I ever did meet Harry, it would be hard to forget these graphic details. Everyone was riveted and the attention shifted away from me. I wondered if anyone had noticed how Julia had used the words 'barbaric' and 'backwards'? It seemed not.

I picked up my bag and waved to Sam.

'Sorry, I need to dash off,' I said.

'Before you go, Faiza, just take a look at this,' said Lizzie, handing out glossy booklets to everyone.

'It's a young Nigerian artist who's just graduated. He's a former scholarship student from my father's foundation and I've organised for him to hold his first show at the art gallery in the Village. I'd love it if you can all come and support him. He's so talented.'

I looked at the intricate paintings of bees, butterflies and trees. They were truly stunning.

'Yes, sure,' I said. 'Oh, but it's on Thursday; I'm so sorry, I'll be at work.'

'That's a shame. Well, I'm asking everyone to pre-order any paintings you like. He's in such a tight spot financially and unless he gets a boost from some sales, he'll have to work full-time and won't be able to paint.'

Julia put a cross against three paintings.

'We invest in a lot of art and these are excellent. I'll hang them up in my house so my guests can see them and maybe spread the word that way.'

'Thank you, Julia. That's incredibly kind of you,' said Lizzie. 'It'll mean a lot to Adedayo, the artist.'

'Not at all. It's our duty, isn't it, in our position.' Julia looked around the table. 'Let's all help this artist.'

The paintings were priced between a thousand to five thousand pounds. I flicked through the booklet slowly. Luckily, Sam bought a painting too and called out the number she'd chosen.

'Faiza? You better pick one before you leave,' said Julia. 'So far, ladies, we've raised ten thousand in ten minutes.'

'I'll look at this later, Lizzie,' I said.

'Sure, just text me,' said Lizzie.

Julia cut in. 'Come on, Faiza, pick something. It won't take a second. I thought you of all people would like to support this artist. As he's, you know,' she paused before saying, 'BAME.'

I ignored her, waved goodbye to everyone and left. I

thought about the way Julia had singled me out. There were others on the table who hadn't bought anything yet. I was afraid I might cry and I didn't want to do it till I was in my car.

At least no one had asked me about work.

Thirty-Three

Sergio handed me a piece of paper.

'Your first VIP client, Fi. Vladimir Omersky. *Times* Rich List.'

'Why's Fi getting this account? You know what happened last time. I have some bandwidth.'

Teresa no longer made any pretence of sisterhood. Ivan also looked displeased.

'Because she is a Wimbledon Mummy and his twins go to school in Wimbledon and his wife lives there. Plus, her Russian background. It's perfect for her. Right, Fi?'

'Yes, thank you,' I said.

I smiled as broadly as I could. Despite my apparent enthusiasm, I agreed with Teresa. There was a high likelihood that I would mess this up. However, unless I showed some results soon, I wouldn't pass my probation, which ended in two weeks. My sales board was still empty, and people commented every day as they walked past.

'Still nothing, Fi?'

Later, outside the private members' club in Piccadilly

where I had my meeting with Vladimir, I saw a pale mauve, metallic Rolls-Royce with an Arabic number plate. As I went up some steps to the entrance, a doorman in a hat and a long green overcoat edged with pink opened the door for me. Just as I was about to go in, my phone buzzed. It was Alex's school. I always panicked when they called. I shook my head at the doorman and stepped back outside to take the call.

'It's Mrs Williams here, the school nurse.'

All thoughts of Vladimir tipped out of my head.

'Alex got hit in the privates when he was playing football and he's got a groin injury. I think you should get him checked out at minor injuries, just as a precaution. Can you please come and pick him up?'

I had ten minutes before my meeting.

'I'm afraid I'm at work, but I'll ask my husband to get him. Could I please have a word with Alex?'

I put the phone on speaker, so I could WhatsApp Tom at the same time.

He was crying.

'When will you get here, Mum?'

'As soon as I can, darling. Dad's coming to pick you up.'

'I don't want Dad, I want you. My willy hurts.'

'Dad will look after you, I promise. He knows about willies and goolies better than I do!'

I heard his small laugh.

The doorman, listening to my conversation, smiled at me.

'Does it hurt?'

'Yes. I want you to come home.'

His voice sounded so far away. I just wanted to hold him close.

'I'll come as soon as I can. Dad's on his way. Love you. I have to go.'

I hung up, and said, 'Fuck!'

Then I remembered the doorman.

'Sorry!' I said.

He smiled, as if hearing a woman discuss her son's genitalia with him and swear on the steps was nothing unusual.

Inside the club, an usher led me through corridors and up a staircase lined with cherrywood panelling and portraits of club presidents through the ages. The clothes had changed over the centuries but the faces staring down at me were interchangeable: male, middle-aged, white.

'*Dobray den*,' I said, shaking Vladimir Omersky's hand and putting thoughts of anything but his portfolio out of my mind...

'Go on then, Fi, write it up!'

Sergio stood by our desk, tie askew, sleeves rolled up, hair dishevelled. He looked like he'd just come out of a wrestling match. As I'd discovered, this was his natural state of being, not the perfect image I'd seen at the interview.

I couldn't suppress my smile, as I went up to the whiteboard, picked up the marker and wrote up my sales figures for Vladimir – one million pounds – next to my name. My first deal.

I sat down, fizzing with excitement. I'd done it! Sergio pulled on his jacket.

'Time to tell the directors. Come on!'

I wanted to ask him to wait a minute so I could brush my

hair and check my make-up, but he was already walking towards the partition. I tucked my blouse into my grey pencil skirt and ran-walked while fluffing up my hair with my hands then smoothing my ring fingers under each eye to make sure my eyeliner hadn't smudged. I was going to meet Julia's husband and I had to be careful what I said. I clenched my teeth and tried to calm my breathing as I followed Sergio.

'Now they'll see I was right to hire you!' he said, rubbing his hands together as if he'd won a bet.

Thirty-Four

Behind the partition I saw a wide corridor with flush mahogany doors.

We started with Tilly, who I'd discovered was called 'The Dragon', though never to her face. She congratulated me and then said, 'You win!' to Sergio.

'Now, Harry,' said Sergio. 'He's the most important one for you to meet, because he covers a lot of the Russian clients too. He's grown the market share more than the rest of us put together and he has kids too. You'll love him.'

My heart was racing. I had to concentrate but the image of Julia's husband pleasuring her, which she had described in such graphic detail, popped into my mind and I didn't know how I'd be able to look him in the eyes.

Sergio pushed the door open slightly and we both looked in. A very tall man, well over six foot, was standing with his back to us, looking out of a wall of glass at London spread out below him, and speaking on the phone. The late afternoon sun streamed in around him, defining his outline as if drawing it in dark pen. He was dressed in starched white shirt and navy trousers.

I stepped back, mouthing, 'Let's go' to Sergio, but he pushed the door open and cleared his throat.

I steeled myself as Julia's husband turned around, showing salt-and-pepper hair and smiling hazel eyes. I forgot about Julia though as I realised that this was the man from the lift! The one who had stopped me stumbling when I'd dropped my papers. A wedding ring glinted on his hand which I hadn't noticed last time. I wondered if he remembered me. Dressed like this, he looked more like the photograph I'd seen on the HH website, although he wasn't wearing glasses now, but in the lift I hadn't recognised him.

I arranged a neutral smile on my face. My mind jumped from the fact that I was standing in Julia's husband's office, to the feeling that he had flirted with me on my first day.

'I'm sorry, can I call you back?' he said into the phone.

He shook Sergio's hand warmly.

'Come in, come in.'

Sergio introduced me.

'I've seen you before,' he said.

I managed not to look away. What if he'd seen me at some school event or dropping off Sofia, even if I hadn't seen him, and he remembered me? Or was he reminding me of that day in the lift?

I nodded. My face burned.

'In the office,' he said.

He led us to the sleek grey sofa. I was acutely aware that I was sitting in the glare of the sun and the harsh light must have been picking out every line on my face. Our eyes met and I saw that his had green flecks in them.

'I'm very glad to finally meet you, Fi. I'm looking forward to our collaborations.'

I couldn't believe the man from the lift was my boss, and Julia's husband.

As we were leaving, I couldn't stop myself looking at the photographs on Harry's desk. Julia's eyes seemed to follow me as she stood in the sleek silver frame in a white slip dress, her blonde highlights and smile beaming. Her daughters were in another photograph, standing on either side of Harry, who had his arms around them.

Harry had no idea that I saw his daughters at school drop-off, or that I'd just emailed his wife about the charity auction committee in my lunch hour. I looked away, my mouth suddenly dry. Sergio was still talking, telling Harry how I won the deal with Omersky.

'I always knew Fi's Russian would give us the edge. Pity she's been hiding herself away in...'

I cut in before he could say 'Wimbledon'.

'Sergio, you're embarrassing me now. But thank you,' I said.

I wanted to leave before Sergio said anything about my children or my also living in the Village. However, when he spoke again, he sent the conversation in a different direction.

'Fi was at Oxford too,' said Sergio.

Harry asked me which college and year and what I'd studied and before long we were reminiscing about the halls of residence, the dinner ladies and the beloved College porter who'd recently died of cancer.

'I can't believe you were in A6 too!' I said. 'Life is so strange isn't it, sometimes?'

He smiled. I thought about Harry sitting on the same benches at breakfast and using the same creaking lift.

'It is indeed. Although I left eight years before you. Otherwise, we might have been neighbours.'

I didn't know if I imagined it or if the words 'or more...' were implied by Harry. His eyes crinkled, as if sharing a joke with me.

I had deliberately looked away from Julia while we spoke but my eyes were drawn back to her. She seemed angry. Harry saw me looking and picked up his daughters' photograph.

'My girls,' he said. 'Do you have children?'

Sergio's phone rang and he went out, leaving us alone. I felt exposed, as Harry looked at me. I wondered if he was also thinking about the day in the lift.

'Yes, two sons. Twelve and six.'

'The opposite of mine. Two teenage girls, Amber and Elle,' he said.

I looked at the photograph that he was holding out, at the faces I had seen many times at school.

Dread seeped through me. Perhaps I should say something after all? If the moment passed, it would be too late. I couldn't bring myself to tell him the truth, though. Things were going so well for me now but I still had to pass my probation and this deal would help towards my bonus. I couldn't let Julia mess it all up for me. I just had to keep up the pretence for another few months.

'They're very pretty,' I said, looking at the photograph.

'They take after their mother in the looks department, thank goodness.'

He smiled at Julia's photo.

Julia smirked at me.

'This is my wife, Julia.'

That was the moment I should have said something like, 'Oh, you're Julia's husband?'

I didn't.

There would be no way out now, if he ever found out. It would be clear that I had deliberately lied.

'You have a beautiful family,' I said.

Before he could ask me any more questions about the children or Tom, I said, 'I'm looking forward to the Omersky proposal. Sergio said we're kicking off with a meeting tomorrow?'

He looked taken aback at my change of topic, as if he was the one who usually led the conversation. Then he smiled, as if impressed.

'Yes, I met him a few years ago. I think we have a real opportunity here. Well done on getting this.'

'Thank you. Sorry, I'd better get back to work. It's great to meet you.'

Harry's eyebrows moved up a fraction. He seemed surprised that I was opting to leave an audience with a director before being dismissed, but by the way he smiled at me as I left, he seemed to like it.

Thirty-Five

I had passed my probation. I had a job for the next five months, at which time, if I met my targets, I would get my bonus. I could then pay off the bank loans and put back most of the emergency fund. Sergio also said that if I carried on like this, they might offer me a permanent role.

I sat at my desk, trying to appear calm and carry on working as normal, but inside my joy bubbled like the champagne Sergio opened at our desk, to celebrate. Besides the relief, I felt a sense of confidence that had disappeared from my life a long time ago. I felt as if I had proven myself, at least at this hurdle. At HH all that mattered was that I could do my job. I remembered that feeling from when I worked in the City before. It didn't matter about my name, or the colour of my skin, or even what I looked like. In the City, the bottom line was that if you delivered the money, you belonged. At least at my level. My confirmation showed that my hard work had paid off and I had been accepted.

I wanted to see Tom's face when I told him. It was a

Friday, so I arranged for the children to be at sleepovers and made sure I left at five.

'Tom!'

I started calling him while my key was still in the front door but there was no reply. Damn. He was out.

I stood still for a second and then spun myself around in the hallway, my arms spread out. We were safe! We could go back to being us. Tom would never need to know what I'd done, and I would never lie to him again.

I heard a sound upstairs. Tom *was* home. I ran up.

He was standing at the window in our bedroom, staring at the sky. This room was always gloomy in the evenings but he hadn't turned on the lamp. I stood in the doorway. Poor Tom, alone in an empty house all day. I couldn't wait to fling my arms around him and see his smile. I knew that he'd be just as excited at my news.

I ran towards him, but stopped when I saw his face. When he looked at me, his eyes were hard as marble and his face taut. The skin around his eyes was blotchy, his hands hung clenched at his sides.

'What the fuck have you done?' he shouted.

His voice was like a slap. I took a step back, so shocked that it took a second before I realised what he'd said. Even then, I wondered if I'd heard him correctly.

He held out a piece of paper that he'd been holding in his fist. I smoothed the creases quickly, wondering what it could be. Then I saw the bank's logo and my eyes filled with tears.

He knew.

'What does it say?' he said.

Each word felt deadly. My hand trembled.

'What does it say?'

He repeated his question with clipped precision.

I sat down on the bed. My heart pounded through my chest, my head, my ears. I wanted to tell him that I was sorry, to beg his forgiveness, say that I'd pay back every penny. I knew none of that mattered, though. Nothing could excuse what I had done.

'I went to the bank,' he said. 'All the money's gone. The emergency fund was our safety net. For our family, for the children.'

His hands gripped my upper arms and pulled me up. His face was distorted, as if in physical pain. I had done this. When he spoke again it was as if in a daze. I covered my face with my hands.

'I got an automated call saying that the account didn't have enough money for the safe deposit box. I thought it was a mistake, or some kind of fraud. The bank said there was no fraud. They gave me the balance from April, a seven-hundred-pound overdraft. There was seventy-five thousand pounds in that account, Faiza, and you only put ten thousand in the current account. Where's the rest?'

I couldn't say anything.

'They said my name's been taken off the account and only you can operate it. I told them there must be a mistake, it's a joint account, but she showed me a form which she said I had signed to remove my name. I never signed anything like that.'

I had no fight left. I wanted to tell him everything. Confess. That was how criminals probably felt when they pleaded guilty, after months of protesting their innocence. My arms felt weak and I suddenly felt very tired. How long could I keep up this pretence? I let myself submit to the inevitability of it all and started to cry quietly.

'Look at me! What the hell have you done with our money? How was my name taken off the account?'

He came closer, standing over me as I perched at the edge of the bed. My breathing was faster, louder, as if I'd been running.

I had to tell him.

'OK, I'm sorry, I did sign your name for you and take you off the account but—'

'You did what?'

His anger filled the room. I had to say something, anything.

'That time you were in Argentina, the bank told me about a great investment bond that was only available for a couple of days. But to transfer the money for the bond, we both needed to sign, because the emergency account was a joint account. I signed a form on your behalf, to take your name off, so then, only my signature was needed, and I could buy the bond. It was such a great deal; I didn't want to miss out on it. I just forgot to put you back on the account later.'

I didn't know if any of it made sense. I had lost control of my lies and of my life.

'You forged my signature? Faiza, that's fraud. I can't believe you'd do something like this.'

He spoke as if in a daze and looked at me as if he didn't recognise me.

'I'm so sorry.' Still crying, I went up to him. 'I know I shouldn't have done it, Tom, but I was just trying to help.'

'That's no excuse! I trusted you, but you've forged my signature like a criminal. Where's all our money? Tell me the truth!! That was everything we had. You've been lying to me, haven't you? Is it all gone? Tell me!'

'Tom, please…'

'Tell me what you've done with the money or I'm leaving now and I'm not coming back!'

Tom never made empty threats. I froze. He started to walk towards the door. I couldn't lose him, not now when everything was going to be all right. I ran after him and blocked his way.

'I haven't done anything! Would I lie to you about something like that?'

'Why is the account empty then?' I heard the hesitation in his voice. He wanted to be wrong. 'Where's all our money?'

My mind raced. He hadn't seen the statements so he had no idea what had happened. Adrenaline surged through me.

'I can't believe you'd say these things to me,' I said, and stared at him accusingly. If I was going to do this, I had to believe my own lies.

I started to speak, unsure of what I was going to say, until I heard the words myself.

Thirty-Six

'I put it in the Post Office,' I said.

I'd remembered a conversation with Sam a few years ago.

'*What?*'

He looked at me as if I'd gone mad.

'Iceland. I moved the money to the Post Office after what happened in Iceland in the last crash. Remember how Jules and David lost millions? Sam and James moved their money to the Post Office because of that. She said the government guarantees 100 per cent of your savings, but if a bank collapses it can take years to get your money back.'

He didn't pull his hand away when I took it. He wanted to believe me. The more he wanted to trust me, the worse I felt as I told him lie after lie. But it was for the best, it really was. When I got my bonus, I'd put everything right. He need never know what I'd done. What would he gain from knowing, anyway?

'I almost had a heart attack when I saw the balance.'

'I'm sorry, Tom, I should have told you,' I said.

I put my arms around him and he sighed. We held on to

each other, each of us grateful that this storm had passed. I couldn't stop myself from crying again, this time with relief. I would put things right and I would never make this mistake again.

I looked up at him.

'Guess what? I passed my probation!'

'Well done! I always knew you would, though.'

He lifted me up and swung me around.

We went downstairs, his arm still around me, talking about going out for dinner to celebrate.

'Darling, please transfer all the money back from the Post Office into the current account.'

I stopped, grabbing the banister.

'Why should we touch that money? We have my salary now.'

'Darling, your salary won't cover everything. We need the money in our current account and we need cash flow. No banks are collapsing, trust me.'

I went into the kitchen and turned on the kettle. I looked for a mug, rifling through the whole cabinet before taking one out.

'The money's tied up in bonds, though. I can't transfer it overnight,' I said.

'OK, twenty-five thousand then. We must sort out the roof before winter, plus the boiler needs to be replaced, remember? Then the school fees will be due next term. Let's go first thing tomorrow – the Post Office is open on a Saturday – so you can add my name to the account too and then I can manage it myself.'

I told him I was too tired to go out for dinner, so we got a pizza, which we ate while watching *Casablanca*. I couldn't stop sobbing at the end and carried on crying till we went to bed.

He was expecting to see sixty-five thousand pounds in a non-existent account in the Post Office in the morning.

Once Tom was asleep, I crept downstairs. I curled up on the sofa and wrapped a blanket around me. I had made everything so much worse. I should've admitted the truth. Instead, I had built a whole new universe of lies.

I drifted off. I felt myself falling, dropping fast through the sky, about to die. I woke up with a jerk, just in time. As the birds started their morning chatter, I held my head in my hands and tried to quash an idea, but it kept getting louder and more insistent. I could see no other way out, even though the thought made me feel as if I was committing the worst kind of crime.

I put my hand on Tom's shoulder as he slept and made my decision.

I would have to take the money from Ami and Baba. I thought about my anger at Farrah, for taking their money, but I was going to do the same.

To save my marriage, I would have to betray my parents.

Thirty-Seven

I used my keys to let myself into Ami and Baba's flat and went straight into the kitchen, juggling a wet umbrella and two bags of groceries. In the living room, I saw the scene that I expected to greet me at ten in the morning, or at any time of the day, in fact.

Ami was in 'her' armchair, with headphones on, watching a Pakistani play on TV, one of several she had on the go at any one time. She was frowning at the usual mother and daughter-in-law intrigues playing out on the screen. She was wearing a freshly ironed floral salwar kameez and tiny matching turquoise earrings.

The room was silent as the headphones blasted the TV straight into Ami's ears. Baba was reading the *International Herald Tribune*. Their neighbour, a millennial banker whose parents had bought him the flat next door, and probably an unused subscription to the newspaper, always saved it for Baba. He was already shaved and dressed in his daily uniform of blue and white checked shirt and navy trousers.

They were both wearing the furry slippers I'd bought for them last year.

'Salaam alaikum.'

I kissed them both.

'I've brought the cleaning things you asked me to pick up. Shall I make some tea?'

On the way to the kitchen, I knelt down and wiped away the drips from my umbrella in the hallway with a tissue. These days, I found myself 'elderly-proofing' their flat the way I had child-proofed my own house years ago – uneven rug edges that could trip them up, or a bedspread corner trailing too low on the carpet. They seemed so vulnerable now, as if anything was a threat.

As I waited for the kettle to boil, I rehearsed my lines. The mugs rattled as I carried the tray with clammy hands.

Baba had asked for some of my business cards and I handed them over. He took a deep breath in as he looked at them. His eyes crinkled behind his glasses. He smiled, nodding his head.

'Very good, Beti. Client Investment Manager. Very good. I'm proud of you.'

'You're proud of me whatever I do, Baba. You were proud of me when I decided to stay home with the children and you're proud of me now.'

'That's true. Why shouldn't I be? You're a wonderful daughter.'

Ami put my card inside her small black phone book.

'Mashallah! I'm going to call all my friends and my sisters and my cousins to tell them about your new job.'

We chatted about their hospital appointments, and news about their friends, and after asking me about work and the children, they went back to their activities. I bent my head over my phone, pretending to scroll through my emails. My resolve was weakening with every passing moment. When I thought about asking them for the money, I felt my windpipe contracting, narrowing, as if it might fuse.

What would I say anyway? I couldn't tell them what I'd done. Besides my own shame, I had to consider theirs. They would blame themselves and talk for months, years even, asking themselves what they had done wrong. That sort of shock and worry was the worst thing for Baba's health. It could kill him.

There was an idea that had been germinating in my mind all night. It was plausible enough. They would believe whatever I told them. That should have made me feel more confident, but it made me want to cry.

I didn't know what to do.

My head was throbbing. If I told Tom the truth, I'd lose him and my family would break up. If I lied to my parents, I'd be betraying them. If I told them the truth, they would be heartbroken and might fall ill.

I was only lying to protect them, I reasoned. I'd pay them back from my bonus. Their savings were their emergency fund, though. It was all they had. They always took the bus rather than a taxi, even when it was raining; they shopped in budget supermarkets; they didn't turn on the heating, or the lights, except in the one room they sat in all day and even then, only for a few hours.

I couldn't do it.

I picked up my bag, desperate to leave. I had no idea what would happen next. I kept imagining Tom's reaction when he realised the lies upon lies that I had heaped upon him. How would my children cope with the fallout? What about Ahmed?

I hugged my parents goodbye. If they knew they could have done something to save me, save my family, they'd have done so without hesitation.

I could see no other way out.

'I almost forgot. I wanted to ask a favour please.'

I clutched the bunch of keys in my hand, pressing the serrated edges into my flesh. Once I spoke, there would be no going back.

Baba lowered the newspaper and peered at me over the top of the page. Ami took her headphones off. I smiled an easy smile.

'The children's schools have come up with a new scheme. If we pay the whole year's fees in advance, we get a 30 per cent reduction. That's a saving of around seven thousand pounds.'

My heart thudded with every word. I held onto the door frame.

Baba looked worried. I realised I was frowning.

'Are you having problems because Tom's not working? Do you want us to help you? Tell me, princess.'

His voice was gruff. He watched my face, as if holding his breath for my answer. My eyes darted instinctively to Ami's medicine basket, where I could see Baba's yellow angina spray peeking out.

'Not at all. We have money put aside for the fees. You know how organised Tom is, but that's the problem. Most of our money is tied up in investments, and he's planned for them to mature through the year for the fees at different stages. We're just a few thousand pounds short, to pay for this scheme upfront. He said to leave it but I think it's such a good opportunity.'

'I think it's a very good idea,' said Baba.

'So, I thought maybe I could borrow some from you and Ami? Only if you can spare it, of course. There are some bonds that mature in five months and I could pay it all back to you then. If I save seven thousand, we can share the money. You can get your bathroom done, maybe, or go on a holiday?'

A part of me wanted them to say 'No', so that I wouldn't have to embezzle two OAPs. Mostly, though, I wanted them to open up their cheque book.

'How much do you need?' said Ami.

'Fifteen thousand... It's just for five months though.'

Farrah had told me they had seventeen thousand left.

'Please don't mention it to Tom, though. He'd hate me asking you for help.'

The success of my plan depended on me getting my bonus, but I was well on track for that.

Baba smiled as he wrote me a cheque.

'Princess, that's what parents are for. We're happy to help. Anything for our lovely grandchildren's education!'

In my car, sobs shook my body. If my parents ever found out what I had just done, their hearts would break and nothing would ever be the same again.

Thirty-Eight

I was in the living room, reading an English essay that Sofia wanted me to check before she handed it in. It was past midnight but I knew I wouldn't get a chance to read it at work. I was feeling too wired up to sleep anyway.

I'd made sure that, between football matches, party pick and drops, and sudden errands for my parents, we couldn't make it to the supposed Post Office account to add Tom's name. I deposited Baba's cheque into the emergency account and then transferred the money to the current account, so Tom couldn't trace it. I had almost been caught out. I couldn't afford any loose ends.

Despite my guilt at lying to my parents, I felt relief. I had bought myself some time. I couldn't let our marriage get destroyed by this one mistake. I picked our wedding photo out on the side table, with those early versions of us staring back at me. We had been happy together every day since, even on the days we weren't happy. It hadn't been easy to get to our wedding day, though. There had been a lot of opposition.

Tom's parents', Victoria and Jason, lived in Guildford, in the same house where Tom and his brother Peter had grown up. The first time I met them was at a barbeque in the proudly tended garden, behind their end of terrace, semi-detached house. They'd also invited their next-door neighbours, 'as they're like family'.

Victoria offered me a coke, whispering, 'I know you don't drink alcohol,' as if commiserating about an affliction or mentioning an embarrassing fact that could not be discussed openly. She turned away when her neighbour, Dave, called out, 'Where are the sausages, Vicky? You always have sausages.'

Tom's voice rang out across the garden as he replied before his mother could.

'Faiza doesn't eat pork, so we decided to skip the sausages today. Let me get you a burger.'

He walked towards the grill where his father stood silently, his face redder than when I'd met him an hour earlier. No one said anything for a minute, but as Tom walked away, Dave's wife muttered to no one in particular, and so to everyone, 'Well, *we* still eat sausages. Why do we have to deprive ourselves?'

I'd whispered to Tom that of course I didn't mind if his parents and their friends had their usual barbeque menu, but by then, everyone's opinion of me, as someone who deprived people of their freedom to eat sausages, was sealed. It wasn't Tom's fault; I knew he'd only been trying to make me feel more comfortable.

I'd done the same when he came to our house for the first time for dinner. I asked Ami to make food that was easy to eat and not too spicy. I warned Farrah not to laugh if Tom used a knife and fork to eat the seekh kebab. My family were also strictly instructed not to slip into Urdu at any point during the evening, although I got told off by Baba for saying that.

'We would never be that rude!' he said, bemused at my request.

The two sets of parents met just once before the wedding. We decided on afternoon tea at a café in Esher, a symbolic midpoint, both geographically and gastronomically. Everyone loved a cup of tea.

Neither side had expressed a desire to meet earlier and I was relieved. I couldn't have handled a double dose of the warnings each of our parents had been doling out to Tom and me, like daily proclamations of doom, as emphatic as those from a psychic. Considering that all the tragedies our parents feared would befall us if we got married were based on the huge differences between our cultures and upbringing, it was ironic that the warnings from Victoria and Jason were almost exactly the same as the ones from Ami and Baba.

'These people are not like us.'

'These kinds of marriages never work.'

'What will people say?'

The meeting was short and sweet. All four parents were on their best behaviour, as if they were our children, eager to make sure they didn't disappoint us.

As well as trying to reassure our own parents, Tom and I also spent more time with our in-laws to be. I tried to think about it like phobia therapy. Like when you're afraid of spiders and you're exposed to them in tiny increments, at some point you stop freaking out at the sight of a spider.

I always thought that Tom and I were the spiders in this scenario, but sometimes I wondered if my in-laws scared me as much as I clearly unsettled them.

Ami and Baba came around more quickly than I'd expected. Maybe it was because they themselves had married against Ami's parents' wishes, or that they'd already made so many adjustments in their lives: adapting to a new country, new food, a new language, a whole new world. Besides, they couldn't resist Tom, once they got to know him.

He took them to see his flat in Fulham to show them how he was getting the place ready for me: the new wardrobe, the bookshelves, the walls he'd painted cream because he knew I'd like that, and the pot plants dotted about, just as they were in my bedroom at home. Baba was delighted that, in the kitchen, there was a long shelf, with a neat line of lever arch folders where Tom filed all his utility bills, insurance papers and bank statements in a frighteningly similar system to my father's, which I had teased Tom about, but which won Baba over.

Slowly, we convinced them that despite his brown hair and blue eyes, Tom ticked every single item on their wish list for a husband for me.

'He is a good boy,' said Baba.

And it was settled.

My parents' seal of approval meant that the objections of the extended family also evaporated, at least to our faces. The aunties talked instead, about Tom's job and salary, which must both be very good as he had bought his flat. They approved that he had studied at LSE, said he was very handsome, and were excited at the prospect of us having good-looking children.

It had been Tom's parents who had struggled more with the situation, though they tried not to show it.

Just before the wedding, Tom's parents had a lunch for some of their extended family. It was July and I wore a floral sundress, which I thought was as English as I could get, with some pastel kitten heels. Everyone was excited about the wedding and I felt the months of tension finally easing. His mother complimented me and said that I looked lovely.

'I can see why Tom fell for you,' she smiled.

I smiled back, glad that she had finally come around.

'I'm sorry I was a little hesitant at first, but you see, he's never dated anyone like you before. He's always gone for blondes, never a "brunette", not a single one. Not until you. So, I was just very surprised. I'm sorry, I wasn't sure if it was anything serious, but I can see how much he loves you. Welcome to the family.'

She put her arm around me and squeezed quickly, before walking away.

The thing I'd been waiting for all those months, for her to accept me and acknowledge that Tom loved me, was swept away under a wave of unease. Tom, it seemed, like the title of the movie, preferred blondes.

Despite that nugget, at least his parents had given their blessing.

I went back to reading Sofia's essay. I had to make things work. We had overcome so much to be together – and I wouldn't let my family be destroyed now.

Thirty-Nine

I got to the office at seven every day, before any of the others. I was still playing catch-up, learning about the products and getting to know Annie's existing clients, as well as building my own portfolio. Now I thought about my parents every time I made a call and every time I prepared a document. I had to return my parents' money quickly and safely.

My new sales targets were terrifying, although Sergio called them 'ambitious'. I was also preparing for a major pitch in Amsterdam that the whole team was competing for. If I won that account, I'd be well on my way to getting the bonus.

I started leaving the house before the children were awake, sometimes even before Tom woke up. I used the extra time to push harder than anyone else on my team.

One morning, when I thought I was alone in the office, I swore at the computer screen in frustration, unable to understand an investment model despite staring at it for ages.

'Fuck you, you fucking, stupid, crazy, fucking, useless bond!'

I heard laughter behind me. I spun around, my face burning. Harry.

'Oh shit, fuck!' I said, before putting my hand up to my mouth. Then I started to laugh.

'And good morning to you too! Don't worry, Fi, this business will drive anyone to profanity. Now, let me go through this with you. Someone helped me the first time I did this one too,' said Harry.

He led me to his office and insisted that, before anything else, we needed a proper cup of coffee, which he made for me using a complicated black machine with lots of little buttons.

Since he'd found out we'd been at the same college, he'd taken me under his wing somewhat.

'It's my duty as a fellow alum,' he said.

To my surprise, we got on very well. There was none of the awkwardness that I had felt in the lift. I realised he'd only been flirting with me that day as men sometimes do, a reflex as inbuilt as smiling or shaking hands. Once he knew I was married and his colleague, there had never been the slightest hint of that again.

I was grateful for his help. Besides Ivan, no one had spent any time teaching me the ropes, and at the end of the day, Ivan and I were still competing with each other for our sales figures.

It turned out that Harry was also in the habit of coming in very early. The morning coffee became a sort of ritual for us and I was grateful for this daily tutorial. He'd make us coffee and I'd bring in apples, peaches or a fresh croissant from the café downstairs on my way in. Then he guided me on the pitches that I was preparing, sometimes challenging my ideas, and at other times, sharing his with me.

Often, I would catch myself wondering how he could be married to someone like Julia. I got a kick out of imagining her outrage if she knew that I was having coffee with her husband every morning. I allowed myself this petty indulgence of having 'one up' on her. I felt I deserved it after all her nasty comments to me.

The others in my team all stayed at the office until nine or ten o'clock, eating dinner at their desks, and I didn't want to be the one who stood out by leaving. Besides, I needed to stay visible and involved, so when it came to bonus time, I was seen as a 'closer' and 'contributor'.

I barely saw the children but stayed in touch through calls at bedtime and so many texts that they told me to stop.

Tom was great. He sent me photos of them all having dinner, or homework sheets with good marks, and reassuring texts, telling me their news from the day: how Alex had asked him about global 'worming', and that Ahmed had played PlayStation online with his friends and Tom had heard him laughing in his room, which reassured us that his recovery was continuing. He told me how he and Sofia had watched *Pointless* together, and that she'd let him look at her 'private' Instagram.

'Everything's OK. Don't worry.'

It was exactly what I used to do for Tom when he was working late.

When I got home, he'd lock up downstairs as I fell into bed and then tuck the duvet around me.

'Another day, another dollar,' he'd say, smiling.

It was what he used to say to me when he was away on a business trip and I asked him how his day had been.

Our lives had flipped.

Tom asked me a couple of times when we could go to the Post Office to add his name but I managed to dodge it. 'Yes, sure, darling. Just let me get through this pitch.' I couldn't stall him forever, though.

Forty

I was becoming obsessed with my job and my work spilled into my evenings and weekends too. Everything depended on my getting the bonus.

One morning I noticed that Sofia was very quiet. I only saw her briefly and she had her ear pods in, clearly indicating her desire to not engage in conversation. I was uneasy all day, although Tom said that she seemed fine. Perhaps it was my guilt at being away from home that was the issue, not Sofia, but I decided to leave work early. I hoped that my absence at the daily Deliveroo desk dinner in the office would not count as a black mark.

I'd been trying to find time to look through her university choices and used this as an excuse to go into her room. She shifted to make room for me on her bed and I lay down next to her as we looked at university courses on her laptop.

'Besides Oxford, I want to choose universities where there's a good international mix. I mean places that aren't too "white".'

I frowned. 'What do you mean?'

'We had a talk by some alumni and there was a girl whose parents were from Pakistan. She went to a university where almost everyone was white. She said I should go somewhere more diverse and I think she's right.'

'OK, but why should that matter? Most of your school friends are white, and you're half white. I mean, I can understand that if her parents are from Pakistan, she may have experienced some racism; sadly, that's far too common. But I'm sure it won't be an issue for you.'

Sofia looked at me then looked away, as if she wanted to say something, but was hesitating.

'What?' I said.

She shrugged.

'It *is* an issue, Mum. I'm English, but then I have the Pakistani half of me. All my genes are mixed up and no one understands what it's like. People can be mean.'

I put my hand over hers and gave it a squeeze. Sofia had never mentioned anything like this before. I knew it wasn't always easy, but things were different now to when I was growing up. Besides, if our children were Pakistani *and* English, I thought their mixed heritage meant that they might get a little more acceptance than I had. There had been the incident at Ahmed's old school. But I thought the bullies would have picked on him about anything because he was shy. Now I wondered if I had been wrong.

'Has someone said anything to you about being mixed race?'

She shook her head. 'No, it was worse than that.'

I couldn't bear the thought of my children being attacked just for being who they were. I put my arm around her.

'Tell me what happened,' I said, already furious that someone had made my daughter look this sad.

She stared at her laptop as she spoke.

'I was at a party on Saturday, someone Meg knows from another school. There was a boy, Ben, who seemed really nice and I think he liked me too. I was talking to him and his friends about a summer job at this coffee shop in Balham, and he said, "It's full of Pakis there."'

My whole body tensed. This was worse than all the times someone had flung that word at me.

'I'm so sorry, baby. That's vile. What a nasty piece of work.'

'He didn't think he was doing anything wrong. None of them did. They thought it was OK to say it. He didn't know I was half-Pakistani. Everyone thinks I'm English, or sometimes Spanish or something.'

'Oh God, that's awful. No one spoke up? Did you say anything to him?'

'I told him it was racist to use that word, but I didn't tell him I was half-Pakistani. I wish I had, but I couldn't...'

I gave her a hug and she sank into me without her usual resistance.

'Don't worry, it's always hard to know what to do when someone is racist like that. I really hoped you wouldn't have to deal with all this crap, but this kind of hatred is creeping back. Most people are nice, though, in my experience. You did the right thing to tell him he was being racist.'

I kissed her head.

I wondered if things really had changed. Maybe I'd just moved my children out of the pathway of the sort of racism I'd experienced, so they didn't come across it every day. They knew it existed though – they'd heard a group of teenagers shout out 'Fucking Paki' to me as we queued up for ice cream on holiday in Dorset, and had been with Ami when someone on the bus told her to 'Go back home!' when she was speaking Urdu. They watched the news.

Even in our bubble, though, I sometimes felt its presence, like a bad smell, that had lingered, though grown less pungent. I wondered if the National Front signs of the Eighties had infiltrated into spaces where I thought we were safe. I remembered the way Julia had said the words 'BAME' and 'your culture' to instantly signal that I was, above all, different.

Sofia shrugged.

'I was just shocked. No one's ever said anything like that to me before. I mean, they weren't even saying it to me, but it was *about* me. Next time I'll know what to say, because it's just wrong.'

'You are lucky to have two amazing backgrounds, Sofia. Don't pay attention to this kind of ignorance.'

She nodded. 'I know, Mum.'

I thought about all the times that I'd heard someone make a comment or say something that felt a bit 'off', and how I never challenged them. I'd felt the way Sofia had, but at least she'd acknowledged that she should have spoken up. Next time, I wouldn't stay quiet either.

Forty-One

The final meeting for the charity auction was at Julia's house. As it was the last session and Julia wanted everyone there, she held it on a Saturday. As soon as I saw the group text, I knew I had to get out of it. Harry would be home on a Saturday. I imagined him opening his front door, his shock at seeing me, Julia's questions, her outrage that I had kept it all from her – and Harry finding out that I had lied to him. I'd have to pretend that I was sick and tell her at the last minute.

The day before the committee meeting, a chance remark from Ivan solved the problem.

'I've got to wake up at five tomorrow, to catch the plane to Geneva. I wish Harry had picked a more civilised time.'

'You're going to Geneva? With Harry? Tomorrow?'

'Correct,' Ivan smiled.

'When are you back?'

'Monday night.'

'So, your flight is tomorrow, Saturday? At what, 7 a.m.?'

'Yes. Would you like to come and see me off?' Ivan laughed.

'Sorry! I just can't believe Harry would drag you off at that time on a Saturday,' I said.

I leaned back in my chair, relieved. Harry wouldn't be at home. He wouldn't even be in the country. I could attend the meeting after all. I didn't want to lose touch with the school crowd. For Sofia's sake I needed to know what was going on with the teachers and the university applications. I'd also see Sam after ages.

The next day I was sitting in Julia's living room, while she held court, checking that everyone had 'achieved their objectives'. She was doing a casual, at-home look, wearing white linen shorts, a white shirt knotted at her waist, with intricate lace cut-outs in the sleeves and Chanel pumps.

Sam sat next to me, her blonde curls scooped up in a messy knot on top of her head. She'd probably taken thirty seconds to do it, but it looked perfect. Lizzie waved to me from across the room. She was in yoga pants and a fuchsia vest, glowing despite wearing no make-up. I was glad that I'd made an effort too, wearing skinny jeans and a pale blue silk top. Despite the range of clothes and hairstyles, there was a level of gloss in the room that could have been prepared for a quintessential yummy mummy photo shoot.

On an antique chest to one side, there were several family photographs. I felt like a trespasser, entering Harry's private world. He had no idea that I could see his holiday snaps and an old photograph from his university graduation. There was a TV on the wall opposite and I wondered if he sat in the same spot where I was, his arm around Julia.

'Thank goodness Harry's away,' whispered Sam.

I grinned and gave her two thumbs up.

'I wouldn't have come otherwise.'

She smiled.

'How about you? How's the party from hell?' I said.

'Hellish.'

'How's James?'

'I don't know, Faiza. This strange power his parents hold over him is ruining everything. He has enough stress from working all hours without all the pressure from them. It's affecting our relationship too. Things aren't good.'

I'd never heard her talk like that. Sam and James were solid.

'I'm sorry, that does sound stressful. Tom said he'd heard about cuts at James's firm. It's not going to affect him, is it?'

Sam's face was suddenly a deep red. She frowned.

'I didn't think Tom was the gossiping sort. Why are you two discussing James with other people?'

I put my hand on hers.

'Hey, I'm sorry, it's not like that. Really, Sam. Tom's headhunter was telling him about all the layoffs in the City, for Tom's job search, and that was just one of the companies he mentioned. Tom only spoke to me. We were worried because we've been through it ourselves. That's all.'

The way Sam had flown off the handle was worrying. It just wasn't like her. She nodded, her colour coming back to normal.

'I'm sorry too. I overreacted.'

'No problem. Are you...?'

Julia's voice was suddenly louder.

'Cora, thanks for arranging *Tatler*, and Anna's sister's husband has persuaded a very famous tennis player,' Julia tapped the side of her nose, 'to be our MC.'

There were murmurs of approval from everyone.

'I'm emailing a list of salons to get your blow-dries, make-up, facials, lash extensions, gel manicure and even,' she stopped to giggle, 'vajazzle!'

I couldn't help a snort of laughter escaping. I leaned over to whisper to Sam, 'Isn't that a cream for itchy privates?'

She smiled. I yawned, wishing that I had skipped the meeting after all.

'Thank you, ladies! I think we're done…'

Julia's phone, which she was holding in her hand to read her notes from, started to ring. She glanced at it with disapproval, then smiled.

'So sorry, it's my husband.'

The others started to chat quietly, but I couldn't tear my eyes away. I imagined what Harry was saying to her. I wondered if he called her whenever he landed, and was telling her he'd arrived safely in Geneva and was missing her. Perhaps they did have the perfect marriage that Julia always talked about.

She hung up.

'I'm so sorry. My husband's flight's been cancelled and he's on his way home with a colleague. I'm just going to leave some sandwiches for them in the study. He'll be home any minute, so please excuse me. Then we'll finish off the checklist.'

Julia left the room and suddenly I couldn't breathe. I looked at Sam.

'It's OK. He won't come in here,' she said.

'How do you know? Even if he doesn't, he'll be in the house. So will Ivan. He's in my team. They'll see me.'

I knotted my hands together, twisting my fingers till they hurt.

'I can't even leave now. I might bump into them in the driveway. Sam...'

'Look, it's fine,' she said, and swapped places with me so that she was sitting on my other side.

'I'll shield you. If he comes in here, I'll sit forward and you can hide behind me. Julia said he had a conference call. The last thing he'll want is to meet a bunch of school mothers.'

I looked at the French windows.

'Maybe I could go into the garden?'

'Faiza, stop. What will you do in the garden? Hide? Listen, Harry's probably going to go straight into his call. He'll stay well away from us.'

Sam was right. Julia came back and said that Harry was locked away in his study.

'He never stops working,' she said.

As we left, going into the hallway as a group, I positioned myself in the middle, so I remained hidden. I just needed to walk a few steps to get to the front door. Sam shielded me on my right as we passed the study door which was closed and I kept my head down. Suddenly, the study door opened. I couldn't help looking at it and, from amongst the throng of women, through one small gap that appeared as someone missed a step, for one split second I looked straight into Ivan's eyes and he stared back at me. His expression changed as he recognised me. I put my finger up to my lips and shook my head, pleading with my eyes for him not to say anything. He nodded, shutting the door again. I scrambled into Sam's car as soon as we were outside.

Forty-Two

I texted Ivan as we drove away: *Please don't say anything to Harry or to anyone. I promise I'll explain everything on Monday.*

He texted back: *Why were you at Harry's house? Why is it a secret?*

I replied: *I promise it's nothing weird. Please just keep this to yourself. I owe you one.*

He texted back a very Russian: *OK.*

I remembered how put out he'd been not to get the Vladimir account, but we had also become friends since then, and I had no choice but to trust him – and hope that he didn't use this to get closer to Harry.

Ivan was back in the office on Tuesday but was in meetings, so it was almost the end of the day when we went for a coffee. Sitting at the wooden table in the café, I clasped my hands around the warm cup. Ivan stared at me, his eyes not hiding his curiosity or suspicion.

'Ivan, you haven't…?'

'No.'

'Thank you.'

I shouldn't have waited three days before telling him, but I hadn't wanted to put anything in writing in a text. It was too dangerous. It may have been a mistake to wait though. He might have conjured up all sorts of scenarios about me in the meantime: a stalker, a liar, a corporate spy.

I decided to tell him the truth, however bizarre the politics of the school run might seem to a twenty-nine-year-old man. The danger was that he'd think my truth was so outlandish that it was a lie. I had to make sure he believed me and keep him on side.

'I knew Harry's wife, Julia, from before – our daughters are at the same school. But when I got the job, I didn't know that Harry was her husband.'

'You have a daughter?' said Ivan.

I flushed.

'Yes, I didn't want to say because she's in the same class as Harry's daughter.'

I sounded dodgy, even to myself. Why would he believe anything I said now?

'Why haven't you told Harry that you're friends with his wife? It would be good for you, wouldn't it?'

I shook my head. 'Harry's wife and I don't get on.'

'She isn't a good woman?'

'No, she's fine. It's just that we've never hit it off. So, I thought she might say something bad about me to Harry and then it would spoil my chances of ever making a good impression. That's why I didn't tell him.'

'Tell me the whole story. If she's a good woman and she

hates you, what happened? Is something going on between you and Harry? I see you coming out of his office in the mornings.'

'Ivan, please! Harry and I are just friends and I'm very happily married. Nothing happened with Julia either. She doesn't "hate" me, she just doesn't like me,' I said.

'Maybe she's a racist? Maybe she hates Asians?'

'No!' My eyes widened. 'Nothing like that.'

Julia often made comments that were a little off-key, that might have been considered inappropriate, but she had never said anything openly racist, either to me or in general. At first, I had wondered, like when she always refused to eat any Pakistani dishes that I made for coffee mornings. 'Oh, too spicy for me,' she'd say, with an apologetic smile. And I'd felt a little unnerved when she'd talked about 'too many people who can't speak English' in London. There was also the vociferous defence of politicians who made Islamophobic comments. None of that was so different from things I heard regularly at smart London dinner parties, though. It was simply culturally unaware, I told myself, not racist.

'Personality clash,' I told Ivan. 'You don't think Harry saw me, do you?'

'No.'

I breathed out in relief.

'So, now I can't let Harry find out the truth. What on earth would he think, if he knew that I had lied about knowing his wife?'

'Don't worry, your secret's safe with me.' Ivan stood up.

'Thank you so much. I owe you one.'

'Yes, you do,' he said.

I grinned, but he looked back at me without a hint of a smile.

Forty-Three

Naila had been messaging me to ask how work was and when we could meet up for a coffee. I hadn't answered, but now I sent her a quick message: *Sorry. Work is manic. Hope all well xx*

If we'd been meeting as we had in the past, then perhaps we could have talked, but my friends and I seemed to be in completely different worlds. I'd only seen Sam and Lizzie briefly a couple of times since I started working. It felt like I'd lost touch with everyone.

That week I was at Ahmed's school for a special class assembly. I'd told Sergio that I had a dental appointment so would be in late. As I was leaving the school, someone called my name.

'Faiza!'

I turned around. It was Naila.

'Hi,' she said. 'I didn't know you'd be here. They invited the new parents too. So, I came.'

'Great,' I said.

She stepped forwards to hug me. I kissed her on both cheeks, keeping my distance.

'I'd better get to work,' I said.

She walked alongside me as I headed towards Wimbledon station.

'What's wrong?' she said. 'You haven't answered my texts.'

'Sorry, I've just been so busy at work,' I smiled.

Say the right thing, avoid any upset, pretend everything is OK. The mantra from my childhood, when I was the only one trying to keep the peace between my warring parents, was hard to override. Every step I took, though, I realised that I was walking away from Naila and our friendship. I stopped, and before I could let my natural instinct of avoiding any kind of confrontation win, I started to speak.

'Why didn't you tell me you were applying to Clissington's?'

Naila looked down at the pavement and pressed her eyes with her fingertips, as if she was rubbing away sleep. I waited, wishing I hadn't said anything. It felt as if I had walked to the edge of a precipice and I wanted to get back to safe ground. What would I gain by being so aggressive?

'I'm sorry, I should have,' she said, finally looking up at me, frowning and biting her lip.

'I found out from Hannah,' I said, 'and I was so shocked. You must have known for months.'

Naila asked if we could get a coffee at the café near the station. My fear at speaking my mind was starting to subside. Nothing terrible had happened, and although Naila was upset, it wasn't with me.

'I was embarrassed, after all the things I've said to you about private schools. I tried to tell you, but I just didn't know how. I was wrong, though. I owed you an apology for being so judgey and now I owe you an apology for not being honest.'

'So why did you apply to Clissington's?' I asked.

It was good to have things out in the open. It felt like us again, talking the way we always had.

'You know those lectures I went to at Lizzie's father's foundation? She invited me after I met her at your dinner. I realised that Adil would benefit from smaller classes. He's been struggling at his school. Anyway, Lizzie told me they had bursaries that we could apply for and I thought, why not?'

She blinked at me, leaning forwards, and sighed. 'I didn't know how to tell you. I still feel a bit embarrassed telling anyone. I'm so sorry. I was also worried, now Tom's lost his job, that you might have to take Ahmed out, and it felt as if we were taking your place.'

We hugged each other properly when we left. In the train, I felt a rush of energy. I was so glad that I'd spoken my mind to Naila. It felt exhilarating and things were better, not worse, because I had told the truth.

I wished things could have been that simple with Tom. I wondered if they ever would be again with this enormous lie between us...

Forty-Four

I was at Sofia's school doing one of my last stints selling the tickets for the charity auction before the end of term.

I told Sergio I had another dental appointment and would be late. He winked and said, 'You know, Fi, you can come late for other reasons too.' He smiled. 'I know how hard you work and we're all grown-ups here. Take it easy.'

I felt embarrassed that he'd guessed I was lying about the dentist, but was grateful that I had somehow found a human and humane boss, a rare breed in the City.

Sam and some of the other mothers were there too, as everyone was going for a class coffee after the ticket sale. Most of the women were in gym clothes, showing off sleek bodies and sleek skin. Lizzie was in pale-pink yoga gear, Sam in black leggings and a T-shirt showing her company's logo, and Julia was all in black – vest, leggings, trainers, almost Cat woman-like, with her blonde hair in a high ponytail.

Since I was going to the office straight from school, I was dressed in work clothes: a black, sleeveless silk shift dress and high black heels. My eyebrows were neatly brushed, I had a slick of eyeliner and berry lip gloss, with my hair blow dried straight. I was wearing turquoise and silver drop earrings.

'You look very smart, so chic,' said Anna.

The women all surrounded me, admiring my outfit and saying how much they missed getting dressed up for work. Several of them asked me about my job and said they thought I was very brave. A couple of women asked if I could give them some advice about restarting their own interrupted careers.

'You look lovely, Faiza,' said Lizzie. 'We're so proud of you, you know, going back to work like this. I'd never be able to do anything like that now.'

'Of course you would, Lizzie! You're amazing. You manage your father's foundation, and I don't know how many houses in how many countries! I could never do all of that,' I said.

At the edge of the crowd, I glimpsed Julia. She was clearly not happy with the attention I was getting. She came forward.

'Form a queue now, ladies, and Faiza, let's be more efficient. Let's leave the chat till coffee.'

While I counted the money and ticked off names, Julia came up and started asking me questions about where I was working.

'Oh, it's just a tiny marketing company in central London,' I said.

I looked down at the list of names again, as though rechecking them.

'So, what do you do? What's this company called?'

Sam asked Julia something about the next ticket sales session to distract her, but she wasn't deflected.

'Actually, it's just a small start-up belonging to a Pakistani family friend.'

As expected, the fact that it was a 'Pakistani' company made Julia lose interest quickly.

'What about Tom? Has he found a job yet?'

Julia had now been joined by a couple of her friends and there were still three or four others waiting to go to coffee, standing nearby. Everyone was listening. I didn't know what to say. I didn't want to say anything.

'He's working on a project,' I said, picking up my bag, and gathering the ticket money.

'I'm afraid you might have to face the fact that he may never find a job again. Not at his age and in this market,' said Julia, as if she cared about his job prospects and well-being.

I ignored her and started to put the money in the metal box. I spoke to Sam and the women standing next to her.

'Sorry, guys, I won't be able to join you for coffee because I have to rush off to work but it was really good to see everyone.'

Julia came and stood in front of me.

'I hope you didn't mind me speaking openly, Faiza. I'm just worried about how you'll pay the school fees for Sofia. Anyway, I hope things turn out...'

'Let's go, Julia, I've booked a table for ten,' said Lizzie.

She and some of the others kissed me goodbye and they all moved off towards the school gates. I was sure that the discussion on our ability to pay the fees, or Tom's descent into long-term unemployment, would continue over lattes and flourless brownies.

I went to put the money in the office safe and when I came back Sam was sitting at the table. I sat down next to her.

'I hate her so much,' I said.

'Hey, don't get so upset. How are things though, with Tom?' she said.

After my talk with Naila, I decided to speak more truthfully to Sam too. I sighed.

'Not great. Nothing new on the job front for Tom and our savings are running out. I don't know how we'll manage if they don't keep me on once the contract ends. I'm quite worried about the money situation, to be honest.'

Sam put her arm around me. 'Faiza, you're doing so well and I'm sure they will offer you the job. Life's never easy, is it?'

'Thanks, Sam.' I felt lighter, after talking to her. 'I just don't need Julia to be gossiping about my private business, that's all.'

A couple of days later, Sam called me when I was on the train home.

'Julia has summoned us,' said Sam. 'I think she wants an update on the ticket sales. and she'll probably give us a pep talk about "giving it 110 per cent" for the next session because it's the last one.'

'I sold quite a lot,' I said. 'I'm sure you did too. Why do we need to spend any more time with her?'

'You know what she's like. Let's get it over with. Shall we go tomorrow afternoon? You have a half-day for Ahmed's concert, don't you? And it's my day off. Next week you're in Amsterdam, and James and I are away for the weekend. He's been working non-stop and I think it will do us good to have some time alone. Julia says you told her that you're going to Dubai to see your aunt, apparently!'

'I had to say that because her husband's coming to Amsterdam with me!' I sighed. 'I'm so glad you and James are getting away for a bit.' This was a good sign. They were getting back on track. 'OK, I'll do it, but only if we split some chocolate cake. If we meet at 2.15, I'll leave at 2.45 latest, for Ahmed's school.'

When I got to the café, Sam and Julia were already at a table. They stopped talking abruptly when they saw me. Perhaps they'd been discussing something that Julia didn't want to talk about in front of me. Sam flushed. She probably felt embarrassed by Julia's rudeness.

Julia started to speak, staring at me with such intensity that my hand instinctively went up and I brushed it across my lips in case there were some crumbs there from lunch. She sat up straighter.

'This is a very difficult conversation to have, Faiza. I was just telling Sam that eight hundred pounds has gone missing from the ticket money in the school safe.'

I looked at Julia, then at Sam, I frowned and leaned forwards.

'Oh my God. Seriously? What happened?'

'That's what I'm trying to find out,' said Julia.

She only looked at me, not Sam, as she carried on. Sam stared at her phone.

'We're retracing the steps, which is why I wanted to see

you both today. So, you and Sam put the takings in the safe after selling the tickets this week. Sam was the last one to put in £1300 yesterday after drop-off. You put £1700 in two days ago. There was three thousand pounds in total and Mrs West was going to take it to the bank. The money should have been deposited in the bank today but Mrs West couldn't do it straight away. When she opened the safe, there was only £2200. Eight hundred pounds are missing.'

'That's awful,' I said. 'Could it have been used for petty cash, maybe, by someone else in school?'

Sam had been silent, but now she said, 'Yes. What if it was taken by mistake, by another member of staff, as petty cash?'

'No, this safe is only being used for the ticket sales. The money's been stolen,' said Julia.

I shook my head.

'Do you think Mrs West could have taken it?' said Sam. Her forehead was a tangle of worry.

'That's the only explanation,' I said. 'I can't imagine her doing that, though.'

Mrs West was an institution; she'd been the secretary for almost fifteen years.

'No,' said Julia. 'Besides, the school nurse was there when she opened the safe. They counted the money together.'

'We couldn't have left the safe unlocked, could we, Sam?' I said.

This was terrible. The school was a secure space. I couldn't imagine how anyone in that community, people we trusted completely, could have done something like this.

'No, you can't take the key out unless the safe is locked properly.'

She pushed a hand through her hair, making her curls wilder than normal, like question marks around her head. She looked as if she might cry and she never cried in public. She didn't cry easily in private either.

'Let's try to think about this systematically. How many keys are there?' I said.

'Three. You and Sam have one and then Mrs West,' said Julia.

'And they're security keys. They can't be copied,' said Sam.

'Then I don't understand it,' I said.

I didn't like the way Julia was staring at me, in a questioning way, as if I had the answer to the mystery. Sam had noticed as well. Her eyes darted from Julia's face to mine.

The waitress came over but Julia asked her to give us a few more minutes.

'It *is* baffling. There were only three people with access to the safe. Mrs West, Sam...' Julia paused a second, 'and you.'

The insinuation in her voice was unmistakable. I looked at Sam to see if she'd noticed it too, or if I was imagining it? My skin was hot and I wanted to take off my scarf but I didn't want to make any moves that might incriminate me further in Julia's eyes. I had to stay calm but couldn't help getting angrier as Julia's murky hazel eyes stayed fixed on my face.

I was about to tell Julia exactly what I thought about her behaviour when Sam said, 'Julia, why don't Faiza and I go through our lists again? The only explanation is that we've got the numbers mixed up. We must have made a mistake.'

Julia stood up.

'Yes, please do that straight away. This is a very serious matter. If we can't sort it out, I'll have to inform the Head. And I'd rather solve the mystery without having to get the authorities involved.'

As soon as Julia left, I let loose.

'What the hell, Sam! Did that awful woman imply that *I've* stolen the money? I can't believe she'd try to pin this on me! Did you see the way she was staring at me?'

'I'm sure there's a simple explanation,' said Sam. 'Let's go through both our lists and recount.'

Sam had the lists and we went through them twice, but the figure was still the same. We sat back.

'I don't understand...' I sank my head in my hands.

'What do we say to Julia?' said Sam.

'Sam, I know it sounds bizarre, but you don't think she's trying to frame me?'

Even as I said it, I knew it couldn't be true. Julia might have disliked me, but that would be a step too far, even for her.

'No, I really don't,' said Sam.

We were silent for a while. Sam looked at the table and spoke in a voice not much more than a whisper. I still heard her, though.

'I feel awful even asking this – and please, please, don't take this the wrong way.' She paused and swallowed. I knew what was coming from the look on her face. 'I know you've been worried about money and using up your savings. You know, what you were saying that day... I know the sort of stress you've been under and well, we do strange things when we're under so much pressure. If you did...'

She stopped, as if even she couldn't believe that she was saying these things to me. Red blotches crept up her neck, then her chin and into her cheeks. Her words left me winded, as if she'd punched me in my face, knocked out my teeth, broken my nose.

I couldn't speak. All the chatter around me became louder, as if someone had turned up the volume dial of the café. How could Sam think that of me, let alone accuse me? A tear splashed from my eyes onto the wooden table. I let my hair fall forwards and wiped my face so no one else could see.

'Faiza, please don't be upset. I asked Julia to let me speak to you first. We can sort it out...'

'You've discussed my being a thief with Julia?'

I pushed my chair back and stood up, then ran towards the door, bumping into people on my way out. As I left, I heard Sam calling my name, but I didn't stop.

Forty-Five

I drove to Ahmed's school with no idea about what I could do. I heard nothing as Ahmed sang songs from *Bugsy Malone* with his class on stage. All I could think about was Julia going to the Head with her suspicions. If they called the police and they started to investigate, they'd discover that we had no money, except loans from the bank and my parents. They would speak to Tom. The accounts would be looked at.

Julia had been gossiping about Tom being unemployed. I wondered how long it would be before she started spreading rumours about my financial desperation, or that I'd taken the charity money? It wouldn't take long for the news to filter through to the parents and into the lower sixth classroom to Sofia, then to the parents next door in Ahmed's school.

If the police started an inquiry, I would lose my job.

There was no way to prove I hadn't taken the cash. If even Sam could think I could steal the money, so would everyone else. My mind kept flipping between how to prove my innocence and replaying Sam's accusation. I was closer to Sam than to Farrah even.

All evening Sam kept calling me, but I didn't answer. Then she sent a text.

I'm so sorry. I am an idiot. I've told Julia we need to recheck our lists but I won't get a chance for at least 10 days because James and I are away and so are you. She won't say anything till then. Please forgive me xx

I couldn't forgive her, though, and I couldn't stop worrying. Julia could not be trusted. She could go to the Head on Monday and report me to the police.

Forty-Six

As time passed, the prospect of a new job for Tom no longer seemed like a natural next step, but more like a remote possibility. Not knowing when the market would pick up again left him with a growing sense of unease and I started to hear the swish of the Solitaire cards on his phone in the mornings again. He was up even before my alarm went off at six.

My attempts at squeezing in quality relationship time with Tom were no longer working. He was feeling low and that needed time to break through, not just a walk on the Common before coming back to cook for the children, or a quick sushi dinner date while Sofia grudgingly babysat. I wanted to spend more time with him but it was impossible. My timings meant that we barely saw each other for half an hour a day during the week, and at the weekends the children wanted to make up for lost time, and I had to check in with my parents too.

I had no choice but to carry on with my long hours, though. The only way out now was to get my bonus and for HH to hire me permanently. It also took my mind off Julia, Sam, and most of all, the distance between Tom and me.

As well as the late nights in the office, I attended a couple of client dinners. For some reason, I hadn't told Tom about these outings, and the one tonight – with Harry and the clients, a fintech entrepreneur from Sweden, and his wife – was no different.

I felt guilty about having dinner at Michelin-starred restaurants, and I felt even worse about how much I enjoyed the time I spent with clients. I was meeting some interesting people, and I also liked spending time with Harry. We had become more like friends rather than just colleagues. When I was with Harry, we didn't talk about families, or children or the hassle of domestic domains. We didn't even talk much about work at these dinners. We discussed the books we were reading, or our favourite films. We talked about our bucket-list holiday destinations. He told me long, but always interesting, stories about his time working all over the world. The conversations I enjoyed most were about our days at university.

'I still remember my graduation. My parents were so nervous with all the pomp and circumstance but the profs made them feel so welcome at the garden party afterwards,' he said.

He told me that he didn't come from a privileged background either.

'Same!' I said. 'My parents were so happy that day.'

'Do you remember how it felt back then? Like we were about to fly? Take off into some amazing adventure,' said Harry as we waited for the clients to arrive.

As he said it, I remembered that feeling again. The fizz of possibility that had flattened gradually, like an open can of Coke, in the many years since. I smiled at him and at the memory.

Tom and I used to talk about the old days, but not anymore. We used to laugh about the first B & B we stayed in after we got married, in Bath. It had no attached bathroom, but a freestanding shower cubicle in the middle of the room and a TV you had to feed fifty pence coins into or it turned off. Now, if I tried to lighten the mood by taking a trip down memory lane, Tom didn't reply.

Chatting to Harry, in the carefree way I used to with Tom, was like getting a much-needed hit of normality, and feeling the way I used to feel. I needed that before I went home to the gloom that had settled as an almost permanent mood around Tom.

Our table tonight was in a secluded corner of the Chinese restaurant and we were waiting for the clients to arrive. Harry focussed all his attention on me as we chatted and laughed, not glancing once at his mobile. I missed my friends and this felt the way I did with them – fun, relaxed, comfortable. For the half hour that Harry and I were alone before the clients came, probably for the first time in ages, I forgot everything else. I even forgot his connection to Julia.

I decided that this time I would tell Tom about the dinner. I didn't want my time with Harry to be a secret because that would imply I was doing something wrong, when of course I wasn't.

The next morning, when Tom and I were in the kitchen having breakfast before the children came down, I said,

'Oh, I got in so late, I didn't get a chance to tell you. I went for a client dinner at this amazing Chinese place. Made a change from Deliveroo at my desk.'

'Who did you go with?'

'It's the account I'm helping Harry with, so just us and the client, a Swedish CEO and his very beautiful wife. They've been together since they were fourteen!'

He didn't say anything and started making Alex's packed lunch.

'Anyway, hopefully I can come home earlier today. I haven't spent an evening at home for ages,' I said.

'If you can tear yourself away from gourmet food and the star of HH,' he said.

'I'd much rather be with your spag bol – and HH is full of stars!'

I laughed and went over to kiss his cheek before I left, but he bent down to get some dishes out of the dishwasher, so that I couldn't get near him.

I stayed where I was for a minute, even though I knew I'd miss my bus. I wanted to turn him around and say, 'Hey! I was trying to kiss you. Come here!'

I wanted to stand on tiptoes, smile at him teasingly, look into his eyes and kiss him. I wanted to say, 'Stop being such a grump! See you tonight!' and see his face break into a grin as he said, 'OK, I'll kiss you, but only so you can let me get on with doing the dishes!'

That was what I would normally have done if he was in a bad mood. I always knew how to make him feel better and he'd always let me, at least in the past.

But he carried on making packed lunches, and didn't look at me again. The set of his shoulders, and the look on his face, stopped me this time, for the first time, from going to him.

I picked up my bag and went outside, running to catch the bus, trying not to think about how things had changed between us, in a way I could never have imagined.

Forty-Seven

After my chat with Sofia, I made sure that I had some regular one-on-one time with each of the children, even if it was only half an hour playing Thomas with Alex, or taking Sofia for a Bubble tea. I was especially careful to keep an eye on Ahmed. I was going away for my first business trip, but before I left, I wanted to make sure he was all right. I hadn't seen him much since I started at HH. Tom had made an effort to keep a closer eye on him, learning one of his PlayStation games so they could play together. But Tom hadn't been with Ahmed every day since he was born almost thirteen years ago. I could pick up things Tom couldn't, like a twinge in my psyche when something wasn't quite right with one of the children.

The weekend before I was due to leave, I took Ahmed for a walk on the Common.

'How's the Biology project coming along?' I said as we sat down on a bench.

What I really wanted to ask was how he was feeling? His sessions with Dr Keane had gone down to once a month and he seemed to be all right, but because I hadn't seen him much, it was hard to know if he was hiding any worries.

'I'm good, Mum. Don't worry. I have some really cool friends now and everything is different. I know it wasn't me or my name that made those boys bully me.'

I nodded, trying to blink away my tears. I stared ahead at the pond, watching the ducks. Ahmed's voice had started to get a little deeper and he'd become even taller in the last few weeks.

'I used to bring you here to feed the ducks, do you remember?'

'Yes, Mum. Look, can I please go to a concert at Wembley next month? Dan's older brother will take us. The tickets are expensive so I told Dan I couldn't go because Dad doesn't have a job but he says it's fine. He's loaded so he's getting tickets for us both. I'm going to pay him back by selling my old trainers on Depop. Also, can he come for a sleepover afterwards?'

There were so many things to process. As he started to eat his cookie and went on Snapchat, I thought about how things had changed. Ahmed wanting to go somewhere he hadn't been before, arranging a sleepover with his friend, talking in such a matter-of-fact way about us not having money for the ticket, and figuring out a way to pay for it. I felt a happiness so intense that I wanted to remember that moment forever. I knew that I would.

Forty-Eight

The whole team were flying to Amsterdam the next day. There was a lot riding on this pitch. If I was chosen to work on the account, my bonus would be guaranteed

We'd been allowed to go home early to pack for the trip. Tom was playing Solitaire on his phone and didn't look up when I went into the living room. I stood in the doorway for a moment.

'Hi. What's wrong?' I asked.

'Nothing's wrong. I'm trying to unwind. Can you please leave me alone for a few minutes?'

'Oh, sure.'

My face was wet by the time I got to the top of the stairs. It was as if my husband's body had been taken over by an alien. Usually, if I went away for a weekend, with my friends or with Farrah, Tom looked through travel guides and time zones with me and found me the best route from the airport to the hotel. He always told me to enjoy myself while I was away.

I sighed. I knew he wasn't himself. It must be awful for

him to be stuck in this limbo, with no idea of when he'd get back to work, and no company or no distraction. I wished I could make him feel better, but I seemed to annoy him even more. Perhaps a few days away from each other would help us both.

On the plane, Harry sat next to me. We talked about an upcoming alumni event at Oxford. He asked if I'd like to go with him and did funny impersonations of Professor Hodge, the literature tutor we had both had. It was the sort of thing Tom would have done in the past, making me laugh so much that I forgot my worries for a while. It was just what I needed, after what had happened with Sam and Tom. I was lucky that I'd made a good friend in Harry.

The night before the pitch, we all went to a bar in the centre of Amsterdam. We were politely thrown out at closing time. The buildings swayed and rippled as I tried to focus. I had broken my 'one glass of champagne' drinking rule, and had two. I wasn't drunk, although I let the others think I was, because it made them so extraordinarily happy.

I still felt a little unsteady, though. Teresa and Sabine had wisely worn flats for Amsterdam, but I'd been unsure about how to dress for the team dinner and had stayed in heels. My shoes slipped on the cobbles and Harry put his arms around my waist to steady me.

'Never thought I'd see the day,' laughed David. 'Now you're officially one of us.'

I'd pretended to drink the non-stop stream of wine and cocktails. In fact, I had either poured my drinks in the plant pots by the pool table, or said that my glass had just been topped up.

Harry hooked his arm through mine.

'I think I'd better hold on to you. We don't want you breaking your neck before you've emailed me the slides.'

We criss-crossed the canals over tiny bridges, the water ink-black and still as glass. My heels wobbled. The rest of the team were already further ahead, except Teresa, who walked alongside us. She clearly did not want me to have time alone with a director if she couldn't. When we got closer to the hotel, her phone rang. She walked a little further ahead as she talked.

The she came back and said, 'I need to FaceTime my daughter so I'd better run. Is that OK?'

She looked at me as she spoke and I frowned. If she needed permission, Harry was the one she should ask.

'Don't worry, I'll look after her,' said Harry, waving her off.

I was glad when she left and it was just the two of us. Fairy lights winked at us from the trees lining our route, like a mass of stars that had fallen down from the sky. We walked on in silence. I enjoyed the warmth of being close to Harry. Tom hadn't been near me for days, not even for a hug or to pull me up against him while we watched TV, and it felt comforting to lean on Harry's arm. My supposed intoxication meant that it was perfectly correct for Harry to take me up to my room at the hotel and open the door for me.

He waited until I was inside and said, 'Will you be all right?'

His hand was on the door handle.

Yes please, can you come in and... I stopped, shocked at my thoughts. My cheeks flamed and I shook my head.

'Goodnight, take some paracetamol,' he said, smiling, and left quickly.

My head started to throb. I knew it was just the drink, which had left me disorientated, and with this unexpected reaction towards Harry.

The next morning at breakfast, Ivan said, 'Be careful with Harry.'

'Pardon?'

'I saw the way you two were last night. I hope you didn't...' Ivan leaned forwards and stared at me. I bent my head and sipped my coffee. I didn't trust myself to speak.

'Harry's a nice guy but he has a "reputation". There were rumours about him and Annie who used to do your job. He usually likes his women younger but you're just his...'

I put down my cup. My ability to keep my face arranged in whatever expression was required for the situation was almost an instinctive skill, so my body knew what it had to do, even though my mind was screaming. I widened my eyes, as if in shock, then burst out laughing.

'Sorry, Ivan! I'm afraid you've misread the situation completely. I may have been a little tipsy but I'm a happily married, middle-aged mother and Harry was the perfect gentleman.'

'OK, good,' he said. 'It's always best not to get too friendly with the boss. If anything goes wrong...' He drew his finger across his Adam's apple, unsmiling.

'Agreed,' I said. 'It's also best not to let your imagination run wild. Honestly, Ivan, this is hilarious. Don't worry, there will be no...' I copied his gesture across my throat.

He seemed satisfied. 'Sorry if I got it wrong.'

I replayed my actions from the night before. No, I hadn't done or said anything inappropriate and there hadn't been anything in Harry's behaviour to suggest that he was in any way coming on to me. Quite the opposite, in fact.

Although Ivan seemed genuine, I wondered if there was something else going on. He'd been so angry about the Vladimir account. He, like the others in the team, was so much younger. Perhaps he felt I had an unfair advantage because I was the same age as the directors and we had things in common, like our social circles and children's schools. Ivan might be trying to drive a wedge between Harry and me. Perhaps I did need to be careful, but about Ivan, not Harry.

Forty-Nine

'I imagined he'd have one of those amazing houses on the Keizersgracht,' I said as we headed towards the coast for our pitch, hurtling down the motorway.

'No, he bought a castle on the beach from the 1800s. Better for the helipad and more security,' Ivan said.

'Do you know him then?' I asked.

I smiled, dread creeping up my chest. Ivan, being Russian and more experienced, already had an advantage over me. But if he knew the client as well, then it was pretty much a foregone conclusion that Misha would pick him.

'Not personally, but we have friends in common,' he shrugged, and nodded his head in time to Phil Collins singing 'You Can't Hurry Love' on the taxi's radio.

My call with Tom earlier kept replaying in my mind. I'd asked him if the headhunter had been in touch about another job they'd been discussing.

'Another "Not hiring yet", OK? Sorry to disappoint you.'

I'd tried not to feel hurt at the way he spoke. He was

bound to be upset. I could hear Alex coughing in the background and longed to be at home with the children rather than in the sterile, air-conditioned hush of the hotel room in Amsterdam.

'I'm sorry, darling,' I said. 'Listen, don't worry. I'm sure something else will come through.'

'Yes, people are lining up to hire me. Anyway, I don't have time for this right now. I have to give Alex his antibiotics,' he snapped and hung up.

I'd wanted to tell him that Alex needed to sleep propped up on pillows with lots of Olbas oil. Ever since he was a baby, Alex couldn't sleep when he had a cough, unless he was leaning against my chest as I slept sitting up against the headboard, but Tom hadn't given me a chance. I kept thinking about how Alex had cried as I was leaving for the airport, and had called out to me just as I got to the bedroom door, 'Today is the day I'm going to die! You'll never see your son again.'

I'd never been away from Alex when he was sick and I was also disappointed that Tom didn't get the job. He had no right to act this way towards me.

The countryside became darker. A sudden right turn took us into a trickle of a road where we were hemmed in tight between a high hedge on one side and what looked like a boundary wall on the other. I pulled my arms towards my body instinctively.

'This is it,' said Ivan, sitting up and tapping his thigh.

I peered out to get a better look and spotted sharp metal spikes glinting along the top of the wall.

'It looks more like a prison than a luxury castle,' I smiled. 'I wonder if there's a moat littered with bankers who didn't deliver results for Misha?'

No one replied.

I leaned forwards, squinting to get my first glimpse of the house but all I saw were clouds of trees bearing down on us in dense woods. Eventually, the landscape opened up. Manicured trees stood to attention like a military guard of honour on either side of the long, ruler-straight driveway, at the end of which was a six-storeyed castle with all the windows lit up, as if on fire. The taxi crunched to a stop on gravel.

A butler handed us champagne and ushered us upstairs to the buzz of conversation on a first-floor terrace which overlooked the sea and a private beach. A low Perspex wall allowed uninterrupted views of the inky sky and a slice of the moon, while flickering candles and white roses lay along the edge of the decking.

'Fi, come and meet everyone!' Harry waved at me.

Misha looked too young to be a father to the four children for whom he had asked us to set up trust funds. His clothes underlined the youthful image; jeans and a salmon-pink starched shirt with a Patek Philippe watch. He shook my hand and then turned straight back to continue his conversation with the Dragon. I didn't know what to do next. Harry was in a smaller group a little to the side with Sabine and some others.

Ivan saved me by calling me over and introduced me to one of Misha's colleagues, Peter.

'Fi is one of us! She knows Russian.'

Ivan's eyes kept flitting towards Misha and soon he

excused himself, leaving me with Peter. He started talking to me in Russian and despite my recent attempts at brushing up my language skills by listening to audiobooks on my commute, I barely understood anything he said.

'I'm sorry, your English is much better than my Russian!' I laughed, trying to cover up my terror that someone at HH might discover my lie.

'I want to hear you speak it! Say something,' he said.

'I can't really remember much, to be honest.'

'Please! You must, for me?'

Peter looked as if he'd started early on the champagne. People were beginning to look in our direction and before he became more agitated, I agreed.

'I only remember a few lines of "Medniy Vsadnik",' I said.

The poem was the only thing that had stuck in my mind since my university days.

I was about to start, while planning my exit strategy, when Peter shouted out, drowning the conversations in the room, 'Silence! This lady is going to recite Pushkin!'

There was an immediate hush and I grew ice-cold. Misha looked annoyed at the interruption; Ivan, Teresa, David and Sabine were standing around him, so he must have been in the middle of their pitches. The Dragon seemed to be relishing the spectacle and I couldn't bring myself to look at Harry. They all turned to face me.

I cleared my throat. Twice.

'Right.'

I took a deep breath. I just wanted to get it over with quickly. I started reciting the poem in Russian, as quietly as I could.

'Na bereguy, pusteenisk voln,
Stayal ohn, doom velikikh poln…'

I fixed my eyes on the trouser hems and ankles surrounding me. My mouth was parched and my face was burning. I carried on for five lines, then stopped.

'Bravo! Bravo!'

Peter's voice rang out and he started to clap vigorously. Less enthusiastic and uneven applause followed from the others. I sneaked a look at the team and saw Teresa and David openly sniggering and the Dragon frowning. I had performed a party trick in front of one of our biggest potential clients at the request of an obviously drunk man, when I should have been pitching my portfolio to Misha.

'Excuse me.'

I moved towards the edge of the group, to escape to the bathroom.

'How do you know Russian?'

Misha was blocking my path. This time he was looking at me, rather than through me.

'I lived in Moscow for a year. And I studied it at university too.'

He began to talk to me about Moscow and we were soon comparing notes.

'Where did you live?'

'Ulitsa Zolotovskaya at Patriashiye Prudy – that huge pond near the Garden Ring. I remembered it from Bulgakov.'

'Which block?'

'The yellow one. Do you know it?' I said.

His eyebrows shot up. 'I grew up there. In that building,

the yellow one with the arch. My grandmother still lives there!'

Misha asked me to sit next to him at dinner so we could carry on talking about the yellow building.

As the waiter replaced my caviar starter with a main of sea bass, decorated with delicate slivers of vegetables on crisp white china, I caught my breath, thinking about how much my life had changed. I was part of a banking team, quoting financial data to my client, with deals being negotiated all around the table and seven-figure sums and global currencies tossed around casually. I was wearing heels, my nails had been painted a communist red at a Vietnamese nail bar, and my hair was blow dried straight. It was so far removed from what I would normally have been doing in the evenings, before I went back to the City: cooking dinner, washing sports kits, helping with homework, before having dinner with Tom, just the two of us.

Throughout the evening I was aware of Harry sitting on my right, his leg inches away from mine and his long fingers tapping the white tablecloth. I was missing Tom that was all. He hadn't held my hand for days or hugged me when I left for the airport. This wasn't about Harry.

I had done weeks of intense research and so when Misha quizzed me about my proposal, I could answer all his questions.

'Let's do it,' said Misha.

I beamed.

'You know why I chose you?' asked Misha.

'Because I lived in the same block as your grandmother?' I teased, excited at how things had turned out.

'Very funny. No. I chose you because you're a mother.

You understand why I want to protect my children, and that this is more important to me than any other business deal.'

I smiled. The one thing that I had considered my biggest handicap in the City seemed to have won the deal for me.

As we left, Harry asked if I could add some additional projections to our proposal before meeting Misha again the next day. It meant two more hours of work back at the hotel, but I was too excited to sleep anyway.

Fifty

I fell back against the padded headboard and shut off my laptop, giving myself two black eyes by smudging my mascara with the backs of my fists. It was 1.30 a.m. I needed to print the projection slides in the hotel's business centre on the next floor up, but I was too tired to get dressed again for a ten-minute dash. I hauled on a massive towelling robe that trailed the ground under my bare feet. The corridors were deserted and no sounds came from any of the doors I passed.

The business centre was empty and while the printers shuddered to life, squeaking in protest before beginning their rhythmic hum, I couldn't help laying my head down on my arms. I just needed to close my eyes for a second.

'No!' I protested as I felt someone tugging at me. 'Go away!'

The children knew they shouldn't wake me up at the weekends. But the hand kept shaking me, pulling roughly on my arm. A man's voice filtered through and I sat up quickly, heart thudding, half-awake. I relaxed as I remembered where I was and a pair of navy and white striped boxer shorts came into focus and below them long, muscular legs.

'Fi?'

It was Harry. I rubbed my eyes, dabbing away the sleep-induced blindness. I felt a wet patch on the side of my mouth and wiped it away quickly with the back of my hand. The skin on my cheek tingled and my fingers went up instinctively to touch it. I felt the imprint of the bath robe stripes and imagined the raised red lines across my face.

'Busted! Sleeping on the job,' said Harry.

Harry handed me my papers and sat down next to me. His feet were bare and he wore a white T-shirt. I was unable to stifle a crocodile-wide yawn, giving him a good view of all my fillings.

'Sorry, I must have just drifted off...'

Embarrassed, I looked down, trying to hide behind my hair, and realised that my robe had fallen open, giving him a clear view of my black bra and stomach.

I pulled the robe together. 'I'd better get to bed. Thanks for waking me up...'

'I need to scan some papers for US clients. They only work to American time zones.'

He looked exhausted. His hair was messy now, standing up like a crown. I wanted to smooth it down with my fingers.

As I stood up, the bottom of my robe got caught in my feet and I fell forward, losing my balance. Harry steadied me as I fell against him. I moved away quickly.

'This is getting to be a habit; you tripping and me catching you.'

It took me back to that day in the lift. My heart raced.

'They should make these robes for small people too,' I laughed and shuffled away, holding up my robe as if walking on a wet floor. He stood watching me as I left.

All that effort I'd put in to look good for the pitch and then Harry ended up seeing me smudged, wrinkled and covered in drool! Perhaps it was for the best.

Fifty-One

I was back in London. Harry and I were working on Misha's deal and when he needed to do some extra work on one of his existing projects at the same time, I offered to help. I wanted to thank him for all his support, but I also knew that a willingness to 'pitch in' would count in my favour for both a permanent job offer, and the size of my bonus.

His office became our base for the week. It was huge, comfortable, and we could spread out our papers without disturbing the rest of the team. One night we worked straight past dinner, not wanting to break our momentum. Harry was sitting next to me on the sofa when my stomach gave a loud rumble.

'It's eleven o'clock! I'm so sorry,' he said.

'I feel that as the source of that impolite sound, I should be the one to apologise,' I smiled.

He ordered us sushi from Sexy Fish and while we waited for the delivery, he said, 'Please excuse me, I'm going to FaceTime my daughters and my wife so feel free to call your husband too. This might end up being an all-nighter.'

I darted out of the room, saying I'd be back in a few minutes. I was horrified to think that he might, like some people annoyingly did, pull me into his call to introduce me to Julia.

I had no desire to FaceTime Tom. When I'd texted him earlier to say I'd be working very late, he'd replied, 'Have fun.'

Harry took out two chilled mini bottles of champagne from a little fridge and we ate dinner sitting on the floor at his coffee table. The overhead lights were off and, in the lamplight, we could see the lit-up skyscrapers outside his huge office window.

'We're eating sushi as it should be eaten, on the floor,' I said.

He started to tell me how he'd taught English for a few months in Japan in his gap year and I said how Japan was top of my travel wish list. He cleared away the packages while I opened up my laptop and sat back on the sofa.

'Take off your shoes, Fi, and make yourself comfortable – we probably need to be at this for another couple of hours.'

I slipped off my heels and tucked my legs under me and Harry also took his shoes off and untucked his shirt.

I kept my eyes on my laptop screen. I had been careful around Harry since Amsterdam and, luckily, it hadn't been hard. Tom had been his normal self when I got back from the trip, he had hugged me, and been excited about my deal with Misha. He'd asked Ami for her secret chicken karahi recipe and made it for me as a surprise, and we'd talked about the amazing coincidence of Misha living in the yellow building when Tom and I also lived there.

I realised that feeling attracted to Harry in Amsterdam

had just been the result of a perfect marital storm with Tom. Our fight before I left, his stress about the job hunt, then the heady feeling of being away from everything: that was all.

When Harry and I finished it was 1 a.m. I stretched my arms over my head and my legs in front of me. I saw Harry glance at my red toenails and then my bare legs but the moment came from nowhere then disappeared. I wondered if I had imagined it...

Fifty-Two

Sam texted me a few days before Julia's two-week deadline.

Let's go through all the sales right from the start. We must have made a mistake counting up xx

I agreed to meet her. She was right, that was the only explanation.

Tom and I had been getting on better. Perhaps he was more relaxed as my salary started to hit our account, and I had also finally stopped worrying about the money. My salary, supplemented by the bank loan, covered our newly streamlined monthly expenses and Ami and Baba's money lay in the account to satisfy Tom's need for cash flow. I was also on track to get my bonus to repay my parents and replace our own savings.

One morning, though, I felt his low mood the minute I woke up. I knew it had something to do with an email that had pinged onto his phone at 5 a.m., which was the middle of the office day somewhere in the world.

I went to hug him from the back before leaving for work and he shrugged me off.

'What's wrong, darling?' I spoke softly. 'Did something happen?'

'I'm unemployed, Faiza. I might never get another job again. We can't live on just your salary forever and our savings will soon run out. We might need to sell the house and I have no idea what we'll do about the school fees. We might have to take the children out of their schools. But you just carry on having your jolly dinners and trips away!'

I couldn't move with the shock of his words. I tried to think rationally. He was just lashing out at me because there was no one else. And the truth was that if I hadn't spent the money then I could be home, supporting him through this time, instead of being out all day. We wouldn't be in such a precarious position. This was all my fault.

However, another voice jostled with this reasoning, ramming it out of the way. All Tom could think about was himself. He was wallowing in self-pity at a time when we were both under stress. I'd never expected him to be this man.

'You shit!' I hissed, closing the kitchen door so the children wouldn't hear us. 'Why are you being like this? Do you think I like leaving the children all day? Do you think I like worrying about my parents all the time? Do you think it's easy to go back into that shark pool and suck up to idiots to win my commission? No. But at least I'm doing something, not feeling sorry for myself or giving up. Why should we sell the house? Why should we take the children out of school? Other people seem to have jobs. Why is it just you that's not working?'

My hurt at his words combined with my guilt had released some kind of piston and my anger came tumbling out. Even as I said the words to the back of his head, tears ran down my face, ruining my morning office make-up. I knew that what I was saying was unforgivable and cruel, but the more he ignored me, the louder I became.

'Get your bloody act together!' I snapped.

Fifty-Three

That night, Tom wasn't home when I got back from work. Sofia wasn't there either, so the boys were alone. Tom had dropped them home after school, they said, then left. Neither Tom nor Sofia replied to my texts.

I started to get worried. It wasn't like Sofia to disappear. I could see she was online, but she wasn't responding. I started calling her, again and again, and eventually I got a text back: *I'm not dead. I'll just be late.*

Me: *Not good enough! You know the rule: Where, who with, when, what. I need to talk to you when you get home.*

I seemed to have lost touch with Sofia completely. I had no idea what was going on in her life. She refused to say more than just 'Fine!' when I asked her how she was.

Tom hadn't replied to my texts either. The duvet on our bed was rumpled in the same folds I had left it in that morning and he'd taken his watch and wallet. I saw that he'd been on WhatsApp an hour earlier, so at least he wasn't dead – but I would kill him when I saw him.

Sofia came home at 11.30 and ran up to her room. She locked her door and wouldn't come out.

'Are you OK, baby?' I called.

'I'm fine. Leave me alone!'

I stood outside her door. She didn't sound fine.

It was well past midnight when I heard a car and rushed to the bedroom window. Tom was getting out of a taxi. He held onto the door for a second to steady himself. He laughed and said something, then waved it off. I got straight back into bed and a few minutes later he walked in as if after a normal day at the office. He was in a suit, with his tie poking out from one of his pockets. He undressed, brushed his teeth and lay down with his back towards me.

'Where the hell have you been?' I said.

'I had a meeting.'

'Why didn't you tell me where you were? I thought something had happened to you. You didn't answer my calls.'

'So what if I went out one evening? You do it all the time. I had a last-minute meeting. You told me to go and get a job this morning, didn't you? You should be able to understand that, after all your evening events with Harry.'

I jumped out of bed and shut our bedroom door. He wasn't bothering to keep his voice down, though he knew I never wanted the children to hear us fighting.

'I never go out without letting you know first,' I said.

He sat up in bed.

'Perfect, perfect Faiza and useless, good-for-nothing me. I can't do anything right. I was trying to get a deal, OK? For us. To get back to work. It was last minute and I had no signal in the club so I couldn't call.'

'I'm just saying that—'

'Fuck off!' he said.

I flinched at the look in his eyes.

The words were like a punch I hadn't seen coming, because they were from Tom.

He lay back down. As I turned off my lamp, I knocked over my glasses and my book crashed to the floor. I stared at the wall as it started to come into focus in the dark.

I pulled the duvet over my head and turned on my phone, then googled 'Why would a husband start acting differently?' The answers ranged from adultery, to financial troubles, job loss, or mental illness. Well, he was under a lot of stress. I shouldn't have been so angry. What if he was depressed? I came across a headline: 'Fears of a mental health crisis in banking after another City suicide.' A man had jumped from a multistorey car park and another had thrown himself under a tube. A banker and a lawyer.

I felt really bad about lashing out at Tom. Stress could spiral out of control. And he definitely wasn't himself.

Fifty-Four

When I saw Tom the next morning as I made coffee in the kitchen, my anger disappeared.

'Hey,' I said.

I stroked his bare arm. He didn't reply.

'Look, about last night. That wasn't like you. I know this is a really difficult time for you, but don't take it out on me. We need to stick together.'

He turned around to pick something up from the table.

I went up to him and laid my head on his chest. He stiffened. I took his hands in mine and lifted them to my waist.

'I think I need to remind you how this works. You have to put your arms around me too.'

I tried to smile.

He pulled his hands away, not meeting my eyes.

'I was thinking that maybe we could see the doctor. It might help if you got some counselling. We could get counselling together?'

'I don't need counselling; I need a job. Which is what I

was trying to do last night. Don't patronise me, Faiza. So, I get angry with you because you're acting like a hysterical control freak and suddenly, I need counselling?'

I could only stare at him in silence, trying to reconcile my Tom with this person. His calm face and his eyes which always had a special look just for me, had been replaced by an angry twist of his lips. The old Tom would have listened to me and, even if he disagreed, would have said why, then kissed my forehead gently as a full stop to his explanation. This Tom hurled his words at me, with a look in his eyes that left me frozen. It was clear, undisguised contempt. He didn't seem angry with life, only with me.

He went up to the door and paused a second before saying, 'Just do me a favour, please: stay away from me.'

I must have caught the bus, sat on the train to Waterloo, picked up my usual takeaway coffee, then walked to the office, but I had no memory of any of it. Tom might as well have thrown a grenade on me at close range.

Fifty-Five

As the day wore on, feelings started to seep back in, like sensation coming back into numbed fingers. I alternated between sadness that Tom had been so cruel, and terror that we would never recover from this. Had we really been happy all these years, or had we wanted to prove everyone wrong so badly that we had convinced ourselves that our marriage was perfect.

I made my way to Harry's office, carrying the printouts of my presentation for the next pitch in New York. This was not a time to make any mistakes, but I hadn't been able to concentrate.

Harry was sitting by the wall of glass, with sunshine flooding in. I perched at the edge of the deep sofa and spread the papers out on to the glass table, making sure I had them in the correct order. This was Harry's client and we were pitching for a huge account. I had been working on this for two weeks, staying up late not just at the office, but also at home once Tom and the children were in bed. I would get an extra ten thousand in my bonus if I got this account.

I started going through the slides, telling him what I would in my pitch. I managed to answer all his questions. It took less than ten minutes.

'This is excellent,' he said.

I sat back, relieved.

'Just one thing, though.'

His words made me sit up again.

'In Amsterdam, your presentation was so full of energy and passion and I think that's what really clinched it for us. You need to ramp that up a notch for New York. You seemed a bit low key just now, not quite engaged. Are you saving all the pizzazz for the clients?'

There was a smile on his face, but I heard a hint of doubt. Harry had put a lot of faith in me and I needed to deliver.

'I'll pull out all the stops for New York. I just have a bit of a migraine today.'

'Fi, why didn't you tell me? This light must be killing you.'

He pressed a button and large blackout blinds descended, like eyelids shutting silently, obliterating the sun, the City, and the expanse of glass. The room was plunged into darkness. It felt intimate, like a hotel room in the middle of the afternoon. It took us a few minutes to adjust to the dark and I was grateful for that because I couldn't help tears springing to my eyes at Harry's small gesture. In the few seconds he took to pour me a glass of water and bring it to me before sitting down next to me, tears were rolling down my face.

'Hey, come. Shall I get you some Nurofen?'

He touched my back softly, just for a brief second, but that set me off completely and I began to cry uncontrollably.

He pushed a box of tissues towards me and I bent my head, trying desperately to stop. Oh God, he wouldn't trust me to go in front of a client after this meltdown. At that thought, I started to shake.

'Fi, what is it?'

He patted my back, as a football coach might do to a player who had been injured or missed a goal.

'Drink some water.'

He held the glass to my lips, as if I were an invalid. I took a sip, then took the glass into my hand.

'I'm s-so sorry. I'm never like this, ever. I *never* do this.'

It was true. My game face never slipped, except in front of Tom.

'P-please don't sack me.'

'I'm not going to sack you. This isn't Wall Street. We are all human, sort of!'

I tried to smile, but couldn't quite manage.

'Are you sure there's nothing else? This seems more than a headache. Look, I'm here if you want to talk. As your manager, but also as a friend.'

He leaned forward. His aftershave, lemon and spice, floated towards me. My knee bumped into his as I shifted on the sofa. I jerked back and, as I did, some water from the glass spilled onto my shirt, a wet patch spreading on the white silk. He grabbed a tissue and instinctively started to dab the spot, which was on my chest, just above my breast.

Harry and I both realised what he was doing at the same time and I snatched the tissue away. To fill up the silence I blurted out, 'Things are a little difficult at home.'

'I'm sorry to hear that.'

His phone buzzed and he glanced at it.

'I've taken up too much of your time. I'm sorry about... I'm so embarrassed. This headache is making me crazy. I won't be like this in front of the client.'

'I thought we were friends, Fi. You can talk to me.'

I needed to talk to someone.

'Everything's fine. It's just – just Tom and I had a fight... I don't know, it's hard... He's looking for a job and the market's not great at the moment.'

'He shouldn't be taking it out on you. I hope you don't mind me speaking openly?'

I shook my head.

'You're an incredible woman, Fi. You've come back to work, you're earning money for the family, you're looking after your parents, you're a devoted mother, and you seem to worry about Tom too. He should be thanking you, not fighting with you.'

'Tom's lovely, really he is. This isn't like him.'

I had been thinking the same things as Harry, but when he criticised Tom, I had to defend him. What if Harry was right, though? I was terrified that this had broken us. Perhaps Tom and I hadn't been as solid as I had imagined all these years. If we had been, then why had we failed at this first test in our relationship?

'I suppose you know him best. But marriage is supposed to support us in the tough times, isn't it?' said Harry.

I kept looking down. He was right, but it felt wrong to discuss Tom like this.

'My loyalty is always going to be with you.'

'It's just a difficult time for us,' I said.

He nodded.

'For what it's worth, you can always talk to me if it helps? Right now, though, you should rest. My driver can take you home.'

'Thanks. You've been so kind.'

I dabbed my shirt a little more. As I stood up, so did Harry. He had to move away from the sofa so I could pass by and, as I got near him, I saw him look down at my shirt. Two of the buttons had become undone and my breasts, in a nude lace bra, were visible. I clutched at my shirt but the movement was too fast and I lost my balance. Harry put his arms out to steady me and had to pull me towards him to stop me falling.

I wanted to make a joke about how I had now made a fool of myself in every possible way, or that he would think I was drunk, or say 'Oops, sorry,' but I stayed silent. His arms tightened and I let my head fall on his chest. I needed someone to hold me. It was as if I were watching myself from the outside, as he started to stroke my back.

'It's going to be OK.'

I nodded into his shirt.

'Sorry,' I said into his tie, raising a hand to my head. 'I'm a little dizzy.'

He was silent. His hand, which had been between my shoulder blades, began to slide down the silk of my shirt slowly, over the bump of my bra and then rested on my waist. I stood absolutely still, not breathing, not moving away. He was more angular than Tom, who was more solid, with broader shoulders and familiar muscles. It felt strange to be in Harry's arms, but also comforting.

'Fi...'

Before he could say any more, there was a loud rap-rap on his door.

'Harry? It's Olivia. May I come in?'

The room was dark and I was standing in clear view of the door, with Harry's arms around me, my blouse was open. I knew that Olivia would come in any second and see everything. Without thinking I rushed into a small alcove at the back of the room where the coffee machine was, behind Harry's desk. I pushed myself against the wall. Harry moved just as quickly and sat down at his desk. I was now completely hidden from view.

'Woah, it's dark in here!' said Olivia.

'Too much sun on my computer,' said Harry.

'I just need you to sign this letter.'

Harry's fountain pen scratched the paper and Olivia's heels walked away, then the door shut.

My cheeks burned. I didn't know how to face Harry. I shouldn't have let him hold me like that. I had no business acting like this with another man, however angry I was with my husband.

Tom had an excuse for the way he was acting, but I had no way to justify my behaviour. Not only could this destroy my marriage, but it would ruin my friendship with Harry, and I might end up losing my job.

I stepped out of the alcove.

'I'm sorry, Harry. You must think I'm completely mad!'

I couldn't look at him. I tried a laugh and started to walk towards the door.

'I'm the one who should apologise,' he said. 'I hope I wasn't inappropriate. I just hated seeing you so upset.'

'No, I'm sorry I hid like that. I thought Olivia might get

the wrong impression. You were just being kind and I'm so embarrassed.'

'There's no need to be embarrassed. Totally under-standable. Let me call my driver.'

He seemed eager for me to leave and I obliged. I told him that I would prefer to walk for a while and then get a taxi. I didn't want his driver to drop me at a house less than ten minutes from Harry's.

On the way home, I tried to think rationally. Harry had just held me while I cried, like a friend would. There had been no kiss, no fondling, nothing inappropriate.

I brushed aside any thoughts about how it had felt to bury myself into Harry and feel his body against mine. That was just a physical reaction. It didn't mean anything. I had only been craving the comfort of Tom's touch and kindness, which he had unilaterally withdrawn from me for weeks.

When I got home, I hesitated before going inside. Tom didn't know that I was coming back early and it almost felt as if I were spying on him.

'Hi, Tom! You home?'

I heard sounds coming from the laundry room at the back, a room Tom had not really known existed until recently.

He was folding the washing and I hugged him from behind, wrapping my hands around him so that they rested against the fabric belt on his Levis. I laid my cheek against his back and kissed his spine. He didn't recoil.

He turned around to face me. He looked like himself again.

'How come you're home?'

'TOIL for New York.'

'Well, I just had a very good call with a headhunter,' he said. 'They called me about a great role.'

We high-fived.

That was the thing about Tom and me. However bad our fights, we were both so happy when they were over that we never rehashed anything. I always wanted to forget about our arguments anyway. I used to think that this was a sign of our deep connection, but now I wondered if it was a weakness, never to probe our fault lines.

He started to kiss me but I jerked my head back. If he knew that less than an hour ago Harry had been pressed up close against me, it would devastate him, and I had a sudden desire to shower.

'I'm an idiot. I should never have said those things to you,' he said.

'Ditto,' I said. 'I'm an idiot and I should never have said those things to you.'

He put his arms around me.

'You smell of aftershave,' he said.

Harry had seeped into my hair and my pores and Tom could smell him on me.

'Oh, it was this ageing Lothario type on the tube. He was sitting next to me and reeked of aftershave. In fact, I think I'll take a quick shower otherwise I won't be able to stop thinking about how sick it made me feel. Urgh!'

I was worried about seeing Harry again, but the next day, he just smiled and said, 'Are you all set for New York?'

I smiled back.
'I can't wait.'
We were back to normal.

Fifty-Six

The doorbell rang. It was late, 9 p.m., and raining outside. Tom and I looked at each other in surprise, then he went to answer the door.

I heard Sam's voice. We weren't meeting until the weekend and I stood up, immediately afraid that Julia had informed the Head and Sam had come to warn me. She came into the room, her face blotchy as if stung by nettles. I stared at her, breathing fast suddenly. What if the police had been brought in?

'I'm just going upstairs to check on the boys,' said Tom, shutting the door behind him.

'I'm sorry to burst in on you like this,' she said. 'But I know where the money is.'

I had to sit down. She sat next to me and covered my hand with hers, as if we were still friends.

'Where's the money?' I said.

'I'm so sorry. It was all my fault. *I* had the money. It's at my house. I've told Julia.'

I couldn't believe that she had stolen it, then accused me.

Her face was red, flooded. She looked down.

'*You* took the money?'

'No! Well, yes – no. I mean yes, but not on purpose.'

'I don't understand. If you had the money, why did you let that vile cow speak to me like that? Why did you accuse me? What the hell is going on, Sam?'

She looked at me.

'It's all been a terrible mix-up. That day, after I'd sold the tickets and I was putting the money in the safe, Mum called. She was crying, saying that her father hadn't come home all night. My grandad has been dead for fifteen years. I've never heard Mum talk like that. I panicked, Faiza. It was awful to hear her talk such complete gibberish. I got scared about what else she might do in that state of mind. I didn't know if she'd walk out of the house or set fire to it. Anyway, I locked the safe and drove straight to her house.'

'Oh, Sam. Is she OK?'

'Yes.' Sam nodded. 'She's back to normal, just like someone flipped a switch. Anyway, in my panic I didn't put all the money in the safe. Some got left in my bag but I didn't realise. I only use this bag,' she held up her luggage-trolley-sized blue tote, 'on my day off. It's so full of rubbish that I didn't see the money till tonight, when I was looking for a pen. It was right at the bottom and I only realised then what had happened. I called Julia immediately and then I drove here like a maniac. I knew you wouldn't talk to me if I called... Not that I blame you.'

I stared, trying to take it all in.

'I've been so worried,' I said. 'I thought Julia would spread rumours about me and tell the Head. She might have done that already.'

'No, she hasn't said anything.'

Sam moved closer.

'The most important thing is that I want to say sorry.'

Her eyes were bright, which was the nearest I had ever seen to her crying.

'I've been going crazy, Faiza. What with Mum and James – I don't know how much more I can take!' She paused, breathing fast. It seemed as if she wanted to tell me more, but was struggling to find the words. Then she shook her head, as if pulling herself together. 'I mean, his obsession with impressing his parents. It's affecting us too. I don't know if I want all this anymore.'

'Poor you and poor James,' I said.

I didn't understand how things had become so bad between them.

'It's hard, Faiza. James has changed and I'm not sure if we can get through this.'

I put my arm around her as she sighed.

'His parents have started doing the same thing with our children. Praising the ones who get an A star, ignoring the ones who don't make the top team. And now James does it too. At the parents evening, he took a notebook to compare the boys' exam results against the others in their class. It was like he was checking how his investments were doing. I'm scared he's going to mess them up the way his parents have messed him up.'

'Not with a lovely mum like you,' I said.

We talked a little more and then she got up.

'I'm sorry, I shouldn't have listened to Julia, though. I hope you can forgive me,' she said.

'Let's forget all about it,' I said, and meant it.

Sam was going through a lot; she'd made a mistake but had apologised. Besides, I had thought about taking the money, hadn't I? Despite my hurt and fury, she hadn't been that far off the mark.

I was worried about Sam and James. It was frightening how quickly a close marriage like theirs had unravelled. The thought chilled me as I fell asleep.

Fifty-Seven

As I packed for New York, Tom was lying in bed, scrolling through the news.

'Hey, do you remember that time we got lost in Central Park and then ended up in the kitschy horse-carriages? Then we had the lobster rolls from the pop-up place near the Apple store?'

He looked up and smiled.

I folded a navy wrap dress that I was planning to wear for the pitch and a red silk sheath that would work for the client dinner.

'Darling, don't forget Ahmed has football camp all next week and we pick and drop Daniel too.'

The summer holiday schedules were tricky if you factored in all the meals, playdates, activities, pickups and drop-offs for all the children.

'Is it just you and Harry on this trip?' said Tom.

'Yes, but we're not travelling together.'

My face flushed. I turned away and bent down to get my earrings out of a drawer, aware that he was watching me. I examined the earrings in my hand, letting my hair fall forward.

'So, you and your new best friend get to have a trip together,' he said. 'That's nice.'

'He's not my best friend, he's my boss. *You're* my best friend,' I grinned.

He didn't reply. I understood he might feel jealous but how many times had he been away with young female colleagues, when I had been pregnant or home with toddlers, too tired to even brush my hair? I had felt as he had, but I hadn't taunted him like this.

I tried to reassure him by going up to hug him.

'You're not feeling a little jealous, are you?' I laughed and took his hand, but he pulled it away.

'It's not funny. Please have a little more respect for me than that.'

'Tom, I was joking because the whole idea is ridiculous. He's a work colleague. I'm going to New York for work, I'm not running away with another man!'

Even as I said the words, I felt a pinprick of guilt. I had explained my time with Harry as just a good friendship at the office. Tom would be furious, though, if he knew that when Harry and I worked late, we sat side by side on his sofa with our feet on his coffee table, balancing our laptops on our knees. I hadn't mentioned the day Harry massaged my neck when I got a sudden crick. I was at his desk, his office door open. It was only a friend, easing my muscle pain, but he had slipped his fingers inside my shirt, to reach the spot on my neck where it hurt. Tom wouldn't understand. In a way, I didn't either, but we hadn't done anything wrong.

As I zipped up my case, Tom said, 'I need access to the emergency money in the Post Office account. You're travelling a lot and I might need it while you're away. Can you please add my name to the account?'

'OK, sure,' I said. My head pounded. 'I'll do it when I get back from New York.'

'Please make sure you do. I've been asking you for months and you keep saying you will but you still haven't.'

I couldn't sleep all night. I'd be back from New York in three days. My bonus wouldn't come in for another two months and the bank manager had said that I had exceeded the maximum loan he could give. Even if I managed to get another loan somewhere else, I had no way to explain away not adding Tom to the non-existent Post Office account.

Tom didn't say goodbye when I left for the airport. It was an early flight and he pretended to be asleep when I bent down to kiss his cheek. I stroked his hair. I wanted to climb back into bed with him and forget everything else.

'Love you,' I whispered, and then I left.

Fifty-Eight

I had never been to New York without Tom before. New York was our place, our first choice for an anniversary celebration or a rare getaway without the children. As I sat in the taxi, the worn ID photo of the driver called Mohammad and the small TV screen talking animatedly to me about a fire in Brooklyn, were all familiar sights. I placed my hand palm down on the plastic-covered seat. It felt strange not to have Tom's hand squeezing mine as we hurtled away from the airport.

I turned on my phone and checked my messages, hoping for a text from Tom, saying that he loved me, or to have a good time, or sorry. But there was nothing. I realised, with a jolt, that this no longer surprised me. Despite everything, I felt myself getting excited as we approached Manhattan. Tom and I were always impatient to catch our first glimpse of the Chrysler building and the skyline twinkled, as if welcoming me back.

I took a photo and wanted to send it to Tom but I remembered his comment about me 'swanning off' on my business trips. Instead, I texted him: *Landed safely, on my way to hotel. Hope all OK at home.* I couldn't help adding *Miss you.* He replied straight back, with a thumbs-up emoji.

I'd been anxious at the prospect of staying at the same place as Harry, but was relieved when his assistant told me he always stayed at an exclusive hotel near Central Park. The team stayed at a different one in midtown.

In my room, I went straight to the window and looked down at constant traffic on the roads and the pavements, feeling the energy float up to me on the thirtieth floor. I sat on the bed and stroked the starched sheets, savouring the silence. It felt giddy not to be needed, without a constant to-do list running like ticker tape in my head.

I hadn't been able to speak to Ami and Baba before I left and neither of them had mastered the text function on their mobiles. They were excited about my trip when I saw them at the weekend, and had given me a shopping list of pain rubs, and other medications for various ailments and Tom had said that he would check in on them.

Harry's plane was delayed in Houston, so we couldn't go through the pitch one last time. He said that he'd meet me at the client's offices, but if he was late, I should go ahead and present by myself.

Alone???? I texted.

Yes. You will be fine. That's an order.

Fifty-Nine

The pitch was over. Harry and I burst out laughing as we stood outside the client's offices near Bryant Park. He high-fived me and then I fist-bumped him.

'Very nicely done, Fi.'

I was still buzzing. Harry had arrived just as I was doing the Q & A and I had introduced the client, Max, to Harry, rather than the other way around. Max had just sold his company and had millions to invest. Once I'd started presenting the slides, I didn't feel afraid. I put my skills of pretence to good use, acting as if I had been doing this for years.

'Are you tired?' asked Harry, loosening his tie.

I shook my head. I wanted to savour the excitement and success, the feeling of having confidence in my work again, for the first time in years.

I also felt as if a huge burden had been lifted. I was almost there with my targets to get the bonus. I couldn't wait to give my parents their money back.

'I'm not tired at all!' I smiled.

'Me neither. Let's have a drink to celebrate. It would be good to jot down a couple of things they mentioned just now about their investment plans.'

I didn't want the celebrations to end either, and as it would be a working celebration, I relaxed. I knew without doubt that he would have done the same if Ivan or David had been with him on this trip instead of me.

At his hotel, Harry led me into a dark, windowless room with low lighting and red velvet sofas. The walls were mirrored in smoky reflections of us everywhere I looked and a woman played the piano in one corner, humming tunes rather than singing them, the sounds vibrating along the room. She had an auburn pixie cut and white breasts under a red slip dress. She swayed hypnotically as she played.

'Wow!' I said, my head swivelling at everything as the hostess led us to a table at the back, even though the bar was mostly empty.

'Your usual, Harry?' she said.

'Champagne, please, Maggie, we're celebrating. Is that OK, Fi?'

'I'll have one glass, thank you. After that, it has to be Coke Zero if you don't mind. I already had my one glass limit with Max but as it's a special occasion...'

I wished I could get something to eat as well. As if he'd read my mind, he said, 'How about some chips? Or something more refined?'

'Chips would be awesome. I'm so hungry – but I was too embarrassed to ask!'

'No one ever gets to eat properly at these work things. Chips and Moët it is, then.'

'Would you please excuse me for a minute? I just want

to check on the children before it gets too late in London,' I said.

I went into the lobby, relieved to get a signal, and called Tom. It was only around 11 p.m. I couldn't wait to tell him how I had presented alone and won the pitch.

'Hi! How is everything?' I said.

'Fine, fine. Why are you calling from our personal mobile? You know it costs a fortune. Use your work phone.'

'You're right, but that battery died and I really wanted to tell you about the pitch. It went really well, darling! Harry was late and so I had to do it all by myself but the clients loved it and I got the account! Harry says—'

'That's great.'

He spoke without emotion, as if eager to get off the call.

I started to get angry.

'You could be happy for me.'

'I'm very happy, OK? I wish I had time to chat about what Harry says but it's late and you're wasting money using this phone.'

'Why are you being such a shit?'

I hung up with tears in my eyes. How long would I have to keep on trying and trying with him? What was the point? What kind of a marriage did we have if it had unravelled so quickly? I was perched on the arm of a sofa in the foyer and hadn't noticed that Harry had come up to me. I hoped he hadn't heard anything.

'I'm sorry, I couldn't help overhearing. Is everything OK?'

'Can we please not talk about it?'

I tried to compose myself.

'Sure, sure. I believe there's a bottle of champagne with our names on it. We also need to plan the strategy. I'm interviewing the niece of a friend from Oxford tomorrow, who wants an internship. Do you think you could spare an hour to interview her with me?'

'Sure, happy to,' I said, as we walked back to the bar.

I started to feel more in control as he carried on talking about some upcoming meetings in London.

I tried to forget the phone call and felt better with the first sip of the champagne. Usually, my inbuilt Pakistani guilt wouldn't let me have more than one glass. That night though, I didn't say anything as Harry poured me another, even though my head was already light from having a glass of wine with the clients

The waitress arrived with a steaming bowl of chips.

'So, what do you think our global strategy should be for Max?'

We ate the chips and in-between sips of champagne, brainstormed investment options. Once we finished, I leaned back into the embrace of the soft velvet chair and closed my eyes. I felt a languid sense of peace, as if my mind had shut down.

'What a day,' I said.

'I don't want to pry, and you don't have to answer, but is everything OK at home?'

I looked at him.

'Yes. No. Oh, I don't know! All our conversations end in some kind of an argument these days. It's not Tom's fault, I know he's under a lot of stress but then so am I...'

I couldn't tell him that every time Tom spoke to me lately, it broke my heart. That I was becoming increasingly scared that our marriage wouldn't survive. I had thought that nothing could shake us. I thought I'd defied my childhood, and Farrah's pessimism about our ability to have successful marriages. What if what I had believed was compatibility and closeness was simply rubbing along nicely because we were busy with the children and nothing really bad had happened to us before now?

I wondered if Tom had only been caring and loving because I made such an effort to be perfect. When he got home from work, the children had been fed and watered, their problems already solved, by me. I was ready, with lipstick and Aqua di Parma, and dinner a deux accompanied by roses from the garden and a relaxing candle. I brushed away most disagreements, happy to give in to him. We had never argued like my parents because I had never let us argue. Until now.

'He seems to be a different person,' I said.

'Listen, I might be completely wrong here, but as your friend I have to mention this. Do you think he might be having an affair? I saw this happen with my friend. He was the one who cheated, but he lashed out at his wife, making her feel as if she'd done something wrong.'

'No! Tom would never do that to me.'

I shook my head several times, but inside I wasn't so sure. The old Tom, *my* Tom, would never have done that, but recently he had hurt me in lots of ways I could never have imagined. I didn't feel as certain as I tried to sound.

I shifted and the flap of my silk wrap dress slipped a little, exposing my thigh. Harry's eyes glanced at my leg then came back to my face.

'Good, because you don't deserve that. You're one of the most incredible people I've ever met.'

I swallowed. His eyes were moving over my whole face

and it felt as if his fingertips were stroking my skin. I looked down.

'You're probably right,' he sighed. 'He's acting like this because of the stress. I do understand what that can do to a marriage. My daughter Amber's had an eating disorder for two years and Julia and I haven't coped well with it. We've ended up arguing about how we should handle it, instead of pulling together. It's like we've suddenly become enemies.'

'I'm so sorry. How is Amber now?' I asked.

I could see the pain etched across his face, a look I'd never seen before, as if he had taken off a mask and set it aside. I knew that feeling of helplessness from Ahmed's illness. Just as he was about to reply, my phone started to buzz. We both looked down at it. It was Tom.

'Go ahead, answer it,' said Harry.

He sat up a little straighter, turning the strap of his watch around between his fingers.

I shook my head. 'It can wait.'

Tom was probably calling to offer a half-hearted apology but I wasn't ready to hear it yet. He had hurt me. This pitch had been such a huge success for me and he of all people knew how nervous I had been and how hard I had been working on it.

I thought of the countless times he'd called *me* over the years, to tell me about a deal he'd won, or a promotion or job offer. I had always whooped in delight, told him how proud I was and had been as happy for him as I would have been for myself. I wasn't going to let him off so easily this time. The phone stopped buzzing, then started again, until eventually it shuddered to a standstill.

A text flashed up: *Call me.*

'I'm sorry about this!' I said.

I turned the phone off and dropped it into my bag.

Who did Tom think he was? Half an hour ago it was 'too late' for me to call him and then, when he felt like unburdening his guilty conscience, he started harassing me.

I turned to face Harry.

'Marriage, huh?' he said.

'Seriously! Did you know that twenty years, the time I've been married, is the equivalent of a life term in prison? Surely, I should be allowed some time off for good behaviour? A sabbatical?' I said, smiling, trying to lighten the mood.

'I think I should get one too. We've been married fifteen years. We got married when Amber was two. I was waiting for my divorce from my first wife to come through.'

Julia had never mentioned an ex-wife and I didn't think anyone knew that Harry had been married before.

'It turned out well, though, because we had Amber there with us as our flower girl,' he said, smiling at the memory.

'How is she doing? I won't say a word to anyone, of course.'

He was quiet for a while, as if deciding whether to say anything.

'I know that, Fi, I trust you. It's just painful to talk about. She's better, but no one can tell us how the future will pan out. I don't know if she'll be able to go to university or get a job or get married, have children.'

My chest tightened. Poor girl. I didn't know what to say. I'd had no idea and I didn't think Sofia or the other girls knew either.

Harry spun his phone around and around on the table and lowered his eyelids, so that his dark lashes brushed against his cheeks.

'I haven't spoken about it to anyone before tonight. I don't want to put a downer on your celebration, though,' he said.

'It's fine, please,' I said.

I reached out and put my hand on his, to reassure him. Before I could move it away, he turned his hand so that our palms were touching. His fingers slipped through mine and gave a quick squeeze.

'Thank you,' he said.

The moment to move our hands apart came and went. Neither of us made the first move to do so. He looked at me. I could feel the hairs on my arms shiver.

The waitress came up and I moved my hand into my lap.

'We're having a laser light show on the rooftop starting in a few minutes, if you're interested?' said the waitress, clearing away our empty glasses.

'I love those!' I said and stood up.

I hadn't wanted to move my hand away and it had scared me, so it was best if we left the table.

'Laser show it is then.' Harry smiled. 'You do get excited about the strangest things.'

'I'm easily pleased,' I smiled. 'I laugh at your jokes, don't I?'

'Hey!'

We laughed as we walked to the lift; the moment had passed and I took a deep breath, grateful for the narrow escape.

When the lift door shut, Harry moved so he was standing

in front of me. I stepped back a little and looked down. When he spoke, his voice was deeper, with no hint of a smile.

'Fi, we need to talk about what just happened.'

Sixty

I had to look up. My heart was racing. I didn't know what to say. The green specks in his eyes flickered and I looked back down at my hands which were clasped together. He carried on speaking.

'When I held your hand just now, I didn't want to let go. I don't want to be disrespectful, but I think you felt it too. I love the time we spend together. I don't have to pretend with you. I can be myself. It felt so good to finally talk about Amber. I really like you.'

He took my hand and held it. I knew I should pull it away but it was as if I was paralysed. It felt good, and I didn't want to stop feeling like that. He had been so kind, had trusted me enough to open up about his daughter. If I heard any doubts, I silenced them. This was just a moment, one single moment in twenty years.

My stomach somersaulted but I wasn't sure if that was the lift shooting up to the rooftop or the fact that Harry was squeezing my hand tight and it felt as if that was how it was meant to be. I realised how much I missed the affection and attention that Tom had withdrawn. His love had been everything, all my happiness and all my protection. The best part of my day was going to sleep next to him and seeing his face when I woke up. Now, all that was gone and I was left wondering if it had been as solid as I had believed. As Harry squeezed my hand, my sadness about Tom was pushed out of my mind. I felt Harry's skin on mine and I let myself forget everything else.

The lift doors opened straight onto the terrace, and I stepped into the warm, dark night. As we stood amongst the crowd, Harry moved his hand to my back, just above my waist. His fingertips lingered and started stroking my back. I refused to think about what was happening. My breaths came faster and I was grateful for the noise and the dark, so he couldn't see.

The show started, and blades of neon pink, blue and green criss-crossed the sky, as if fighting each other. The music pounded and Harry moved his arm to circle my waist, singing along to a David Bowie song. He knew all the words and told me to join in, and soon we were singing at the top of our lungs. We craned our necks to look up at the lights and then down at the skyscrapers glittering below. I felt as if we were on a spaceship, hurtling away from reality.

There was a sudden surge of people behind us and Harry's arm tightened around me.

'Let's move back a little,' he shouted above the music and led me away from the crowd. He was still holding my hand as we stood back from the others, in the shadows. He tipped up my chin with two fingertips.

'I've never met anyone like you, Fi, I think I'm falling for you.'

'Harry, I like you too, but we're friends...'

'I know, I know. But tell me honestly, doesn't it feel good when we spend time together? I can't talk like this to anyone else, not even Julia. I know you felt the same downstairs. What were the chances that you and I would ever meet and get close like this? If you and Tom are that good together, then why are you standing here with me?'

He was right about everything. He *did* make me feel good, I looked forward to seeing him every day. I didn't know what to think. I took a step back until I was leaning against the wall.

He came to stand in front of me and put his hands on the wall either side of me but made no attempt to touch me. I looked up into his eyes. He didn't move. I was breathing fast, watching his mouth. He started to bring his face towards mine, as if in slow motion. I closed my eyes and then he was kissing me. He kept his hands on the wall and I started to kiss him back, feeling his mouth, arching towards him. My head started to spin. His arms went around me and we kept kissing. He parted my lips with his, pushed his tongue gently into my mouth and squeezed my breast. My eyes snapped open. What was I doing? I saw Tom's face and imagined him seeing me with Harry. It would break him. I loved Tom. I knew that. I pulled away and put my hands up against Harry's chest.

'What is it? Do you want to go to my room?' he whispered, breathing into my face, stroking my hair, and pushing it back gently. He gazed into my eyes.

I shook my head. 'I'm sorry. I can't do this.'

I pushed him away and stepped into the middle of the rooftop.

'What?' He looked confused.

'I love my husband, Harry,' I gasped, and covered my face with my hands.

'If you love Tom, then what just happened with us? You know you wouldn't have kissed me unless you felt something. Fi, I want to be with you and I know you want it too. We can't ignore how we feel.'

I opened my eyes. His face was lit up by the flashing lights of the laser show and I could see that he was smiling. His fingers touched my cheek. I took a step back. His hand fell away. He frowned.

'I'm married. It's wrong. And it would kill Tom if he ever found out. I can't do this, Harry. I think we both got carried away.'

His smile vanished and he glared at me. He shouted above the music but I thought he would have shouted even if we had been in a silent room.

'You were also married five minutes ago when you had your tongue in my mouth! What's changed suddenly?'

It was as if his features had rearranged themselves. He didn't even look like himself as he spat out his words.

'Were you just leading me on? I thought you were different, but you're nothing but a fucking prick-tease!'

I turned and ran. The lift was around the corner. I waited, pressing all the buttons repeatedly. I hoped he wouldn't follow me. He didn't.

Sixty-One

I jumped into a taxi, still afraid that Harry might appear. He had spoken to me with such contempt. But he was drunk, surely? He would never have said those things to me otherwise. And he was right to be angry. I had held his hand, kissed him, let him touch my breast. I had thrust myself against him. If I hadn't thought about Tom at that moment, would I have gone up to his room, and got naked and let him fuck me? That's the way things had been heading.

However much I liked Harry, I couldn't believe how close I had come to being unfaithful. I had gone against all my beliefs, against everything my parents had taught me, and everything I had taught my children. What had I become? I had been prepared to cheat on Tom, to commit adultery. I had kissed another man, and I had betrayed Tom again. My breaths were shaky, like sobs without tears.

None of this would have happened if I hadn't spent that money. Every lie I'd told had led me here, to a point where I couldn't recognise myself. I had told so many lies that I had become a lie myself. I didn't know who I really was anymore. I had to stop all this and get back to Tom.

In the cab I scrambled for my phone and switched it on. I needed my marriage back and this was not the way to do it. I wanted to hear Tom's voice. I would listen to his apology, give him mine for calling him a shit and hanging up the phone. We couldn't lose each other.

As soon as the phone came on, I saw a stream of missed calls from home and from Tom's mobile. The phone pinged several times as multiple texts flashed up on the screen, one after the other, all from Tom.

Can you call me please? We need to talk.

Then, *Where are you? I've called your hotel but no answer. Please call as soon as you get this message.*

Finally, the latest text, sent twenty minutes ago:

Darling, please call me whenever you get this message. Don't worry about the time in London. I love you.

I fumbled with the phone and he answered on the first ring.

'What is it? What's wrong?' I asked.

'It's Baba, Faiza.'

I didn't want to hear any more. I held my breath, wanting the world to stop.

'He's alive. He's in intensive care at St George's. It's his heart. He's getting the best care, but it's probably best if you come home.'

Sixty-Two

I prayed for Baba throughout the flight back, unable to sleep at all and took a taxi straight from Heathrow to the hospital. It was early in the morning and Tom was waiting for me outside the ward.

He folded me in his arms, stroking my back and spoke against my hair. 'He's stable, a little better and out of ICU. We're just waiting for the consultant.'

I wiped my tears but more kept coming. He kissed the top of my head.

'I can't lose my Baba, Tom.'

I saw Ami first, slumped down in a plastic chair by Baba's bed, a doctor standing nearby.

My father's eyes were closed, his face hidden under an oxygen mask. A monitor screeched and beeped next to him, with tubes and leads sprouting out from all over his body. The gown had slipped off one of his shoulders.

I stopped, not wanting to go forwards, not wanting to believe this was real. Ami's eyes were closed and her lips moved silently as she prayed, counting off the beads on her turquoise tasbeeh with quivering hands. Her face crumpled when she saw me and I bent down and put my arms around her.

Then, I forced myself to turn around and face Baba. I went up to the bed and took his hand, taking care not to touch the cannula. Tom put his arm around me, and I leaned into him.

The doctor, a cardiologist, led us into the corridor.

'He needs to have heart bypass surgery but because of your father's age, you need to weigh up the risks. It's open-heart surgery. Without it, though, he's at risk of a fatal heart attack. We call this the "widow-maker" blockage.'

My eyes darted to Ami, then back at the doctor, frowning at the phrase.

'I thought bypass surgery could be done via keyhole these days?' said Tom.

'Yes, but I'm afraid we can't guarantee that on the NHS, and then there is a waiting list too. We'll do our best and keep an eye on him in the meantime.'

Sixty-Three

Once Baba was home, I took him to a private surgeon who specialised in keyhole surgery and could do the operation within the week, but Baba did not want to pay.

'We have the best health service in the world, despite its problems. I'll just do it on the NHS.'

'I asked Mrs Khan's son, who's a cardiologist, and he said you should have keyhole too, and make sure it's a senior consultant. They can't guarantee that on the NHS. We'll tell them we're OAPs and ask for a discount,' said Ami.

'Yes, Baba, and the waiting list is too long if you don't go private.'

'I'm afraid it's not that simple; even if I did want to have the surgery privately, which I don't, I haven't got that kind of money,' said Baba.

My eyes filled with tears and I looked down at my hands.

'Baba, you have enough money for the surgery, OK? My bonds matured weeks ago but I haven't had time to put the money back in your account. I'll do it tomorrow.'

This surgery could be the difference between life and

death for Baba. Despite that, there had been no request for the money and no reproach that I had taken it. I would put the money back, so he could have the operation.

As I drove home, I was suddenly uneasy. I had no idea if the money was all still in our account. I knew that my salary had not covered everything and I just hoped Tom hadn't spent any of it yet.

I tried to log on to the online banking site, but I'd never used it before, and I couldn't remember my login. After a few attempts, I was locked out. There was no way to check the balance that night.

I was the first person at the bank counter the next morning. I put my debit card in the machine and asked to see the balance. The cashier wrote it down on a piece of paper and slipped it to me under the partition. There was nothing left in the account.

I swallowed hard and forced myself to speak.

'But there was over fifteen thousand pounds in here!'

'I'm sorry, this is the current balance.' The cashier was looking at me warily, unsure what I would do next.

'I want the statements, please, for the last three months.'

I grabbed them as he held them out to me. There was a transfer of fifteen thousand into another account four weeks ago.

'That's your savings account. Nothing to worry about then. There's a direct debit set up to transfer three thousand into the current account on the thirtieth of every month.'

'So, the money's still there? I can use it?'

I transferred the money back to my parents' account. Now, all our accounts were empty.

Sixty-Four

Mr Zhang, the consultant, nodded towards Baba through the glass partition.

'It was very wise to proceed as we did. If we'd waited, it might have been too late.'

Once he'd left, I leaned against the wall. My ankles were the only things holding me up and they trembled. My handbag dropped to the floor with a thud.

'*If we'd waited it might have been too late.*'

Not a single soul knew the danger I'd put Baba in by taking his money. I was lucky that the money was all still in our account. If we had already spent it, I would not have been able to give it back. Baba would have stayed on the waiting list, which was twelve weeks long. He wouldn't have made it.

I bought a cup of tea and a croissant for Ami from the hospital café before I went to work. Naila was coming that afternoon, to check in on Ami. I folded her scarf into a square and placed the makeshift cushion in the small of her back on the plastic chair.

'I texted Farrah and she's flying in on Thursday,' I said.

I had told Farrah that we had to stop blaming our parents for messing up our lives, and take responsibility ourselves. She knew Baba had almost died and something had clicked. She was coming home. Her ex, Shahed, had been coming to see Baba in hospital and I'd texted her that he had asked about her. *Shahed still loves you...* I'd written.

Before I left the hospital, I rubbed Baba's leg under the regulation white sheet. *I'm so sorry.*

I bent down to kiss Ami's soft, crinkled cheek.

'Khuda Hafiz Ami.'

'You're such a good girl.' Ami kissed my hand as I was leaving. 'You and Tom have saved us. You know he takes us to Tooting every week, and he put the blind up in the kitchen when it fell? He's bringing me lunch later. You know, Faiza, he's not my son-in-law, he's my son.'

I ran through the labyrinth of corridors thinking about Tom taking Ami and Baba shopping, carrying in their bags, and probably making them a cup of tea. He'd never even told me. *Tom* hadn't changed. He was still the kind, solid, caring man he had always been – I had been the one who had messed up. While Tom had been looking after the children and my parents, I had been kissing Harry.

Outside, it had started to drizzle. By the time I got to the car park the wind had blown my hair into a tangle and left my face numb. The rain got heavier as I drove home. I turned on the radio, but no amount of political discussion or debate could drown out the clamour in my head.

Now that Baba's money was gone and my salary was not yet in the account, the bank would send Tom a notification when the mortgage payment bounced later. It was due any day. My hands were clammy on the steering wheel. He would have to be told. About the emergency fund, the Post Office account, the money from Ami and Baba to cover my tracks. I slammed on the brakes as the lights turned red.

The wipers grated on the windscreen: tell him, tell him, tell him. If I told him one thing, though, I would have to tell him everything. The driver behind me pressed his horn and I lurched away.

At the roundabout, I didn't take the exit for home. I couldn't bring myself to. I kept driving around in circles, missing the exit a few times before making up my mind and driving off to the station instead. I couldn't face Tom.

Sixty-Five

The station car park was empty. The rain was hammering down. I had to catch the train to work, but it was too early. The sound of the rain began to lull my thoughts. No one knew where I was and, in my makeshift cocoon, away from everyone, I felt safer than I had in months. I could have been anywhere in the world.

Fat raindrops exploded then disappeared on the windscreen: a million tiny waterbombs. I leaned my head against the side window. Rain ran down the windscreen in vertical tracks like an endless stream of tears. It reminded me of my trips to the car wash with Baba when I was a child. I imagined Baba finding out that I had lied to them to get the money. Then finding out about everything else.

I had failed Baba. I had failed them all. Everyone who loved me and trusted me, who thought I was someone to be relied on. Tom, my parents, my children... I had destroyed everything good. I closed my eyes and listened to the rain falling endlessly. I had nothing left to give them.

I started to shiver. I was still on New York time, and had

spent my nights praying for Baba's recovery and my days at the hospital with Ami, looking at Baba's heart monitor. My body ached but, at the same time, felt numb. I closed my eyes. I wanted to stay in the car forever, or just disappear. I thought about Sofia, Ahmed, Alex. No, I couldn't give up. I sat up and wiped my face. I still had a chance to put things right for my children.

I was meeting Harry and Sergio at the GlobalCorp offices at ten, three hours from now. This was the pitch when they would decide whether to offer me the permanent role. If the GlobalCorp CEO wanted me to manage his portfolio, it meant at least another two years for me at HH.

I took out my notebook and a pen, trying to remember the outline of my presentation, but the more I tried to retrieve the information, the more it slipped away. Perhaps I could concentrate better at the office.

Sixty-Six

At the station I walked towards the far end of the platform; it was quicker to get out at Waterloo from there. My head was down, braced against the wind slapping my face. I tried to remember the details of the GlobalCorp portfolio again, but all I could think about was Tom's face when he saw the bank balance.

The board started flashing: all trains into Waterloo were delayed. I might not even have time to print my report. I wouldn't win the pitch, or get the job. I heard my voice echo in my head, over and over again: you've destroyed everything.

I pushed my hands, balled up tightly, into my pockets, and stopped for a minute, trying to still my racing heartbeat. My eyes travelled to the tracks in front of me. There was a green salt-and-vinegar crisp packet lying between the steel tracks, Ahmed's favourite. As I kept looking, more things started to come into focus, as if my eyes were adjusting to the dark. I saw a train ticket, a clump of beige elastic bands, a biro, a palm-sized square of blue plastic. A tiny yellow and red tube caught my eye. It was the lip balm Sofia used. I remembered reading that the train tracks were live, just touching them would electrocute you.

The trains were delayed further. I wouldn't make it in time to prepare for the meeting. My mind emptied, as if my thoughts had been tipped out, and I felt everything seep out of me.

I walked to the opposite platform, the one someone had jumped from back in May, and examined the debris on the other tracks. I could see nothing, not a speck. As I was searching for clues between the rocks, my view was suddenly obliterated by a flash of blue and red, juddering past me. It was so close that I felt the vibrations in my jaw as a train raced past. I didn't have time to step back and the force made my eyes sting and pushed my hair back, as if someone was jerking it from behind.

The train was gone in a second and the platform was silent and still again. It was almost as if it had not been there. This must be why people chose this platform and this train for their suicides. Everything would be over in a second. No wait for pills to dissolve in your stomach and seep into your blood stream. No messiness or inaccuracy of cutting arteries. The pain of that would be terrible. No well-meaning stranger jumping into the freezing Thames to rescue you, if you had gathered your courage to jump from London Bridge. I could see why the train would be the best option. The metal track would hurt as you fell; it would be hard and cold. But you would only fall a millisecond before the train would hit... and then it would be over.

'Please stand away from the edge of platform six. The next train is not scheduled to stop at this station.'

319

The warning boomed out from the loudspeakers. The next fast train was due in a minute. I saw a guard out of the corner of my eye. They were paranoid about anyone being on this platform now. I walked back to platform five before he came and asked me to move.

My train finally had an arrival time: due in ten minutes. I heard the fast train thunder past behind me without stopping. The guard had disappeared, so I walked back to platform six.

I thought about the people who had stood in this same spot. The distance behind the safety of the yellow line painted away from the edge of the platform and the tracks was around two feet. That was all that it took. To stop everything. Peace.

An image of Tom and me, divorced and alone, flashed in my mind. I had left the children unprotected. My father could have died because of my lies. I had let everyone down. I was no good to anyone and now I had lost my chance to put things right by getting the permanent job. A thought burst through like an answer: There was still my life insurance; Tom would get it. I could return what I had stolen.

The fast train appeared at the bend. All sounds faded away and I watched the front as it approached; it was hard, heavy, solid. My chest fluttered, then pounded. I stood on the yellow line. I had to run forwards. The train got closer. I had to do it now. But my feet wouldn't move. The train thundered past. I dropped my head. I couldn't even do this for my family... Another train was due in two minutes. My heart was still racing.

Then my phone started to ring, urgent and grating in my

coat pocket. It was Sofia. She never called. I was immediately worried. My children! I started to shake and stepped back from the yellow line.

'Mum, tell Dad I can have Coco Pops on Fridays! He's saying I have to have porridge.'

It was Alex.

'Alex? Why are you calling from Sofia's phone?'

'I'm hiding from Dad and Sofia's in the shower but I know her pin! Can you tell Dad I can have Coco Pops?'

I sank down on a bench. The sounds of the station were seeping back: the morning chatter of schoolchildren, loudspeaker announcements about the arrival of trains and the need to be vigilant if you saw anything suspicious on the train. I felt as if I were regaining consciousness after fainting. How could I have thought that my mangled body, squashed to mulch on a train track, would in any way make things better for my children? I started to shake, my teeth chattering.

'OK,' I managed to say.

'Wait, you can tell Dad now!'

I hung up. I looked at the steps going up to the exit. *I needed Tom.* I started to go up, then stopped. Someone swore at me as they bumped into me. I walked back down to platform five. I'd catch the train to Vauxhall instead and meet Sam. I needed someone to hold me and keep me safe. I knew that she would call Tom, though.

The Waterloo train was pulling in. I rushed towards it, swallowed up in the crowd. There was no need to tell anyone. There was nothing to tell anyway. It had just been a second of madness. All that stress. I felt ice cold despite the muggy heat of the carriage. The image of the train and the tracks kept flashing in front of my eyes. Fear crawled up my chest, into my jaw and along the nerve endings of my face. My lips were numb.

The people around me would never guess what I had thought, even for a split second, just a few minutes ago. I bit my lip. How could I have contemplated leaving my children, and in that way? Suicide was a sin, I knew that. There would have been no peace for me. God would not have forgiven me. No one would.

Sixty-Seven

When I got to the office, I sat down at my desk and
turned on my computer. I tried to look at the GlobalCorp
documents, but I was still numb. Harry's door was open
and I needed to tell him that I couldn't do the presentation.
I hadn't seen him since I had run away after kissing him in
New York, but he had texted me once he found out about
Baba.

*I misread the signals, Fi. I'm sorry about the things I said.
I was horribly drunk, but that's no excuse. Please can we
forget about New York? I hope your father is better. Don't
worry about work. I hope we are still friends. Harry.*

Since then, he had texted me to ask after Baba and then a
couple of times to check some details about the GlobalCorp
account. His texts were proper and friendly and I told
myself that if I had made a mistake in kissing him, he could
have made a mistake too. I was grateful that it would not
have any impact on my job. I felt embarrassed but reassured
that we had moved past New York.

I knocked on his door.

'Good morning! You're in early. I was just going to email you about the slides. How's your father?'

I stayed standing inside his door, unable to speak.

'Has something happened to him?'

He led me to the sofa by the window and sat next to me in a chair. He leaned forward and was about to reach for my hand, but then linked his hands in front of him.

'Fi?'

I swallowed.

'My father's fine, thank you.'

I kept looking down. My hands were writhing in my lap, clutching each other, as if independently of me. I wanted to scream.

'I can't do the pitch.'

I struggled to get the words out. Harry was still a director. There was no valid excuse to miss a pitch as important as this one. I may as well have been handing in my resignation.

'No problem. I can do it. Just email it to me. I know how hard you've worked on the pitch. Don't worry about the meeting today – I'm more worried about you. What's the matter?'

The train track flashed in my head. I saw the yellow line. My shoulders started shaking. Harry stood up and came back with some water.

'Look, you've had a difficult week, but your dad's going to be all right. Are you worried about what happened in New York? Don't be. You were right. It was a moment of madness, the curse of the business trip. We just got carried away. Let's forget it ever happened – and I promise you that it won't affect your position here.'

I hung my head down.

'What's the matter? You can tell me anything, you know that.'

I didn't know if that was true. He was my boss and Julia's husband. He knew other parents at Brookwood High who knew me. His hand had been on my breast. He could hold whatever I told him against me when they decided on offering me the job. I had no choice, though. I had to get the words out of my body.

That was how Harry's office, with its views of St Paul's and grey linen sofas, became my confessional.

'I tried to kill myself today.'

It was a whisper. Harry leaned forwards. He hadn't heard me, I thought with relief. It had been a mistake to say it out loud. I had spoken the words. That was enough.

'What happened? What did you do?'

It was too late. Now I had to carry on. He took my icy hand and rubbed it briskly.

'I'm sorry, that came out wrong. It was a split-second craziness and I didn't do anything. I'm not hurt. It's just that a thought came into my head that I could jump in front of the next fast train while I was waiting at the platform and it frightened me. It's probably just the stress of my father's surgery, and the fact that I haven't slept since I got back.'

He dropped my hand and stood up. His voice was deep when he spoke.

'Are you all right? I'll call Tom. Give me his number.'

When he mentioned Tom, I started to cry.

'No, please, I don't want him to know! I just got spooked because I had that thought. This won't affect my permanent job will it? Please, please don't fire me.'

'Of course I won't fire you. And we don't need to call

Tom if you don't want. I'm glad you told me. It can be our secret. But why would you even think about harming yourself? You're devoted to your family, to your children. What's happened?'

He sat down next to me and waited.

Then, through my sobs, I told him everything.

Sixty-Eight

'I'm going to transfer £50,000 into your account,' said Harry when I'd finished.

He grabbed his phone and stood up. The initial rush of letting everything pour out had now settled into a cold pit of shame. Tears trickled down my face and onto my neck. This was a huge amount of money. What did he want in return?

He sat back down opposite me. 'Fi? I'm doing this as your friend. Nothing else, OK?'

I wondered if I had spoken my fears out loud. I didn't think so.

'I'm sorry about my behaviour in New York. Neither of us wants to risk our marriages, and I don't want to lose our friendship. Please let me do this for you.'

'Harry, I can't take that sort of money from you. It's too much. I...'

'I have the money; you know I do, and plenty more. I can't just stand by and do nothing, not after what happened – almost happened – today.'

He passed me a tissue from a box on the coffee table and I wiped my face. The air conditioner hummed. I hadn't asked him for the money. He had offered. I would have done the same for a friend, wouldn't I?

'Just give me your account details. The money will go through immediately.'

Harry had been my champion and my friend since I had started the job. The only reason I was hesitating was because of New York, but he seemed to regret that as much as I did. I had told him about deceiving my husband, tricking my parents out of their savings, and all my thoughts as I waited on platform six. He had continued to pat my back without missing a beat, as if soothing a child. I thought about the children: Harry's money could keep their world intact.

His tone was brisk. 'You don't have to deal with this alone. Let me help.'

I ran my fingers through my hair and looked up. My voice was hoarse.

'I'll pay you back, I promise, Harry. As soon as I get my bonus. Thank you!'

He exhaled, as if he'd been holding his breath.

'There's no rush. Wait until you guys get back on your feet. Now, give me your bank details.'

He tapped the banking app on his phone and, within a minute, the money was in my account. It was like magic. The money that I had spent months chasing, agonising over, the money that had almost destroyed my marriage, taken away my peace of mind and even made me think the unthinkable that morning, had been at Harry's disposal in an instant.

All he had done was place one fingertip on his phone screen...

'The money's in your account,' he said.

I felt at once untethered and lost, light-headed without the weight of worry that had held me captive for months. I needed to be alone. I excused myself and walked slowly to the ladies, holding on to the walls as I made my way down the corridor, clutching my bag in one hand.

I took out my make-up case and looked in the mirror. My eyelids were twice their usual size and mascara streaks ran like black scratches, right down to my chin; my lip was split, as if I had been punched. I needed to erase any evidence of my tears before the others arrived. My hand trembled as I tried to unzip the make-up case. I gave up and held onto the sides of the sink, gripping the cold ceramic. I leaned forwards and looked in the mirror. My eyes stared back at me.

'It's true,' I told my mirror-self. 'It's really happened.'

I closed my eyes. The new reality seeped into my head, expanding and exploding. It moved down my face, into my chest, down my arms and then my legs, dissolving the tension that had burned in every nerve ending for months. My body fizzed. I opened my eyes, and then, I smiled. I said a silent 'Thank you' to God, promising to say my prayers when I got home.

When I got back to my desk, Harry placed a bowl of Teresa's Rice Krispies in front of me. There was a thick layer of sugar sitting on top.

'Eat this up like a good girl,' he said.

'Thank you, Harry. Look, you know I can't tell Tom about this, but if he knew, he'd be so grateful too. You've been so kind. I still can't believe it. Thank you for doing this.'

'It's only a bowl of Rice Krispies, Fi.' He winked and we both laughed.

The others wouldn't be in for another hour and I started to work on the presentation. As I went through the slides, I knew exactly what I needed to add and I felt a tingle of excitement as I tapped in the figures. The pitch was good and I had decided to attend it after all, even though Harry would present it. Everything seemed possible now that the money was in the account.

I was printing the slides twenty minutes later when Harry came out, carrying his raincoat. He called out to me as he went past my desk, 'I'll meet you and Sergio at GlobalCorp. I have another meeting now.'

I waved goodbye. He stopped when he was almost at the door, then walked back quickly.

'Damn, I forgot some figures I need for this meeting. I've turned off my computer and my Uber's here. Do you mind just looking it up on your computer for me, please?'

'Of course,' I said.

I brought up the documents that he needed on the screen while he stood behind me, scanning the numbers.

'There's too much here to jot down. Do you mind emailing it to me? Just put "Info from Fi – confidential" in the subject, so I can find it easily.'

I emailed it as fast as I could. I was surprised he'd asked me to label it confidential, but I didn't get a chance to ask him why.

'It's sent,' I said.

'Thank you,' he said, and left.

I was relieved that I'd felt no awkwardness or attraction between us when I was in his office. Whatever I had felt towards him had disappeared the minute Tom had pulled me into his arms at the hospital. I did not want anyone else, I never had, really. I had just been missing Tom and the way we used to be.

I took out my phone and texted him: *I love you.*

Ivan came in at 8.30 and started to tell me about his Tinder date the night before. I laughed as he described how the girl had played footsie a little too energetically under the table and had ended up hitting a sensitive part of his anatomy by mistake. As he went off to make some tea, I realised that, for the first time in months, I'd been able to talk to someone without thinking about the emergency fund at the same time.

Later that night in bed, Tom opened up his arms and I snuggled onto his shoulder. His hand rested on my arm, stroking it gently. A tear rolled out of my eye and fell on his T-shirt.

'He's going to be fine. The doctors say he should be home soon,' said Tom.

'I know. I just love you all so much, that's all.'

'That's good, because we love you too!'

He smiled then shifted and picked up the stereo remote. He put on the first song that he had played for me, the day after our wedding, 'Heartbeat' by the Pet Shop Boys. I remembered the sheer excitement of waking up together, married. We had done it. We had overcome all the objections and pessimistic predictions.

It felt the same now. We had been through so much since Tom lost his job, but here we were, lying together, listening to the Pet Shop Boys, twenty years later.

I fell asleep and didn't wake up until the alarm rang the next morning.

Once Baba was up to it, I took the children to see him. He was recovering well in hospital. He sat up in bed, with Ahmed on a chair near him, as they played Rummy.

'I used to play this with my grandfather. I've been playing it for years,' said Baba, 'but your brain is young and quick. You'll beat your Nana!'

Ahmed smiled. 'I'm afraid I will, Nana!'

'Look at this one, Nani,' said Sofia. 'This dress is perfect.'

Ami was sitting in an armchair, with Sofia perching on one arm of the chair, and Farrah on the other. Sofia was showing them wedding dresses on her phone. She'd found a Pakistani designer's Instagram account. Shahed and Tom, along with Alex, had gone to get some takeaway from Tooting for us for later, to celebrate Shahed and Farrah fixing a date for the wedding.

'Farrah Khala will look so good in red,' said Sofia. 'How are you going to do your hair?'

Ami reached out and took Farrah's hand.

'I'm so glad Baba is still alive to see you get married,' she said.

Farrah smiled.

'Ami, it's good he's still alive, period. Not just for the shadi!' I said.

We all laughed.

'Have you and Tom started saving for Sofia's wedding? It's your responsibility. Our weddings cost a lot, you know,' said Ami.

'Sofia is half-English, Ami. Maybe she can just have a nice little registry office affair instead of a big fat Pakistani wedding, and Tom and I can use the money to go on holiday!'

As we all joked, I looked around, thankful that, after everything that had happened, we had made it to this place.

But it couldn't have happened without Harry's generosity and I would always be grateful to him.

I tried to ignore the fact that I was still lying. Tom didn't know where I'd got the money. Soon, though, I would have my bonus and return Harry's money, then everything would be back as it should have been. It was only a matter of a couple of weeks.

Sixty-Nine

'Are you coming to Lizzie's anniversary party?' said Sam.

I wrinkled my nose and shook my head. We had managed to catch the same train home from Waterloo and, even more miraculously, found two seats together.

'I really want to but I'm not sure.'

'Oh, come on! It'll do you good, both of you. Naila and Tariq are coming, so Tom will have a buddy there. You and Tom have isolated yourselves. It's time to get back out there.'

'Well, Naila did say that I needed to come as her "brown person plus-one" so she doesn't feel like there's a lone diversity tick hanging over hers and Tariq's heads at the party.' I smiled. 'And Stewart has told Tom he's going to introduce him to some friends who might have an opening at their company so he's quite keen.'

'Fab. Come then!'

She offered me a crisp from her packet.

'Mmm. There's one more thing I'm worried about, though. Harry and Julia are going to be there,' I said.

I'd told Sam all about New York, but not about the money Harry had lent me. There was no reason to ever think about the emergency fund again and I wanted to forget it had ever happened.

'It's too risky to be with Julia and Harry together. They'll find out that I know them both and that I've been hiding it from them.'

'Well, at some point it's bound to come out. Your kids are at the same school, for goodness' sake.'

I shook my head.

'It's not just that. Even if Tom doesn't know that I kissed Harry as a mistake, introducing them together feels unfair to Tom. It's humiliating for him. Harry and I will know what happened but Tom would have no idea.'

'Ah, I see. That might be awkward, but you and Harry have agreed to forget about that. Besides, nothing actually happened, did it? All the more reason to act absolutely normal, as if New York was just an ordinary business trip. And so what if Julia finds out you're working for her husband? It's not a crime.'

'OK, we'll come,' I said. 'Is James in town? It will be nice to see him too.'

'Yes, he's coming. His awful brother Rupert is going to be there too, but I hope we can avoid him. There will be enough people there.'

'We can form a ring of steel around you two,' I smiled.

'That might not be a bad idea!'

I still felt uneasy but perhaps it would be one less thing to worry about once Julia and Harry knew the connection – and once Tom and Harry met, it would confirm that nothing that terrible had happened in New York, and any discomfort around it would be dispelled. I was crossing out secrets one by one and each one made me feel lighter.

I had to find a way to let Harry know that I was also going to be at Lizzie's party, so that it didn't look like a big deal when he saw me there. I still wouldn't tell him that I knew Julia. Not yet.

The next day at work, as I sat in Harry's office, I said, 'It's such a small world, I didn't realise you knew my friend Lizzie and her husband Stewart. When she found out I was working at HH she said that one of her friends is a Director there!'

When the inevitable moment came at the party, when Julia realised that I worked for Harry and Harry discovered that I knew Julia, I would simply have to pretend that I had no idea about the connection until then. It was too late to backtrack now.

As for Harry showing me Julia's photograph, it was perfectly plausible that I hadn't paid attention. I was meeting a Director for the first time, who had also turned out to be the man who had flirted with me in the lift. I wouldn't necessarily have examined the photograph of yet another blonde corporate wife in much detail. I had planned how I would react at the party. My pleasantly surprised face, the shake of my head and a delighted squeal of, 'Wow, this is incredible! I can't believe you're married to Julia. I had no idea!'

Seventy

September

I was going to the party straight from work, so Harry had offered to give me a lift and I took my outfit to the office that morning. My friends had gone to Butterfly and clogged up my WhatsApp with photographs, asking which dress to choose and trying to persuade me to join them. I'd resisted the urge. Something had shifted inside me. I felt happier to have the money in the bank than spend it on a new dress. It felt strange, but good.

Instead of going shopping, I had taken out one of Ami's saris which she had worn when she was pregnant with me, over forty years ago. It was red Chantilly lace and I had found an old red sari blouse of mine that fitted fine, once I'd let the sides out a little. I wouldn't normally have worn this to one of my white friends' parties, opting instead for a dress from Whistles or Joseph, but wearing the sari had meant that I would spend nothing. I hoped this group of friends knew me well enough now not to be alienated by my wearing a sari. There was always a chance, though, that some of them, especially the guests who hadn't met me before, would think that I was some kind of religious fundamentalist, even though my blouse was backless, with barely-there spaghetti straps.

The Dragon said I could use her office to get dressed and when I emerged, wearing my sari and feeling unusually tall in my nude Jimmy Choo sandals, I was greeted by cheers and clapping. I felt embarrassed, but I had no choice. I had to walk across the open plan office. I held my clutch bag tight against my chest and pushed my hair back from my face. I'd straightened it into a sleek sheet myself, instead of spending money on a blow-dry, and I tried to compose my face so that it didn't betray my discomfort.

I would have liked to slip away unnoticed. The only person I couldn't wait to show myself to was Tom. I hadn't worn a sari for years and I wanted to see his face when I found him at the party; and later, I wanted him to unwrap the sari from my body. It felt as if we had become separated while out for a walk in a foreign city and, after a frantic search, had found each other again. I didn't want to get lost ever again.

'Not bad, I suppose,' said Ivan, shrugging his shoulders, then he laughed. 'You look very beautiful.'

'Thank you, guys,' I said to the people looking at me from the other teams as well.

'I love your sari,' said Sabine. She came up to feel the lace between her fingers. 'French, non?'

'Oui!'

To divert attention from myself, I started to tell them the story behind the sari and how Baba had bought it for Ami in Paris before I was born. As I spoke, I sensed a movement behind me. I looked around. Harry, stood in the corner, watching in silence, his eyes like stones, unprepared to be caught out. I turned to face him, feeling embarrassed. I had draped my long hair forwards to one side of my face, and my back was almost completely bare.

'I'm sorry, Harry. I hope I haven't kept you waiting?'

His expression changed. He smiled.

'Not at all. I only just got off a conference call.'

A black Mercedes was waiting and Harry's driver, Rob, opened my door. Once I was in the car, all my worries which I had stacked away with logical explanations about how it would be fine for Julia, Harry, Tom and me to be in the same room, came crashing back. I tried to slow my breathing, telling myself I had to keep my game face on, and that once I got over this hurdle, things would only get better. At least I knew what to expect, unlike the others, and so I could make sure I stayed calm.

The sun hadn't quite set as we drove along the Embankment and I watched the bridges along the Thames as we sped past them. We turned onto Albert Bridge. Tiny lights studded the bridge like gems and glittered above us. As a child I had called this the fairy-tale bridge and always asked Baba to cross the Thames there when we drove into London. The sunset was streaked with pink and City skyscrapers stood out against it in the distance, the Shard standing taller than the rest.

I texted Tom: *Can't wait to see you.*

I smiled as he messaged me straight back: *Love you.*

Harry was watching.

'Sorry, I'm just letting Tom know we're on our way.'

I regretted mentioning Tom. At the end of the day, I was still in a car with my boss.

'Sergio and I are meeting GlobalCorp again next week. He said that I have "earned my bonus"! I'm going to start paying you back once I get it.'

'I don't want your money,' he said.

He sounded strange and I looked out of the window in silence. Perhaps I had to stop pestering him about paying off my debt. He pressed a button on his door and the tinted glass partition swished up between us and the driver.

'Is everything OK?' I asked.

'No!'

He seemed angry but I didn't know why.

'Do you want to talk about it? Can I help you? Is it something at work?'

'Yes, yes and yes, to all three. In fact, you're the only one who *can* help.'

It had grown darker outside and his face was in the shadows. I looked out of the window, giving him time to reply, so I didn't see him move, and before I could even register what had happened, his hand pushed down between my legs. I jumped and cried out. His hand was heavy on my crotch and he started to rub the dip between my thighs over the material of my sari.

'Stop! Get off, Harry!'

I tried to push him away but his arm was stiff, immovable. He dipped his fingers deeper, pressing down. I pushed my thighs together and dug my nails into his hand. Still he carried on, pressing harder. I thought that he was going to tear Ami's sari.

'Stop this, Harry! Have you gone mad? I'm going to tell the driver!'

The driver wouldn't have been able to see anything, even if the partition had been open. I leaned forwards and knocked on the glass, shouting through it.

'Rob! Please can you stop the car?'

We were on the A3, but still a good twenty minutes away from Lizzie's house. Harry pressed a button and spoke into the intercom.

'It's all right, Robert, keep driving. We've changed our mind.'

I tried to push myself down into the seat, away from his hand, but I couldn't escape. I was worried that his hands might reach out for my breasts next.

'I'm going to call my husband and then I'm going to call the police. I'm going to tell Sergio. Stop this!'

I spat out the words. My fear turned to fury. How dare he do this to me?

He finally moved his hand away and, shaking with rage as much as fear, I put my clutch bag in my lap. I thought I was going to be sick and retched into the footwell, but nothing came out. I wished I could have puked all over the bastard. I tapped Tom's number, edging closer to the door.

'Call him. I'd be happy to tell him how you French kissed me on the rooftop and then fucked me in my hotel room.'

'That's not true!'

'Some of it is though, isn't it? Are you so sure he'd believe you and not me?'

I swallowed. 'If you tell Tom, I'll tell your wife.'

He shrugged.

'Go ahead. I don't mind. We have an arrangement. This wouldn't be the first time she heard about a liaison.'

'Tom will believe me, not you,' I said.

'Really? You kissed me on the rooftop. You can't deny that.'

I knew it would destroy Tom to hear about New York. It would destroy *us*.

'Harry, I don't know what's happened. You're not like this. What do you want?'

'I want you to sleep with me. I want you to finish what you started. If you don't, I'll tell Tom everything.'

I froze.

'I will also make sure that you're fired and you never work in the City again.'

'You can't fire me just because I won't sleep with you. I'll take you to a tribunal if you try. Sergio's already told me that I'm getting a permanent job based on my performance. You've lost your mind!'

'You've let me breach a Chinese wall – well, our version of it. The information you emailed me that day was never supposed to be seen by me. This is what I'll tell the directors. You told me that you'd lie to the directors, saying I had asked for this information, when I hadn't. You then demanded £50,000 to stay quiet. You committed fraud and then you blackmailed me.'

'That's not true!'

My feet turned to ice. My hand flew to my mouth, smudging my red lipstick.

'That's what I'm going to tell them unless you cooperate. You have until Monday to make your decision. Under the circumstances, it shouldn't be a hard choice.'

Tom would find out everything. Harry's money, which was lying in my account, suddenly felt like dirty money, not the lifeline I'd thought it had been to save my marriage. If Harry told Sergio about the Chinese wall, I'd get fired and I wouldn't be able to get another job. Everything would crumble. My children would find out the truth about me – that I was a liar and a cheat.

'Why are you doing this? What have I ever done to you?' My voice was a rasp. A spear of pain pierced my eye and my head started to throb.

'You're a prick-tease. You left unfinished business in New York. I was prepared to give you more time when we got back to London but then you gave me all that crap about loving Tom. I saw you tonight, preening in front of me, half-naked. You knew we'd be going to the party together. You can't act like that and not carry it through.'

I started to shake. If he told Tom his lies, Tom would ask me about what had happened in New York. He already got annoyed every time I mentioned Harry's name. What if Tom believed Harry and not me? If he heard about my supposed infidelity with Harry, or even the kiss, he might not forgive me. Harry would also tell him everything I had confessed about the money and my lies.

'Just take a minute to think about all of this. I'm doing you a favour, Fi. You're stuck in an unhappy marriage and Tom has acted abominably towards you. When people connect the way we did, you can't ignore it. I want you. We would be so good together. You need me to do this. So you don't feel your good-wife, perfect-image guilt. Stop pretending. You want to fuck me as much as I want to fuck you. I've just made it easy for you.'

I looked out of the window, trying not to cry. Whatever happened now, Tom would get hurt and my marriage would be over, if Harry went through with his threat, unless I slept with him. I started to shake. He had attacked me. Even if I told him I would never sleep with him, he could attack me again.

The car stopped. We were outside Lizzie and Stewart's house. Candles blazed along the driveway up to the front door, which was covered in red roses.

'You have until Monday,' said Harry.

Seventy-One

Tom was standing there. He smiled as he helped me out and I put my arms around him.

'You look beautiful,' he whispered in my ear.

'Thanks. Let's go in.'

I took his hand but before we could move, Harry was introducing himself to Tom, shaking his hand. Then Naila and Tariq arrived. As we said hello and Naila hugged me, I saw Harry walk away. He turned back and smiled at me.

Tom and I moved along in the crowd of people going into the white marquee set up in the back lawn. The dress code for the women was 'red for love', and the enormous marquee had rustic white chandeliers hanging above round tables decorated with tiny wild red roses and tea lights. It could have been a wedding.

The sea of tall, blonde women, with slim bronzed limbs, all exuding a specific brand of confidence, was a familiar sight. Several people stopped me to compliment my sari and say hello. I waved back and smiled automatically but kept walking. I clutched Tom's hand, aware that any moment I might come face to face with Julia and Harry.

After we had congratulated Lizzie and Stewart, I felt my breathing get faster. The image of what had happened in the car hit me with force again.

Tom pulled me aside. 'What's the matter? Are you OK?'

'Yes – no, actually, no. I have a terrible headache.'

I thought about telling Tom I was sick and we needed to go home, but before that, I had to talk to my friends about what Harry had done.

'Shall I ask Lizzie for some paracetamol?'

'I've got some and I'll take it now. Just give me a minute. I'll be right back,' I said.

I moved through the crowd until I spotted Naila, her red silk salwar kameez shimmering in the crowd.

'Can I talk to you?'

She came closer, smiling.

'We need to find Sam too, Naila. Can you help me?' I said.

Naila placed her hand on my arm. 'Hey, *kya hua*? Is something wrong?'

Her face was blurring as I blinked back tears. I nodded.

'I think Sam went upstairs,' she said.

She took my hand, which was icy in hers, and we climbed up the curved oak staircase, which had more red roses pinned along the banisters. Naila didn't ask more questions. We spotted Sam coming out of the loo and hurried towards her.

'Come back in,' Naila said to Sam. We all went inside the bathroom and Naila locked the door. She flipped down the lid of the toilet and guided me there as if I was unable to manage it myself, and sat me down.

'What's wrong?' said Sam.

Naila shrugged and shook her head. They both trained eyes full of worry at me.

'Harry stuck his hand between my legs in the car.'

'*What?*' gasped Naila.

'What do you mean? I thought New York was a mistake? Are you two back on?' said Sam.

'No! He pushed his hand between my legs and I told him to stop. But he said I have to sleep with him, that I'm a prick-tease. He kept...'

I started panting, unable to say any more.

Sam put her arm around me and rubbed my back.

'Look at me, Faiza,' said Naila. 'Breathe with me. In. One, two, three. Now out – one, two, three.'

I looked up at her, trying to focus on her eyes as she counted. My heart stopped hammering in my chest.

'We have to report this. This is assault. Have you told Tom?' Sam's voice trembled with the outrage I could no longer feel or express. I felt myself watching us all from behind a screen.

'No! I can't tell Tom anything. Harry's going to tell Tom that I slept with him in New York.'

'We'll tell Tom he's lying,' said Naila. 'Tom will believe you, not Harry.'

'I did kiss him though, didn't I? I let him touch me. I won't be able to deny that, will I?'

My friends were suddenly silent.

'He says he'll get me fired. He got me to email him some information that he wasn't supposed to have access to, but I had no idea. He says he'll tell the other directors I was blackmailing him. He gave me £50,000. He's threatened to tell the FCA that I was extorting money from him.'

Sam crouched down in front of me and took my hands. She spoke softly, as if to a child in pain. 'I don't understand. Why did he give you so much money? Why on earth would he do that?'

There was an edge of doubt in Naila's voice, as she said, 'Why would you take that money from him?'

Someone knocked on the door.

'Excuse me, there's a queue out here!'

'I'm sorry but I'll be a while yet, and you won't want to come in here after! Please use another loo!' Naila spoke into the door.

A burst of swear words exploded then drifted away.

My friends were waiting. I looked down as I spoke.

'I was desperate. The money was just a loan, until I got my bonus in November. When Tom lost his job, he said we had to use the emergency fund we'd put aside years ago. That was all we had left. But I'd been spending that money for ages and when I checked, it was all gone. Thousands and thousands. There was nothing left for school fees, or Ahmed's therapy, or the mortgage – for anything. I couldn't tell Tom I'd spent it. He would have left me. So, I've been trying and trying to put that money back. That's why I got a job. But it wasn't enough and Tom was going to find out what I'd done. Then Harry lent me the money and it was the solution to everything.'

'Shit!' said Naila.

'You stupid girl!' Sam exclaimed, sitting down at the edge of the bath.

'I knew you'd think I was stupid. That's why I didn't tell you. And you're right, I *was* stupid.'

'Not stupid for spending the money – although Jesus, Faiza, what were you thinking?' Sam said. 'I mean stupid for not telling us! *I* could have lent you money. Why did you go to that snake?'

'But you said you had a rule – never mix friendship and money. You told me! Anyway, I was too scared to tell you. I couldn't bear for you to find out what sort of a person I am.'

Four arms wrapped themselves around me like life vests and Naila stroked my hair and Sam patted my arm.

'We all need to think about what we can do to stop this bastard but first, tidy yourself up and go to Tom before he starts wondering where you are.'

Naila opened my clutch and handed me my brush and lipstick. She took a tissue and, tipping my chin up, wiped softly under my eyes.

Sam paused at the bathroom door and said, 'I'm going to ask James about how things are from a legal standpoint. I won't say it's you, just one of the mums from Ed's school. I'll meet you downstairs in twenty minutes.'

I walked downstairs with Naila, both of us watching out for Harry. I couldn't see him anywhere.

Tom had texted that he was in the garden, just outside the marquee entrance, and that's where I found him. He was the tallest person in the group and was smiling, his head nodding occasionally, his smile lines crinkling into fans at the side of each eye. The breeze blew his hair softly, as if whispering in his ear. He was wearing a starched white shirt without a tie and navy linen trousers. He looked happy.

He was chatting to Lizzie, Stewart and Anna. James joined the group and Lizzie waved me over. She had tiny red roses in her hair and they were all laughing at something Tom had just said. He took my hand and squeezed it, took a glass of juice from a passing tray, and gave it to me.

Stewart took Tom to meet his friends, and Lizzie and Anna moved away, while I stayed chatting to James. I wanted to text Sam that James was with me, but before I could, a man I couldn't place, but who looked vaguely familiar, joined us. James stopped talking mid-sentence.

'Hello, big brother,' said the man.

I realised it was Rupert. He looked like James, but more aggressively polished, with slicked-back red-blonde hair and whitened teeth, wearing a pristine cream linen suit.

James seemed to have frozen. Remembering my promise to Sam to shield James from his brother, I stuck out my hand and stepped between them.

'Hi, I'm Faiza, a friend of Sam and James.'

He shook my hand for the shortest possible time then dropped it and walked up to James.

'I heard what happened to you. It's the talk of the City. Bad luck,' said Rupert.

'Rupert...'

James sounded as if he was warning him off. His face was so red that it looked almost purple.

I felt as if I was intruding, but also knew I shouldn't leave James alone.

'You're a laughing stock.'

Rupert's words were icy, but his smile showed that he was enjoying himself. James's fists clenched as Rupert carried on speaking.

'Passed over for promotion, doomed to stay a junior partner, at your age too. I heard they moved your desk to the stationery cupboard! I can have a word with them if you want. Ask them to keep you on as a charity case.'

'You bastard!' said James. It came out as a wheeze.

I didn't know if Rupert was telling the truth. If he was, James must have been devastated. His job was everything to him. I wondered if Sam knew? It didn't seem so. She was always talking about how busy James was at work.

'Listen, I don't think this is the right place...' I said.

Rupert ignored me.

'That's no way to speak to me when I'm trying to help you,' said Rupert. 'Have you told the parents yet?'

James was starting to sweat. The anger in his eyes had been replaced by terror. I thought I saw tears. He looked as if he was being hunted and had no chance of escape.

James turned and walked away towards the house and Rupert moved off. I saw him grab a drink and join another group, already shaking hands and kissing.

I texted Sam that I needed to see her and that I was in the garden. Tom came up to me and I told him what had happened.

'Can you please go check on James? I'm scared he might have a heart attack. I'll try to find Sam.'

'I don't really know the bloke that well,' Tom said. Then, looking at my face, 'All right.'

I was suddenly alone. I looked around, afraid that Harry was nearby, but I didn't spot him or Julia.

'Hi.'

Sam tapped me on my shoulder and I spun around.

'I just saw your text. Where's James gone? Have you seen Harry again?'

'No, but James was talking to me and Rupert turned up. They had words and I think you should go check on James. That brother of his is vile!'

'What did he do? What did he say?' said Sam. She was panicking, her eyes blinking fast. 'Was James OK?'

She had that same look of fear that I had seen in James's eyes.

'I've sent Tom to look for him. He was saying things about James's work and telling their parents.'

Tom texted that he'd found James in the library and I told Sam who stumbled in her heels as she tried to run.

I got another text from Tom.

James was in a bad way. He was crying.

Something was very wrong. James's brother had been nasty but this reaction was worrying. So was Sam's.

I had to go to Tom. I didn't feel safe alone.

I walked through the darkness, under the lights intertwined in the trees, and went into the house.

'I need to speak to you.'

It was Harry. I almost screamed when I heard him behind me. He smiled, as if he were greeting me with pleasure. I shuddered.

'I'm sorry, I'm going to see my husband. I can't.'

'Your choice. I would advise you to listen to me though.'

I couldn't ignore the threat in his voice. If he had other ammunition that he intended to use against me, it was better if I knew.

'OK,' I said, stepping out of the way as a waiter carried a tray of champagne bottles outside on a silver tray.

'Not here. Follow me.'

He started to walk away from the party, towards a staircase at the far end, shrouded in darkness.

'No, we'll talk here,' I said.

I stepped to the side of the large hallway. He turned back and shrugged and walked towards me. We moved to the back of the room, out of the way, but still visible to the others. He couldn't do anything to me there.

Seventy-Two

'Well?'

I raised my chin and stared at him, hoping that he would see my disgust. I wondered if I could still persuade him to drop this, to be reasonable. He had been so vulnerable when he'd talked about his daughter. He'd helped me so many times at work, had listened while I sobbed in his arms. A chill ran through me. I wondered if all those things had been part of his plan. He knew what he was doing when he got the client data from me. The story about his daughter was probably just to soften me up, his form of foreplay.

His eyes travelled down my body.

'I like you in this dress. Very exotic, erotic.'

His words were as much of an assault as his actions, but I kept my face a blank.

'What do you want?' I snapped.

'Look, there's no need to be like this. I'm sorry I said those things, but why don't you just admit it? Be honest, you wanted it as much as I did. I remember the way you kissed me. I keep thinking about your tongue in my mouth. You know you...'

His words were drowned out by a scream and I heard a woman's voice shout, 'You Paki slut!'

Julia had suddenly appeared next to him. She was wearing a strapless red dress and her blonde hair fell in a straight bob to prominent clavicles. Instinctively, I started to walk away from her and Harry, towards the centre of the room.

She continued to shout as I saw Tom near the French doors. He was soon at my side and took my hand.

'What's going on?' he said.

More people had started to come in. There was a rustle of whispers punctuated by gasps.

'You can't say that to Faiza,' said Lizzie, standing in front of Julia.

'Who is that woman?' said Tom. 'This is unacceptable.'

I frowned, still watching Julia. I couldn't believe that she had called me 'Paki'. The force of her words had hit me like the waves from a nuclear explosion.

'How dare you say that to me you racist—' I said.

She didn't let me finish. She moved closer, shouting into my face.

'I know you're fucking my husband!'

'Julia!'

Harry grabbed her arm to pull her back.

Tom's hand fell away from mine and I shook my head at him.

Naila appeared next to me, along with Lizzie. Tariq and Stewart stood next to Tom. Julia shook Harry's hand off her arm.

'I know you gave her fifty grand! I checked your phone. You bastard! I know everything!'

She turned to me, her wine glass gesticulating wildly as if any minute she would throw the contents on my face.

'How many times did you fuck him to get that much? You bitch! Why didn't you tell me you were working for my husband? I know you were in New York together, and I know you've been sleeping with him. Fucking whore!'

The room was beginning to sway and I leaned into Naila who put her arm around me.

Tom took my hand, but I didn't feel any comfort in his touch. I let him lead me through the spaces between the other guests, who moved apart reluctantly.

Somehow, I was in our car and we were driving away. The world was black outside and I realised that I was crying. It took too much effort to hold my head upright and I let my chin sink almost till it touched my chest. Tom was driving too fast, not slowing at bends. A car beeped its horn in anger as we passed it around a corner, the headlights blinding us, but Tom still continued at the same speed. I shut my eyes. What would be would be…

Seventy-Three

He parked on a side lane by the Common, near the pond. There were no street lights there, just the deadly stillness of trees in the night. He did not touch me or look at me. After a minute or two he spoke, so softly that I almost didn't hear.

'Are you sleeping with Harry?'

'No!' I turned to him. I looked into his eyes. 'I swear to you. I love you. I would never...'

'Why was his wife saying that you had?'

'I honestly don't know. I was talking to him and she just started screaming. She called me a "Paki bitch", for God's sake. She probably just saw us talking and...'

Tom's hands were clenched around the steering wheel. He gazed into the darkness in silence. He hadn't asked me about the fifty thousand. Perhaps he hadn't heard it. Julia had been screaming, almost spitting her fury into my face. It was such an outlandish thing to hear that maybe it had gone unnoticed, except by me and Harry.

I touched Tom's arm. It stayed stiff.

'Darling, you can't really imagine that I'd ever cheat on you. I swear—'

He cut me off, his voice slicing through the air.

'What was she saying about fifty thousand pounds?'

My mind flashed with possible answers. I'd say that I had no idea. That Julia was drunk? Confusing me with someone else? I had never met her before? I was about to provide a suitable excuse when Tom turned his head and his eyes locked on to mine. The face that I had loved for twenty-one years looked at me. He didn't deserve any more lies. I closed my eyes and bent my head.

I told him everything.

Seventy-Four

He didn't speak at all as I told him about the emergency fund and lying to him about the Post Office. I told him I'd sold my jewellery, taken out loans and a new credit card, and tricked my parents into giving me all of their savings. I told him that I had been lying to him about the money for the last six months – longer, in fact. He showed no emotion as I told him about that morning on platform six, about Harry giving me the money and then blackmailing me by saying he would tell the directors unless I slept with him.

As I said the words, the enormity of my lies hit me for the first time. I wanted to stop. It felt unbearable to say it and I knew it would hurt him to hear it. I forced myself to carry on and told him everything that I had tried so hard to hide.

I felt the heat coming off his face, saw his clenched jaw in the dull moonlight. Finally, I told him that Harry had kissed me. That I pushed him away but I waited a millisecond too long and kissed him back, but just for a minute. In that moment my world had split open and I regretted it straight away.

'I am so sorry.'

I paused. His breathing was harder and he bowed his head and gripped the steering wheel tighter.

I couldn't bring myself to tell Tom about the attack in the car, though. He would be devastated and he would probably go and attack Harry himself. I would tell him about it later. At that moment I needed to tell him what I had done. I had to tell him all of it.

'I'm so sorry I lied about the money. I made a terrible mistake, but I was trying to put it right. I couldn't bear the thought of you hating me or leaving me if you found out. I thought that if I could just replace the money, we could go back to being us. That's all I ever wanted.'

Without saying a word, he started the car and drove home, to number 30 Firewood Lane, the house we had bought with such excitement, in the right postcode, close to the best schools, with the perfect garden for the children to play football and have a trampoline. The home that I had decorated with our family photographs and countless drawings made at school, with Murano lights and marble countertops, studding the walls with oil paintings and the floors with oak parquet and expensive silk rugs It was no use to me now. The planning, the memories, the dreams, the careful construction of the perfect life. None of that could protect us in the end.

I thought that the money would insulate us against Life. In the end, it had proved useless.

The truth was that if Tom had lied to me for months, spent all our savings, and kissed another woman, I would have thrown him out of the car and told him never to come back. I could ask him to forgive me all I wanted, but I knew that I would not have forgiven him. He wouldn't forgive me either.

I didn't want the house or any of the things in it. I just wanted us. But the closer we got to our home, the more I realised that I was going to lose everything.

Seventy-Five

Tom fumbled as he unlocked the front door and we staggered into the dark hallway like survivors from a car crash. I turned on the lights and saw his eyes were glazed. I put my hand on his arm and he shrugged it off with such force that I stumbled back a little. He walked away to the living room. I wanted to run after him, but something in the way he held his body made me stop. I decided to wait a few minutes.

I stepped out of my heels and left them near the front door, then I pulled myself up on the banisters and went upstairs. My legs ached as if I had run a marathon and my arms felt bruised. I passed the children's empty rooms, grateful that Sofia was staying at Meg's house for the weekend, and the boys were with my parents. I had made the arrangements so we could have a romantic night alone. Now, it meant I didn't have to pretend that everything was all right. I didn't think I could have, anyway.

I paused on the landing, listening. I heard Tom in the kitchen, taking out a glass, turning on the tap. There was the scrape of a kitchen chair on the floor, then silence.

I pulled off the sari, bunching it into my hand as it unrolled from my body, then I dumped it on the bed and took off my blouse. Stepping out of the petticoat, I left it pooled on the floor. On my bedside table I saw the tuberose candle I'd put there that morning, along with a bottle of massage oil.

I had imagined Tom unwrapping me out of my sari, and had planned to do a jokey, sexy striptease in the candlelight for him, revealing the matching, see-through red underwear I had worn in anticipation. I thought that we had finally come back to 'us'.

Instead, I pulled on black leggings and a T-shirt, tied my hair up in a ponytail and ran downstairs.

He didn't look up when I went into the kitchen. He was at the table, staring into his glass. The ice tray lay on the counter with two ice cubes melting next to it. I refilled the tray and put it back into the freezer, then wiped the counter with some kitchen towel, before taking a deep breath and turning to face him.

He looked as if he had been knocked down by a punch and was still shaken from the fall. Every instinct in me wanted to go to him to smooth away his hair from his forehead, kiss his lips and hold him close. But these were empty gestures now. I couldn't undo the damage that I had caused with a hug or a kiss.

'Tom, I'm so, so sorry about everything. I've been so stupid. I don't know what happened, I just...'

He looked up. I forced myself not to look away and he started to shout.

'I'll tell you what happened! You've stolen all our money and left us penniless. God knows what you've done with it all! You've lied to me, you've lied to your parents, you've betrayed us all!'

'Darling, I promise you, I never meant for this to happen. I was always going to put the money back, I swear. And I know I should never have lied to you but...'

I stopped when I saw the look on his face.

'You were with another man. All these years, I trusted you completely and you cheated on me. I never thought you could do that to us. I was an idiot.'

My voice was hoarse. 'I know I shouldn't have kissed Harry, but I promise you, it was just for a second. I pushed him away as soon as it happened. I realised I'd made a terrible mistake. Tom, you have to forgive me! You have to. I didn't cheat on you. I would never, ever do that. I love...'

'He's a millionaire, right? Much more your type. I just never made enough money for you, did I?'

'You know that's not true.'

I spoke quietly, even though his voice had become louder and louder. He had a right to shout at me. I sat down opposite him.

'Harry is vile. He's blackmailing me. I was the idiot, not you.'

His hand was on the table. I wanted to reach out and touch it, but I didn't dare.

'Why did he give you that fifty thousand? No one gives out that kind of money, not unless there's something in it for them. Do you think I'm stupid? Tell me the truth for once. Are you sleeping with him?'

I felt as if I couldn't breathe.

'Don't you believe me? I *told* you I didn't sleep with him.'

His eyes searched my face and I didn't know how I could arrange it to convince him that I wasn't lying.

'Did you sell him that information, then? To get that money? Is he telling the truth?'

'How could you even think that!' I cried out.

He pushed his chair back. It crashed to the floor and he came towards me. His face was red, his eyes the darkest shade of blue as he brought his face right up to mine, his breath hot on my cheeks.

'How do I know what's true and what's not? I can't believe anything you say, ever again.'

I flinched back into my chair and when he spoke again, I could barely hear him.

'I don't know who you are any more.'

'Yes, you do, Tom! Of course you know me. What I did isn't me – I made a mistake, a stupid, terrible mistake.'

He walked out of the kitchen. I went after him.

'Stay away from me!'

He grabbed his car keys from the console table and I ran to him.

'Tom, please, I beg you. Don't go. Let me explain. I never meant any of this to happen. Just stay and talk, please.'

He walked towards me, his hands clenched into fists and I was suddenly aware of his height and the anger coiled up in his body. I shook my thoughts away. This was *Tom*. I trusted him with my life.

'What did you spend it on? Spoiling the children with useless stuff? Clothes, shoes, the house? To impress your friends? You risked everything for that? I told you not to touch that money but you don't give a shit about anyone except yourself. Not me, not the kids!'

I couldn't bear the hate in his eyes. I backed away and my hands found the edge of the sideboard behind me. I held on to it.

'That's not true! I'd do anything for you and the kids. I know you're angry, but don't say this. Please. We love each other.'

He opened the front door, then turned to look at me.

'You disgust me.'

The black floating frames that we had bought together in Rome, with photos of the children as babies, shook as the door slammed and his car screeched on the gravel as he drove away.

My knees buckled and I sank to the floor, my spine liquid. I drooped until I was lying down flat, hugged my knees to my chest.

'*You disgust me.*'

The words spun around in my head, getting louder and louder. I disgusted myself too. All these months that I had been telling him lies, I'd told myself that they were just little ones, that I was protecting him. I hadn't even noticed them after a while. But now I saw that the deceit had permeated my whole being and I couldn't stand what I had become.

I put my hands over my ears and shut my eyes, sobbing silently, unable to get up again...

I must have fallen asleep. When I woke, I was still curled up into a ball and it was 1 a.m.

I went upstairs and got into bed but I couldn't sleep. I

texted Tom but he was offline and none of my messages were delivered.

Please come home. I can sleep in the other room. Just come home.

Later.

Baby, just let me know you're OK.

I called his phone, but it kept going straight to voicemail. At 3 a.m. I started to get worried. I knew there was no point in texting Tariq or Tom's brother, Peter. He wouldn't tell anyone what had happened. Not yet anyway. I threw back the duvet and stood by the bedroom window, looking at the driveway. I googled 'car accidents in south west London', but didn't find anything. The police would have called me if there had been an accident, anyway.

An image flashed in my head of Tom in a hotel, in bed with another woman. If he believed that I had slept with Harry, he might see it as simply redressing the balance in our marriage. He could have gone to a bar, got drunk and taken someone to bed.

I started to walk up and down the small space between the window and the bed. He couldn't have meant the things that he'd said. He was angry and hurt, that was all. I prayed that was true.

I got back into bed, clutching my phone. I sat propped up against the pillows but eventually fell asleep again, waking in a panic at 6 a.m. to find no text from Tom. He hadn't been online since he'd left the house. I ran to the guest room and then the children's rooms in case he was sleeping there, but all the rooms were empty. There was no sign that he had come back.

I texted Martha to ask if she could collect the boys from my parents later and got into my car. I couldn't just sit at home. I had to find Tom.

Seventy-Six

I drove around the Common first, looking in the lanes where we went for walks with the children and where Tom and I had a snow fight last winter. I drove past our favourite Sunday lunch pub and then to the hotel nearby. I checked the car park but there was no sign of his car. I drove down the High Street and the back roads in the Village too, and then down to Wimbledon.

I called his mother in case he'd ended up there. I knew she woke up at the crack of dawn.

'Good morning, Victoria.'

'Is everything OK, Faiza? Why are you calling so early?'

Her question gave me my answer. He wasn't there. Her immediate worry had sounded almost like Ami. Perhaps after two decades she had picked up some of the inbuilt neurosis of a Pakistani parent.

'Yes, sorry to call so early. I wanted to ask you what you used for the lemon icing for Sofia's birthday cake. I'm making cupcakes for Alex for a sleepover and I was just off to the supermarket to get the ingredients.'

I knew that she would panic if I told her Tom was missing. It was best not to say anything yet and I knew exactly what I could pretend to phone about.

I tried to get off the call as soon as I could, which was hard, as Victoria gave me detailed recipes for lavender and orange icing as well. I parked the car and checked my phone again. Nothing. I would never find him like this, I knew that. But I couldn't face going home either. I drove to the A3 and headed towards central London. I knew where I needed to be.

It was still early and I found parking in a side street off Piccadilly. I got a takeaway coffee then darted across the road towards the Ritz and walked to the entrance of Green Park. When I reached the gate, I stopped. I remembered standing at that same spot, twenty-one years ago, debating whether to go in or not. Tom had been waiting for me inside.

It was our first date. My head was crammed with all the reasons I should not go in: the different cultures, my parents' ban on my dating anyone at all, let alone a non-Muslim and non-Pakistani. If I went into the park, I'd be going against every expectation and tradition that had been drilled into me. I would be entering uncharted territory.

I was already in love with Tom but I didn't know exactly how he felt. I was aware, though, that a twenty-eight-year-old English guy would not be thinking love and marriage, when they hadn't even been on a proper first date. I was setting myself up for a fall. On the day of the date the sensible thing would have been for me to turn around, walk back to the tube station and go back home, to the path expected of me.

Even though I was in love with him, at that stage I could have got over him, eventually, I'd thought. We had been circling each other for months, coming closer and closer, until Tom had asked me to come for a picnic.

'It's a date,' he'd said. 'Just so there's no confusion.'

On that April afternoon, against all logic and self-preservation, I'd walked into the park for my date with Tom. He had laid out a red and white picnic rug under a tree and he smiled when he saw me and stood up. I waved to him and ran the rest of the way.

That tree would later be christened 'our' tree. Four months later, Tom and I lay on the same blanket in the park, looking up at the sky. I was crying, and he was holding my hand.

'You don't have to do this anymore,' I said. 'I'm sorry, but I just can't sleep with you unless we're married. I want to, more than anything, but I can't go against my beliefs. It's just not something I can do. I know it would be bizarre for you to marry someone before sleeping with them so it's an impossible situation. I'll understand if you want to end things.'

My tears blinded me and I could no longer see the frothy clouds in the sun-blue sky that we had been staring at earlier. Tom squeezed my hand. He was silent for a heartbeat before he spoke.

'Or, we could just get married.'

I stopped crying instantly.

'What?'

It was such a casual remark. If he was joking, I knew that my heart would break. I held my breath and he nodded, then was absolutely still. His eyes were a serious, deep blue, waiting to see my reaction. When he saw it, a smile spread across his entire face. He pulled me closer.

'Good. You know I'd do anything for a shag.'

His arm tightened around me, and I smiled.

For the last twenty years, Tom and I had come to Green Park every April. As I walked into the park, I realised that we had missed our date this year.

The memories were painful, as I took a sip of my coffee. It was the first time I'd been here alone, and the first time that I had no idea where Tom was, or if he still loved me.

I sat down under our tree and took out my phone. I had to keep texting him until he replied. I held my breath when I saw he'd just sent a message: *I'm OK. We need to talk. I'm coming home.*

I let out a shaky sigh. Thank God he was all right. I gripped a chunk of grass in my hand.

I typed back quickly: *Don't go home. Kids there with Martha. We can't talk there. I'm out. Can you come and meet me?*

Where?

Green Park.

There was a pause.

OK.

I wanted to tidy myself up before he got there. I had a brush in my bag and some mints. I was still wearing the leggings and T-shirt that I'd slept in. I hadn't brushed my hair or my teeth before I'd left the house and last night's red lipstick and eyeliner were smeared and smudged on my face. I pushed my tangled hair back, tucking a strand behind my ear. I didn't have the energy to fix myself. I stared at the grass at my feet and waited.

Seventy-Seven

'Hi.'

I hadn't heard him come up. He sat down opposite me. His eyelids were pink and his eyes bloodshot. His white stubble stood out in the morning sun.

'Where have you been?' I spoke without emotion, careful to keep my voice neutral. I didn't say that I had been worried or that he should have called.

'I needed some time to think.'

He spoke without the anger of the night before. We could have been discussing what we had for lunch.

'We missed our Green Park date this year. But we made it after all. Twenty-first date,' I said.

When he spoke, it was as if he hadn't heard me. He had prepared what he was going to say.

'I can't do this. I'm sorry.'

The quietness of his voice and the layer of kindness between his words were worse than the fury from the night before. These weren't words thrown in anger. It was his verdict after hours of consideration.

I watched an old woman with a grey plait and a striped rainbow jumper who was feeding the pigeons across from us. She was singing to the birds and the sounds carried in the air towards us. Her arm cut a perfect 'C' in the air as she scattered breadcrumbs.

'Are you leaving me?'

He didn't reply.

'Tom, darling, please...'

'I don't know who you are any more, Faiza. Last night I found myself wondering what was true and what was a lie. I always had complete faith in you – now I doubt every word that comes out of your mouth.'

I looked away from his eyes, from the pain and bewilderment there. I'd done that to him.

'I love you, Tom. Don't you believe that?'

'Maybe love means different things to you and me.'

The calmness of his voice was deadly. I felt as if my heart had stopped. I didn't know how I was still breathing, still listening. This was it. The thing I had always feared.

The irony of it hit me. We had dismissed the warnings and cautions from both sets of parents about the strains and stresses of a mixed marriage, but I hadn't forgotten their words. They had stayed in my head and walked down the aisle with me. We had reassured each other that we wouldn't let religion or culture or clothes or traditions or the societal pressures on us from two very different worlds ever break us. And they hadn't. After the first three or four years, those issues faded into non-issues. I had never imagined, though, that the threat to our love would come not from culture, but from cash.

'Look, we need to sort things out,' he said, brisk and

business-like while my head felt as if it was underwater. 'Let's get a coffee and think about what needs to be done.'

The old woman was gazing at the birds now, the way I used to watch my children eat when they were toddlers: with exhaustion but a deep satisfaction.

Tom took my hand to pull me up, then dropped it. He walked a little ahead of me and I watched his shoulders, wanting only to lay my head on them. I couldn't imagine never holding him again.

He left the park without a backward glance and I stepped through the gate where I had started our story, knowing that it would now end.

Seventy-Eight

We went to the coffee shop in Waterstones, and Tom borrowed a piece of paper and a pen from the waitress when she brought our coffees and croissants. He started to make a list. I drank my coffee, but couldn't swallow anything else.

Tom was going to leave me. The words were like acid burning into my brain. I didn't think that I could survive. He clearly felt no such emotions.

'The first thing we need to do is to give Harry his money back. I'll do it on the laptop when we get home. Can you give me his account number, please?'

My face flamed as Harry's name was mentioned. I had a confirmation email for the transfer from the bank so I took a screenshot and sent it to Tom. He opened the text, his lips a tight line of disapproval.

'You have to tell Sergio that Harry tricked you to get the information – I can bet he's done other things too, if he's done this with you.'

'But what if they don't believe me? They could just fire me.'

'You have no choice. Has he contacted you since the party?'

I shook my head. I didn't want to tell him that Harry *had* texted, to say that nothing had changed, and I should tell Tom that Julia had mistaken me for someone else he'd been seeing – to her, all brown women with long black hair looked the same – and deny anything about the money.

His text said: *There's no way he'd know about the money. Just stay quiet and I'll keep your secret. I told Julia it was a company payment and she had it all wrong. You're a dark horse. Looking forward to Monday.*

I still couldn't tell Tom about Harry attacking me; he would definitely make me go to the police and I couldn't risk anything that might jeopardise my job and my bonus. I had to carry on as normal, and stall Harry for another two weeks until I got the bonus.

'But we're giving Harry's money back and then, if I lose my job and don't get my bonus...' I said.

Tom was brusque. 'We'll just have to deal with it.'

I couldn't help my hand from moving towards his. I didn't function without touching Tom. He moved his hand away and put it under the table. I slid mine back and picked up my phone. I looked at him but he looked away. His eyes had always been my anchor. I didn't know where else to look.

Outside, we went in opposite directions to our cars. As I walked away, I looked back, wondering if he would too, some part of me still hoping that this was just a tiff that would dissolve and disappear – my mind could not envisage a reality where Tom no longer loved me. But he was already on the other side of the road, taking long strides away from me.

He never looked back.

Seventy-Nine

When I got home Tom was already there, and the small blue suitcase that we used for weekends away in Bath was lying on the bedspread. I wrenched open the wardrobe door. His side was already half empty and the hangers shook mournfully as I stared at them. I hadn't thought he would move out like this…

Later I watched Tom from the kitchen window, his laugh loud enough to reach me as he picked up Alex and swung him around in the garden, while Ahmed kicked a ball into the goal and raised his arms in victory, running in a circle around Tom and Alex. No, I told myself, Tom would calm down once he'd had some time to think about it all. He couldn't throw all this away. He would stay for the children, even if he didn't want to stay for me.

After lunch, when we were alone, he said, 'I've transferred Harry's money back.'

'Thank you.'

I was glad we had returned that monster's money but I couldn't help shivering as I thought about Harry's text. He was still expecting me to go through with his 'offer'. What if he tried to attack me again? I couldn't tell Tom though, I just couldn't...

Tom's eyes were fixed on his phone. I wanted to reach out and touch his cheek, kiss his forehead, do something to take away all that pain. I needed to show him that I was sorry. It was almost twenty-four hours since he found out about the money. I hoped that he would now let me explain what had happened and tell him how much I loved him.

'Tom, listen...'

'I've packed my things, Faiza. We should get the children together and tell them that I'm leaving...'

'Tom, no! Please, come on. You don't have to leave.'

'I'm sorry, I can't stay here.'

'This is too much for the kids to take in. Let's just say you're going on a business trip.'

'And then what? Have them feel cheated when we tell them the real reason I left? No more lies, Faiza. They need to know what's going on and I need to tell them that I'll still be there for them, even if we aren't together.'

He called the children into the TV room. Alex sat on my lap and I put my arms around him, pulling him close. I wasn't sure if I was comforting him or myself. Tom sat next to Ahmed. He put his arms over our son's bony shoulders, then patted the seat next to him, for Sofia to sit down. She stood impatiently by the sofa, her eyes flitting to her phone, her feet poised to flee, as if at the start of a race. She stayed where she was.

I let Tom start, still hoping that, as he said the words, their horror would make him come to his senses. He could still change his mind and his script.

'We wanted to tell you about something very sad that's happened.'

Ahmed flinched and Sofia was suddenly still.

'Don't worry, no one is sick or anything like that, but Mum and me haven't been getting on very well for a while now and so we've decided that it's best if we have some time apart. I'm going to stay with Uncle David, my friend from university, remember?'

Sofia burst out laughing. 'Very funny. Although it's not the best joke, Dad.'

'Darling, I'm sorry but this isn't a joke. I wouldn't joke about this.'

The silence was suddenly louder than all the noise the children had made over all the years put together. Sofia's face was a mask, her jaw stiff just like Tom's. Ahmed stared at his shoes. I wanted to jump up and pull all my children to me, in a close hug, but I couldn't move. I tried to take one breath after the other, and quieten the screams in my head. I just wanted it all to stop. I concentrated on keeping my face calm for the children and holding back my tears.

'I'm going to move out, but this doesn't mean you won't see me.'

Alex wriggled out of my arms and ran to Tom, who hugged him.

'I don't want you to go!' said Alex.

Ahmed was silent, biting his nails. Sofia looked at us both and shrugged. Her cheeks were red, her eyes glittered.

'It makes no difference to me. I'll be out of here soon anyway!'

'Listen, you know these things happen. You all have friends whose parents are divorced—' said Tom.

'Divorced?' exclaimed Ahmed, and Alex started to cry. Sofia took his hand and pulled him towards her, hugging him.

'Stop it, Tom!' I was furious, and I could see that he was now regretting telling the truth.

'No one has said anything about divorce,' he said, trying to backtrack.

'It's OK, my darlings, it's going to be OK,' I said. 'We wanted to tell you what was going on. I know it's upsetting – Dad and I are upset too – but we love you…'

'Say sorry, make friends, be happy, Daddy!' said Alex, his tiny voice wobbling, as he repeated the phrase I always said when the children got into spats.

'But you and Mum are always saying how much "in love" you are,' said Sofia. 'You're happier than all my friends' parents. What's happened?'

I had never wanted the children to see any discord between us, always protecting them from any arguments or disagreements in our marriage. But my pretence of perfection had left them unprepared for any kind of reality, especially the reality of their parents' marriage collapsing seemingly overnight. I couldn't stop my tears any more. Ahmed came to sit next to me and put his arm around me.

'Have you found someone else? Like Emma's Dad?' Sofia glared at Tom.

'No, Dad hasn't done anything wrong. I-I…' I said, trying

to stop my tears by pressing the tips of my fingers onto my eyelids.

'So, it's your fault then!' Sofia was shouting now and Tom went up to her.

'It's not anyone's fault. I'm so sorry, so is Mum. We never wanted this to happen. We just want to be honest and tell you what's going on. It's for the best.'

He touched her arm and she shrugged him off.

'Why's Mum crying then? I've had enough of this! Come on, Ahmed, let's go.'

She took Alex's hand and Ahmed followed her as they all went upstairs and then her door banged shut.

I sat down in the kitchen, too numb to cry any more, as Tom went upstairs. I heard muffled voices as he opened Sofia's door. He must have been saying goodbye to the children. Then I heard him walking down the stairs. He left without saying anything to me.

I was grateful for the frantic start of Monday morning, but it suddenly felt overwhelming to do it all by myself. Even though the morning routine had been mine to manage alone for eighteen years, I had become used to Tom finding Alex's reading book or last-minute pound coins for 'wear your own clothes' days. I looked forward to having breakfast with Tom and our little chats, the quick kiss before I rushed off to work. As I drank my coffee, I noticed Ahmed watching me. His eyes were assessing me, as if trying to gauge what he should be feeling by the expression on my face. I smiled, and he smiled back. I couldn't fall apart in front of them.

All through breakfast, I was worried about going to the

office. Harry would be waiting for me. I thought about all the times I had been alone in his office with the door shut, the late nights when the others had all gone home. He could have attacked me any time – and now that he had crossed that line, what if he grabbed me again? Stripped away of his Savile Row suit and the charm he wore like a disguise, I had seen him for what he was: a thug.

Eighty

I felt my body tense as I got closer to my office.

Sergio and the Dragon were their usual selves when they met me; as far as I could tell, Harry hadn't said anything to them yet.

It wasn't long before Harry emailed, asking me to take a report into his office. I knew I couldn't avoid him. I had planned what to do. I would leave his door open and stand nearer to the door than to him so he couldn't do anything to me. Still, I had to force myself to walk over to him.

He was sitting behind his desk, but he started to get up.

'Please stay where you are,' I said.

'Why are you being like this? I won't bite. Not unless you want me to.'

That smile spread across his face, the smile of a tormentor. I wanted to fly across the room and hit him, but I kept my face composed and lifted my chin slightly, not moving my eyes away from his, not letting him see my fear. I couldn't stop shaking, though, and I saw his eyes gloat when he noticed.

'Tom knows everything, so you can't threaten me with telling him,' I said, keeping my voice steady. 'And I've returned your money so you can't say I blackmailed you. It's really quite pathetic that you have to go to such lengths to get someone to sleep with you.'

I hoped my face showed my disgust.

'Not with someone – with *you*. And you *will* sleep with me if you want to keep this job, and if you want to have any job in the City in future. Otherwise, I'll tell Sergio that you gave me confidential information on your client and then blackmailed me. I'll say you returned the money when I threatened to expose you.'

I changed my tack.

'Harry, this isn't just about me. You have children. This will destroy my family too. I've worked so hard and I'm about to get my bonus. Please don't tell Sergio these lies.'

His eyes settled on my breasts. I felt my anger growing. My voice grew colder, as I continued.

'If you do, I'll tell Sergio you attacked me in the car! Haven't you heard about sexual harassment? Or Me Too? You can't get away with this kind of behaviour. It's a crime.'

'Who says I did anything to you? You can't prove it and Sergio will believe whatever I tell him. If you love your family so much, you know what you have to do. I'm flying to Stockholm today but when I get back, we can take up where we left off in New York. Stop acting so outraged, Fi. You know you'll have a very good time.'

I turned and fled, rushing towards the loos. I locked myself inside the cubicle. My heart thumped through me and my hands shook as I took out my phone and pressed the white playback icon. There was silence and then some scratching sounds. My phone had been in my pocket. I couldn't have risked Harry seeing the record button flashing on the screen. Every passing second felt like it held my entire future. Then, there it was. Harry's voice pouring out like slime through the speakers. It had worked. Harry's threats were now on my phone.

I sat down on the toilet lid, my relief making me ice cold then hot. I emailed the file to myself straight away, so I wouldn't delete it by mistake. I listened again, to make sure it had gone through.

I decided not to give it to Sergio yet. Harry might still try to wriggle out of it if Sergio confronted him with my accusations and it could mess up my chances of keeping my job. The directors might see me as a problem, even if it went to HR. I just needed to get my bonus and an offer letter, then I could get another job.

If he threatened me again, though, I would tell the directors that I would sue for sexual harassment unless they fired Harry. I could use the recording as proof. It had to be the last resort, though.

Eighty-One

Tom had texted to say that if I was OK with it, he would carry on picking the children up from school, giving them dinner and leaving before I got back from work.

The evenings without Tom were unbearable, especially as I knew he'd been in the house just moments earlier. I saw traces of his presence everywhere – his mug on the draining board, the lunch boxes and dinner plates he'd stacked in the dishwasher, his shape in the sofa cushion. I chased his aftershave all over the house.

In bed, I turned my back on Tom's empty side. One night at 2 a.m., unable to sleep, I texted him: *Come back. Please. Give me another chance.* He didn't reply. There wasn't even a blue tick that he'd read my text.

Harry was back from Stockholm. It was the day of the agreement signing with the GlobalCorp CEO, and as I was leading the meeting, I couldn't stay home. Since all the directors would be at the meeting, I hoped I could avoid being alone with Harry.

I had planned to wear a pale-pink, closely-fitted dress

for the meeting, but when I thought about Harry watching me, I put on a navy skirt suit with a loose jacket and buttoned my white shirt high. Afterwards, Sergio pulled me aside to congratulate me. He joked about my outfit, saying he'd never seen me looking so prim, but that I could wear whatever I wanted, now that I'd signed such a huge client. He said that I would get my job offer and bonus email in a couple of days.

The Dragon wanted photographs with the clients for a 'wall of success' she was putting up in the lobby, and we all lined up in front of the HH logo as the receptionist took the photos. I could do nothing when Harry came and stood next to me, shuffling closer as if to make room for the others, until the side of his body was touching mine. I felt myself sweating and moved away as soon as I could.

Later, we took the clients to dinner at City Social, where the CEO toasted me and Sergio looked on like an indulgent parent. I should have been feeling excited; instead, I was on edge as Harry stared at me all evening.

When I stood up to leave, Harry also got up.

'Let me give you a lift,' he said. 'Fi and I are neighbours – in fact, our children go to the same school.'

There were murmurs of surprise and smiles. I forced myself to smile too.

'No thank you. My husband's picking me up.'

I rushed out of the building, not sure where to go, afraid that Harry would come after me. I ran towards the tube station, down the steps at Bank, through the ticket barriers, and down the travelator. The Waterloo and City line train didn't move for two minutes and the tube doors stayed open.

I stood with my back pressed against the end of the carriage in case Harry had worked out where I'd gone and came to find me. When the doors closed with a sigh, I collapsed on the nearest seat.

When I reached Wimbledon, I got a text from Harry.

See you on Monday. I've booked a very nice hotel. I've told Ivan that we have a meeting so you won't be back for the rest of the day. Have a good weekend.

In bed, I kept staring at the text. I thought about sending Harry the recording to warn him off, but what if that gave him time to think up some excuse?

I called Sam.

'Is everything OK? It's so late.'

'No, I'm so scared, Sam. Harry's booked a room at a hotel for Monday. He wants me to sleep with him or he's going to tell Sergio about the info I gave him. I don't know what to do.'

Although it was a relief to tell Sam, to tell anyone what was happening, I knew she couldn't help me. No one could. Even if Sergio believed that Harry had attacked me, he might still believe that I'd given Harry the information to blackmail him. They might report me to the police. At the very least, Sergio would think me incompetent for not knowing about the Chinese Wall and I could lose my job. I started to cry.

'What does Tom say?'

'Tom's left me. He doesn't know any of this.'

'Why didn't you tell me? Where is he? When did this happen?'

'The day after the party. I couldn't tell you, Sam. I haven't told anyone. I kept thinking that he was just angry and hoping he'd come back. But it's been over a week. He's taken his clothes and he won't even answer my texts.'

'Does he know that Harry attacked you and is harassing you?' said Sam.

'No. I was afraid he might beat Harry up and report him to the police, and that Harry would say I'd slept with him in New York.'

'Well, you can't go to the office with Harry there, not when he's threatening you,' said Sam.

'I have no choice. We're penniless, Sam. I should be getting my bonus in a couple of days so I just need to stall him till then. We need that money. I just don't know what to do about Monday.'

She was silent.

'Today was so awful. He stood with his body touching mine when we were posing for a photo, then he tried to get me in his car. I'm so scared of him. Even if I don't go to the hotel, I think he might attack me again.'

'He's dangerous, Faiza.'

'But I can't lose this job! If I say anything to the directors, you know whose side they'll take. Oh, listen to this...'

I played the recording for her.

'This is very good. Play it for your boss on Monday.'

'No, I need to wait till my permanent contract's signed.'

'OK, but please be very careful – and tell Tom what's going on. I can't believe what you've been through. I'm sorry I didn't check in on you, but James...'

'How is he? Was he OK after the party?' I said.

'Yes, yes, don't worry about him. Try to get some sleep now, OK?'

I went downstairs to make sure that the front and back

doors were locked and no windows had been left open or unlocked. I sat up in bed trying to read, but the words ran away from me. I turned off the light and was staring at the ceiling, thinking about Monday, when I heard a noise in the hall. Someone was in the house! I sat up in bed, thinking about the boys across the landing, and grabbed my phone.

Then I heard Tom's voice downstairs.

'Faiza, it's me.'

Eighty-Two

I ran downstairs, forgetting everything else. Tom had come back!

He had switched on the hallway light.

'Sam called me – why didn't you tell me?'

He put his hands on my arms, looking at my face. I wanted to lean into him but he made no attempt to move closer.

'What did he do to you?' Tom's mouth was set in a hard line. There was several days' stubble on his chin and dark shadows under his eyes. I could feel the tears on my face.

'Don't cry. Come.'

He placed his hand on my back and guided me to the TV room. I wanted to reach for his hand, to throw myself against him, but there was something about the careful way he stood apart that stopped me.

'Are you all right? Did he hurt you?'

I shook my head.

'Tell me what happened, all of it.' He spoke gently, as if aware that even the tone of his voice might hurt me.

I tried to zone out as I replied, telling him the facts, like the placement of Harry's hand in the car, and quoted his threats, then told him what had happened at the office and the text about the hotel. I knew that Tom would be devastated too, to hear it all, so I didn't say how I had felt, and tried to speak calmly.

He nodded as I spoke, not showing any emotion either, but I saw the tightening of his jaw and his eyebrows frowning. He took both my hands in his, rubbing them, as if trying to restart my circulation.

'We need to report him to the police, Faiza. If I ever get my hands on him…! I'm so sorry this happened to you.'

Then he led me upstairs, saying, 'We'll sort this out, OK?'

He got into bed with me, and Harry and his threats tipped out of my mind. Tom still loved me. He had forgiven me.

I shuffled closer to him and he put his arm around me.

'Tom, I'm so sorry about everything.'

'Go to sleep, it's late.'

He kept holding me but though his touch was firm and protective, it was not tender or loving. It didn't feel the same as it had before. He didn't kiss me.

When my eyes snapped open the next morning, Tom was sitting up against the headboard. He started speaking before I could say anything.

'I should have been here for you,' he said.

'It's not your fault. I just couldn't bring myself to tell you about Harry. Not after everything else that I'd done.'

'I'm not just talking about Harry. I've been thinking about it all over the last few days. I should have been here for you all these months when you were worried about the money, when you were too afraid to tell me, when you got into so much trouble. You should have been able to talk to me. I should have noticed that something was wrong.'

'It's not your fault. I'm just good at hiding things.'

'You shouldn't have needed to hide things from me. I'm sorry.'

I was about to lay my head on his shoulder but he got out of bed and went to stand near the window. He stared out and shook his head.

'When I think about what you must have gone through. Forcing yourself to go into work, knowing he was there. You must have been terrified. I know you were doing it for the family. I can never forgive myself that you couldn't tell me what you were going through.'

I leapt out of bed and took his hand.

'I just wanted to put everything right,' I said.

He squeezed my hand. 'I know.'

'The worst thing out of all of this was when you left. I can't be without you, Tom. Are we OK?' I said.

He didn't reply.

Things didn't improve between us as the weekend went on. I told myself to be patient. It was like a cut that needed time to heal before we could brush against it and I hoped that it was not too late for us. Even though he was back, everything felt fragile.

Eighty-Three

That night we slept at different ends of the bed and when I woke up on Sunday morning he wasn't there. I wondered how long this would go on, and when he would forgive me. He didn't seem angry though. It was more as if he wasn't even willing to try to get back to where we were before it all went wrong. It felt as if he had given up on us. I got dressed quickly, thinking about how I could flip him out of this mood.

When I went down, he was having breakfast with the children and cutting Alex's egg on toast into small squares.

We had told the children that Tom was back and we were no longer angry with each other. All three had nodded and Alex had jumped into the air and said, 'Yay!' They could tell that things were not back to normal though,

'Family dinner tonight,' said Tom. 'You too, Sofia! I'm going to make my famous leg of lamb extravaganza.'

'Yesss!' Ahmed and Sofia high-fived and Alex pretended to faint in his chair, while shouting, 'Yum!'

I smiled. This was a good sign.

'Can I help? Sous chef reporting for duty!'

'No thanks. I'm good,' he said.

He called out to the boys as they left the kitchen. 'Be ready in ten minutes, boys. We don't want to be late for football.'

Tom stayed away from me all day. If I passed him, he moved aside and I started to feel afraid. What if, despite his regrets about not being there for me all these months, he realised that he couldn't forgive me after all? Maybe he was just staying to make sure that I was OK until the Harry situation was resolved?

Tom wouldn't look at me or speak to me, but he was cheerful with the children and I realised how much he had become involved in their lives. He knew which times table Alex had to learn for his test on Monday and discussed Ahmed's fantasy football strategy, something I had never been able to understand. Sofia told me that he had helped Meg to tell her parents that she was afraid she had an STD. He had talked to Meg, when Sofia told him how terrified Meg was that she had an infection but was just as afraid of her parents finding out.

'It's all sorted now. Her parents are fine and she's been checked out but Dad was so cool. He didn't get angry, but just talked to Meg and calmed her down.'

I shook my head, wondering how I could have missed all this.

'That's why I was spending so much time with her. I had to go to the hospital with her that day I came home late and you were so angry with me. She thought she had Aids.'

'I wish you'd told me.'

'It's OK, Mum, you were working – and Dad was here.'

That evening, when I laid the table, I took some roses from the garden and put them in a vase. Ahmed, now taller than me, was helping me to lay the cutlery and at one point he put his arms around me.

'I love you, Mum,' he said.

I swallowed back my tears

Tom looked at us, catching my eye as he cut the broccoli. He looked away quickly.

'Love you too, my darling,' I said, and stood up on tiptoe and kissed the side of my son's head.

The dinner could not have been more perfect. There was an intense sunset, the type you get in the last days of summer. Sunshine streamed in, falling on the china and the glasses, making everything sparkle. We chatted about Sofia's university choices and Ahmed's annual school camping expedition. Alex wanted Ahmed to save all his old clothes for him and asked him if he had something that would fit him now.

'Mum,' said Alex, 'I think I'm getting too old for my Thomas engines. But can we save them? For *my* children?'

I smiled at Tom and he smiled back. Our eyes locked.

'Mum, please may I have another crunchy potato!' Alex demanded my attention.

Perhaps everything could still go back to normal? All being well, I'd have my bonus soon. I'd repay the money in a few weeks, I still had a job, the children were fine, and Tom was back. Everything was perfect – and yet I knew that it wasn't.

Despite Tom sitting a few feet away from me, I felt we

were further apart than ever. Worry burrowed itself into my heart. What if all the time that I was imagining us reuniting, he was planning the opposite? He hadn't said that he was back for good.

'Ready for school tomorrow?' Tom said to the children. 'I've had a great summer with you all. Do you know, this was the first summer holiday I've spent at home?'

Sofia got up and hugged Tom from behind. 'You did good, Dad!'

'I'm very glad to see you have all grown into kind, mature people. I'm proud of you.'

The children fell silent. Tom never spoke like that.

'I love you all.'

He was saying goodbye! I put down my fork and took a sip of water to try to swallow my food. Just as I feared, he had come back but realised that it had been a mistake. It felt as if this was the last time that we'd be together like this. The children continued to eat, unaware of what lay ahead.

'Love you too, Daddy!' said Alex.

After dinner Tom took the children into the living room. I stayed back in the hallway and peeked in. He was hugging all three of them at the same time, and I felt uneasy as I watched them. Something was wrong about the scene in front of me. He was holding them as if he was never going to see them again.

Eighty-Four

That night Tom and I both lay awake in the dark, lying on our backs. He started to speak.

'Why didn't you just tell me you needed more money?'

'I just didn't want us arguing. I was scared you'd get angry and I hate it when you're angry with me. We were so happy. I didn't want to spoil things,' I said.

'You were scared of me?' he said.

'I was scared of us fighting. It was stupid, I know.'

He was silent and then sighed. 'I'm sorry. I didn't realise that you couldn't talk to me.'

'You would've been right to be angry, Tom,' I said.

He didn't say any more and it felt as if there was nothing left to say.

When he was asleep, snoring softly, facing away from me, I slid across the bed and moulded myself into him. I held him close, pressed my lips gently to his back through his white T-shirt and breathed him in. He didn't move and I wondered if he was, in fact, asleep, or just pretending, allowing me to hold him one last time.

The next morning his leg was thrown over mine and he was holding me. I smiled, warm and groggy, and it took a few seconds before I remembered. I curled my hand around his arm and he tightened his grip. I turned to face him and he pulled me closer. I held my breath. He had forgiven me! He kissed the top of my head and I put my hand between us, finding the waistband of his pyjama bottoms, but his hand clamped onto my wrist.

'No.'

He rolled away and got up.

'I have a meeting in the City this morning. We might go for lunch too, so I've asked Martha to pick up the boys this afternoon. I'd better get ready.'

I started to get dressed for work too. I didn't understand what was happening. He'd held me, then moved away. He hadn't left me, but nor was he with me.

He was in his suit, putting on his Hermes tie, as I got ready to leave.

'Just tell Sergio everything,' he said. 'Do it as soon as you get in. Harry's dangerous – he needs to be reported for assault. We'll go to the police together. If I ever see him...'

'I'm scared. What if I lose my job?' I said.

'I don't know. We need to sort out our finances quickly. There's nothing left in the account and all the bills are due – the school fees are already late – and it will take some time to sell the house. I know how hard you've tried to put things right, Faiza. It's not all your responsibility. I should have got a job by now. I know I've failed you all.'

He pulled me close.

'No, Tom. You've been amazing. This is all my fault.'

'I should never have let you get into this mess: Harry, the loans, all of it. I should have protected you.'

He fell silent.

'Tom… We're OK now though, right? You're not going to divorce me, are you?'

His arms tightened around me, but he didn't reply.

I closed my eyes and sank into him.

'I love you, Tom,' I said.

'I have always loved you. Remember that.'

His anger had gone but, in its place, there was a subdued melancholy, which was worse. His words were dull and his arms felt like dead weights.

'That's all that matters, Tom. I mean I know we're broke but…'

'I'm working on that,' he said. 'I think there's a way we can solve our money problems. I'd do anything for the children, you know I'd give my life for them…' He turned away, putting his watch on.

'Are we OK?'

'I'd better wake everyone up. Good luck with Sergio.'

His voice was a monotone, his eyes empty. They were not a dark angry blue, or a worried swirl of blues and brown, or a resigned calm blue. They looked almost colourless, as if all the life had drained from them, as if he had disconnected.

On my way to work, I kept picturing the expression on his face that morning. It was one I had never seen before. I tried to push the thought away but I knew it was true: he had made up his mind. It was over.

Eighty-Five

On the train, I tried to rehearse what I'd tell Sergio. I had to tell him everything and play him the tape.

When I entered the office, I could tell something was wrong. People stood around in groups and were not at their desks. Hushed chatter rippled through the air instead of the usual morning banter. I saw three police officers coming out of the Dragon's office. What if Harry was angry that I hadn't replied to his text? If he'd told Sergio his lies about me, had the directors called the police to arrest me? I sank down on my chair and started to scratch the eczema on my hand.

Ivan leaned across and whispered, 'They're looking for Harry.'

The police officers were walking towards our desk, along with the Dragon who waved at me, calling me over.

I felt my heart thumping as I walked towards them, trying not to show my panic. One of the policemen held a tiny notebook, his pencil poised.

'Can you please tell me your name and address?' he asked.

I couldn't speak.

'She works with me. Fi, I mean Faiza, Saunders.'

Sergio had appeared next to me.

'When did you last see Harry Wentworth?'

'Friday evening, at a client dinner,' I said.

They asked if I'd heard from Harry since then, but they didn't arrest me and I sat back down in my chair, feeling the sweat under my bra.

'Harry's been taking money from the company. Looks like he's done a runner,' said Teresa.

If they were investigating Harry, it would only be a matter of time before they came across my email.

I wanted to call Tom, but he was probably in his meeting. I was holding my phone, debating whether to text him, when Harry's name popped up on my screen. He was calling. I went to the ladies and called him back.

'Thank God,' he said. 'I need your help. Please don't tell anyone, don't tell the police. I have something for my daughters. Can you meet me in Costa by St Paul's? I don't have long.'

'What have you done? The place is crawling with police.'

'Please help me, Fi. I've got letters for my daughters and I'm not sure Julia will give them to Amber and Elle.'

I was silent.

'Please! Look, I'll write a letter to Sergio to tell him that I tricked you.'

If he could give me something to clear myself, I had to get it. 'OK,' I said.

I told Ivan and Sergio that I had an eye test and I'd be back in an hour. The Dragon was now leading the police back into her office.

Eighty-Six

In Costa, I stood by Harry's table.

'Sit down for a minute,' he said.

He was dressed as normal, down to his silver cufflinks, but his face was grey and drained of blood.

'No.'

He handed me two white envelopes.

'I know I'll be arrested soon – if the irate clients don't catch up with me first. I'd be safer in custody,' he laughed, then stopped abruptly. 'I've written a letter for each of my daughters.'

'I'll make sure they get these,' I said.

You deserve everything you get, I thought, but I didn't say it. I wanted to get away from him as soon as I could and never see him again. I kept looking at the door, afraid the police had followed me.

'My letter?'

He handed me a piece of paper and I read it quickly. It said clearly that he had tricked me into giving him the information and that he was blackmailing me. It was signed and dated.

'Thank you.'

I put everything in my bag and, without saying another word, ran out.

I started walking back to the office as fast as I could. The police might still be there. I'd tell them I'd spotted Harry at Costa and where to find him. My legs suddenly felt shaky though and I had to sit down in a café. I couldn't believe that I hadn't seen Harry for what he was. My phone buzzed. It was a text from Tom. I read it quickly.

Did everything go OK with Sergio?

Yes, all good thanks.

I'd tell him the details later. He replied with a thumbs-up emoji.

Then I sent another text, even though he was already offline.

I love you Tom.

I doubted that he would reply, even when he turned his phone back on. I knew he still cared what happened to me, but that didn't mean we were OK. I was the mother of his children and Tom would always look out for me, even if he didn't love me. He was that kind of man.

As I was about to go into my building, Sam called. She spoke in such a rush that I couldn't understand anything she was saying. Her voice trembled and she didn't sound like herself. All I could hear was panic. I wondered if something had happened to her mother.

She spoke between gasps. 'James's stormed off to see Rupert. He was so angry. He said he was going to kill him. What if he does something to him?'

I stopped walking and someone bumped into me from behind. I stepped out of the way.

'Of course he won't. I'm sure they'll have words but nothing else. Take a breath,' I said.

'You don't understand, Faiza! I've never seen him like this. Rupert called and said he was going to tell their parents about James's job. James just lost it and stormed out, shouting he was going to teach Rupert a lesson.'

'Oh no!' I said.

'James has been under a lot of stress at work. I knew he was having issues with his boss, but I didn't realise how bad things were until Lizzie's party. He broke down and told me they've demoted him, and taken away his office! I had no idea. If his parents find out about all this, it will destroy him.'

'Poor James. I'm so sorry, Sam.'

'He's not answering his phone. I'm so worried.'

'Listen! James's never done anything violent in his life – you know that. I'm sure he'll just go and have a huge row with Rupert and then come home. The work stuff is awful, and so is his family, but he knows he has your support and you love him. I'm sure it will be all right.'

'I hope so,' she said. 'I'll keep trying his phone.'

Eighty-Seven

By the time I got back to the office I felt completely drained. Poor James; the prestige and status of his job were so much part of him. And poor Sam, sitting alone in her office, trying to keep her husband safe.

As soon as I sat down, Ivan said, 'Harry's been spotted. The police just left.'

I felt a rush of relief.

'Good. Where's Sergio?'

'Out for meetings then a client lunch,' said Ivan.

Until I told Sergio about Harry and cleared everything up, I couldn't relax. I wanted to tell the police exactly where I had 'spotted' Harry. I sent them an email, and also described what he was wearing. I hoped the details might help them catch him. I was grateful that I had to do a presentation for a team meeting. It kept me busy while I waited to see Sergio. I was in the glass conference room to the side of the open-plan office with Ivan, Teresa and David, writing up sales figures on a flip chart, when there was a commotion outside. Marianne, one of the secretaries, was sitting sobbing on a chair and a few people were standing around her. We all went out. Marianne spoke between sobs.

'He fell right past me. Oh God! The sound when he landed on the ground!'

Someone handed her a tissue.

'What's happened?' I asked the man standing next to me.

'Marianne was getting coffee from the arcade near Bank and a man jumped from The Cinq. He fell right past her. She'd be dead, too, if he'd hit her.'

'He died?' I said.

Andrea from HR joined in.

'That poor man and his family.'

'Do you think it's Harry?' someone asked. 'The police said he was spotted near Bank this morning but then disappeared. It could be him.'

Several people gasped.

'Well, he would never take to being banged up.'

'No, he loves himself too much to kill himself,' someone else said.

'He did fleece some very powerful people,' said David, his face uncharacteristically sombre.

There was some nervous laughter, but people also looked worried and it *was* a possibility. Harry had looked frightened earlier. I thought about the letters he'd given me, and how he'd begged me to make sure his daughters got them. What if that was what he'd been planning? Despite everything, I didn't wish him dead.

The Dragon came and put her arm around Marianne.

'Are you OK?'

Marianne nodded. She wiped her constant tears with the tissue. 'Oh God, what if it was Harry?'

The Dragon looked at us. 'I've just had his wife on the phone. She's hysterical.'

My phone started to buzz. For a second, I wondered if it was Harry again and he was OK. It was Sam.

I stepped away from the group.

'Did you find James?' I asked.

'Someone's jumped from a building right next to Rupert's office!' She was gasping, talking too fast. 'What if it's James? There's something I didn't tell you. After Lizzie's party, he told me he had a sort of mini breakdown. They called it work-related stress but his boss had been bullying him, humiliating him for months. The GP sent him for counselling, but he was too ashamed to tell me. That's when you saw him at the hospital. His career is over and he thinks he's going to lose his parents. He said he was going to teach Rupert a lesson, but what if he meant...?'

My mouth was dry, but I tried to calm Sam.

'Sam, there's no reason to suspect anything like that! Did he even go to Rupert? Have you called him? Where *is* Rupert's office?'

'It's in Tower Twenty. That's where this man jumped. I just saw it on the news.'

My heart was racing. I had a flash of Sam and James with their children at a barbeque at our house, all of them squeezed together on one sofa. I asked her to call Rupert first and I'd try to find out exactly where the suicide had been.

'Which arcade was it? Is it near Tower Twenty?' I asked Marianne.

'Yes, near the tube station. That's the sixth suicide from The Cinq rooftop. It's just so awful,' said Marianne.

I'd been hoping that it wasn't in the same place. I closed my eyes and took a deep breath. I'd have to tell Sam. I prayed that it wasn't James. But there was something else that had made me uneasy as Marianne talked. I frowned, trying to pinpoint it. Then I realised. The name of the restaurant. My head had been so full of Sam and Harry that it had only just registered. Tom had mentioned The Cinq that morning. He said he might have a meeting there. He'd mentioned anther place too but I couldn't remember.

My stomach turned. I told myself that I was only thinking this because of my conversation with Sam. There must be almost a hundred people at The Cinq at lunchtime. Only one had jumped. I was being irrational, I knew it, but I couldn't stop myself from shivering.

I decided to text Tom, to calm myself down, but when I opened my phone, there was already a message from him.

I'm sorry.

There was nothing else.

I called him straight away, walking out of the office towards the corridor, but I only got voicemail. I leaned against the wall. He was fine, of course he was. He couldn't answer his phone because he was in a meeting. Things had been so unsettled between us. It was natural for him to text me that he was sorry. Maybe he was saying that he didn't love me after my last text?

I started to pace and texted him again.

Are you OK? Tom, darling, please text me or call me. It's urgent.

As I waited for his reply, I thought about how strange his

mood had been all weekend, and I remembered his words that morning: 'I'd give my life for the children.'

My nails rasped against my skin and my hand became covered in red streaks. I was acting like Ami, as if my life was the plot of some Pakistani drama. I had to get a grip and push these irrational fears out of my mind. Sam was the one who had to worry. Tom was fine. Tom was solid.

As I walked back to my desk, though, the stories about the people who had jumped at platform six replayed in my head. The men, and it was almost always men, worked or had worked in the City. There were middle-aged, like Tom; they had families, like Tom – but something had gone so wrong that they'd jumped.

If I could have considered suicide, even for a moment, that day on platform six, how could I be sure that Tom wouldn't think about it too? We had lost each other; our family was shattered. He'd said something about his life insurance when he was job hunting. I tried to remember what. We'd been trying to laugh off another job rejection and he'd jokingly said, 'I could earn more if I dropped dead. My life insurance is £150k.'

My thoughts were like jagged pieces of a jigsaw, slotting together. Tom's hug that morning, that felt like a goodbye; the unexpected family dinner and the way he'd held all three children; Tom had been out of work for months, we were facing financial ruin and I had kissed another man. I thought about the sudden meeting in the City and the text saying that he was sorry. It was the perfect storm. He had mentioned The Cinq that morning. I was sure he had.

I remembered the way he'd stopped getting dressed and meeting people, the out-of-character anger and apathy. I'd been so stupid. He wasn't being unsupportive; he had been depressed. I started to call his phone repeatedly. If it was on silent, he might still feel the vibrations if I kept on calling. It might shift on the table in front of him if he had put it face down during his meeting.

I thought about a long-forgotten conversation we had years ago, about getting older. I'd said that if only it wasn't for my beliefs, I'd love to 'check out' when I got to eighty-five or ninety, in a civilised way at some spa-like facility in Switzerland. Suicide was forbidden, though. It wasn't an option for me.

Tom had smiled and said, 'I'm not sure if that would stop me checking out!'

I shook my head. No, no! I was overreacting. The suicide could be anyone and it was more likely to be Harry. I hoped it wasn't James, and it couldn't be Tom, of course not. He would call me any minute.

I decided to get back to work, watching my phone screen out of the corner of my eye, waiting for Tom or Sam to call. I started typing a reply to Misha's query about one of his funds when, without warning, an image flashed in my mind: Tom lying on the concrete, his legs and arms splayed and broken, dark red blood pooling slowly around his hair.

The worry that had been a vague ache in my chest suddenly became clear. I remembered what he said: 'I've failed you.' He told me he'd found a way to fix our money problems. What if he'd thought the same thing I had? That if I died, at least I would leave behind my life insurance.

Eighty-Eight

I ran to the lobby and waited for the lift, all the time calling Tom. I had to get to The Cinq. Once outside I didn't take a taxi; the police might have closed off the roads nearby. I started to run towards Threadneedle Street, weaving through people, shouting, 'Excuse me!', when I wanted to say, 'Get the hell out of my way!'

Outside The Cinq there were four police cars parked in the middle of the road as well as an ambulance. I stopped, panting, afraid to go forward now that I was here. A crowd was gathered around the building, police tape keeping them back. I craned my neck to look at the rooftop. Green plants dotted the Perspex railings around the edge.

Now that I had stopped, my feet hurt, and I hobbled closer. I checked my phone. Nothing. A journalist was being filmed by a TV crew. He was holding a microphone in front of an older woman whose eyes were wide as she relived what she'd seen.

'I saw him jump. I don't usually come into the City but my son was treating me for my sixtieth. I saw a man walk to

415

the far end of the terrace. He was just standing, looking at the view. You know you can see the whole City from there? I saw him because my son got me a seat with the view. And then, next minute... Oh, it was awful. I saw him climb over and then he jumped.'

'This must have been very distressing. Can you describe him?'

'He looked like anyone in the City. He was wearing a suit, in his forties I think, brown hair, though I didn't see his—'

Her voice was drowned by a roar of blood in my ears. I pushed forwards through the crowd, bodies hitting against me, until I reached the cordon. A blue plastic sheet lay on the ground but it was flat. There was no body. A group of police officers stood next to it.

'Excuse me!'

I slipped under the tape and was about to walk to the officers when they all shouted at me to stay back. One of them came over and took my arm, pushing me back under.

'This is a police scene. You can't come in here, madam.'

'You don't understand! I need to know the name of the man who jumped.'

The policeman's face softened. I was crying.

'I'm sorry, we can't do that.'

Another officer came and stood beside us. The crowd had formed a circle around me. I thought I saw someone filming me on their phone.

'Please, please can you tell me his name?'

I wrapped my arms around myself, my teeth clenched.

The officers looked at each other and one of them took my elbow, leading me away from the crowd.

'I th-think it might have been my husband,' I gasped.

He took a sharp breath in.

'I'm sorry, but the man had nothing on him to identify him. No wallet, no ID.'

'What did he look like? Did he have light brown hair, streaked with grey? Tom has light blue eyes. He was wearing a blue and pink tie. He has a small scar on his left eyebrow.' I cried out as if in pain, 'Please help me!'

'Look, the best thing would be for you to go home. If, for whatever reason, we need to contact you, we will.'

I'd been expecting them to say that I shouldn't worry and it probably wasn't my husband, but instead he took my name and mobile number, then went back to join his colleagues by the blue plastic sheet.

I called an Uber. I couldn't go back to the office. I'd go home and wait, in case the police contacted me. We'd just reached the Strand when I remembered that I didn't have my keys. My bag was still on my desk. I asked the taxi to turn back and texted Ivan to bring the bag down for me.

'You look terrible. What happened?' said Ivan, as I took my bag through the lowered car window.

'I'm not feeling well. Thanks, Ivan, I just need to go home.'

'Did you hear? Harry's been arrested,' he said.

In the taxi, I kept checking my phone. Nothing from Tom. I tried to call him again and felt anger rip through me. Why hadn't it been Harry? Then I closed my eyes. No one deserved that, not even Harry. I thought about Harry in jail and felt numb. I knew that's where he belonged. He was dangerous, and now I was safe, but I couldn't feel anything, not relief, not anger. Nothing. My chest got tighter and tighter. The more time that passed without hearing from Tom, the more I felt hope slipping away.

I started to silently recite a prayer that Ami had taught me, over and over again.

When I was almost home, my phone flashed. It was Sam. 'He's safe! It wasn't him,' she said joyfully and I started to cry with relief, and with terror.

At home I kicked off my heels and sat down on the sofa. I plugged my mobile into the charger and put the house phone next to me. Then I waited.

No news was good news, I told myself. Except they might still be trying to identify Tom. I kept praying he was OK, while trying to push away the image of Tom lying on a dirty pavement, his head cracked open, his future lost, because of what I had done.

If I hadn't started all of this, using the money, telling my lies and destroying our marriage, none of this would have happened.

He should have answered my texts by now, or come home.

I stood in the middle of the room and started to scream, 'Tom! Tom! Tom!' as if it might bring him back.

I kept shouting his name over and over again, until my throat was raw.

Eighty-Nine

The children would be home soon. I couldn't let them see me like this. Martha was picking the boys up and was going to cook supper for them. I texted her that I had a migraine and was going to bed to sleep it off.

I locked my bedroom door and climbed into bed, pulling the duvet over my head. The house phone lay next to my stomach and the light from my mobile was a flare inside my duvet tent.

I must have fallen asleep and awoke to banging on the bedroom door.

'Open the door, Faiza!'

It was Tom. The room was dark and I ran to unlock the door. I threw myself at him, clutching his jacket, touching his cheek, running my hand down his arm. It *was* him. My head spun. He held me and I leaned into him then started to cry.

'Tom...'

My knees buckled and he half-carried me back to bed.

I heard him on the landing, telling the children that I

wasn't well, then he came back into the room and locked the door again. He fetched me some water from the bathroom and sat next to me, holding it to my lips. I sank back on the pillow, my eyes darting over his forehead, his eyes, his lips. I took his hand and kissed his knuckles. He took a tissue from the bedside table and dabbed my face.

'Martha told me you have a migraine. Have you taken some painkillers? I'm sorry, I switched my phone off during my meeting and then they took me to lunch, then drinks. I forgot to turn it back on and I've only just seen all your texts. Are you OK? I saw your text saying that everything went well with Sergio, so what's wrong? Did something happen at work? Did they fire you?'

He pushed my tangled hair back from my face.

'You don't have to deal with all of this alone any more. We'll sort it out together.'

He took my hand and kissed the middle of my palm, as if he still loved me.

I held his hands and looked directly at him. 'Tom, I can't live without you, so you can't leave me. I won't let you. I'm begging you to forgive me.'

'I'll never leave you, Faiza. I'm sorry too. I texted you, didn't you see? It wasn't all your fault; I know that now.'

'It *was* my fault. I lied to you, but I'll never do that again.'

'Shh, it's OK,'

He stroked my hair.

'You don't hate me, do you? I mean really? I'm a terrible person. I almost destroyed everything.'

'You're not a terrible person and you don't have to take all the blame. You should've been able to talk to me instead of worrying about what I'd say.'

He leaned forward to kiss me, but I pulled away.

'I thought you were dead! I thought you'd killed yourself.'

'What?'

'You said you were going to The Cinq for lunch. Then I heard about the man who jumped and I couldn't contact you and I thought... I ran to the restaurant but the police wouldn't tell me anything and I couldn't get through to you. You were so devastated by what I'd done, by the job, everything. I thought I'd lost you, Tom. I can't, I couldn't...'

He didn't say a word. He stood up and took off his shoes and socks and then his trousers. He dropped his jacket and shirt on a chair and climbed into bed. He lifted me off the pillows, as if I might break, and pulled me close, resting my head on his shoulder. He turned me towards him until we were face to face then he rubbed my back and kissed my cheeks, my eyes, my tears and my lips. I saw tears in his eyes.

'I'm so sorry, I had no idea. I would never leave you. All those things I said, I was just angry. And I was angry at myself too, not just at you. There's nothing you could do that would ever stop me loving you.'

I wiped his eyes with my thumb and sat up.

'I can't believe I spent all that money. I just didn't think...'

'I had no idea what you were going through,' said Tom. 'I know I can be a little controlling about money. "Never touch savings." That was our family motto, but I should have talked to you instead of just setting impossible budgets.'

'I hated us fighting, Tom. I was scared to end up like my parents. I tried not to spend the money but I couldn't stop myself. I was afraid that if I didn't keep up with the other women, they wouldn't be my friends, and then the children wouldn't have friends. I didn't want them to feel different, the way I had.'

Tom tipped my chin up.

'We're not your parents, OK? And the children will not have to go through what you did. I know you were only trying to protect them, but their experience won't be the same as yours and, even if it is, we can help them to deal with it.'

I sighed.

'I was trying to shield the kids but maybe I've done more harm than good. I suppose, in a way, it's good you lost your job. They've had to wise up and, actually, they've been really good. I didn't want them to feel bad about not having the same things as their friends, or not going on school trips or on holiday, the way I had. I was wrong though: they have everything and I didn't even realise it.'

I understood now, that I hadn't needed to reassure the children. I was only trying to reassure myself.

'I spent money on myself too, though. It wasn't just about the kids.' I bit my lip. 'I went a little crazy. Everyone was looking younger and having these anti-ageing treatments. I didn't know if you'd still like me with wrinkles and saggy bits.'

'Darling, wrinkles are good, getting older is good. These things are all part of life. It doesn't mean I won't love you anymore. I have wrinkles and my hair is turning grey. Trust me, getting older is good. It's much better than the alternative!'

I nodded and tried to smile.

There was another reason I had been trying to look as

good as I could, for as long as I could. It had been worrying me for years, probably since the day we got married, but the feeling had become stronger as I'd started to see signs of ageing. I had never been able to ask him the question though, because I'd been too afraid of the answer. Now, it was going to burst out of me. I had to say it. I pleated the edge of the duvet between my fingers, unable to look at him.

'It's not just the getting older, Tom. I can't stop thinking about your ex-girlfriends. Every single one was tall, blonde, English. I've always wondered if you married me just because, you know, I wouldn't sleep with you unless we were married. Then, when the children came along, you just stayed, because you're a good guy.'

'Faiza! No one put a gun to my head to marry you, or to stay with you. You're the most beautiful woman I've ever seen. I love your face, I love your body, I love your craziness, I love how caring you are, I love how funny you are, and how you pretend to be tough. I love *you*, and I still want to grab you every time I see you. Is that clear?'

A knot loosened somewhere deep inside me at his words. I knew that he wouldn't lie.

'It is now! You could have bloody told me that at some point in the last twenty years, couldn't you? It might have saved us a lot of hassle!'

'I thought you knew,' he said, and we both laughed.

He started to kiss me again – and this time he didn't stop. He kissed me harder and started to undo the buttons on my shirt, then slipped it off and kissed the side of my neck. I'd missed the feel of his skin on mine and the weight of his body pushing into me. He held me tighter and I wrapped myself around him, holding on to him, until everything else faded away.

Afterwards, Tom said, 'I forgot to tell you. I went for an interview today – and I got the job.'

Ninety

Naila, Sam and I sat in silence and stared at our drinks, partially shielded from the rest of the coffee shop, in a booth in the corner.

We were silent for a few minutes, as our updates to each other began to sink in. I had tears in my eyes and saw that both of them, even Sam, were tearful.

'I can't believe we all went through so much shit and we didn't even tell each other,' I said. 'If I'd told you, maybe I would've had the courage to tell Tom too, and things wouldn't have got that bad.'

They nodded. We had all shared the things we'd been trying so hard to carry alone. Now, with my friends, as with Tom, and with everyone in my life, I just wanted to be myself.

I needed to stop hiding.

'I wanted to tell you but I felt so ashamed,' I said.

Naila passed me a tissue and Sam put her arm around me. They huddled together to hide me from the rest of the café.

'Faiza, you nutcase, we love you. I'm so glad you told us,' said Sam.

I smiled, looking into their eyes, which showed no disgust or reproach.

'Spending all that money, lying to my parents, leaving my kids unprotected, and for what? My mum told me how she used to spend money to impress her parents and her sisters, who made her feel second best because we weren't as rich as them, until one day she realised that she already had everything she wanted. I think the same thing happened to me. My life was great, it really was, now I think about it. I had Tom, the kids, my parents, you guys, but when I compared myself to the glam women around me and their glossy, perfect lives, I just forgot. I felt I had to be just like everyone else to fit in, but I didn't.'

I realised now that being around that crowd had touched a nerve in me that I had no control over; the Achilles heel from my 'scholarship girl' days, the chip I had carried so well hidden on my shoulder.

'Nothing good ever comes of comparing yourself to other people!' said Sam. 'There's always going to be someone thinner, or prettier or richer, or more successful. That's what James's toxic parents have done to him all his life, comparing him to Rupert. That's why he fell apart when things went wrong at work. We didn't need the money and I loved him, promotion or not, but he felt he was a failure when he compared himself to his brother.'

Sam had just told Naila about James as well.

'I'm so sorry. How is James now?' said Naila.

'Better, thanks. He's left that job – and I told his parents to fuck off.'

Sam never swore.

'Go Sam!' I said.

'I've never even had an argument with them before but I marched in, told them that we would not be seeing them at all for three months and that the anniversary party would be a family dinner at our place – take it or leave it. James was horrified when he heard, but I think he's relieved too. I wished I'd told you both, but James was so embarrassed by it all...'

Naila told Sam about Adil starting at Clissington's.

'I'm sorry I kept it a secret, but I felt like such a fraud, after all my talk about private schools.'

'Naila, we're not friends with you because of where your son goes to school,' said Sam.

'Remind me again: why *are* we friends with her?' I asked.

Sam and I started to laugh but Naila didn't join in. She was staring at the fork in her hand as if she'd never seen a fork before, rubbing the handle.

'There's something else. I'm only telling you both, in the strictest confidence. Seema's got a boyfriend. She's been getting drunk, going to parties, smoking weed. I had no idea until she passed out at a friend's house and they called us. I don't know what I've done wrong,' she said, and wiped her eyes with a tissue.

'She's just being a teenager,' said Sam.

'No, Sam, you don't understand. We can't do these things in our culture. If anyone finds out what happened – my parents, or Tariq's parents or other people – her reputation will be ruined. So will ours.'

I passed Naila the plate with the brownies. She took a bite and I said, 'Naila, listen, things are different for our children. Their experience is not going to be the same as ours. And, by the way, this is not just because I'm married to a white guy. Haven't you heard me talk about all the desi dinners and weddings I've been to with full bars and everyone getting wasted? The same people pretend to be teetotal when they're with a more traditional crowd. All I'm saying is, everyone is trying to find their own way. At least now things are in the open, you and Seema can talk. Explain to her why you don't want her to do these things – and don't say "because it's our culture". First, their culture is not the same as yours and mine, and second, because there are plenty of Pakistani families in London *and* in Pakistan, who do all the things you're telling her not to. Find out what works for you and for her. You're a great mother and Seema is a great kid, OK?'

'Thanks. Maybe you're right,' said Naila.

'That's what I'm trying to do with my kids. Tom and I can't really understand their experience, because they have this lovely cultural mix, so we need to find a way that works for us, for them, *and* for what we believe. Why is life so hard? Give me a brownie!'

We all smiled. My friends were looking the way I felt: lighter, relieved, happier.

Later, they asked about Harry.

'He has a court date coming up. For the fraud but also for the assault. I found out that Annie, the woman whose job I took over, had made a sexual harassment complaint about him too but they paid her off and she left.'

'No!' said Naila.

'It gets worse. Apparently, she was Indian and Harry was known in the office to have a thing about Asian women.

428

Annie's real name was Anoushka. Ivan tried to warn me but I wouldn't listen. I never got that vibe from Harry, though, not until the night of Lizzie's party. That's when he showed his true colours. He kept saying how exotic I was.' I shuddered. 'It also explains why Julia has always hated me. Maybe she knew about his desi fetish?'

'It's still no excuse for the things she said to you,' said Sam. 'I'm sorry, I didn't even realise.'

I had explained to Sam why Julia's comments about Ami not speaking English, or constantly talking about 'my culture' and trying to 'other' me, had upset me so much. Sam had understood straight away. She said she'd never realised those comments had caused such distress and asked me to tell her if she herself or someone around us said something like that without realising the connotations, or if they did it deliberately.

Julia had texted Sam.

'She's moving back to Notting Hill and the girls are going back to their old school. She's not divorcing Harry. She says everyone in the City does what Harry did in those deals and HH are just making him a scapegoat. She also thinks you overreacted, Faiza. I can't believe she had the nerve to say that after what he did, and to say it to me, knowing you're my friend!'

'Julia and Harry deserve each other. I'm just glad they won't be here anymore,' I said.

By the time we left the café, each of us had cried, all of us had hugged, and we had promised to not keep secrets from each other, just for the sake of keeping up the image we thought people, even our closest friends, had of us.

Tom was waiting for me at home and I snuggled up on

the sofa, feeling a sense of peace that I never had before. I didn't need to pretend to be perfect. Tom and my friends knew the worst about me – and they hadn't left me. They still loved me.

Ninety-One

Three months later

'Where's my reading book?'

Alex demanded that we all stop what we were doing and attend to his needs. Tom and I looked at each other and shrugged.

Sofia found the book, which was propped next to the toaster and put it inside Alex's bag.

I mouthed a 'Thanks' to her.

'Mum, can I borrow your blue cashmere jumper? I'll be careful, I promise,' she said, timing her request perfectly to coincide with her good deed for Alex.

'It's very expensive, Sofia.'

'But you never wear it anymore,' she said. 'I haven't bought any clothes for ages and this way I can just use yours.'

That was true. My Butterfly clothes did not really have space in my new life.

'OK, but please be careful!'

She gave me a hug.

'So, Aunty Naila's taking you home after school, Ahmed,' I said.

'Cool,' he said.

I put my jacket on and checked when the next bus was coming.

'Five minutes, darling,' I said to Tom.

'And Alex, you're staying on for football club and I'll pick you up today,' said Tom, handing Alex his after-school snacks in his new Chelsea lunch box.

'Where's the form for my football kit?' asked Ahmed.

'Shit! Shit! Sorry,' I said, 'I forgot. Wait a sec.'

I ran up to my bedroom and found the form where I'd left it two days ago, next to my make-up. I ran down to the kitchen shouting, 'Pen, pen! Quick!'

Tom handed me a pen and I filled the form in, leaning on the console table while everyone stood in a line, ready to leave the house.

Outside, Naila was waiting for Ahmed in her car with Adil, and Sofia set off with Alex to drop him off at school. She held his hand, while speed-texting on her phone at the same time with her other hand. I frowned. Alex loved talking on his way to school. Then I saw Sofia pause and bend down to her little brother as he pointed to something on the ground. My body relaxed. Tom saw it too and smiled.

'She's a good kid. They all are – Mashallah!'

'Well, well, who knew you could integrate so well!' I laughed.

We missed the bus and decided to walk down the hill to the station. I made my morning call to Ami.

'Wa-Alaikum salaam, Beti. I'm just getting ready because the bus is coming to pick us up.'

She sounded excited. They were off on a day trip to Eastbourne arranged through an elderly outings scheme run by the council. They loved taking the trips.

'Oh yes, I forgot. Have a great time! Give my love to Baba. Khuda Hafiz!'

Farrah had found out about this service, and about a hospital transport scheme to take them to their appointments when she and I were both at work. I still worried about not being around for them as much, but so far, they were happy and Farrah was also helping me look after them.

When I hung up, Tom said, 'Can you listen to the pitch I'm doing this morning? Tell me if it comes across well?'

He ran through his ideas and I told him a couple of changes that might make his points clearer.

On the Waterloo and City Line, we managed to get seats next to each other and held hands until we got to Bank, then walked off separately towards our offices.

Tom called on my mobile a few hours later.

'Shall we meet outside the Royal Exchange?' he said.

'Yes, I'm just leaving.'

I picked up my bag and went around the team desk to kiss my friends goodbye. Two cheek kisses for Teresa and Sabine, and three for Ivan. I waved when I got to David.

'Bye, children! Be good!'

I'd realised that Teresa and Ivan had both tried to warn me about Harry but I hadn't listened.

'Are you moving this weekend, Faiza?' said Sabine.

They all called me by my real name now – Fi was in my past, thank goodness.

'Yep. First move in fifteen years! I'm a bit nervous. But excited too. The kids are moaning, of course!'

'You have very big balls, Faiza!' said Ivan.

'Why, thank you, Ivan! That might be the nicest thing you've ever said to me!'

Teresa and Sabine joined in with our laughter.

'See you all in a week!'

Tom had started his new job, but I didn't want to stop working. We still had to repay the loans and, despite selling the house to free up some money, we had to be careful. Tom's job was initially a two-year contract and my bonus hadn't been as high as expected, although I'd managed to put back some of the emergency fund.

Besides the money, though, I loved my job, and I was good at it. I had become the go-to consultant for trust funds that our clients wanted to set up for their children. They liked the fact that I was a mother and understood why these were the most important funds of all, for them.

I'd discovered a budgeting app and used it to keep track of my spending for myself, whipping it out every time I went into a shop, and explaining to the bemused Wimbledon Village sales assistants why I could only spend what my app allowed. I had even used it in Butterfly. Tom had stopped going through the items on the credit card bill, or compiling spreadsheets with budgets.

We'd made a pact to talk to each other about money: how much we had, how much we were spending. It had felt strange, at first, and made me nervous, but the more we did it, the less of an issue it became. We were a work in progress, but now it felt like we were living a partnership, rather than parallel lives.

I left the office and walked towards Bank. I looked up as I passed The Cinq. Tom and I had laid a bouquet there, for the poor man who had jumped. I felt a stab of sadness for him and his family and realised yet again how lucky we had been.

Christmas lights were already up on almost every building, and the City sparkled in the pale winter sun. Tom was waiting for me.

'What do you fancy for lunch?' he asked, putting his arms around me, warming me up as I shivered in the cold December air.

I went through a mental list of our usual City haunts, all of them either in skyscrapers with dazzling views, or with delicious food, but hefty bills that always made Tom's eyebrows jump up in fright. Nor would they comply with my budgeting app. Then I had an idea.

'Happy Days?'

'Sounds good,' he said.

He took my hand and slipped it into his coat pocket, holding it tightly as we walked away, talking about our work and the new house. I was surprised at how excited I felt. It was a fresh start.

We left behind the skyscrapers and glossy global brands and walked towards narrower streets and dirtier pavements, passing high street coffee shops and sandwich kiosks, interspersed by key cutting services and walk-in barbers. We turned into Petticoat Lane market and passed stalls selling rows of leggings, T-shirts and leather jackets, suspended high above us.

We found a small table in the corner, in the middle of the Friday lunchtime rush at Happy Days, a local fish and chip shop where we used to go when we first started dating.

After we'd eaten, Tom moved aside the salt and pepper

shakers and the bottle of vinegar, one by one, and took one of my hands in his, on the plastic, red-and-white checked table cloth.

'That was delicious,' he said.

'It really was. It was perfect.'

I reached out for his other hand and looked around at the bustling restaurant, with its bright red tinsel and laminated menus. I smiled at Tom, looking into his eyes. He was right. We would mess up, we would fight, we would change, but we would always love each other. I squeezed his hands as my eyes filled with tears. It didn't matter where we were, or what we had been through. *This* was all that I needed.

He started to rub circles, soft as a feather, in the palms of my hands. I felt myself shiver. He was watching my face and I swallowed, trying to slow my breathing, aware of my chest rising and falling. He smiled.

'I know that look,' he said. 'I know what's going to happen next.'

'Do you now? Let's see if you're right.'

We both stood up and leaned towards each other across the small, rickety table.

Then we kissed.

Acknowledgements

Thank you so much for reading *Would I Lie to You?* A reader is the ultimate prize for a writer and I'm thrilled to share this story with you.

When I started writing my debut, I had no idea about how many people would play a role getting me to this magical moment. I'm so grateful to them all.

Thanks to my wise and kind MA classmates at Royal Holloway, Allison, Catherine, Megan, Prescilla, Ross, Sam, Zoe, and Julia. Thank you to everyone in my Curtis Brown Creative writing group, especially Geoff, Louise, Swithun, Wendy, Ziella and to Ian, for spending Boxing day reading my manuscript! Writing this novel would have been harder, lonelier and much less enjoyable without all of you. Andrea Mason, thank you for being such an inspirational role model for my writing and for life!

I am very grateful to my lovely sister-in-law Fawzia, for your encouragement, and for being a careful, gentle and insightful early reader. Thank you to my dear, late in-laws for our long discussions about books.

A special thanks to my nephews and nieces for cheering me on, and to Seyhr for that long conversation about my writing. Thank you to my dearest siblings for their huge love and support, for celebrating every step with me, and for being so understanding about my disappearing acts. Thanks to my brother for always telling me to hurry up and finish writing my book!

Shelley Weiner, Anna Davis and Nikita Lalwani, thank you for believing I could do it, even when I wasn't sure. Thank you to Dr John Moran. Without your help, I may still be writing this book!

Working with my brilliant UK editor Laura Palmer has been an amazing experience. Thank you for loving the book right from the start and for understanding it so well that it spooked me out! You are a genius and your insights have made the book stronger and shinier in ways I could not have imagined. Thank you for your constant encouragement, calm approach and collaborative style, which made everything seem easier and made my confidence soar. I would also like to thank the lovely Anna Nightingale for your support, and every single person at my incredible UK publishers, Head of Zeus, for all your hard work and for championing my book with such energy, expertise and enthusiasm. I am lucky to have you all on my team.

Thank you very much to my US editor, the fantastic Beth deGuzman. I am fortunate to benefit from your expertise, your passion for my book and your impeccable, invaluable guidance. Thank you for being so collaborative and supportive and for sharing my excitement. I am very grateful to the whole team at my wonderful US Publishers, Grand Central Publishing for taking such great care of my book, so I always felt it was in safe and expert hands. My thanks also to Kirsiah McNamara, for all your excellent help and support.

I would also like to say a big thank you to Jenny Bent, for championing my book so brilliantly in the US.

Thank you to my children for understanding and supporting my writing dreams, and never complaining about all the time I spent with my laptop! I am grateful for Yusuf's encouragement, Asad's clear-sighted advice, and Zoya's invaluable input on edits, for making a stunning cover reveal video, and for reassuring hugs. You three are my world.

A massive thank you to Juliet Mushens, my superstar agent. You are an amazing ally and an amazing person. None of this would have been possible without you, or been as much fun. Your energy, kindness and razor-sharp business brain blow me away, and your belief in my writing makes me braver and more excited about my work. Thank you for always being in my corner, for stellar advice, for problem-solving, for style inspiration and for making me laugh. You made my dream come true. I also want to thank Liza DeBlock, for your cheerful emails and for making me feel so well looked after.

I don't know how to start or how I could ever finish, thanking my beloved parents. Your pride in me and love for me, have been limitless and constant. It has been the biggest gift to have such wonderful, good people as my parents. Dad, I can absolutely feel you cheering me on, and Mum, your joy and excitement at each step of the publication process has meant everything. I am so happy we could share it together and grateful for your wisdom as I navigated it all.

The biggest thank you to Irfan, for a lifetime of love and support. The only thing you ever wanted was for me to be happy and once that involved writing, you did everything you could, to help me have the courage, time and space to make this book happen. Thank you for valuing my work when it was nothing but some random ideas in my head, and for holding my hand through every high and every low of this journey. In the words of that card from Leicester Square; 'I know lots of good people, but you are the best.'

Book club notes

1. Faiza's story in *Would I Lie to You?* stems entirely from one lie. Throughout the book, we see the effects of lying, but why might we lie? Would you have lied about the emergency fund or would you have told Tom right at the start?

2. What was the last lie you told? Are some lies more acceptable than others?

3. Money worries are one of the biggest reasons for relationships to break up. How should couples handle their finances? Can relationships work when you have very different approaches to money?

4. Faiza and Tom's relationship undergoes some serious pressure, but it's not like they haven't faced difficulties in the past. What do you think about Faiza and Tom's relationship? What makes a good marriage?

5. Alongside their differences regarding their finances, Faiza and Tom also have different cultural and racial backgrounds. How do their backgrounds impact their

decision making? What did you think about their children's experience of being biracial?

6. The women in the book are all in their mid-forties. How does life change in this age group for women?

7. The yummy mummies of Wimbledon are very present in the novel and in Faiza's life, but how much agency do they have in their own lives? How much is their status dependent on their husband's salary? What do you think about this in the twenty-first century?

8. Though we might find it difficult to admit, we've probably all felt the pressure to 'keep up with the Joneses' at some point in our lives. When was the last time you can remember feeling this pressure? Do you think that having credit card debt is a symptom of social pressure?

9. Faiza knows that she made a massive mistake by spending her family's emergency savings. Can we ever recover from huge mistakes and can others truly forgive us?